Havoc

By Jamie Shaw

Mayhem
Riot
Chaos
Havoc

Havoc

JAMIE SHAW

AVONIMPULSE
An Imprint of HarperCollinsPublishers

This book is a work of fiction. References to real people, events, establishments, organizations, or locales are intended only to provide a sense of authenticity, and are used fictitiously. All other characters, and all incidents and dialogue, are drawn from the author's imagination and are not to be construed as real.

Digital Edition FEBRUARY 2017 ISBN: 978-0-06-256939-4
Print Edition ISBN: 978-0-06-256941-7

FIRST EDITION

17 18 19 20 21 LSC 10 9 8 7 6 5 4 3 2 1

For every reader who falls in love with Mike.

Chapter 1

There's an elbow on my head.

My boobs are smashed against a barricade, a Converse sneaker almost just kicked me in the face, and there's an elbow . . . on top of . . . my head.

"ADAM!" my cousin screams over the music that's blasting out of gargantuan speakers piled high at the sides of the stage. I pull my neck down just in time to avoid the arm she throws over the railing, and the elbow on my head follows me deep into my turtle shell.

"Adam!" she yells again as she jumps on an invisible trampoline in the front row. "Down here! Adam!"

The lead singer of The Last Ones to Know is crouched down at the edge of the stage, his fingers reaching out toward the mash of girls gathered at his feet. They're climbing over each other to try to yank him into the crowd, and I'm just here, trying not to die.

"I fucking love you!" Danica shrieks as Adam serenades the fans front and center. His knees poke out of the bare threads of his jeans as he stretches his black-nailed fingers toward the crowd, and the way his lips caress his mic . . . well, it's no wonder half of these girls have gone rabid.

All week, I've had to listen to Danica talk about her rock star ex-boyfriend. About how madly in love with her he was. About how he worshipped her all throughout high school. About how his band is finally making it big.

The only problem is, her ex-boyfriend isn't the lead singer.

At the back of the stage, in a black T-shirt that's damp with four songs' worth of hard-earned sweat, Mike Madden beats on the drums with arms that have been sculpted to do nothing else. He wields his drumsticks like they're extensions of his own body, radiating power as he sets the beat for the war song in the club. He's not lanky or dressed in distressed clothes like the rest of the band, but there's no mistaking it—he's a rock star.

"I thought you were here for the drummer?" I shout, but my voice is as tiny as the rest of me, lost under the swell of the music and the frenzied screams of the crowd. I try to hold my own as I get jostled left and right, but I'm at the mercy of the waves upon waves of people that slam into me from all sides.

"I WANT TO SUCK YOUR COCK!" some chick further behind me screams at Adam as she tries to jump past the gigantic sweaty guy molded to my back, and Adam smiles wide under the glowing blue lights without missing a single lyric. The crowd is absolutely insane, but the band has obviously seen it a thousand times before. Even Danica's frantic shrieking can't get their attention.

"Shawn!" she desperately pleads when she notices the lead guitarist glancing down from his spot at Adam's right. In a vintage tee, with messy black hair and a thick layer of stubble, he shreds his guitar and shouts backup lyrics into his mic. He and Adam weave a song, line over line over line, and I almost start to enjoy it—right up until my hand gets snatched from the railing.

"Help me get his attention!" Danica orders as she yanks my arm high over my head.

I'm fighting for control of my limbs, in serious danger of getting sucked backward into the music-fueled chaos, when Shawn finally locks his sights on Danica.

A crease forms in the center of his brow, reminding me of this stray cat that used to live on my family's farm . . . It was only friendly when it went into heat, and then suddenly its favorite thing to do became weaving figure-eights around my dad's denim-clad legs. My dad hated cats, particularly this one, and he used to make this face—a face almost exactly like the one Shawn makes at Danica.

"OH MY GOD!" Danica squeals, clamping a freakishly strong hand onto my shoulder. She spins me to face her, and I latch on to her arms to avoid getting knocked sideways into a thrashing whirlpool of elbows and armpits and hair. "Did you see that?! He looked right at me!"

A violent wave crashes into me when Adam hits the chorus of the song, and I struggle to keep my head above water. Blue and purple lights cut across my skin as I get slammed back against the metal bars in front of me and Danica shouts her undying love to every single guy on the stage.

Adam! Shawn! Joel! Mike!

She doesn't waste her breath on the female guitarist, introduced earlier as Kit, but I don't bother commenting—because I'm too busy ducking to avoid getting kicked in the head by another crowd surfer. A security guard drags the screaming fan over the barricade and ushers her away, and at the weary expression on my face, he gives me a sympathetic look that promises, *It'll be over soon.*

Only, it's *not* over soon. It doesn't end until an eternity and two kicks-in-the-head later, when the music ends and the lights finally cut. I inhale a deep, much-needed breath—and get pushed hard to the side. "Let's go," Danica orders as she shoves me directly into someone's back.

"Where do you expect me to go?" I bark as she continues pushing me into the crowd.

"Just GO."

She uses me as her battering ram the entire way out of the pit, and I almost regret not getting trampled to death while I had the chance.

"You can stop now," I snap at her as soon as I have enough room to spin around.

"Shut up for a minute."

I'm biting my tongue—literally, because it's all I can do to keep from growling at her—when Danica rises onto her tiptoes and begins scanning the venue. We're in a club called Mayhem, in the city we both just moved to. I moved here to get my bachelor's and eventually doctoral degrees in veterinary science, and Danica moved here for . . . well, who knows why Danica does anything.

She's always been the star of the ballet. The captain of the cheerleading squad. The Juliet in school plays. The queen of the homecoming dance.

She's never had to want for anything, and she does whatever she wants.

"How do we get backstage?"

"Um," I say as I peel my shirt away from the sweat on my back, "I'm pretty sure we don't."

"Don't be stupid, Hailey," she scoffs. "Didn't you see the way Shawn looked at me?"

Like my dad looked at that horny barn cat? Yeah, I definitely saw that . . .

"There!" she interjects, and when she begins walking away, I gaze longingly at a big red sign that promises EXIT. I wonder how much I'll regret it later if I make my escape while I have the chance. It's not like Danica would have trouble finding a ride home. She has the kind of beauty only money can buy—salon-tended copper-brown hair, trainer-sculpted curves, cosmetically whitened teeth. And aside from all of that are pretty almond eyes and naturally flawless skin. Since moving in with her almost two months ago, I've stopped counting the number of guys that have stopped by our apartment to pick her up or bring her home.

All of them have been cute. But none of them have been rock stars.

"Are you coming or what?" Danica shouts from a few steps ahead of me, and at the impatient look on her face, I sigh and follow her.

It wasn't always this way. When we were kids, she sometimes let me be the leader in follow the leader. In Simon says, she sometimes let me be Simon. In house, we took turns being the mom and being the dad. And when her family moved away when Danica and I were in elementary school, I was actually pretty sad.

But that was before she started at her new school, where she became a mean girl made for movies. Our families continued to get together for holidays—Christmases, Thanksgivings, Easters—but each year, Danica turned more and more into someone I didn't know. She grew into someone beautiful and someone ugly, while I stayed more or less the same. I never imagined we'd end up roommates, but at our family dinner this past Easter, when I mentioned wanting to transfer to Mayfield University someday since they have one of the best pre-veterinary programs in the country, she jumped right in and volunteered her father to pay my tuition. She said she wanted to go back to school too. She said we should *both* go to Mayfield and be roommates. She said it would be *so much fun*.

AT A DOOR near the back corner of the room, my fun-loving cousin marches right up to the first security guard she sees, who also happens to be approximately five zillion times her size, with muscles made of stone and a face to match. "Who do I need to talk to to get backstage?"

At her bossy tone, Muscle Man lifts an eyebrow. "The Easter Bunny?"

"Excuse me?"

"No one's allowed backstage." The arms he crosses over his chest warn that he isn't messing around.

"I'm with Mike," Danica lies, and after studying her for a moment, Muscle Man laughs.

"Sure you are."

"I am!"

When Muscle Man just smiles at her like she's a petulant child, Danica resorts to acting like one. She demands to see his boss and threatens to get him fired. When that doesn't work, she resorts to curse words. And when those have no effect, all hell breaks loose.

She's torpedoing her finger into his chest and shouting something about his inbred gene pool when I try to pull her away from him. But Danica is on a rampage, and all my efforts get me is a hard shove that nearly knocks me on my ass. At five feet tall, one hundred and three pounds, I'm not exactly in a position to throw my weight around, and I don't make a second attempt to try. I'm rubbing my tender collarbone when the security guy picks my assailant up off her feet, and I helplessly follow as he carries her outside.

After serving as an armrest for a sweaty gigantor inside the club, after obliterating my eardrums in front of the world's biggest speakers, after getting knocked around like a bratty child's toy all night, all I want is to take a hot shower and crawl into my own bed to sleep for a week straight. Instead, I stand on the sidewalk outside Mayhem, frowning at the furious look on Danica's face as she glares at the big metal door the security guard just shut behind him.

She came here for one thing, and I know she's not leaving until she gets it.

"You didn't have to push me," I mutter, and her eyes flare.

"You should've had my back!"

"And done what? Bite his ankles?"

In her four-inch wedge boots, Danica towers above me. I stare way up at her, trying to remember the girl who played dolls with me up in my parents' hayloft. But she's lost somewhere behind fake lashes and fifteen years of getting everything she's wanted.

"You've been nothing but a bitch this whole time," she snaps, and I sigh and pull my shirt away from my skin again, letting the cool night air dry the sweat beaded on my lower back. There's no point in trying to defend myself. In Danica's mind, she's always simultaneously the victim and the hero, and as her non-rent-paying roommate, I've learned to just accept that.

I appreciate everything she's done for me. I do. If she hadn't been the little voice in her father's ear, persuading him to fund my schooling and begging him to make some calls to get us enrolled, I'd be home mucking stalls, not following my dreams. Her dad pays *all* of my bills—my tuition, my insurance, my living expenses, all of them. And while I suspect that Danica's sudden interest in my life wasn't entirely genuine—she'd flunked out of college before, and I think her dad was only open to the idea of her going back if she was living off-campus with a responsible roommate, aka her boring farm-girl cousin—I owe her. I owe her the roof over my head and the massive student loan debt I don't have.

When her phone rings, she wastes no time dismissing me to answer it. "Katie?" she says. "Guess who just got kicked out of the fucking club. Yes! Because this asshole bouncer wouldn't let me backstage." She gives me a dirty look. "Just stood there doing nothing. I know! No, she didn't even try. Getting a place with her was stupid."

An icy chill slithers up the back of my neck, and I chew the inside of my lip. Because of my uncle's insistence that I focus all of my energy on school right now instead of also finding a part-time job, I have no income. My only "job" is not pissing off his daughter. And it's a job that I'm learning I am very, very bad at.

With my mouth shut, I slink away before my mere presence can enrage Danica further, and when she asks where I'm going, I make up the lamest excuse ever. "To read this flyer over here."

I walk to a telephone pole to give us both time to cool down, choosing to poison myself with the second-hand smoke coming from the chain-smoking girls standing nearby rather than spend another second listening to Danica's passive-aggressive trash talk.

"He is so fucking hot," a girl in cheetah-print leggings gossips as she blows a string of smoke from her bloodred lips. The streetlight hanging above her pours a harsh glow over her bruised-purple hair, making it look even darker against her pale white skin. "And you know what they say about drummers."

"No, what?" her friend asks, scratching the back of her fishnet stockings with the scuffed toe of her black leather boot.

"Drummers really know how to bang."

A quiet chuckle escapes me as their drunken cackles echo down the city streets.

"You are so bad!" the girl in the fishnets says. "But I hear he never hooks up with fans."

"Ever?"

"Ever. You'd have better luck with the bass player."

"But I hear his girlfriend is batshit crazy . . ."

"Crazier than you?" Fishnets asks, and Cheetah Print pushes her while they giggle and continue fantasizing about my cousin's ex.

It makes me gaze down the sidewalk at Danica,

wondering if in some alternate universe, we could still be friends. Maybe I'd actually have fun at rock shows. Maybe she'd stop being so mean. Maybe we'd *like* living together.

Maybe we'd even gossip about boys.

Presented with two options—banging my head repeatedly against the telephone pole until this night finally ends, or extending Danica an olive branch—I take a deep breath and walk back toward the club.

"I have an idea," I offer as she hangs up her phone.

"First time for everything."

Ignoring her jab, I ask, "Don't bands like this have tour buses?"

While she stands there staring blankly at me, I wait for her to tell me what an idiot I am, or how stupid my idea is. But instead, the corners of her mouth start pulling up, and she smiles. *Really* smiles.

"See," she says, beaming down at me, and she's so sincerely happy, I can't help smiling back.

"See what?"

"I knew you weren't completely useless."

Chapter 2

"Didn't I tell you he was hot?" Danica asks as I sit on the pavement in front of the band's double-decker tour bus, picking a rock out of the sole of my sneaker. I scratch at it with my nub of a fingernail, mentally tallying how many times she's said that word over the past week.

Mike's band has gotten so hot.

They performed with Cutting the Line. Cutting the Line is so hot.

Mike wasn't this hot in high school. Look at this picture. Do you think he's hot? Hailey, are you even looking?

"Hailey, are you even listening?" Danica scolds, nudging my knee with the toe of her boot as I chip a short fingernail on the rock still wedged in my shoe.

I stare way up at her, wondering if she kicks everyone when they don't give her their undivided attention, or just me. Was she this bossy with Mike when they were together? What did he even see in her?

"Yeah," I finally answer. "He was okay."

"*Okay?*" she scoffs. "Are you blind?"

I'm not blind. I just don't feel like answering stupid questions at one o'clock in the morning. Of course I saw how hot he was. Everyone did. The girl in the cheetah print did, the girl in the fishnets did, and I'm guessing a hundred other girls did too, and each one of them will be jealous of Danica, and I'm pretty sure that's exactly why she's making me sit out here in the cold next to a locked behemoth of a tour bus. What does she want me to do? Congratulate her on how hot her soon-to-be boyfriend is?

"Adam was hotter," I lie.

"Huh?" Danica scrunches her nose, and my expression changes to match her confusion.

"What?"

"Who do you even think I'm talking about? The lead singer. Adam. Do you ever listen to anything I say?"

I free the rock from my shoe and stand up, dusting off the back of my jeans. We've been waiting out here for so long, my ass is numb and the rest of the fans have left. "If you're so in love with Adam, why didn't you date him instead of Mike?"

"Yeah, right," Danica scoffs, and when I just stare at her, she rolls her eyes. "They have some stupid bro code or something," she explains as she combs her fingers through the smooth hair hanging over her shoulder.

"Mike was always in love with me, so Adam wouldn't go for it. Believe me, I tried."

I don't even know how to respond to that, and I apparently don't need to because Danica orders, "Stop looking at me like that."

"Why are we even here?"

I can guess, but I've spent the past few weeks trying to give her the benefit of the doubt. Now, I'm tired, I'm bored, I'm cold, and any sense of self-preservation I had got smashed somewhere inside the pit of Mayhem. I don't care if I make her mad or that she has the power to make my life hell—I just want an explanation for why I smell like armpit and can't feel the tips of my fingers.

"I want Mike."

"Why?"

"I miss him," she lies. I can tell because she smiles when she says it. It's her sweet smile—the one she uses to get what she wants from her rich father, a smile that's *too* sweet. It's the same kind she gave me tonight when she asked if she could wear my hoodie "for a minute," even though we both knew she had no intention of giving it back.

I cross my arms tight over my thin thermal to ward off the cold, and Danica must be able to see the doubt on my face, because she continues explaining.

"Mike was an amazing boyfriend," she insists. "He treated me like a princess. He used to carry my books and bring me little gifts. On Valentine's Day, he always put flowers in my locker."

Her smile softens into something almost genuine, but it disappears when I ask, "Then why'd you dump him?"

In that condescending, usual tone of hers, she says, "Because we were graduating and he wasn't doing anything with his life. He was totally broke, but he wouldn't even *think* about going to college. He didn't have real goals. He was just a loser in some stupid little garage band."

Judging by the legion of fans jammed in front of the stage earlier tonight, it's clear he *did* have real goals and he's accomplished them with his "stupid little garage band," but I don't bother pointing that out. I also don't bother pointing out that Danica dropped out of college after only one semester and has spent the past six years living off of her parents' credit cards.

Sixty years ago, our grandparents bought a farm. Twenty-six years ago, her dad and my mom inherited it, and my parents made it their home. Fourteen years ago, Danica's parents made a lot of smart connections and investments, breaking into the corporate level of the livestock business, making a fortune, and moving far away from our small town and the modest plot of land that started it all. Now, Danica works for their company when it suits her.

My parents and younger brother still live on the same small farm our grandparents bought, and up until two months ago, so did I.

"And this has nothing to do with what Adam said at the beginning of the show about their band signing a big record deal?" I challenge, and Danica's eyes harden, but she doesn't bother arguing with me. Instead, movement toward the club steals her attention, and her almond eyes swing toward Mayhem.

Seven people walk across the dark parking lot toward the buses. Adam and a girl under his arm. Shawn and the female guitarist, Kit. Joel and a bombshell in high heels. And Mike.

Danica strips off my oversized hoodie before any of them can see her in it, tossing it to the ground and running toward her ex. "MIKE!"

It's like a scene out of a movie. Her long legs race across the parking lot. Her hair flies in the wind behind her. She jumps into her ex's arms.

But when his arms should lift to wrap around her—so he can spin her around like any good movie heartthrob would—Mike's simply hang motionless at his sides.

I stop brushing the dirt and dried leaves off my green Ivy Tech hoodie—the one my parents bought me one Christmas when they couldn't afford to get me much else—to watch the curious scene in front of me.

"Aren't you happy to see me?" Danica squeals, and the female guitarist makes a sound that causes Shawn to tighten his arm around her. Her black eyes are murderous, and I notice that the rest of the band looks more or less the same. They watch Mike and Danica like the scene unfolding before them is a horribly offensive horror movie instead of the timeless romance Danica wants it to be.

I watch too, and when Mike's arms eventually lift to hug Danica back, I sigh and return to inspecting my hoodie. There's a stain on the sleeve. It smears as I rub my thumb over it.

"What are you doing here?" Mike asks, and Danica flippantly tells him that she lives here now as she moves on to hug the rest of the guys. She puts on a performance worthy of an Oscar, and it doesn't falter until Shawn steps out of reach when she tries to catch him in her arms.

"What are you doing at our show?" he asks.

"I wanted to see Mike." She pouts without casting Mike even a second glance.

"Why?" When Mike speaks, it strikes me how well his voice suits him. It sounds like it belongs to someone with big brown eyes, thick brown hair, and sculpted arms. He's hotter than Adam, even if Danica can't see it, and I find myself feeling irritated—maybe because someone like him *would* love someone like Danica, maybe because someone like Danica would never love him as much, maybe because I'm tired and it's freaking cold and I smell like someone else's BO and my favorite hoodie in the world has a freaking stain on the sleeve and I have to go home tonight with the bitch who put it there.

"Yeah, Dani, why?"

She glares over her shoulder at the sound of her childhood nickname—the one that started getting under her skin when she decided it was too boyish—and I try not to stare down at my shoes.

Since we moved in together over the summer, I've held my tongue. I've been her housemaid, her personal chef, her babysitter, and her doormat. It's the price I've had to pay for the roof her family puts over our heads and the tuition they pay on my behalf. But three hours of waiting in line tonight, followed by five hours of no personal space and then two more hours of ass freezing, has severely compromised my filter. Which is a dangerous, dangerous thing.

I'm thankful when she lets my comment go and instead gives her attention back to Mike. "Can we talk?"

His expression is unreadable as he stares at her. I look for the guy who was in love with her, the one who put flowers in her locker. I look for the rock star I saw onstage tonight, the one who could have had any girl he wanted. I look for the dreamer, the one who knew better than to let Danica hold him back.

But they're all locked behind guarded brown eyes, and I stop looking for them when Mike says, "Sure," and leads Danica toward the bus.

Chapter 3

"ISN'T IT PAST your bedtime?" I taunt as I creep up on an enemy stronghold with a small but coveted weapon in my hand—a satellite phone linked to Command.

"Your mom's too busy sucking my dick for me to go to bed," the prepubescent voice in my headphones quips, and a bunch of other little boys laugh belligerently while a smile sneaks onto my face.

My thumbs move over the game controller in my hand, and with one final push of a button, an ungodly loud alarm begins to sound in the game.

"OH MY GOD," the first boy screams over the wailing alarm. The screen is flashing red with the sound, and I try to smack-talk through my laughter as the rest of the boys descend into panic.

"What's that you were saying about my mom?"

"HOW THE HELL DID YOU GET FUCKING AIR SUPPORT!" another boy yells, and on the TV screen in front of me, I watch as a group of camouflaged soldiers flee the distant building.

"Too late, newbs!" I shout as the whoosh of an Apache helicopter nears. A second later, deafening gunfire begins cutting down everyone in front of me, and the cries of little boys on the other end of my headphones warms my cruel, unmerciful heart.

I'm laughing hysterically as they shout a cacophony of curse words and accusations of me being a hacker, when the air inside the tour bus changes and I lift my eyes to see its door opening.

I've been alone on the bus for hours now. The first to leave were Mike and Danica, when she ran a finger over his arm and asked if they could talk in private. I guessed she was tired of the looks everyone was giving her, since it was obvious Mike's band and its entourage all hate her, but I doubted that what she had on her mind was "talking." I'm not sure if seeing Mike up close changed something for her, or if she's simply a very talented actress, but once we were all on the bus together, she barely paid Adam, Shawn, or Joel another glance. And the heat she threw at Mike must have worked, because he took her to a different bus in the parking lot, and they haven't been seen or heard from since.

I passed the time by playing war games with Adam's girlfriend, Rowan, on a flat-screen TV in the main sitting area, until two by two, everyone left to get some sleep. I assured them I'd be fine on my own while I waited for Danica, and I lost track of time as I slayed preteens who had no idea what they were in for.

Now, I set my headphones and controller down on the bench beside me and watch as Mike steps onto the bus, his hair disheveled and his eyes cast down. The door closes behind him, and I realize Danica's not with him.

"Where's Danica?" I ask, and Mike's tired eyes slowly lift when he realizes he's not alone.

"Sleeping." His voice sounds as exhausted as he looks, the air whooshing from the gray leather bench as he sinks into a seat across from me. His elbows come to rest heavy on his knees, and he rubs his fingers roughly over his eyes. "She fell asleep after . . ." He trails off, shaking his head to himself. I don't need him to finish the end of that sentence, and I'm glad when he doesn't. "It might be a while."

I should ask if she drank too much, or if she's safe sleeping alone on the other bus. But as I stare across the aisle at this man I don't know, at the way his broad shoulders slump like they're carrying an impossible weight, I find myself asking instead, "Are you okay?"

It's a silly question. He's a rock star. He obviously just got laid. Of course he's okay.

But when he lifts his chin, the look in his eyes makes me think that he's not.

"I need a beer" is the only answer he gives me as he rises to his feet. "Do you want anything?"

He walks toward the back of the bus without waiting for me to ask any more stupid questions about things that aren't my business, but before he crosses through the divider, I tell him I'll take whatever he's got.

I resume playing the game on the screen, and when

Mike returns with two beers in hand, I set mine beside me and give him my thanks, all without taking my right hand off the controller or my eyes off the screen. I'm probably going to be waiting for Danica for a long, long time. I might as well make the most of it.

"This is Deadzone Five," Mike observes as he watches me play, and I glance at him out of the corner of my eye.

"Shit," I say as I continue playing. "Are you the one beta testing this? I thought it was Rowan."

"You managed to get air support?" he asks, ignoring my question.

"Yeah. And I found a bug. I can keep—"

I trail off after glancing at him again. His eyebrows are tightly knit, and he's staring at me like I've sprouted tentacles out of my ears.

"Sorry," I say as I set the controller down. "I didn't mean to—"

"I've been trying to get air support for *weeks*!" he interrupts with nothing but awe in his voice. I hide my smile behind a simple explanation.

"I'm pretty good."

"You'd have to be! Holy shit."

That forlorn expression is gone from his face, and this time, I let myself grin. "And there's a glitch that lets me keep using it. Do you want to see it in action?"

I hand Mike the headset, and when the alarms in the game start sounding and the screen flashes red, his face brightens with excitement. I can hear the frantic screams of ten-year-olds from his headphones, and when Mike starts laughing, I do too.

"Do me a favor?" I ask, and when he waits for me to continue, I say, "Tell PussySlayer69 that my mom says hello."

Mike laughs so hard, he sends himself into a coughing fit. "Oh my God, that little shit has been working on my nerves for weeks." He pulls the mouthpiece to his lips and says, "Hey Kyle, you realize you're getting your ass handed to you by a girl over here, right? Her mom says hi."

I can't make out what Kyle is saying, but I can hear his signature high-pitched screaming, and judging by the way Mike doubles over with laughter, it must be good. I'm beaming with pride when Mike finally sits back up and lets out a satisfied sigh. "That was amazing. I needed that."

"Rough night?" I joke, but Mike's smile falls away, and I curse my stupid mouth.

Not my business, not my business, not my business. Danica's business is so *not* my business, it's not even on the same map. She is Antarctica, and I am the moon.

"Your name is Hailey, right?" Mike asks.

I nod, still trying to think of a way to erase the last thirty seconds of our conversation.

"I'm sorry for being such an asshole, Hailey. I didn't know you'd end up on your own here all night."

"It's alright—" I start, but Mike shakes his head.

"No, it's not. I wasn't thinking."

The sincerity in his gaze makes me swallow hard, and when he frowns at my silence, I shake my head. If anyone should feel bad about tonight, it's Danica. She made me drive her here, forced me to follow her around like her personal butler for hours, and then fell the hell *asleep*. "Really, it's okay. I haven't been alone for long. I spent most of the night gaming with Rowan."

Mike stares at me a moment longer before a small smile graces his face again. "She's pretty good too. She can wipe the floor with me half the time."

It's true—she *was* pretty awesome, both in the game and out of it. We apparently go to the same school, so we exchanged numbers and made plans to have lunch together—along with Joel's girlfriend, Dee—on campus on Wednesday. It's the only good thing I got out of tonight.

"Not as good as me though," I brag, and Mike chuckles.

"No, you're something else. I still can't believe you got air support in, what, just a few hours."

I lift my beer bottle into the air for a toast, and he clinks his to mine.

"I play DZ4 with my little brother a lot," I explain.

"And you're Danica's cousin, right?" he asks after taking a long sip of his beer. When I nod, he adds, "She never mentioned she had any cousins."

I take another drink, remembering the way she just tossed my favorite hoodie on the ground. It's currently lying wet in the bathroom sink of the bus. Shawn tried to help me get the stain out of the sleeve, but we only made it worse.

"Probably because she's a self-centered bitch who doesn't think about anyone but herself," I spit, and as soon as the bitter truth leaves my mouth, my eyes go wide and my lips clamp shut.

I can't believe I just said that. Out loud. To the very guy she just finished doing God-knows-what with not more than twenty minutes ago. I've lost my damn mind.

I hold my breath while Mike stares at me, and then he gives me an amused smile and teases, "Why don't you tell me how you *really* feel."

I take a humongous swallow from my bottle to clear the even bigger lump in my throat. "Sorry."

"For what?"

"I didn't mean to insult your girlfriend."

"Girlfriend," he repeats, frowning. He sits back against the leather seat and lets his head fall back. "Tonight is so fucked."

I repeat my mantra. Not my business, not my business, not my business.

"Do you want another beer?" I ask, dropping my eyes from the dusting of stubble on his chin to his empty bottle. Mike is an enigma. A rock star who doesn't hook up with groupies. A guy who just got laid, yet acts like someone just died. I don't know what's bothering him, but even if I asked, I'm guessing I wouldn't understand. The guy was in love with Danica, and that's something I could never comprehend regardless of how many years I spent playing tour bus psychiatrist.

"There's not enough beer in the world," he answers, but I hand him what's left of mine before taking his empty bottle and walking in the direction of the kitchenette in the back. I know I can't get involved, so instead, I do the next best thing.

"Where are you going?" Mike asks, sitting up.

"To see if you have anything stronger than beer."

Chapter 4

WHEN DANICA STEPS onto the bus early the following morning, Mike and I are sitting shoulder to shoulder in an open space on the aisle floor, game controllers in hand, beer and liquor bottles littering the benches surrounding us. He's drunk, I'm overtired, and the combination of us has resulted in a night filled with so many laughs, I have a permanent cramp in my side and the muscles in my cheeks ache.

"Hey, Danica," Mike says after a glance toward the door, "watch this."

He activates the air support, and when the alarms in the game begin wailing, so do we. We've been doing this for the past couple hours, but it's still the funniest thing I've ever heard, and I struggle to mimic the sound through the snorts that interrupt my laughter. They make Mike laugh even harder, which makes *me* laugh even harder, which makes us an absolute mess.

I'm laughing, crying, and snorting when I make the mistake of glancing at Danica, and then I'm choking. She's looking a little worse for wear—with finger-brushed hair and day-old makeup—but is still gorgeous in a black top that clings to her curves, skin-tight jeans that hug her legs, and knee-high boots that are probably worth more than every shitty hand-me-down car I've ever owned.

She's staring right back at me, and the look on her face is deadly.

I lock my eyes on the TV, feeling her death glare burrow through the side of my skull. I don't even want to *know* what I look like. I've gotten no sleep, I probably still smell like armpit, and I've cried countless tears while giggling the night away with Mike Madden. I'm guessing that last part is why she currently looks like she's going to chainsaw me to death in my sleep tonight.

When she approaches us, every muscle in my body tenses in anticipation of the attitude she's about to throw at me. But instead of bitching me out for stealing her boyfriend from the other bus—since, in Danica's world, I'm sure it's all my fault she woke up alone—she simply sits on the bench beside Mike, leans down to press a kiss against his cheek, and says, "What are you playing?"

"The new Deadzone," he answers without peeling his eyes from the screen. He continues landing head-shots left and right—an impressive feat considering how much Guinness is probably sloshing around in his stomach—while I stare at Danica like *I'm* the one who's drunk.

She's being . . . nice? Nice. Did I imagine that look she gave me when she came on the bus?

When she glances at me, I'm practically cross-eyed with confusion, but she simply grins and twirls thick chunks of Mike's brown hair around her slender fingers.

"Are you winning?" she asks him.

"It's not really that kind of game . . ."

"Then how do you play?"

Her voice, sweeter than pink cotton candy, makes me want to hurl. "Since when do you care about video games?" I ask, and she gives me that I'm-going-to-chainsaw-your-face-off look again. Nope, definitely didn't imagine it.

"Don't be ridiculous, Hailey," she scoffs, her hand coming to rest possessively on the nape of Mike's neck. "You know how much I love watching you and your brother play."

I have some kind of stroke. That's the only explanation. My jaw drops open, my character gets shot in the head, and my brain does some kind of sputtering thing that leaves my game controller hanging from limp hands. "Say whaaa?"

Since my twelve-year-old brother and I are now separated by hundreds of miles and won't see each other until Thanksgiving break, I make it a priority to play games with him online on a regular basis, and two nights ago, we were playing Deadzone Four when Danica burst into my room demanding that I shut it off. It was one o'clock in the morning, but I was apparently slowing down the wifi and it was more important for her to look up manicure designs on Pinterest than it was for me to help my lonely little brother forget about the asshole who'd bullied him in gym class that day.

My head is tilted to the side like an extremely confused teacup Chihuahua, and Danica gives me another look.

Keep your mouth shut, her eyes threaten.

"You used to hate it when I played," Mike remembers while I'm still trying to recover from my stroke.

"Did I?" Danica's eyes glitter with deceit that I hope Mike can see. "That was so long ago. I was such a bitch back then." When Mike just stares at her, she slides down into his lap and clasps her fingers behind his neck. "Forgive me?"

Mike dated her for four years. Four *years.* He should know better than to buy this crap, right? Right?

Say no, you giant idiot! Push her fake ass off your lap!

When Mike continues studying her with those big brown eyes of his, she leans in and kisses him. She squirms tight against his body and threads her fingers into his hair, and I roll my eyes and stand up.

If batting eyelashes and pink lip gloss are all it takes to get under his skin, then those two were made for each other.

"Alright, well, I'm going to get going." Ignoring my disappointment in the drummer who made me laugh harder last night than I have in years, I grab my keys from the bench beside me and jingle them in the air while Danica whispers something in Mike's ear—or does *something* in Mike's ear. I don't even want to know. "Dani, are you coming or what?"

Mike is the one who pulls away to stare up at me, and I avoid looking at him. The bottles lying everywhere are testament to what it took for him to sort through his feelings for the girl on his lap, but even though he's had a lot to drink, it hasn't been nearly enough to excuse letting that two-faced leech suck his face.

"No," Danica says, still staring at Mike like he's a gold-plated banana split. "I'm going to stay here for a while."

"You're leaving?" Mike asks me, and when he shifts Danica off of his lap and attempts to stand, I have to launch forward to keep him from falling.

Okay, so maybe he *is* that drunk. Shit . . .

"I, er . . . yeah. I mean, I was just waiting for Danica, so . . ."

My eyes drop to my hand, which is pressed tight against the hard curve of Mike's waist, and when I hastily pull it away, he nearly stumbles forward again. His arm wraps heavily around my shoulders in an attempt to catch himself, and I help him find his balance while ignoring the deadly look that Danica gives me.

"Mike," I say, staring up into his big glassy eyes. "Do you need a ride home?"

"Why are you offering him a ride home?" Danica snaps at me.

"He's drunk . . ."

"And?"

"And—"

I'm about to explain some choice phrases like "designated driver" and "decent human being" when Mike interrupts, "Are you trying to hold me up?"

I lift my gaze to his and watch as an amused smile stretches across his lips.

I have one hand firmly on his back and the other on his stomach, like I'm some kind of pocket-sized Wonder Woman capable of keeping a guy twice my size on his feet. "You were going to fall," I reason, ignoring the amusement in his voice.

"You're like two feet tall," he teases with a chuckle.

"Five feet," I argue, and when Mike laughs hard, I try not to smile.

"He's fine here with me." Danica's arms are crossed tightly over her chest, and she has one foot planted forward in an aggressive stance that isn't lost on me.

I should stay out of it. Danica will make my life a living hell if I piss her off. And Mike is *so* not my business.

Except that I'm the one who got him drunk. And I'm the one who drove Danica here. And I'll never feel right about it if I leave this innocent man with the she-devil herself when he can barely stand upright.

My conscience sighs.

"Don't you want to take a shower?" I ask Danica, ignoring all sense of self-preservation and instead hitting her weak spot. I slip out from under Mike's arm and lower my voice so only she can hear. "I mean, don't you want to wash your hair?"

TEN MINUTES LATER, I'm on the road home with Danica in my passenger seat, and she's still periodically inspecting the ends of her perfect hair. Mike said he would sleep on the bus, so after rooting him out some carbs and bottled water and repeatedly making him swear he wouldn't drive, I left.

I felt like I should thank him for the fun time I had with him last night, or like I should . . . I don't know, shake his hand or hug him or something. Hanging out with him felt like hanging out with someone I'd been friends with for years, and I secretly want to play Deadzone Five with him again, but he's Danica's boyfriend, and all of that felt too weird, so instead, I simply told him he should brush up on his sniping skills, and I left.

Danica's goodbye was much more dramatic. A kiss that lasted so long, I waited for her outside the bus.

"So *all* you did was play video games all night?" she asks me for the hundredth time as she studies a lock of her penny-colored hair.

"No, Dani, we had an orgy all night. The opening band joined in. So did some circus performers that were in town. Things got a little weird with the car full of clowns but—"

"Do you always have to be so annoying?" she complains, shielding her eyes from the sun. Without Mike to impress, she's gone into full morning-mode Danica, slunk down in her seat with her bare feet up on my dash.

"I already told you no a thousand times."

"You were too friendly with each other this morning," she accuses.

"Because I'm like everyone's kid sister."

Danica grunts her acceptance, and I curse the fact that the radio in my car doesn't work. Right now would be the perfect time to turn it on so that I can't get dragged into any more conversations about—

"Well, did he at least say anything about me?"

After we started drinking and playing Deadzone, not a word. It was like Danica ceased to exist, and the truth is, Mike wasn't the only one to forget about her. I forgot that I'd brought her along. I forgot about the show. I forgot about the throngs of fans that jumped to the deafening beat of Mike's drums just a few hours earlier. Instead, I laughed and played games and had an *amazing* time.

With Danica's boyfriend.

"He wouldn't shut up about you," I lie, and when Danica orders me to give her details, I scrape for something to appease her. "He said you're even prettier now than you were in high school."

"He said that?" she asks, straightening in her seat and beaming at me.

"Yeah," I answer, surprised that she's buying it, since she can normally see right through any fibs I try to tell.

"What else did he say?"

"Oh, you know . . ." When she won't stop staring at me, I jump out on a short limb. "He said he had a really good time with you last night."

Satisfied, she sits back in her seat and smiles. I smile too, relieved that I no longer have to talk to her, but then she opens her gloss-coated lips again.

"Last night was amazing."

I really don't want to talk about it. Or hear about it. Or think about it.

"He's so much hotter than he was in high school, too. Like, I know you couldn't tell because of his T-shirt, but oh my *God*, Hailey, you should see what he's hiding under there. And he was so fucking *good*." She stretches out her body like it's still aching from the night's activities. "I've never . . . He was never . . ." She starts giggling, and I seriously might need to crash my car into a tree or something. Maybe Danica's dad would take pity and buy me a new one. "I hate you for making me leave this morning. I could've gone a few more rounds."

I'm singing outdated pop songs in my head when Danica makes a sound in the back of her throat. "Ugh. I can't believe he still plays video games though."

And like an idiot, I break my vow of silence. "You acted like you didn't mind."

"Of course I acted like I didn't mind," she scoffs. "We just started talking again. It's not like I'm going to start telling him all the things I can't stand about him."

She shifts in her seat to face me, indignant. "And were you *trying* to call me out back there? Because I don't see why you'd want to be mean like that."

Me. Mean.

"I'm just not as good of a liar as you," I say, and Danica rolls her eyes.

"Whatever. Keep telling yourself that."

I narrow my eyes across the console at her. "What's that supposed to mean?"

"Why don't you figure it out," she says, busying herself with crawling her feet back up my dash.

"Why don't you just tell me?"

Her brown eyes swing over to me and harden as she sets both feet firmly back on the floor. "You think you're so good, Hailey. You think you're too good to have a fun time with me."

"You bossed me around all night . . ."

"You mean I tried to order you to have fun for once in your life? Tried to get you to jump up and down in the crowd with me? Oh, boo-hoo, Hailey. Cry me a fucking river."

I pick at a chip in my foam steering wheel, wondering if she's right. Was it my own fault I had such a miserable time? Was Danica just trying to get me to have fun?

"Sorry," I say, and she grunts.

"Whatever. I'm not your enemy, Hailey."

"I know that . . ." *Do I?*

"We're family."

"I know."

"We should act like it."

I couldn't agree more.

I'm feeling all sorts of confused when Danica says, "Friends?"

Friends? With Danica?

I think back to riding horses with her when we were little girls, to the way we used to braid their manes and pretend they were My Little Ponys. Those are some of my most cherished memories, but the cousin I loved moved away a long time ago, and I haven't seen her since.

"Okay," I say after a while, and Danica gives me a smile before gazing out the passenger window.

"We should find you a boyfriend," she says, and even though that is so *not* happening, I try to stay positive for the sake of our new truce.

"Maybe."

We pass by the college, we pass by the local Starbucks, and we're close to home when she laughs to herself. "I still can't believe I ever thought something happened between you and Mike last night."

"You know I'd never do something like that to you," I say, and when she looks over at the sincere expression on my face, she laughs again.

"And plus he's a rock star, Hailey."

"Yeah?"

"And you're just . . ."

"I'm just what?"

"You," she says with another laugh. "You're just you."

Chapter 5

My truce with Danica looks a little like this: I bake cookies, she eats them. I suggest watching a movie, she picks the movie. I compliment her on her outfit, she offers to help me burn my clothes.

On Wednesday morning, I dress in calf-high polka-dot rain boots, thrift-shop jeans, an oversized sweater, a bright blue raincoat, a sunshine-yellow scarf that my mom made, and a black knit cap that's topped by what has to be the world's biggest, purplest pompom.

"You really should let me take you shopping," Danica critiques as I grab my umbrella, and I close the door behind me.

I have a hectic morning—first, dog walking at the local animal shelter where I'm interning; and then not one, not two, but *three* intense exams that I am *so* not prepared for. The whole morning is crazy, and it gets even crazier when I meet Rowan and Dee for our scheduled lunch.

"Finally!" Dee shouts as soon as I drag my sopping wet self through the college café's heavy double doors. Her long brown hair is twisted into Hollywood curls, her dark eyes bright as she watches me approach her table. My brow furrows as I attempt to uncoil the sunshine-colored scarf from my neck, and I check the time on a clock on the wall.

"Am I late? I thought we said—"

"You're fine," she interrupts, standing up to pull my cap off my head as I continue fighting with my boa constrictor of a scarf. "But I'm not."

"What's wrong?"

Rowan gives me a small wave from where she's sitting, sucking on the oversized straw of an iced coffee, and I wave back as Dee takes my coat and says, "I'M DYINGGG."

"Uh?"

She practically pushes me into a seat across from her, and then she leans across the table. "Last Saturday. After we left. Tell me everything."

"There's not much to tell—" I start, but Dee presses her finger against my lips and shakes her head while *tsk, tsk, tsk*ing.

"Hailey. *Hailey.* Let me stop you right there, okay? We're going to be friends, right?"

All I can manage is a lift of my eyebrow.

"As my friend, you need to know something about

me. I'm practically an old married woman now. I've settled down. My scandalous days are behind me. I've gone vanilla. I'm balled and chained—"

"You're *balled*?" Rowan snickers, but Dee's pleading brown eyes remain glued to the confused expression on my face.

"I *need* you to give me details. I want a story. I need the low-down. Give me some juice. I want the—"

"She's had too much caffeine," Rowan teases, and Dee never breaks eye contact with me as she reaches a hand back and starts batting at her friend.

"Uh." I attempt to comb my fingers through my damp short brown curls since they've somehow managed to tangle in and around and over themselves. My hand gets stuck, and I wiggle my fingers in the knots as I say, "Well, not much happened. Danica fell asleep, and Mike and I played video games until she woke up."

"That's it?" Dee complains, slumping in her chair. "That's seriously *it*? You played *video games*?"

I shrug, and in spite of the pout on Dee's face, Rowan smiles. "What did Mike think of your Deadzone skills?"

The corners of my mouth tug up at her question. "He was impressed."

"Of course he was. Did you two have fun together?"

Too much fun. I've replayed that night in my mind too many times over the past four days, smiling at the jokes that were told or the stupid things that were said or the way Mike's chocolate-brown eyes brightened when he laughed so hard, they filled with tears. I've remembered the way he wiped those tears on his shoulder since his hands were holding his game controller.

And I've remembered earlier: the show. The way he looked at the back of the stage, his messy brown hair tipped with sweat as blue light danced over his shoulders, his neck, his arms. I've remembered the way the entire room jumped to the beat of his drumsticks as they pounded an unforgiving rhythm against his drums. I've remembered the pulsing of the club, and the way Mike's eyes lifted at breaks in the songs to take it all in.

And then, I've remembered that he's Danica's boyfriend, and I've focused on that, and focused on that, and focused on that.

"Yeah," I finally answer Rowan. "It was a lot of fun."

"Mike's a sweetheart, right?" she asks with that bright smile still shining on her face.

"Yeah—"

"And hot, right?" Dee asks, her smile matching Rowan's. I stare back and forth between them.

"I guess?"

I've never been one to gossip about boys. And I'm not about to start with the guy who is banging my cousin.

"I think he's hot as hell," Dee offers. "I mean, those arms, right? Even Joel doesn't have arms like Mike. Joel's arms are kind of lean, but Mike's arms are—"

"Do you have a crush on Mike or something?" I ask, and Dee's face twists, her brows knitting over a severely crinkled nose.

"What? No!"

Rowan stifles a laugh, and I ask, "Are you sure? I mean, if you do, I won't tell Danica, but—"

"Hell no, I don't have a crush on Mike! Jesus. I'm with *Joel*." Dee leans across the table and emphasizes his name. "I have a *boyfriend*."

"O . . . kay?"

She rubs the line between her eyebrows, and Rowan laughs a little before asking, "What about you, Hailey? Do you have a boyfriend?"

"I did," I answer, slowly pulling my eyes from Dee. "But we broke up before I moved here."

"Oh." Rowan's mouth turns down in a frown, her blue eyes sympathetic behind black frame glasses that are slipping down her nose. "I'm sorry to hear that."

"Don't be," I say as I squint my eyes to try to read the coffee menu behind the register up front. I wonder if there's anything I can afford with the three dollars and two dimes in my pocket. "We're better as friends anyway."

"So nothing serious?" Rowan asks, and I give her my attention.

Serious? I'm pretty sure I've never had a serious relationship in my life. The few boyfriends I've had were more like guy acquaintances I just spent extra time with, and all of my breakups have been easy. Nothing worth losing sleep over.

"No," I say, shaking my head. "Definitely nothing serious."

Rowan's smile widens, and I ask her what she's drinking before excusing myself to splurge on a cup of coffee, desperately needing the caffeine after this morning's runaround. Walking a kennel's worth of dogs is always exhausting, but walking them in the beating rain is brutal, especially when I have three back-to-back exams to suffer through after.

By the time I sit back down, my coffee is already half gone, and I search for the phone I left on the table only to find it in Dee's hands.

"What are you doing?" I ask as she maneuvers her thumbs over my screen, and she answers without looking up.

"Giving you all the necessary numbers."

"Hey," Rowan says before I can ask the next question lingering on my tongue, like *Who told you that you can touch my phone?* "We've got to get going, but I almost forgot to give you this."

She pulls a plastic grocery bag from her backpack, and at the sight of a sliver of familiar green fabric, I help myself to the contents before she can finish laying the bag on the table. "I never thought I'd see this again!" I squeal, lifting my treasured hoodie into the air.

The week before I started taking classes at the Ivy Tech community college, my parents came with me to the bookstore. Since neither of them had ever gone to college before me, none of us had any clue what we were doing or how to shop for textbooks, but we figured between the three of us and my seven-year-old brother, we could probably figure it out. We talked to a nice employee who helped show us how to find used books for each of my classes, and she assured me I'd be able to sell them back at the end of the year. With all of my books successfully piled in my dad's arms, my whole family was buzzing with excitement over the fact that I was starting college—college!—next week, and I grabbed some folders, notebooks, pencils, and a pretty green Ivy Tech hoodie to throw in front of the checkout register as well. A face-splitting smile stretched onto my face as the nice employee checked us out, and it stayed there right up until my father's credit card was declined, and then declined again.

Outside the bookstore, with all of my textbooks and school supplies abandoned inside, I tried not to cry. State grants had covered most of my tuition, and my dad had assured me we could afford the rest, but apparently that wasn't true. He called the credit card company, who told us our balance, and I begged my mom to wait with my brother outside while my dad and I went back inside to figure out exactly what we could afford. I put the folders back, I put the notebooks back, I put the pencils back, and finally, I hung my hoodie back up on the rack.

I told myself that I had my textbooks and that that was all that mattered—I could make do with my high school folders and notebooks and pencils, and I did. But that still didn't stop me from bursting into tears when I opened up my first present that following Christmas morning to find the hoodie I had hung back up on the rack. My parents went back to buy it as soon as they could afford to, and even though it's now five years old and its green color is a little less green, it still means the world to me.

"You forgot it on the bus," Rowan says as I hug the soft material against my face, emotion catching in my throat.

"I know," I say as I breathe in the fresh-washed scent. I spread the hoodie out on the table, adding, "In the sink. Shawn tried to help me clean it, but . . ." I trail off as I flip the right sleeve over and over and over. My eyebrows knit together, and I start doing the same to the left sleeve. "Where's the stain?"

"What stain?"

"The one on the sleeve," I say, continuing to flip and flip and flip. "It was right here. It was like . . . mud and oil, or something. We couldn't get it out. It—"

"Mike must have done it," Dee interrupts, and my eyes search hers for answers, but Rowan is the one to offer them.

"Mike gave me that to give to you," she says with a soft smile. "I'm just the messenger."

My head spins with the knowledge that Mike—*Mike*, rock star, gamer, my cousin's boyfriend—got the stain out for me. The stain on my favorite hoodie that meant more to me than he could ever possibly know. The stain Danica put there.

"You should call and thank him," Dee advises, standing up while Rowan packs up her backpack.

"I don't have his number . . ." I say, sounding as confused as I feel. But Dee just grins and hands my phone over.

"Sure you do. Like I said"—she leans in and whispers—"necessary numbers. You owe me a story."

Chapter 6

IN MY ROOM, in my hoodie, with one hand fidgeting with my phone and the other pinching my bottom lip into a weird, squishy U, I'm a cliché. I'm every nervous teenage girl calling a boy in every straight-to-DVD coming-of-age movie ever. Which doesn't make any damn sense, considering that Mike is just some guy I played video games with one night. Just some rock star I watched perform in front of an entire club full of screaming fans. Just some dude who went through the effort to get an impossible stain out of my favorite hoodie that I never thought I'd see again ever.

I tap my phone against my forehead.

He's Danica's boyfriend, for God's sake. I'm just calling to say thank you. This isn't a big deal. This isn't even a *small* deal. This is no deal.

Resigned, I pull my phone away from my forehead

and go into my contacts. Only there's nothing under Mike.

Nothing under Madden.

I'm scrolling, scrolling, thinking about forgetting the whole thing, scrolling some more—and then there it is. Under S.

I shake my head and hover my thumb over "Sexy as Fuck Drummer," imagining that Dee's entire phone is programmed this way. Rowan is probably under "Best Bitch" and I'm probably under "That Awkward Girl Who Smells Like Wet Dogs."

I groan and press my thumb against Mike's number before I can chicken out, swallowing hard and holding the phone to my ear.

Please don't pick up, please don't pick up, please don't pick up—

"Hello?"

Mike's smooth voice makes my eyes shut tight. "Hey. Um, is this Mike?"

"Who's asking?"

Is it too late to say wrong number? It's probably too late to say wrong number. . . . right?

"This is Danica's cousin. We met last Saturday?"

"Hailey?" he says, and my heart stumbles at the sound of my own name. "Hey, I was just thinking about you."

My lip gets clamped tightly between my fingers again before I ask, "You were?"

Why is Danica's boyfriend thinking about me? *Why is Danica's boyfriend thinking about me?!*

"Yeah. Kyle the PussySlayer asked about you."

The laughter that bursts out of me is probably louder than it should be, the product of unfounded nervousness and a long, wet day. "Did you tell him I was busy sleeping with his mom?"

"Better," Mike promises, and I hear the grin in his voice. I collapse back against my mattress, feeling the tension escape my body as my smile shines up at the pale green stars on my ceiling. "I told him that you were so good, they recruited you to beta test Deadzone Six."

"There's a Deadzone Six already?" I ask, and Mike laughs.

"Nope."

My soft chuckle rasps against the phone. "But he believed you?"

"Yep. You should've heard him freak out. You know that scream he does—"

"The one that sounds like a meerkat with its nuts in a clamp?"

Mike barks out a laugh before I hear him half choking on his end of the line. "You made me spit out my beer!"

My cheeks ache from smiling so wide, and I poke at one with my fingers. "Sorry."

"Don't be," he says, but it doesn't matter, because I wasn't anyway. "Hey," he asks after neither of us says anything for a while, "how'd you get my number?"

I stop poking at my cheek. "Dee gave it to me. I hope that's okay. Rowan gave me back my hoodie today, and I just wanted to say thanks."

"I'm glad you got it. That stuff you got on the sleeve was hard as hell to get out."

I'm holding the edge of the sleeve against my nose, breathing in the freshly laundered scent and forcing myself not to correct Mike. I want to tell him that his girlfriend was the one who got the stain on the sleeve, not me, but instead I simply ask, "How'd you manage it?"

"I called my mom," Mike says with a little laugh, and a warmth pools beneath my cheeks.

"You called *your mom*?"

"She worked as a housekeeper for a few years when I was a kid. I figured she might know how. I called Shawn first, but he said he already tried, so—"

"Mike . . ." I interrupt, overwhelmed by his kindness. "You didn't have to go through all that trouble."

"It's nothing—" he starts, but I cut him off.

"No." I stretch my arm above my head and admire my rescued hoodie. It almost looks newer than it did when I first got it. "It's something."

"Well," he says, his voice softening, "you're welcome then."

With no idea what to say next, I say nothing. I let the silence stretch and stretch until I'm rushing to find *anything* to fill it. "I'll go ahead and let you get back to your game," I stammer. "I really just called to—"

"Hey, do you want to play?" Mike interrupts.

"I don't have Deadzone Five . . ."

"What about Deadzone Four?" he counters. "I'm getting tired of this one anyway."

My lip is in a U again as nervous little butterflies

attempt to take flight in my belly. I curse the three-day-old leftover Chinese I ate for dinner, shaking my head and saying, "I can't . . . I have a gaming date with my little brother."

"The one who plays Deadzone?"

Last Saturday, Mike and I had a lot of time to pass. We talked about drums, games, jobs we've had, and most of all, I talked about Luke. "Yeah," I say about the twelve-year-old I miss so much, it hurts. "But tonight he wants to play this weird role-playing game he's getting into."

"Which one?"

"Dragon something? I can't remember. It's some fairy tale game or something."

I expect Mike to laugh and jokingly tell me to have fun, but instead, he asks, "Can I play with you?"

"You want to play?"

"Yeah, why not?"

"Because you'll probably have to play as a fairy princess or something?"

"Are you worried I'll look better than you in a dress?"

My face cracks into a big smile as Mike and I fall into the easy banter we had last Saturday. "It's not my fault I have stubby little legs."

"Whatever you say, Stubs."

The laugh that comes out of me sounds more like a giggle, and I smother myself with the baggy sleeve of my hoodie to prevent another one from breaking free.

"Now are you going to let me play with you," Mike asks, "or do I have to cry myself to sleep?"

I attempt to sound angry when I say, "Let me ask my brother, *Princess*." But by the way Mike chuckles, I fail.

TEN MINUTES LATER, in a three-way chat, Mike and Luke make easy introductions. Luke takes it upon himself to explain the game to Mike in typical Luke-fashion, leaving absolutely *no* detail out. He explains things I'm sure Mike already knows—like which keys to use on the keyboard, and how to change the way he chats—and as he talks, and talks, and *talks*, Mike listens, and asks questions, and engages him in a way that melts my heart. I become a third wheel except for when Mike brings me into the conversation, and by the time midnight rolls around and I order Luke to go to bed—for what has to be the tenth time—I am thankful to Mike for more than just my hoodie.

"He loved you," I say when I answer my ringing phone at 12:02 A.M. I expected that we were *all* going to bed, but then Sexy as Fuck Drummer showed up on my phone and my heart skipped into my throat.

"I'm going to see if I can get the Deadzone people to let him beta Five," Mike says, and my eyes widen.

"You don't have to . . ."

"I want to."

"Why?"

"Because your brother's cool," Mike says, and I snicker.

"He's twelve."

"He's the coolest twelve-year-old I've ever met."

"I'll have to tell him that," I say with a genuine smile in my voice. "Oh! And he doesn't even know you're a rock star. He's going to die."

"Rock star." Mike laughs.

"What's funny?"

"Adam is the rock star."

In the dark, I wonder, *Is that what he actually thinks? Does he really not know what a star he is?* And I suddenly feel a deep-seated need to correct him.

Maybe it's the big sister in me. Or maybe it's the indebted hoodie owner. Or maybe it's just the girl who knows deep down that Mike deserves to understand how special he is.

"You should've heard these two girls outside the club talking about you last Saturday," I say.

"Oh yeah? What were they saying?"

"They were talking about how hot you are." I try to sound as casual as possible in spite of the fierce red blush creeping across my cheeks.

"Go on," Mike says, his amused tone making even the tip of my nose glow red.

"Something about drummers really knowing how to bang."

Oh God, my entire face is on *fire*. I flip the pillow over and bury my flaming cheeks in it as Mike laughs.

"They said you never hook up with fans though," I rush to add, and Mike's laughter slowly quiets.

"Yeah, I don't."

"Why not? Isn't that one of the perks of being a rock star?"

A long, long moment of silence passes, and then Mike says, "Can I be honest with you?"

"Of course."

He takes a deep breath, and I hold mine.

"I don't think I ever really got over your cousin."

"Oh." I pull the covers over my head to hide from the heavy awkwardness that just swallowed this conversation whole. It's like I forgot that he's Danica's boyfriend.

Danica's. Boyfriend.

"I'm supposed to take her out this Saturday . . ." he says while I continue hiding in the pitch-black.

"Sounds like fun."

"Yeah."

"Hey, Mike?"

"Yeah?"

"I'm going to head to bed, okay?"

The line is silent for a while, and then he says, "Okay. Thanks for letting me play with you and your brother tonight, Hailey."

I thank him again for my hoodie, and we eventually end the call. But not before he wishes me sweet dreams.

I fall asleep thinking of the way his deep, quiet voice sounded when he said it.

Have sweet dreams, Hailey.

I sigh against my pillow.

Goodnight, Mike.

Chapter 7

"YOU SHOULD GO out with Mike," my brother informs me on Saturday afternoon as I shoulder my phone against my ear and pick up dog poop while simultaneously trying to untangle three dog leashes from my legs. Apparently, walking a poodle, a dachshund, and a wolfhound all at one time was a terrible freaking idea.

"He's dating Danica," I reply as I try to kick my foot out of a dog-leash noose.

"So?" Luke counters.

"NO!" I shout at the world's horniest poodle when he gets excited and tries to hump my leg. I push him down, but the wolfhound thinks I'm playing and tackles me to the grass. *Again.*

"Geez, *sorry,*" Luke says while I get my face licked by three dogs at once.

"Not you." I make spitting sounds as I writhe on the

ground trying to keep dog tongue out of my mouth. In the distance, I hear someone laughing, and I guess the shelter director, Barb, is getting a kick out of me being assaulted by a horny fluff ball, an overweight hot dog, and a shaggy horse-mutt all at once. No amount of college internship credits could possibly be worth this. It's taking all of my concentration to not roll onto the bag of poop that fell somewhere on the grass nearby. "Hold on a second, Luke."

Approximately five hundred NOs later, I'm finally on my feet again with three very sorry-looking dogs sitting on the grass in front of me. "These dogs are going to be the death of me," I huff as the wolfhound hangs his head.

"They can't be worse than Teacup."

"Teacup is an angel!" I protest in defense of the adorable potbelly pig I had to leave back home. Sure, she had a thing for eating people's shoes. But who needs shoes anyway?

"She ate Dad's slipper yesterday."

"Oh no."

"He threatened to eat her."

"He always threatens to eat her."

"Do you think Mike likes pigs?"

He must, since he's dating one. I grin to myself as I walk the dogs back toward the kennels. "Why are you so hung up on Mike, bud?"

I'm guessing it has something to do with the fact that Mike came through and got Luke a code to beta test Deadzone Five. My brother had been so excited, he could barely form a complete sentence on the phone—just lots of "oh my God"s and "this can't be real life"s.

"I like him. He's cool."

"Do you know he's also in a band?"

"No way."

I chuckle at the awe in Luke's voice. I can just imagine the way his chunky blue glasses slipped down on his nose when his mouth fell open. "Yeah. He's a drummer. His band is pretty big around here."

"Please date him," my brother whines.

"Why, just because he's in a band?"

"And he plays video games."

"Chuck played video games," I remind him of the boyfriend I had for a four-month stint five years ago. Chuck and I were friends in high school until one night when we both got tipsy at the town fair and ended up making out in front of the kissing booth. We both felt weird about it afterward, which is why we forced ourselves to give the couple thing a try over the next few months, until I eventually told him that I was too busy with school and the farm for a relationship. I left out the part about just being bored. I shouldn't have been thinking about math homework when he kissed me, but there I was, mentally solving algebraic equations while he wiggled his tongue in my mouth.

I didn't blame him for the lack of sparks. In all of my relationships, I've never felt them. I'm pretty sure it's just me—I don't spark.

"But he wasn't any good at them," Luke argues, and I laugh.

"I told you, Luke. Mike's with Danica. And even if he wasn't, that's a terrible reason to date someone."

"Why?"

"Why what?"

"Why is it a bad reason? You have stuff in common."

A line forms in my forehead as I swing open the door to the shelter and the sound of barking bounces off the walls. Since when did my twelve-year-old brother become a relationship expert? "You know what we don't have in common? An undying love for Danica."

My brother makes a sound. "Why is he with her, anyway? Just 'cuz she's prettier?"

"Gee, thanks, turd."

"I just mean, like, well," Luke stammers. "Well, you just don't wear as much makeup and stuff is all."

"Digging yourself a deeper hole," I singsong over the sound of barking, and Luke chuckles.

"You're prettier on the inside."

"I'm going to give you the noogie of your life next time I see you," I threaten, and Luke surprises me with a witty quip.

"I'll probably be taller than you by then. I'll just hide the stepladder so you can't reach me."

I gasp, and at the chuckle on the other end of the line, I try not to smile. "You are so dead."

Luke finishes laughing and asks, "Are you coming home to visit soon?"

"Probably not. But I'll see you in two months at Uncle Rick's for Thanksgiving."

"Do you think he'll pay for my college too when I go?" Luke asks, and even though I'm thrilled he plans on going to college someday, I frown.

Allowing Danica's parents to pay for my schooling was a last resort, and it's one I don't take lightly. Last year, after applying to Mayfield University on a whim and getting accepted, I tried applying for scholarships and more federal aid than I was already getting, but I wasn't eligible for enough money to afford the ridiculously expensive tuition. All of the student loans and state grants in the world weren't going to cover Mayfield U's veterinary science program, and without any substantial savings of my own, I asked my parents to apply for parental loans to help.

And that was how I discovered that they have debilitatingly low credit. I had no idea they'd taken out so many loans to keep the farm from going under, but they had, and apparently they'd been unable to pay any of them back. When I quietly asked if the bank was going to seize our home, my dad took another sip of his beer and solemnly shook his head.

My uncle Rick had paid the loans off. All of them. He saved our farm from going into foreclosure, and all it cost was the deed. Our home is now *his* home, and my family is just living in it.

I never want to be in that position. I never want to have to rely on someone else to keep me in my home, or worry that I won't be able to help my children follow their dreams. Right now, I have to worry about myself and Luke, and that's bad enough. It's the only reason why I said yes when my uncle offered me his help. It's the only reason I'm living with Danica.

"I'll have a good-paying job as a veterinarian by then," I assure Luke. "I'll help you pay."

"What if I want to be a chemical engineer?" he asks, and I groan as dollar signs flash in my eyes and the wolfhound gives my elbow one last big lick before I herd him into his kennel.

"Then I think you better get a summer job and start saving up now." I pat the wolfhound on the head, knowing that in spite of how overexcited he gets, he'll be adopted soon. Just like the poodle and the dachshund. I have good feelings about all of them, and I'm usually not wrong.

"I could be richer than Uncle Rick someday," Luke dreams, and my voice turns wistful as I leave the wolfhound's cage.

"I hope so, bud. I really do."

I SMELL LIKE dog when I leave the shelter that night. I *always* smell like dog when I leave the shelter, but after eight hours of cleaning kennels and leash-training new arrivals, I really, *really* smell like dog. The full moon lights the drive back to my apartment, and my legs are heavy as I drag them through the door. I only get two small steps inside before Danica's voice yells from down the hallway.

"Hailey?!"

"Yeah?"

She pops out of her bedroom wearing nothing but a lacy hot pink bra and a matching pair of panties. "Oh my God. You need to help me!"

She disappears back inside her room, and I rub the corneas off my eyes as I slowly make my way back there.

"Are you coming?!"

I turn the corner into her room and take in the absolute destruction. I don't even know how one single person can have so many clothes. And every single piece is strewn across the room. There are shoes piled on the bed, bras tossed over the lamp, skirts discarded on the dresser, a thong wrapped around my shoe.

I'm frantically kicking my foot when Danica flies out of her walk-in closet holding a red mini dress in one hand and a gold-speckled white top in the other.

"Which one?" she says. "This dress"—she lifts the dress—"or this top? I'd pair it with a black mini. Or maybe my—oh my God, where is my fuchsia skirt?!"

Both outfits go flying as she tosses them behind her and practically dives onto her bed. She's a human hurricane, throwing expensive clothes around like they're nothing but cheap oil rags. I jump to the side as a high heel soars toward my head and bounces off the wall.

"Can you help me instead of just standing there?!" Danica barks, and I kneel down to root through the clothes on her floor.

"Is this it?"

She launches off the bed, snatches the skirt from my

hand, and disappears into the closet. "Don't go anywhere!"

I groan and sit on the edge of her mattress, dreaming of a hot shower and the leftover pizza waiting for me in the fridge. I smell gross, I'm starving, and I'm stuck in a bubblegum-pink jail cell. "What are you dressing up for?" I ask, and Danica shouts from her closet.

"Mike's taking me out tonight, remember?"

Judging by the way my throat closes up, no, I didn't remember. Mike and I haven't spoken since Wednesday, except for a text conversation we had when he messaged me to ask for my Deadzone Four username and Luke's email address. I gave them to him and thanked him profusely for doing such an amazing thing for my brother.

Are you sure you don't want a beta code too? he asked.

You just want me on your team, I joked, remembering the way Kyle screamed as I slaughtered him and all of his little dickhead friends.

> Of course I want you on my team. You're on my team in the zombie apocalypse too.

If that team involved Danica, I was pretty sure I'd rather get eaten alive. But I kept her name out of the conversation. You'll have to clear that with Luke. He already has a bug-out plan.

What is it?

And so I told him about Luke's zombie apocalypse plan, and we discussed the pros and cons, and in the end, he made me promise I'd save him from the zombies.

Okay, I finally relented. I'll save your sorry ass from the Walkers.

I smiled as I waited for his text, and I laughed when it finally came through.

Thank you.

You're welcome.

"I wonder where he's taking me," Danica calls from the closet, and I stop fiddling with the buckle of one of the heels in her mountain of misfit shoes. "I hope he takes me to this seafood place across town. That guy from Alpha Sig took me there three weeks ago, and their lobster risotto was *so* good."

I've never had lobster risotto in my life. In fact, I don't think I've even had regular risotto. What the hell is it? Like, rice?

"Yum," I say before catching a quiet yawn in my hand.

"Oh, Hailey, you have no idea. It was so good, I just wanted to die."

"Sounds amazing," I say, my stomach growling even though I don't even really like rice. Or lobster.

I eye the pink quartz clock on her wall, wondering how it's only seven o'clock when it feels like midnight passed hours ago. "What time is Mike picking you up?"

"Any minute!" she shouts as another top flies out of her closet.

I look down at my own clothes—an oversized navy-blue sweatshirt and a pair of mom jeans that smell like sausage-infused dog breath.

"Okay," Danica says as she reappears in her room. "How do I look?"

The golden sequins of her draped top catch the light in just the right way to accentuate her soft curves, meeting a tight fuchsia skirt that is long enough to be decent, but short enough to be suggestive. Long copper hair that she must have spent hours straightening falls over her exposed shoulders, meaning that she must have skipped her classes today. Again. Her makeup is just as flawless, and even the way she stands seems professional, like she's ready to walk onto a runway built just for her.

"You look beautiful," I say, and Danica frowns.

"You think so? This skirt just feels so—"

The doorbell rings, and her eyes go wide.

"Oh my God, I'm not ready!"

I lift a tired eyebrow. "You look—"

"I look like shit!" She bulldozes me off her bed. "Answer the door. Tell him I'll be out."

My clothes suddenly feel a whole lot grungier; that dog-breath smell a whole lot smellier. "Uh—"

"Go!" Danica orders, forcing me out of her room

and slamming the door behind me. The doorbell rings again, and I stare across our apartment at the white front door and sigh.

One heavy footstep after the other, I make my way down the hallway, through the living room, and to the door. I straighten my sweatshirt—for God knows what reason—and swing the door open.

And there Mike stands, flowers in his hand, a nervous smile on his face. His hair is trimmed and styled, with only a few rebellious pieces escaping onto his forehead.

"Hey," he says as I run my fingers through my own short curls.

"Hey."

"Hi!" Danica peeps from the other side of the room, and I turn around just as she careens past me and into Mike. She throws her arms around his neck and kisses him on the lips before lowering down from her tiptoes. She's wearing the same sequined top, but an even shorter fuchsia skirt, and I stand off to the side wondering exactly how many fuchsia skirts she owns.

"Wow," Mike admires as he takes a look at her, and she spins around, her face lighting up like a one-thousand-watt bulb.

"These are for you," Mike says, handing her a big bouquet of red roses just as I start to walk away. "And these are for Hailey."

I turn around to see him holding a small bouquet of orange sunflowers, white daisies, and purple wildflowers. He smiles and extends his arm, and I just stand there staring.

"Why?" Danica asks, and Mike's eyes and mine both swing to where she's standing with her brow furrowed at the tiny bouquet in his hand.

"Why what?" Mike asks.

"Why'd you get flowers for Hailey?"

Her narrowed eyes lift from the sunflowers to me, like the answer will burn itself into my forehead or something. I'm fidgeting under the heat of her gaze when Mike says, "Because I thought it would be a nice thing to do?"

"You thought it would be nice to get flowers for my roommate?"

"She's your cousin," Mike reminds her. A baffled line etches into his forehead at the attitude Danica is copping. "I used to get them for your mom . . . What's your problem?"

Watching Danica change her attitude is like watching winter turn to spring. I can't see the moment it happens, but then there's suddenly no ice in her voice. Only blistering sunshine. "No problem. I was just wondering." Her megawatt smile is bright and pretty right before she coils her arms around his neck again and gives him a lingering kiss on the cheek. "You're so sweet. I love that about you."

Her feet drop back to the floor, and she shoots me a first-degree burn of a smile before telling Mike, "I'm going to go put these in some water."

I'm watching her walk away when Mike steps

toward me and extends the flowers again. "I thought they might remind you of home. Most farms have sunflowers, right?"

I stare up into kind brown eyes, and then down at sunflowers even bigger than the ones that used to grow outside my bedroom window. Eventually, I take the bouquet and muse, "The ones back home aren't nearly this pretty."

When Mike says nothing, I gaze up at him again to find him smiling down at me. His cheek is dimpled, his eyes are soft, and I'm swallowing thickly and taking a step back. "So . . . where are you taking Danica tonight?"

Mike lifts his hand like he wants to run it through his hair, but then he remembers it's gelled and he drops it to the side. He drums his thumb against the seam of his pants pocket instead. "They just opened a Primanti Brothers across town."

"Primanti Brothers?" I ask. "That famous Pittsburgh restaurant?"

"Yeah."

"I saw it on the Food Network channel . . . Isn't it like sandwiches and stuff?"

"I think they have pizza too," Mike offers, and I almost laugh.

After glancing toward the kitchen, I ask in a lowered voice, "Want some advice?"

Mike stops drumming his thumb and asks, "Advice?"

"Danica wants you to take her somewhere fancy. Primanti Brothers sounds cool, but . . ." But this is

Danica. "Danica mentioned some seafood place downtown. She kept raving about their risotto."

"Rice?"

"Yeah," I confirm, even though I'm still not sure. "I think she's hoping you'll take her there."

Mike and I break our whispered huddle just as Danica reemerges from the kitchen.

"So where are we going?" she asks as she grabs a jacket from the coat closet.

Mike glances at me. "Uh . . . Well, there's this new restaurant that just opened across town—"

"Oh, I love new restaurants!" my cousin cheers as she pushes through the million jackets stuffed into the closet. All of them are hers, since there wasn't room left for any of mine.

Mike's shoulders relax, and he says, "It's called Primanti Brothers, and—"

"Isn't that a sandwich shop?" Danica says, turning around with her nose scrunched in disapproval.

"Well, yeah," Mike says as she hands him her jacket. He holds it open for her, and as she slips into it, he adds, "but they're famous."

Danica turns around and pouts, "But I dressed up . . ."

Mike's fingers get caught in his hair when he attempts to rake his hand through it. He tugs them loose and says, "I . . . was also considering this seafood place."

"Harbor 1921?" Danica squeals, and Mike's eyes dart to mine before returning to the excited girl in front of him.

"Yeah. Do you want to go there instead?"

"Yes!" Danica exclaims, grabbing her purse and swinging open the door. "They have *the* best lobster risotto! It's so amazing. You have to get it."

Her voice trails off as she walks out the door, and Mike's eyes meet mine just before he follows her out. I force a smile and give him a thumbs-up, and he drums his fingers on the door jamb before scratching his hand through his hair again. He effectively ruins all the styling he did to it, and then he closes the door behind him.

Chapter 8

THAT NIGHT, MY eyes pop wide open in the dark when a crash sounds in our kitchen. And another.

I grip my bedsheets.

And another.

In the dark, I roll out from under my covers and hit the floor, because I am home alone, at night, and I am being fucking *robbed*.

Someone outside of my room is tearing the entire place apart, and my eyes are frantically struggling to adjust to the dark to find something, *anything*, to defend myself with.

This is what you get for moving to the city! an unhelpful voice shouts in my head as I stand up, and my disoriented, panicked body spins around and around in the middle of my moonlit room. I'm searching for a baseball bat or a crowbar or *anything* except the mountain of pillows on my bed. Why the hell do I have so many pillows?!

When the heavy footsteps draw closer to my room, I'm standing there clutching a half-empty bottle of water in my hand. And when those footsteps grow too loud to ignore, I launch myself into the hallway screaming like some demon-possessed tiger-woman.

"AAAAAYYYAAAAAAHHHHHHHHHHHH-HHHH!"

The water bottle flies from my hand and through the air, and Danica's voice yells "WHAT THE FUCK!" as it whizzes past her head.

"Dani?"

"WHAT THE FUCK ARE YOU DOING?"

Her eyes are even wider than mine, slicing back and forth between me and where my water bottle shattered one of our living room table lamps into a million tiny pieces.

"I thought . . . I thought you were a robber . . ."

"So you threw a water bottle at me?!" When I just stand there like an idiot, she yells, "Did you even call the cops before you tried to murder me?"

That probably would've been the smart thing to do, so . . . "No . . ."

Instead, I sprung into the hallway like a five-foot-tall, Aquafina-sponsored assassin, complete with heart-print pajama pants and a puppy face printed on my T-shirt. I push my wild hair out of my eyes. "Sorry."

"Whatever," Danica scoffs, nudging her way past me. "You are *so* lucky you didn't hit me."

"Why were you making so much noise?" I ask with adrenaline still fueling my racecar heart as I follow her back to her room. She attempts to slam her door, but it meets my open palms and I continue following her.

She doesn't bother going into her closet before she starts stripping off her clothes.

"Because I'm pissed!" she answers as she skillfully unzips her golden top, yanks it over her head, and hurls it at her bed.

"Why?" I ask, watching as she kicks a purple heel into her closet and disappears in after it.

"Because when I asked Mike to come inside tonight, do you know what he said?"

"What?"

Danica reappears barefoot, her pink toenails matching the thin cami she now has on with the fuchsia skirt she wore out tonight. "He said he has to wake up early!" She throws her hands in the air. "What the hell kind of excuse is that?"

"Maybe he really does . . ." I reason, but Danica jabs a finger at me.

"No, Hailey. *No*. Mike's changed."

"How?" She shimmies out of her skirt and kicks it into the wall before disappearing into her closet again.

"Like tonight, I told him he should get the lobster risotto, but he wouldn't. I told him how good it was, but he didn't even care!"

"That's it?" I ask, and Danica practically teleports back out of her closet, her face a mask of anger.

"That's *it*?"

"I mean . . . maybe he just doesn't like risotto. Mike doesn't really seem like a risotto kind of guy."

"How would *you* know?" Danica sneers. "You don't even know him." She stares me down, her eyes narrowing. "Just because he buys you some shitty little flowers because he feels sorry for you doesn't mean you know anything, Hailey."

"I was just trying to help . . ."

"Yeah, well, you can help by paying for that three-hundred-dollar lamp you just broke, but like *that's* ever going to happen."

It's a low blow, and she knows it, but of course I don't think of any good comebacks until I'm lying in bed later that night.

Yeah, well, not everyone has a rich daddy like you, Dani.

That's what I *should* have said. But then she probably would've replied with something even meaner. Or worse, maybe she would have told said rich daddy about how I tried to murder her, and then she'd kick me out and he'd stop paying for my school and I'd have to move back to the same little farm in the same little town and live the same little life my parents did, just like their parents did before them.

It's not that I didn't like growing up on the farm. I did. I got to feed baby cows and play hide-and-seek in cornfields and run barefoot through the mud. But the world has *got* to be bigger than cows and cornfields and mud. *My* world has got to be bigger than cows and cornfields and mud.

After spending another twenty minutes imagining the blow-out argument between Danica and me that never happened, I give up on sleep, roll out of bed, and pad over to my desk, sinking into the canvas camping chair I use as an office chair. My computer screen lights my room as I crisscross my legs in my lap and let out a heavy breath, the shattered lamp and Danica's words weighing on me.

I'll pay for the lamp. Even if it's ten years from now, I'll pay for it. But right now, I just want to forget it. I want to forget the suffocating feeling of living in a glass house across enemy lines. I want to forget that I sleep just one wall away from someone who can't stand the way I dress or talk or act or look or breathe.

I click the icon to Deadzone Four and lay my cheek on my desk as it loads, my line of sight falling on a glass vase filled with the sunflowers, daisies, and wildflowers that remind me of home, just like Mike hoped they would.

Why didn't I throw this at Danica? my mind chastises. I thought there was a robber here to murder me, and I passed up a heavy glass vase for a freaking half-empty water bottle?

I turn my forehead into the wood laminate desk, feeling like an idiot. I'm an idiot for throwing a water bottle. I'm an idiot for not calling the cops before busting into the hallway. I'm an idiot for the way my stomach flipped when Mike gave me the sunflowers. And I'm an even bigger idiot for the way it does it *again* when I lift my eyes to see that his username is active on my friend list.

You don't even know him. Just because he buys you some shitty little flowers because he feels sorry for you doesn't mean you know anything, Hailey.

I don't know why those words hurt so much, but they do. And I don't know why the one person I want to talk to right now is the one person I shouldn't, but here I am, staring at his name on my screen.

Danica was wrong about me not knowing him. In the week since I met Mike Madden, I've learned some things. I know he loves his job. I know he sucks at sniping. I know his mom is some kind of stain-removing guru. I know he's great with twelve-year-old kids. I know he's thoughtful and funny and kind.

I know he loves Danica. I know he never got over her, because he told me so. I know that he bought her a dozen roses redder than any roses I've ever seen.

Hey.

His message appears on my screen while I'm lost in my thoughts, and my stomach does that flipping thing again that's really starting to annoy me.

I stare at the message for a long time before typing something back.

Hey.

What are you doing up?

Breaking 300 dollar lamps.

I press my fingers into my eyes, wondering how I'm going to pay that damn lamp off and wondering why the hell I brought it up. To *Mike.*

When a new message pops up, I pull my fingers away and read it.

Sounds like an expensive hobby.

A small, unbidden smile sneaks onto my face, and I type back, It's a long story.

I've got time.

I start to type back, I thought you had to wake up early? But then I delete it and sit there staring at my screen. Just an accident, I finally type. What about you? Why are you up?

Because I'm talking to you.

I sit there for a long time having *no* idea how to respond to that, until a second message pops up.

If I ask you something, will you be honest with me?

That doesn't sound ominous at all, I nervously type back.

Will you?

It takes me a minute, but I finally type back, Yes.

And five seconds later, my phone rings.

"Hey," I answer, and Mike's voice makes my heart trip in my chest.

"Hey."

"Sooo . . ." I nervously roll the ball of my mouse down and down and down.

"This feels like a really awkward question."

"Probably would've been easier to ask it through a text," I suggest, and Mike chuckles.

"You're probably right." A long pause, and then a heavy sigh. "Just remember what you said about telling me the truth, okay?"

"I don't lie, Mike."

"I know. That's why I'm asking you, even though I know I shouldn't." Nervousness twists my insides as my finger goes double-time on the mouse, and finally Mike says, "Why is Danica with me?" When I don't respond right away, he says, "I know I'm an asshole for asking you, since you're cousins, but there's no one else I can ask."

"What about her?" I counter. "Why don't you ask her?"

"Because I don't trust her like I trust you."

"Then why are you with her?" The words sound more confrontational than I mean them to, but there they are, a challenge that floats between us—how could someone like him be with someone like her?

It's the million-dollar question—one I've had no right to ask. But it's late, and I'm tired, and he's asking me to gossip about my own family. He's asking me to take his side.

"Because I don't want to spend another seven years thinking about her," Mike answers, and my face pulls with disgust.

"So you're just trying to get her out of your system?"

"No!" Mike rushes to say. "No. Jesus, Hailey, do you really think I'm that much of an asshole?"

I immediately regret my gut reaction, because no, I don't think he's an asshole at all. "No. I'm sorry."

Mike's heavy sigh sinks under my skin. "I'm giving us a shot because I don't want to spend the rest of my life wondering, you know? But I can't read her anymore. She's not being real with me, and I'm not sure if it's just because she's nervous and wants to impress me, or . . ."

"Or what?"

Mike hesitates, and I know he's drumming his fingers on something. "Or if she's no better than every other groupie."

The truth is, I don't know either. I know that his growing fame is what put him on her radar, but I also know that they have history, which involves feelings, which I know Danica must have, even if she doesn't show them. I remember how nostalgic she got when she told me about the flowers he used to put in her locker in high school. And I saw how genuinely flustered she was when she was getting ready for their date tonight. But was that because she wanted to impress Mike? Or was that because she wanted to impress the rock star?

"I don't know, Mike," I confess. "I'm the last person in the world who should be giving out relationship advice."

"Why?" he asks, and I can think of, oh, a thousand different reasons. "You've been in relationships, right?"

"Yeah, I've had boyfriends . . ." I say, and Mike picks up on the things I'm leaving unsaid.

"But?"

"But . . . I don't spark."

"You don't what?"

"Spark," I say as I think about banging my head against the desk. I stare at it and scratch my fingers through my bed-tangled curls. "I don't spark."

"What does that mean?"

This time, I actually do scoot my chair back to let my forehead thump against the desk. I squeeze my eyes shut against the dark as I reluctantly answer Mike. "You know, like the sparks you're supposed to feel when you kiss someone." I groan internally. I could drop dead right now and it would be better than continuing this conversation.

"Maybe you've just never been with a good kisser,"

Mike says, and I'm surprised my burning face doesn't light the damn desk on fire.

"I'm pretty sure they've been good."

"You just haven't met the right guy yet."

"Can we go back to talking about your messed-up love life instead of mine?"

Mike chuckles, and I unglue my forehead from the desk. "You never answered my question," he says, and I finally try to tell him why Danica would be with him.

"Probably because you're smart and funny and sweet and talented and—I don't know, Mike. Why *wouldn't* she be with you?"

A long beat passes before a soft chuckle drifts through the phone.

"What?" I ask.

"I was just thinking."

"Thinking what?"

"I should call you more often."

Rolling my eyes at his reaction to the ego boost I just gave him, I pad toward my bed and crawl under the covers. "I'm going to bed now."

"But I want to hear more about how awesome I am."

"Goodnight, Mike."

"Don't you want to play Deadzone?"

"I'm already back in bed."

"Play with me tomorrow then?" he asks, and I snuggle the covers up to my neck.

"Okay."

"Okay." I close my eyes at the smile in his voice. "Sweet dreams, Hailey."

"Sweet dreams, Mike."

That night, I dream the sweet dreams Mike wished me. I dream them in spite of broken three-hundred-dollar lamps and in spite of angry cousins sleeping down the hall. I dream them because Mike told me to, and because the last thing I think about before I fall asleep is the way he looks when he smiles.

Chapter 9

"IT'S TOO RISKY," I caution, my brows knit with concern.

Mike's voice stays calm, collected. "We knew that going into this."

"We'll get caught."

"Maybe."

"What if they see us?"

"What if they don't?"

My fingers fidget with nervous anticipation. "This is dangerous . . ."

"It could be worth it, Hailey."

"Oh my God," Luke groans through my headset. "Will you two stop being so dramatic? Are we raiding this place or not?"

Mike and I both laugh, and I switch out my Deadzone player's weapon, opting for an M1014 semiautomatic shotgun instead of my trusty M16 assault rifle. My fingers flex before settling back against my keyboard.

Alone in my room, I say, "Okay, but I'm pretty sure we're all going to die."

"I'll protect you," Mike offers, and I roll my eyes at my screen with a grin on my face.

"I'm a better shot than you."

"Are not," he argues, and I start to object, but my little brother beats me to it.

"Yeah, she is, dude."

"Traitor," Mike accuses, and at the sound of my brother's laugh, I smile.

"Okay, are we really doing this?" I ask, and Luke starts the countdown.

"One . . . Two . . ."

"Shit!" Mike barks as a torrent of shots are fired. All hell breaks loose, and the three of us scramble in different directions, firing on the enemy team as we run for our lives. I race away from their hideout, through the streets of the post-apocalyptic city, and duck inside a decrepit building. Rats squeak through my surround-sound headphones.

"Where is everyone?" I ask into my mic as I find a good stakeout position and switch the gun in my hands to a Remington 870. Luke, Mike, and I are in team mode, so I know our enemies can't hear me as I try to figure out our next plan.

"I'm with Luke," Mike says, and my brother's voice is in serious gamer mode when it sounds over the chat.

"Do you think we lost them?"

"You definitely lost them," I answer, my finger hovering over the trigger key.

"How do you know?"

I shoot the idiot who runs in blind through the doorway of my building, and then I toss a grenade outside and race up the broken stairs as gunfire begins splintering the rotted wood exterior. "Because their whole team is outside my building. I'm surrounded."

"Where are you?" Mike asks, and after I describe my location, he asks Luke, "Should we try to save her?"

"What do you think?" my brother replies, his tone grave.

"I don't know, man," Mike says. "She makes fun of me a lot."

I chuckle as I crouch down and shoulder my grenade launcher. It's my last grenade, but the enemy team doesn't need to know that.

"Yeah," Luke agrees. "And she told me she was going to give me a noogie next time she sees me."

"I'm your sister!" I argue as I continue watching the bottom of the stairs. "What about all those weekends I took you to the movies?"

"You made me watch a musical," Luke complains, and I launch my grenade when the enemy team sends one of their men on a suicide mission up the stairs.

"That was one time!" I argue over the sound of the explosion blasting in my headphones. "And it was an accident! How was I supposed to know that Crocosaur vs. Sharkopus was a musical?"

"Uh, a little something called the Internet?"

"Dude," Mike interrupts. "Crocosaur vs. Sharkopus was awesome."

"See!" I bark as I sneak down the dark hallway stretching away from the top of the stairwell. My fatigues-wearing player holds my final big-bang shotgun at the ready.

"What about that scene where the crocosaur launches off the cliff and the sharkopus impales it on a tentacle?" Mike challenges. "That scene was the sickest thing I've ever seen."

"It was pretty cool . . ." Luke reluctantly admits as an enemy player bends down to pick up the rare knife I intentionally discarded. I shoot him in the head, race over to collect his weapons and my knife, and slip back into my stakeout position—a hole in the rotted wall.

"I wish I had a sister cool enough to take me to movies like that," Mike says, and I smile at my computer screen.

"Okay," Luke finally agrees. "I guess we'll save her."

"Hailey," Mike says, the smooth tone of his voice doing weird things to my stomach. "Remember when I said I'd protect you?"

"Yeah?"

"You might want to back away from the windows."

I have a second and a half to race from my hiding spot, into an open room on the opposite side of the hallway, when the entire front face of the building explodes. "Holy shit!" I gasp, realizing that Mike and Luke must have been converging on my location the whole time they were pretending to weigh their options.

The players from the opposite team—the ones who

weren't taken out by Mike and Luke's twin rocket launchers—race up my stairwell in a panic, and I fire my M16 like Tony freaking Montana, mowing them all down. Their player counter goes from six to three to one to zero, and then a medal stamps onto my screen, boosting my player to a new level of game play.

"That was AWESOME!" Luke squeals, and I lean back in my desk chair with a triumphant grin on my face.

"Dude, look at Hailey's stats," Mike praises when the scoreboard appears, and I grin even wider.

"Hailey's a badass," I agree, and Mike's answering laugh turns my cheeks a very *not*-badass shade of pink.

"I'd save your badass any day."

"Do you guys want to play again?" Luke asks, and I hate to burst his bubble, but—

"It's a school night."

"Aw, Hailey, come on. Just one more?"

"You said that last night, and we ended up staying up past midnight—"

"But it's not even eleven yet."

"Bedtime," I order, and Luke groans.

"Play again tomorrow?" Mike asks, and my brother finally relents.

"Okay. Thanks for playing with us again, Mike."

"Are you kidding? You're a rock star, kid. That rocket launcher move was sick."

"Thanks," Luke says, and I can hear the smile in his voice even from halfway across the country. When he tells me goodnight, I tell him I love him, and he bashfully says it back before saying goodnight to Mike too. Then, Mike signs off without another word, and three seconds later, my phone rings.

"What was that you were saying about me being a bad shot?"

I pull my feet up into my chair with me, a big smile consuming my face. Tonight is the third night in a row that Mike has played Deadzone Five with me and my brother, since he finally talked me into beta testing it, and it's also the third night in a row that the clock has passed eleven with me listening to the sound of his voice.

"Kind of hard to miss when you have a rocket launcher," I tease, and Mike laughs.

"You're just jealous you didn't get to blow up the entire side of a building."

"Yeah, well . . ." Honestly, I bet that looked cool as hell from the outside. "You don't need to rub it in."

Mike laughs again, and I rest my cheek against my knees, content to listen to the sound of it. Eventually, I say, "I'm glad it was you and Luke though. He really looks up to you."

"Do you miss him?" Mike asks, and I answer without needing to think about it.

"Every day." My eyes close, and I add, "He's the main reason I didn't move away a lot sooner."

I've always loved the idea of going to Mayfield University, since they offer a very hands-on pre-veterinary program and have an extremely well-known veterinary school, but the truth is, I could have gone to a cheaper school—one that federal loans and state grants would have actually covered—and gotten a degree in animal science much earlier. But even the more affordable schools would have been a few hours from home, and applying to them felt like abandoning my little brother, so I never did. Instead, I worked part-time at random jobs, worked part-time around the farm, took part-time general education classes at the local community college, and hung out with my little brother as often as I could. I probably should have been saving my wages to put toward tuition at Mayfield U someday, but instead, I paid off as many student loans as I could and spent the rest on things like making sure Luke got to eat popcorn at the movie theater and always got more Christmas presents than I did growing up.

"What made you move to Mayfield?" Mike asks, and I shy from the answer. I don't want him to think of me as a charity case, even if that's exactly what I am. When Danica's dad offered to pay for my tuition, my books, and *all* of my living expenses until graduation . . . I knew I couldn't turn the offer down. It was too good to refuse.

"Luke's older now," I answer simply, reopening my eyes. "And Mayfield is my ticket away from the farm."

"You don't like living on a farm?"

"It's complicated." I stare at a picture of my family on my desk—my dad and his battered relic of a baseball hat, my mom and her mother hen smile, my brother and his farmer tan, and me, looking like I belong there with cornstalks dying in the background.

"I love my family," I tell Mike. "I love the animals . . . I love most of what growing up there was like. But . . . I don't know." Mike waits in patient silence, and I peel my cheek away from my knees, leaning back in my chair. "I've always wanted to make a life, not just inherit one."

Mike is silent for a while, and I wonder, "Does that make sense?"

"A lot of sense," he answers, and I relax into my chair.

"Sometimes it makes me feel like a traitor."

"It shouldn't," he assures me. "You should never feel bad for going after what makes you happy."

"What makes you happy?" I ask, even though I know I shouldn't. Danica doesn't know about these late-night games or these late-night chats, and something tells me she wouldn't like me asking her boyfriend what makes him happy.

"Little things," Mike answers after a while. "Hearing the crowd sing our songs. Writing new beats with the guys. Eating a good pizza. Playing games with you."

I swallow, and he rushes to add, "And Luke."

"Right. Luke."

"Luke is great."

"Luke is awesome."

"He's practically my best friend."

I chuckle and walk to my bed, crawling under the covers. "Are you touring in Indiana any time soon?"

"No. Why?"

"I bet he'd love to see you play."

"That would be cool . . . But we're actually flying overseas soon. We're doing a six-week international tour."

"Where?"

"Asia. Australia. We even have a show or two in Europe, I think."

"Really?" I ask in disbelief as I roll onto my side and nestle the phone against my ear.

"Yeah. It's crazy. Our record label had another big band signed up for the tour, but the band broke up, and since the dates were already booked, they asked us to headline it instead. It's pretty last minute, but—"

"That's amazing," I interrupt, and Mike lets out a breath.

"It's nuts. We're shooting a big music video in two and a half weeks, and then we're leaving for Singapore the very next day."

There's a long moment of silence, and Mike eventually asks, "You still there?"

"I feel like I should get your autograph or something."

He laughs, and I smile against the phone. "Yeah, you should probably get a picture with me before I leave."

I like that idea, but I don't dare say so. "What's Danica think of all this?" I ask, wondering why she hasn't mentioned it. It's not like we talk much, but I figure this is something she'd want to spend an entire year bragging about.

"She's excited," Mike says, but I get the feeling he's leaving something out.

"That's good . . ."

"Really excited."

"Yeah. Just imagine all the cool places you're going to get to see and—"

"She can't stop talking about how much money we're going to make."

"Oh."

"Yeah."

I roll onto my back and study the glowing stars on my ceiling. Part of me—the part that laughed with Mike on his tour bus and has spent the past few nights getting familiar with the sound of his voice—wants to tell him that he's too good for my cousin, that he should find someone who deserves him. But the other part—the logical part that knows he's a grown man who can make his own choices, and that maybe he sees a side of Danica I don't—knows better than to get involved.

"Well," I say, "I mean . . . having a private theater in your mansion *is* going to be pretty cool."

Mike laughs, relaxing the tension in my shoulders. "I'm going to have a private theater in my mansion?"

"Where else would you have it?" I chide, and Mike chuckles again. "I mean, I guess you could put it out by your private grotto."

"Right, the grotto."

"Which will be right next to . . ." I tap my fingers against my comforter, wondering what Mike would spend an extravagant amount of money on. "Right next to your microbrewery," I decide, smiling to myself.

"Well, it's settled then."

"What is?"

"You're designing my mansion."

Laughing, I say, "Then can I get all the autographs I want?"

"And beer and private movie screenings," Mike says, and my smile brightens.

"It's a deal."

We sit in comfortable silence until I glance at my clock and reluctantly tell Mike, "It's getting late."

"Yeah."

"I should probably get some sleep. I have a big presentation in the morning."

"Play again tomorrow?" Mike asks, and I snuggle deeper under my covers.

"We already promised your best friend we would," I joke, reminding him what he said about Luke.

Mike's voice is happy when he teases, "Think we'll have to rescue you again?"

"Goodnight, Mike," I growl, trying not to let him hear the smile trying to sneak back onto my face.

"Sweet dreams, Hailey," he says, and then he makes me hang up first.

Chapter 10

"So LET ME get this straight," Dee says in the college café on Wednesday afternoon, one day after Mike's epic wall-exploding trick and three days after I nearly decapitated Danica with a water bottle. When I sat down and Rowan asked what I've been up to, I decided to focus on the Danica thing instead of the fact that I've spent the past three nights gaming with her boyfriend. Disdain drips from Dee's voice when she finishes, "You actually had the chance to take that bitch's head off, and you *missed*?"

"I wasn't *trying* to hit her." Actually, I *was* trying to hit her, but that was before I realized she wasn't a robber-slash-murderer-slash-rapist with a fetish for pajama-wearing farm girls. I take a sip from the thermos of coffee I brought from home, trying to concentrate on how good it tastes instead of how second-rate it makes me feel. My uncle gave me a credit card to use while I'm in school, but I hate using it for things that aren't necessary. Bills, groceries, gas—those things are essential. Coffee is a luxury I can bring from home.

"I don't know how you can stand her," Dee complains from across the table. "If I had to live with her, one of us wouldn't be leaving that apartment alive. I almost choked her out when she came to band practice on Sunday."

Rowan chuckles and scoops the whipped cream off her iced coffee. "I think she's scared of you."

"She should be!"

"What happened?" I ask, and Rowan finishes eating the whipped cream off her spoon to answer me.

"She wouldn't stop criticizing everyone—"

Dee makes finger quotations in the air. "Giving *suggestions*."

"And she actually suggested that Mike try singing this one song—"

Dee throws her hands in the air. "Mike! Sing!"

"And even Mike thought that was hilarious, but Danica was dead serious. She started getting all frustrated. But Dee was so fed up by then that—"

"*So* fed up."

"That she told Danica to find some other band to go play Yoko in—"

"That was what Yoko did, right? She broke up the Beatles?"

Rowan smiles and nods as she continues talking. "And then they started arguing, and Danica told Dee that groupies come and go, implying that Dee is a groupie or something—"

Dee growls. "I could have killed her."

"And basically everyone had to end practice early because Dee flew completely off the handle—"

Dee's face stretches into an unremorseful grin. "As one does."

"And none of us really wanted to hold her back."

"Hence the reason you should have saved us the trouble and decapitated her when you had the chance."

I rub a line between my eyes as I stop looking from Dee to Rowan to Dee to Rowan. I'm about to take another sip of my coffee when Rowan finishes eating the whipped cream off of hers and adds, "I don't even know why Mike brought her."

"Adam brought you," I point out, and when Dee's dark eyebrows knit, I add, "And Joel brought you."

"But no one can *stand* Danica," Dee argues.

"But she's still Mike's girlfriend."

Dee makes a sound in the back of her throat and says, "He's probably going to bring her with us on Saturday."

Rowan groans and rubs her silver-painted fingernails along the bridge of her nose. "Of course he is."

I'm looking back and forth between them, wondering what's happening on Saturday but not wanting to ask since it might seem like I'm trying to invite myself along, when Dee's gaze settles on me, like a magnifying glass that makes me fidget in my seat.

"Hailey, what are you doing this Saturday?"

"I usually spend Saturdays walking dogs at the—"

"Good, so you're free then," she says with a mischievous grin sliding onto her face. "We're scouting a location for a music video the band is shooting. Make sure you wear some boots."

ON WEDNESDAY NIGHT, I check to see if I brought my hiking boots from home, and I frown when I realize I didn't. On Thursday, I check out a few thrift stores, but I don't find any boots in my size. On Friday, I suck it up and buy some from the clearance rack at Wal-Mart. And on Saturday, I curl my toes in them as I stand in a blanket of barn-red leaves, staring out over a vast open meadow in the middle of a forest far from the city. Rustling autumn trees form a perfect circle around the wooded oasis, standing sentry around the glittering pond in the very center of the meadow.

"Finally," Dee and Danica complain in unison, cutting each other with dirty looks when they realize their mistake. I never thought I'd see the day when they actually agreed on something, but it didn't take long today before they both started grumbling about the long hike here. Even Rowan started drifting toward the dark side, repeatedly asking if we were close yet and if the guys were sure they knew where they were going. Forty minutes and a nagging blister on my pinky toe later, the trees finally broke and revealed this secret pond.

"How did you ever find this place?" I ask in a quiet voice, not wanting to disturb the serene beauty of it. Long whispers of clouds float across the blue sky, teasing the long grass that dances in their shadow.

"We went to a party up here once," Shawn says from somewhere to my left. There are a bunch of us—me, Shawn, Kit, Adam, Rowan, Dee, Joel, Danica, Mike—and we all stand in a line with the trees.

"Our friend Driver has friends that knew about this place," Adam adds, finally taking the first step. He turns around and walks backward, a beaming smile on his face. "This video is going to be so sick."

"How are you going to get all the stuff up here?" Rowan asks, and Adam chuckles.

"With Mosh Records' money."

Shawn follows Adam into the field, and the rest of us follow. "So we're going to set up on that dock out there," he says, and my eyes travel the length of a steel grate dock that stretches onto the pond, leading to a large circular platform, "and we're going to light up the pond with all sorts of colored flames floating on top, and maybe glow sticks or something hanging in the water." His long legs push through thick tangles of grass that wrap around his ankles, and he turns around and gestures at the surrounding trees. "And since the song is called 'Ghost,' we're going to have tons of people in the trees, but we're going to get the special effects team to make them look really washed out, and, like . . ."

He struggles to find the word, and Joel finishes, "Like ghosts."

"Kind of, yeah," Shawn says. He turns around and continues walking toward the dock. "And as the song continues, the extras are going to start coming out of the trees."

"It's going to be so fucking creepy," Adam gloats. He turns around to walk backward again, practically dancing with excitement.

Shawn casts a grin at him before continuing. "So they're just going to get closer and closer, and it's going to be really eerie, but the closer they get, the more their color is going to start to come back. By the time they get to the edge of the pond, their faces and clothes are going to be really vibrant, and they're going to start jumping to the song."

"And they're just going to keep coming and coming and coming," Adam says.

"We have hundreds of extras signed up for this," Shawn agrees. "They're going to keep coming out of the trees until this entire meadow"—he gestures at the huge expanse of open land—"is completely filled with kids dancing to the song."

And as if that wasn't enough, as if I wasn't over here going into some legit shock at the sheer weight of their stardom, Mike adds, "We're getting drones."

"Drones?" I ask, and Adam laughs outright.

"Oh man, this is going to be so badass."

"Yeah," Shawn says, and even he starts to lose his professional composure, a boyish smile stretching onto his face. "They're going to get aerial shots." He gives his whole smile to Kit, who gives one right back to him.

It's no wonder they're all bubbling with excitement—

between the video and the international tour Mike mentioned, Mosh Records is investing a *ton* of time and money in them. I smile as I imagine what it must feel like for Mike and the rest of the guys to have so many huge dreams coming true all at once.

"Do you know what else you should do?" Danica suddenly chimes in, and Shawn's smile disappears. Adam's smile disappears. Kit's smile turns into something murderous. "You should have like one star ghost in the video. I mean, the song is about her, right?"

"Who says the song is about a girl?" Kit challenges as her heavy combat boots bang onto the steel dock, but Danica just smiles as we walk.

"Well, isn't it?" Kit's jaw ticks, and Danica continues. "And she'd be super hot. I mean, think about it. What hit music video doesn't have a hot girl? You wouldn't even have to pay anyone."

Shawn stops walking when he gets to the end of the platform in the middle of the pond, turning around with his eyes narrowed. "And why is that?"

Danica's alligator smile widens, her long brown hair snaking behind her in the breeze. "Because I'd do it for free."

She's dead serious. *Utterly* serious. Which, I'm guessing, is why Kit completely loses it. She starts laughing, quietly at first—normally, like a normal person. But when personal offense writes itself all over Danica's face, she starts laughing harder, and harder, and harder. Dee joins in, and Joel tries not to, but fails.

Shawn tries to suppress a smile that won't stay hidden, and eventually, Kit laughs so hard that she descends into a full-on coughing fit.

Sneezes and coughs from nearly the entire band made up the soundtrack of our hike through the woods, but Kit coughed more than anyone else, wiping her nose with her sleeve and insisting that she was fine every time Shawn lectured that she should have stayed home. Now, those coughs get the better of her, and she doesn't stop until she hacks something up and spits it into the water at Danica's side.

"Gross," Danica scolds, which only makes Kit laugh again. "What is your problem?" she snaps, and I wait for her to murder Kit, or Kit to murder her, or *someone* to murder *someone* and turn this place into a real-life crime scene, when Mike wraps his arm around Danica's shoulder.

"Kit's just delirious," he says, giving Kit a pointed look. He turns to stand in front of Danica, his big hands on her shoulders. "And they've put a lot of thought into this. We all have."

"I'm just trying to help." Danica pouts, and Mike studies her for a moment before replying.

"I know. I appreciate that."

"My idea wasn't bad," Danica insists, looking past Mike to implore Shawn. "I could take this music video to the next level. Having a sexy girl in it would make—"

"You realize Kit is sexy as hell, right?" Dee snaps, and I can't tell if Kit's cheeks are red because she's embarrassed or red because she's sick, but I don't remember her being that flushed a minute ago. "Look at her. She's a fucking bombshell. This video will *already* have a hot girl in it."

"Well, yeah," Danica reluctantly concedes, "but—"

"Are you going to shoot the video at night?" I interrupt, and everyone's eyes swing to me. I don't even know why I open my mouth, except that something about sharing the same bloodline as Danica forces me to protect her from putting her foot further into her mouth. "To make it more ghostly?"

Shawn stares at me while I use my nonexistent powers of telepathy to beg him to go along with my subject change, and finally, he says, "Yeah." He scratches his fingers over the stubble on his jaw. "But the film crew is going to bring up all sorts of high-tech lighting to help light the dock so we'll be visible."

"It sounds like it's going to be really amazing," I offer, and an easy smile finally returns to Shawn's face, lighting his forest-green eyes.

"Thanks, Hailey."

"Whose idea was it?"

The guys and Kit start telling me who came up with which ideas, and I listen. I smile back at Shawn, my attention skipping between him, Adam, Joel, Kit, Mike, and even Rowan and Dee—until it accidentally lands on Danica.

She should be happy I changed the subject. The guys weren't going for her idea, and I was just trying to keep her from looking fame hungry. Or from offending anyone. Or from . . . I don't know . . . causing Kit or Dee to fly across the dock and strangle her with their bare hands.

But she isn't happy. Not when she locks eyes with me. Her tight lips and her hard gaze make me an unspoken promise.

She is going to kill me.

Chapter 11

When Danica decides later that afternoon, after the guys have fully scouted the woods surrounding the meadow, that she needs to pee and that she needs *me* to go with her—which requires a private trek into the trees, just the two of us—I'm fully certain I'm never leaving this forest alive. I know she's still stewing about the way I derailed her "I should be the star of your music video!" campaign, and I also know that the only punishment for such an offense is certain death.

But instead of clubbing me with a fallen tree branch or pushing me off a conveniently located cliff, Danica simply tramps her designer boots through the tall field grass alongside me and complains, "I hate having to hang out with his friends all the time. I hated it in high school, and I hate it even more now."

"Why?" I ask, and she gives me a poignant side-eye.

"They hate me."

"They don't ha—" I start, but Danica rolls her eyes.

"Don't lie, Hailey. You're terrible at it. You always have been."

She's right, of course. Whenever we got into trouble when we were younger, I'd always have to let Danica do the talking, because if *I* attempted to spin the truth, our parents would be able to tell in two seconds flat. I'd end up giggling, or worse—crumbling under the pressure and spilling every tiny detail, even ones they didn't ask for. Once, when Danica and I got caught driving my dad's tractor, I ended up selling us both down the river *and* confessing that we had done the same thing a week earlier but never got caught. We were both grounded for three lonely, boring, miserable weeks.

"Okay," I admit as we finally reach the tree line and I muscle a thick bush out of my cousin's way, "they hate you."

"I'm aware," she mutters, walking through the passage I make. "They don't hate you though."

In the shade of bloodred leaves that stubbornly refuse to fall, Danica treats the wilderness like she does everything else in her life: she holds her head high and tramples it beneath her feet. She somehow marches easily over branches and bramble and grass that seem to come to life just to coil around our legs, while I hop and skip and trip behind her, cursing under my breath like a pint-sized sailor the entire way.

"Did you think my idea was stupid?" Danica asks just as I get ensnared in a pricker bush. She pauses to look over her shoulder while I carefully attempt to dislodge a thorn from the baggy sleeve of my orange zip-up hoodie, and I stop fighting with the bush to look up at her. She must be able to tell that I'm deciding whether or not to try lying again, because she immediately scolds, "And don't you dare lie."

I cast my eyes back to the thorns stuck in my hoodie, removing them one by one with surgical precision. "No, but I think that the way you suggested it was."

"How?"

I don't need to look at her again to know that her eyes have narrowed into her signature mascara-lined slits. But she told me not to lie to her, so I'm going to follow her orders for once. "You didn't think of them. You didn't think of all the time they put into their idea before you started telling them everything you thought was wrong with it. And you didn't wait to hear what they thought of *your* idea before you insisted on changing their whole video and starring in it. You made it all about you."

"I—" Danica opens her mouth to protest, but I finish before she can.

"You bulldozed them. You're a bulldozer, Dani."

I think about continuing my lecture—about unleashing all of the feelings I've bottled up since I moved in with her two months ago, back in August—but I don't. Just like the band's video wasn't about Danica, her question wasn't about me. If I can get her to understand *this*, if I can get her to see why she was wrong in this one, *tiny* situation that doesn't even involve me, that would be a humongous step in the right direction.

Danica stands there for a long time, her arms crossed tightly as she digests everything I said. Her long hair dances around her shoulders with the breeze, the rest of her prettily statuesque. With my sleeve finally freed from the brambles, I face her, listening to time tick in the space between us.

"But you did agree with what I said?" she finally asks.

"Huh?" I'm not sure what I expected—a revelation?—but her question throws me off guard.

"You think the video would be better with a lead ghost?"

"Yeah," I stammer. "I guess. I mean, I think—"

"Okay, good," Danica interrupts, a smile settling in her happy brown eyes. "Then maybe you can help me." She links her arm with mine as we continue walking through the forest, and I lose all sense of direction as I chase her train of thought.

"Help you?"

"Help me convince them to go with my idea. I know I went about it the wrong way, Hailey. You were right." She bumps my shoulder in a disconcerting show of affection. "But it is a really good idea. It will make the video more popular, which will help the band. And I bet they'll listen to you. Plus, I'll owe you one."

I trip over a rock, but Danica catches me with our linked arms and helps me find my balance. "Why would they listen to me?" I ask as I find my feet.

"Because you don't lie," she says, turning her head to smile at me.

"But you do?"

"Of course not," she says with a too-big smile just as we step from the tree line. The afternoon sun crashes into me, and my gaze swims over waves of golden grass to a large dock in the middle of a pond, where all of my friends are still laughing and carrying on.

"I thought—" *I thought you had to pee?* I start to ask, but I never get the chance.

"Come on," Danica peeps, dragging me toward the dock and, consequently, toward the confused looks I get once we arrive there.

Since when are you best friends? Rowan's look asks.

Why are you letting that she-devil touch you? Kit's look presses.

I glance away from both of them, to Dee's pinched brow, narrowed eyes, and tight lips. *Did she make you drink the Kool-Aid? Are you brainwashed? Are you silently screaming for help? Should I drown you in this pond and put you out of your misery?*

"Did you two get lost or something?" Mike asks, and I let his deep voice kidnap my attention. I turn to see him smiling up at Danica and me from the end of the grated platform, where he's sitting on a plum-purple blanket with Joel. He's wearing a black and green Dallas Stars snapback hat and a matching green hoodie, and looking at him now feels like staring into the sun.

I've tried to avoid doing it too much since meeting up with the group today. It's strange, hanging out with him in person. Listening to him talk. Watching him laugh. Just . . . being around him.

I've ended every night this week by playing Deadzone with him. And every single night, with the exception of the nights we've talked on the phone, my phone has dinged with a text from Sexy as Fuck Drummer just before I've drifted off to sleep.

Sweet dreams, Hailey.

I find myself waiting for those three simple words. The text doesn't always come right away, and on those nights, I've tossed and turned, trying not to think about him.

I know I shouldn't fall asleep thinking about my cousin's boyfriend. I probably shouldn't even play games with him. I never mention our Deadzone games to Danica, and I'm pretty sure Mike doesn't either, seeing as how I haven't been axed in my sleep.

Deep down, I know she wouldn't be okay with it. But if Mike is okay with it, why should that matter? We're just friends. He knows we're just friends. Even if he wasn't with Danica, we'd *still* be just friends—because Mike likes girls like Danica, and I am *so* not her.

Only . . . standing here breathing the same air as him, I don't *feel* like Mike and I are friends at all. This Mike is someone I can't talk to. This Mike belongs to Danica, and the other Mike is someone else. Someone who texts me to wish me sweet dreams.

I wonder if he does that for Danica . . .

"Hailey got stuck in a thorn bush," my gorgeous older cousin teases, finally dropping my arm to go and sit on her boyfriend's lap. He makes room for her but doesn't take his eyes off of me.

"Are you okay?" he asks, and the genuine, open concern in his voice makes my cheeks heat with embarrassment. The two Mikes I know come together in those three little words—the gamer I spend my nights with, and the rock star dating my cousin. The guy my little brother idolizes, and the man who commands venues full of screaming girls.

"Yeah." I attempt a laugh, but it sounds so awkward, I try to transition it into a cough instead, earning me confused looks from everyone who hears it.

"Are you getting sick too?" Shawn asks, referring to the plague that seems to be spreading within the group. His nose is red from wiping it with his sleeve all day, and Patient Zero—aka Kit—still looks like she could just lie down and die right where she's standing. Joel is fighting a cough, Adam has exhausted Rowan's entire supply of travel tissues, and even Dee looks like she had to put on extra makeup today to accomplish her normally effortless Covergirl glow.

"No," I hurriedly answer, willing my cheeks to return to their normal pale color.

"Are you sure?" Shawn presses, his brow crinkled with worry. "You look kind of flushed."

"You do look really red," Mike agrees, and I consider jumping into the pond and living at the bottom forever and ever and ever.

Why did I have to laugh like that? What kind of loser *pretends* to cough?!

"Are you running a fever?" Rowan asks, pressing the back of her hand against my forehead while everyone watches me turn from blush red to beet red to really freaking just-kill-me-now red.

And just when I think things can't get any worse, Danica proves me wrong. "Was that a fake cough?" she accuses, and I'm sure the look on my face must be something akin to a slow loris about to be obliterated by a steamroller.

"What?" I squeak, scraping at a cover that's about to be blown to bits. "What the hell kind of question is that! Of course it wasn't a fake cough. Why would I fake cough? Why would anyone pretend to cough? God, Danica! Who would do that?"

Me. I would do that. Me me me me meee, oh God.

"I'm fine," I insist when everyone just stares at me—including Mike, with his concerned brown eyes, his frowning lips, and a perfect layer of scruff on his jaw that might make a smarter girl try not to act so stupid. "I just, I mean, I'm, it was—" Oh my God. I've forgotten how to use words. I've forgotten how to sentence! "It was a really strenuous walk," I finally manage, wiping nonexistent sweat from my brow simply because I need something to do with my hands that doesn't involve hiding behind them.

I don't know why I can't speak or laugh or cough or even breathe like a normal person right now, but the suspicious look on Dee's face doesn't help.

"Do you want to sit down?" Mike asks, gesturing to a spot beside him on the blanket that Rowan spread out earlier. My eyes flit to Danica, who watches me from his lap with just as much bewilderment as everyone else.

"Uh, yeah," I say, taking Mike up on his offer simply because I don't trust my knees to keep doing their job of holding me up if I don't sit down soon. "Okay."

I plop down cross-legged next to him, feeling like the biggest idiot in the history of idiocy. *Why* did I fake a cough? What the hell was that even supposed to accomplish? Like a weird fake cough is any better than a weird fake laugh? Why am I so freaking *weird*?!

"Water?" Mike asks, holding his half-finished bottle of water out for me, and I shake my head while trying to figure out some way to get everyone's attention off of my nonexistent, delirium-inducing fever.

Luckily, Danica rises to the occasion. "So Hailey and I were in the woods talking about your video, and—"

"Motherfucker!" I interrupt, my pointer finger wiggling inside the hole I just found while nervously fiddling with the sleeve of my hoodie. I don't know why I have *the* worst luck with clothes lately, but I was counting on this hoodie to be one of my go-to jackets for fall. And now it has a freaking hole in it. A goddamn hole. A mother—

"What?" Mike asks while I mutter enough curse words to make my mom disown me, and I angrily wiggle my finger at him.

"That damn thorn bush murdered my hoodie!"

Mike captures my pointer with his calloused fingertips and lifts my hand over my head, inspecting my sleeve and then sticking his finger in yet another tiny rip. "Here's another one."

I pull my arm away and crane my neck to see the underside of my sleeve. "Dammit."

"It's not too bad," Mike lies. "Give it to me when we leave, and I'll get my mom to patch it up for you."

My first instinct urges me to tell him that his mom has already done enough for me, but since I never told Danica about Mike's mom helping with my stained hoodie and I'm guessing she'd read a whole lot more into it than she should, I don't. "Your mom would be able to fix this?"

"Mike's mom can fix anything," Joel praises, his long legs stretched out on the purple blanket. He tosses a pebble into the water, his blond mohawk waging a silent but valiant battle against the brisk afternoon breeze. "She can get blue hair dye out of yellow T-shirts."

"And lava cake out of white carpet," Mike says to Shawn, and Shawn chuckles as he coughs into his arm.

"And grass stains out of zebra-print boxers!" Adam throws in from where he's smoking a cigarette at the side of the dock, and all four guys crack up laughing at some private memory they share.

"She made me a scarf once," Danica interrupts, her cheeks dimpling with the memory. She shifts in Mike's lap to give him her smile. "Do you remember that?"

"For your sixteenth birthday," Mike recalls, and Danica practically squeals at his jogged memory.

"Yes! She gave it—"

"You said you hated that scarf," he interrupts, and Danica's smile vanishes.

"I did not."

"Yes, you did," Mike says, his voice devoid of all the nostalgic warmth it held a second ago.

Indignant, Danica begins to argue, "I would never—"

"You said you'd never be caught dead in it, but it might look cute on one of your family's pigs."

My jaw drops open, and Danica's expression changes. Her eyes widen, her lips unpurse, and she shakes her head wildly because she *knows* she messed up. "I wouldn't—"

"You would," Mike says. "You did. I wouldn't forget something like that, Danica."

My cousin's expression hides nothing as a million excuses race through her head. I have no idea how she's going to get out of this one, and I'm not sure she deserves to.

"What a bitch thing to say," Dee remarks unapologetically, and even though Mike doesn't owe it to Danica to come to her defense, he does. It's the chivalry in him, and I should know by now never to expect less.

Or more.

"Hey—" he warns, looking over my cousin's shoulder at Dee, and with stark clarity, I can see it happening: I can see all of Dee's Yoko predictions coming true. This is the moment Danica is going to put a wedge in the band. This is the moment she'll come between Mike and Dee, and Mike and Joel, Mike and everyone.

"Danica just puts her foot in her mouth sometimes," I blurt. "I'm sure she didn't mean it."

"I didn't!" she hastily agrees, even though I'm sure no one believes her, because I sure as hell don't.

"Why are you defending her?" Dee snaps, and I shrink under her steel gaze.

Rowan speaks for me when I can't find my voice. "Can we all just stop fighting?" she pleads. "This is ridiculous. We're in a freaking meadow, for God's sake. It's pretty." She sneezes and wipes her nose on her sleeved elbow. "It's like . . . something out of Twilight. There are probably vampires around here or something, and they're probably . . . like . . . glittering."

Adam chuckles and wraps his arm around her shoulders, kissing her hair. "Only rock stars, Peach. No vampires."

"So I won't get to make out with Robert Pattinson today?" Rowan pouts, and Adam picks her up and threatens to throw her into the pond. She's screaming and laughing and kicking, and then he's tickling her and she's crying with laughter. The next thing I know, they're kissing, and then they're disappearing into the woods while the rest of us hang around wondering what the hell just happened.

"I'm eating their sandwiches," Kit informs everyone, walking to the other side of the dock and kneeling down to unzip Rowan's backpack. Shawn, Dee, Joel, and I follow her lead, claiming spots on the checkered picnic blanket at that side of the dock to give Mike and Danica some privacy.

"I'll fight you for them," Joel challenges, crawling to sit by Kit.

"I'll throw you into the pond."

"So?"

"You're a shit swimmer," she says, pulling out handfuls of Saran-wrapped sandwiches and tossing them onto the blanket. "You'll probably drown before you reach the shore."

"You'd let me drown?"

"I'd be too busy enjoying my sandwiches to notice," Kit says, unwrapping a sandwich and taking a big bite out of it to prove her point.

Joel chuckles and wisely picks up only a single sandwich, and the rest of us follow suit—all of us except Mike and Danica, who stay where they are to have a hushed conversation that the rest of us pretend not to notice.

Well, most of us. Dee doesn't try to hide the fact that she's watching them like her own personal soap opera.

"So Kit," I start as I unwrap a ham and cheese sandwich. I take the ham off and offer it to Joel, who shoves the whole slice into his mouth. "You went to school with everyone too?"

Kit nods, her mouth full and her hands holding two half-eaten sandwiches. It takes her a minute to finish chewing, and then she swallows and says, "Yeah. I was a few grades lower though."

"Did you all run in the same circles or something?"

"Not really," she says, and then she amends, "Kind of. Uh. Well, one of my brothers knew the guys. They weren't really friends or anything, but they went to the same parties."

"Sometimes Kit came to those parties too," Shawn adds, smiling as Kit's cheeks turn bright red.

"And Danica?" I ask, too curious about my cousin to try to find out why Kit is blushing from head to toe.

"What about me?" Danica asks, joining us at our side of the platform as the guys laugh at my question. I make room for her to sit down, and Mike sits on her other side just as Adam chases Rowan back onto the dock.

"I was just asking if you guys were all friends in high school or something," I repeat, and to my surprise, Danica laughs just as hard as Shawn and Joel did.

"No."

"Let me guess," Dee says, pointing a manicured finger across our makeshift circle at her. "Cheerleader."

"Captain," Danica boasts, and Dee huffs before going back to ignoring her.

"So how did you two end up together?" I ask, turning my head to question her and Mike.

Mike looks from me, to Danica, to me—and Danica finally gives me an answer.

"He asked me out at the school talent show our freshman year." She gazes lovingly at Mike. "He'd had a crush on me forever."

"Since third grade," Mike agrees on his cue, and the

few bites of cheese sandwich I ate nearly make a reappearance.

"Before the last song," Danica continues, her gaze returning to mine, "he walked up to the mic, told everyone that the next song was for the prettiest girl in school, and then pointed his drumsticks at me."

"He was so fucking nervous." Adam laughs, digging his whole braceleted arm into a bag of barbecue potato chips.

"I thought he was going to throw up," Shawn teases, and Mike's cheeks turn a bashful shade of pink.

"Shut up."

"My friends thought he was hot as hell," Danica brags. "They freaked out. And after the show, when Mike walked up to me and asked me out, I thought my bestie, Katie, was going to faint."

I've met Katie. She's a raging bitch.

"What about you?" I ask, noticing that the most important details in Danica's memory are of how her friends felt. Not how *she* felt.

"Well, I said yes, of course," she says with a look-at-me, I'm-so-fabulous smile. "How could I not?"

"He gave her his drumsticks," Joel remembers with a laugh. "Like he thought he was some kind of rock star even back then."

Mike moves to his knees to reach out and punch Joel in the arm, and Danica's smile widens. "And after that, it was happily ever after."

"Right up until you dumped him," Kit mutters as

murky clouds drift across the sky, forming a puzzle of shadows that assemble themselves on our faces.

"It was for the best," Danica says without missing a beat. "I regret the way it happened, but I needed time to grow up. I needed time to realize what I really want." She links her arm with Mike's, fluttering her long lashes up at him when he looks down at her. "I never would have realized what I was missing if I hadn't had time to miss it."

I don't remember her missing him a few weeks ago. I remember her coming home late from dates with guys from Alpha Cheeto Alpha, her hair a mess and her mascara smeared. And before that, I'd never heard of Mike. I'd never heard of Mike Madden or The Last Ones to Know or this eternal love that Danica claims to have for him.

"Hailey, are you okay?" Rowan suddenly asks, and my stomach makes a noise that can only be described as the avenging battle cry of the cheese-mayo-mustard sandwich I just ate.

"I feel like I'm going to puke."

"You're not the only one," Dee grumbles as Mike loosens himself from Danica to lean forward and study my nauseous face. I scramble to my feet because I am absolutely, *definitely* going to hurl.

"You're probably seasick," Mike says. I'm on my feet with my hands gripping my knees when he wraps his fingers around my biceps, and I nearly jump out of my skin. "Let's get you off this pond."

"I'll come with you," Danica peeps as Mike leads me from the platform. She's rising to her feet when I hear Shawn call behind us.

"Wait!" A brief pause. "I . . . actually wanted to talk to you about your idea for the music video . . ."

Danica's footsteps stop echoing off the dock, and I want to look back to see if she's still following us, but I'm too busy holding my hand over my mouth and letting Mike haul me toward dry land. We step off the dock, we walk through the grass, and when our group looks like nothing but tiny figurines in the distance, Mike finally releases my arm.

"Are you okay?" He reaches out to squeeze my shoulder, the breeze covering me with the subtle scent of his cologne. His eyes are shadowed under the brim of his cap, and something about the perfect shape of his jaw makes my stomach cave in on itself.

I shake my head. My arms feel weak. I'm pretty sure he needs to stop touching me.

"Do you want to go for a walk?" Mike asks, and I glance back to our group. Back to where Danica is.

I probably shouldn't, but I nod. I nod my head yes, and I walk with him into the woods.

Chapter 12

I'm lost. Walking alongside Mike, I'm completely, hopelessly lost. I'm a million thoughts scrambling for purchase in my head. I'm the icy wind and the restless leaves and the erratic pulse hammering wildly under my skin.

I focus on my one-size-too-big boots, stepping carefully over rocks and branches and untamed weeds. We don't speak. We just walk. We walk while I concentrate on the cyclone churning in my stomach and the storm brewing in my chest. We walk until my nausea subsides and I can finally gaze over at him without tripping over my own feet.

With his eyes cast down at the decaying orange carpet rolled out before us, he seems just as distracted as me—here, but not here. His thick lashes are lowered over thoughtful eyes, his black and green cap hiding his face from the fading October sun. I wish I knew all of the silent thoughts locked inside his head, and I must stare at him a little too long trying to figure them out, because without looking away from the invisible path he's following, Mike says, "This is weird, right?"

Does he mean us walking alone in the woods? Or the fact that Danica stopped following us? Or the middle-of-the-wilderness pond in general? Or maybe him being a rock star in redneck country? Or his band making a big music video? Or—

He gazes over at me when I take too long trying to figure out what he's talking about. "Hanging out. You and me."

Does he mean because of Danica? *Is* this weird? Is it wrong? Should we go back? Should I—

Mike slides his cap off to scratch his hand through his hair, and then he pulls it back on. "It's weird hanging out face to face, isn't it? After gaming together all the time. You're one of my best friends now, but we only really hung out that one time a couple weeks ago."

He waits for me to answer, but all I can manage to say is exactly what I'm thinking. "I'm one of your best friends?"

Mike's gaze lingers on mine for a moment longer before sliding away. He pushes his loose sleeves up to his elbows and concentrates hard on where he's walking, and then he looks over at me, and the corner of his mouth twitches into a self-deprecating smile.

"I sound like the biggest loser on the planet right now, don't I?"

In the middle of a cold autumn day, a summer

warmth stretches its rays inside of me. He looks so sincere, so vulnerable, and I ignore all of the self-doubt twined tight in my belly to assure him, "You're one of my best friends too."

Mike's lips curve into a soft smile. He pulls his hat off and folds it into his back pocket, his hair a wild, abandoned mess. "Good, that means I'm not pathetic."

"I'm pretty sure that just means we're both pathetic," I say, and he laughs a laugh that makes my cheek muscles hurt from trying not to smile. He hasn't laughed like that all day, and I didn't realize how tired the day had seemed without the sound of it.

"Are you feeling better?" he asks, stepping on a sprawling pricker bush with his big boot so I can walk over it. He takes my hand to help me over a fallen tree.

"Yeah."

"Do you want to head back?"

With one leg dangling on the other side of the tree trunk and my hand still in Mike's, I sit and ask, "What else would we do?"

My heart jackhammers against my ribs even after he releases my hand. I press my palms against the rough bark, wishing I could dissolve into it to escape the last five words out of my mouth. I didn't mean for it to come out sounding so . . . dangerous. It feels dangerous, that question, and I wish I could take each word back, but I can't, because there they are, hanging in the air.

What else would we do? Nothing.

Not go for a walk like I might with Rowan. Not

climb trees like I might with Kit. Not chase clouds like I might with Luke.

Nothing. *Nothing.*

Mike's eyes hold mine, and mine hold his, and when thunder cracks like a whip through the forest, I nearly fall off the log.

One raindrop falls while I steady myself. And then another. And another.

"Shit," Mike hisses, turning his eyes up to the invisible threat slithering through dark clouds in an even darker sky. We're far from the pond now, which means we're really, *really* far from the cars. Which means we're going to get absolutely drenched—if we don't get struck by lightning or have a tree fall on us first.

Mike lowers his chin and wipes wet droplets from his forehead. "When I was up here last year for that party, I found an old cabin. I think it's the way we're heading."

"You *think*?"

"It should be close." The corners of my mouth turn down, and Mike tugs his cap from his back pocket. "Do you want to try for it?" he asks, twisting his hat onto my head.

The question remains in his eyes even as lightning snakes across the sky. Another crack, another flinch, more rain.

"And you're pretty sure it's this way?" I ask, tucking my frizzing hair behind my ears.

Mike nods, but his expression doesn't look confident. "I think so . . . but I could be getting us lost."

I cling to the log and worry my lip, and Mike watches me cling to the log and worry my lip.

"Let's go for it," I finally say, swinging my leg to the other side of the fallen tree. I drop to the solid earth and wait for his feet to hit the ground next to mine.

Mike leads the way, and I follow him deeper into the woods. I follow him through lightning and thunder. I follow him through weeds and mud. I follow him even when the sky breaks open and unleashes hell on us.

I'm running ahead of him a couple minutes later, when the rain is beating us unmercifully to death. Each swollen drop feels like it's been shot from the sky. I'm pelted again and again as I do my best to race through the trees, slipping on wet grass and narrowly avoiding being eaten alive by bushes with teeth. "We're going to die because of you!"

Each strike of lightning is a heart attack in my chest as my lungs struggle to pump oxygen into my legs. I'm in the woods, *lost*, in the middle of a storm that's howling and raging like a living beast. I'm being drowned by rain.

"I'm sorry!" Mike shouts, but he doesn't sound very sorry.

"Are you laughing?!"

"I'm sorry!" Mike yells again, this time laughing in earnest.

I'm about to spin around and save this serpentine storm the trouble of murdering him, when the forest suddenly clears enough for me spot it—a set of old wooden stairs leading up to an old wooden porch attached to an old wooden cabin.

"Thank God!" I shout, doing a final mad dash through twisting sheets of rain. My boots slap one-two-three up the porch stairs, and I throw myself into the door, twisting the knob and practically tumbling inside. I double over with my hands on my knees, trying to catch my breath. And when I finally do catch it, I find Mike in the same position. Doubled over, hands on his knees.

Only, he's *laughing*. His entire body shakes with it, and when he peeks up at me and sees the indignant expression on my face, he laughs even harder.

"I should have left you out there," I say through a sternly suppressed smile, and any last sense of composure leaves him as he laughs hysterically.

"I never swam with a manatee!" Mike laugh-shouts, making fun of the frantic things I cried as I ran through the monsoon, watching my life flash before my eyes. "I never learned to water-ski! I never hugged a koala!"

The sounds he's making no longer even sound like laughter. He's howling, coughing, crying, and I can't help laughing too.

"Stop making fun of me!"

I playfully chuck his hat at him, and he stands upright to catch it. "I never ate pizza in Italy!" he teases.

"Pizza in New York!" I correct, and Mike grins with streams of rain trickling down his happy face. He's soaked, from the ends of his hair to the laces of his boots, and I'm not in better shape.

"We're going to catch pneumonia," I warn, but Mike just shakes his head and chuckles.

"You're going to live to cuddle a koala someday, Hailey, I promise."

He takes off his drenched hoodie and hangs it on a wall hook to dry, revealing the black T-shirt he has on underneath, and then he sits on the floor and stretches out his long legs, watching the rain pummel the forest outside.

The cabin is empty, save for about ten years' worth of dirt and dust. I swipe my shoe over a filthy spot on the wooden floor, and then I sit down too. "How long do you think it's going to rain?"

Mike pulls his phone out of his pocket like it's going to tell him the answer. "No idea."

"No service?"

"None." He leans back on the palms of his hands, and I crisscross my legs.

"Do you think everybody else is getting soaked too?" I ask, and Mike chuckles.

"I wouldn't be surprised if Rowan had a popup tent and a space heater in that backpack of hers."

If she doesn't, I'd bet good money that Danica is *not* going to be happy when we get back, but I keep that little prophecy to myself. I'm sure Mike is well aware.

"You've really never had New York pizza?" he asks, glancing over at me. Rain pounds against the roof and batters the dusty windows, but Mike sits near the open door of the cabin, content to cross one ankle over the other and talk to me about pizza.

"I've never been to New York at all," I confess. I've been to, like, three states. Indiana, where I'm from. Virginia, where I am now. Delaware, where my family vacationed sometimes when I was a kid. And if you want to count the drive-through states, like Ohio, Pennsylvania, and Maryland, I guess you could call that six, even though they all looked the same to me—long highways and wooded rest stops.

"You're not missing much," Mike says. "The state is okay, but . . ." He cups his hand over his mouth and whispers, "Minnesota has better pizza."

"Minnesota?" I laugh, and Mike sits up and begins messing with his phone.

"Look," he says, holding it out for me to see a picture of a slice of pizza. I take the phone from him, and he says, "This is the best pizza I've ever had in my entire life. This place has all sorts of toppings, like, you can even get potato chips, Hailey. On your pizza. But this prosciutto . . ." He closes his eyes. "This is why I won't do U.S. tours unless we do a show near Minneapolis."

Laughing, I ask, "Are you serious?"

His brown eyes pop back open, amused at my skepticism. "Dead serious. I'm pretty sure Shawn even put it in our contract with Mosh Records."

I hand his phone back and say, "I'd have to get the potato chips. I don't eat prosciutto."

"You don't eat prosciutto?" he gasps, like he's offended on its behalf.

"I don't eat meat. I'm a vegetarian."

Mike's brows slam together, his jaw hanging open and his eyes drilled into mine. "You . . ."

"Don't eat meat."

"You don't . . ."

"Eat meat."

"You're kidding."

"I'm not," I assure him, trying not to laugh.

"But you're a farmer!"

"My parents are farmers," I correct, and Mike stares back out the doorway of the cabin, clearly disturbed.

"I've been friends with all kinds of people, but . . ." He looks over at me with exaggerated disgust on his face. "A vegetarian?"

I laugh, and he has the decency to pretend to be pushed when I bump my fist into his shoulder. "And here I thought we were BFFs."

"That was before I knew the truth about you, Hailey Harper."

"Whatever, Mike Madden. If I can deal with the way you constantly drum on everything, you can deal with my aversion to prosciutto."

His fingers stop drumming on the floorboards of the cabin. "I do not drum on everything."

"You're drumming right now!" I argue, pointing to his other hand, and Mike starts laughing. He flexes his fingers.

"It's a drummer thing. I can't help it."

"It's fine," I say, and by *fine*, I mean *cute*. But *cute* is forbidden, and *fine* is . . . fine.

"Danica hates it," Mike says, and I roll my eyes at the rain.

"Danica hates everything."

Me, hiking, secondhand clothes, puppies, rainbows—

"At least she likes prosciutto," Mike jokes, and my spine stiffens.

"Sounds like you're perfect for each other."

"Hm," Mike hums, and I can sense him staring at me, probably wondering why such a harsh tone possessed my voice all of a sudden, but I don't dare look at him. I try not to question my sudden shift in mood, but I'm pretty sure I'll find the answer if I turn my head, if I search his eyes, if I let myself really look.

"The rain's letting up," I say, pushing to my feet and walking to the doorway. I step out onto the porch, listening to the last of the rain patter against the wooden roof and the dying leaves and the soaked-through earth. The scent of it wraps itself around me and nips all the way through three layers of wet clothes.

"I could live with cheese pizza," Mike's voice says from back inside the cabin. I turn to look at him, but I don't know what I expect to see. He finishes pulling his hoodie on, pushes his hat back onto my head as he walks past me, and leads me back to the pond.

Back to Danica.

Chapter 13

THE WALK BACK to real life is quiet, and dark, and wet. Even after the clouds begin to clear, the shadow of them hangs over and inside and around me. Mike helps me traverse the parts of the forest designed to devour five-foot-tall country girls, but we don't say much. We just walk, and walk, and walk. I had no idea we'd traveled this far, but by the time we get back to the clearing, the blister on my pinky toe is throbbing against my boot.

Rowan takes off running the moment she sees us, her wavy blonde hair even frizzier than mine. "I thought you were dead!" she shouts as she closes the distance between us, catching Mike in a hug, pulling away to inspect him, and then squeezing me to death. "How are you not dead?!"

"We found a cabin," Mike says, and Rowan pulls away to look at me. Her blue eyes flit up to Mike's cap on my head, and then they dart back down.

"A cabin?" She turns her chin to question Mike, and he nods.

"What about you?" Mike asks. "How are you so dry?"

"Oh, that blanket I brought is waterproof on the inside. You just fold it inside out and—"

When Mike starts laughing, I can't help smiling.

"I told you she brought a tent!" Mike says, and I hold in a laugh at Rowan's confused expression.

"But the real question is, did she bring a space heater?"

"The waterproof side of the blanket is thermal . . ." Rowan says, and Mike chuckles and wraps his arm around her shoulder, leading us back to the platform on the water. It probably isn't the smartest idea to be standing on a steel structure right after a storm, but the sun is fighting to push the clouds away, and who am I to tell a bunch of rock stars what to do?

Before we get to the pond, I take Mike's hat off and wordlessly hand it back to him, and he removes his arm from Rowan's shoulder to take it. His brow furrows, and I look away from it.

Yes, I understand that he is the type of guy to lend his hats to his female friends and wrap his arm around their shoulders, but his *girlfriend* is my cousin, and while I've worn the hats of other male friends, wearing Mike's hat doesn't feel as harmless as all that.

Maybe it's the look Danica would give me if she saw me in it . . .

Then again, maybe it's something else.

Turns out, it doesn't even matter. Three sets of boots clang onto the dock and then out onto the platform, but Danica is too busy talking on her phone to even notice.

"Did you two have fun in the woods?" Dee suggests, and I school my expression.

"Maybe if your idea of fun is running for your life through mud and lightning."

"I had fun," Mike says from behind me. His hat gets pushed down onto my head a third time, and I squint at him over my shoulder. "Did you know Hailey is a vegetarian?"

"You don't eat meat?" Joel asks, zipping up his fly after he finishes pissing off the end of the dock. He joins our conversation, and I'm wading through the usual shock and awe over me being a vegetarian, when Danica suddenly bounds up and wraps her arms around Mike. She nearly drags him to his knees.

"Did they tell you the news?!"

"What news?"

"She's going to be in the music video," Dee says with a suspicious amount of approval, and Danica beams.

"Shawn likes my idea! I'm going to be the star!"

"The star ghost," Dee corrects, and Danica smiles wide.

"Right. Right. The star ghost. It's going to be amazing! I—" Her phone starts ringing, and she checks the screen. Without excusing herself, she answers it. "Katie, you whore! I've been trying to call you all day! Guess who's going to be in the music video. Yes!" My cousin wanders to the edge of the platform, and Mike sighs.

"We ought to get going," Rowan suggests, and as if on cue, warning thunder growls in the distance. "It's supposed to rain again." She calls to Adam and Shawn, who are sitting at the other side of the platform, and asks them to start packing up.

"Did they finish everything they wanted to get done today?" I ask, remembering that Adam and Shawn spent a lot of time scouting the woods before Danica asked me to take that walk with her earlier this afternoon. I'm not sure if they accomplished everything they came up here to do today, but I hope so, because the video is shooting in just two weeks.

Rowan answers me as I help her roll up the picnic blanket. "Yeah, they found places for good shots, and they got a rough idea of how many extras and lights they'll need. I think everything is good to go." She glances up at Danica and sighs. "Can you get her? I don't think she heard me."

Sure enough, Danica is walking all along the edge of the dock as she chatters on her phone, her hands animating her words and proving just how oblivious she is to everything going on around her. I reluctantly walk over and invade her blast zone.

"Hey, Dani—Danica."

With the phone to her ear, she flashes me her irritated face, the one I've grown exceedingly familiar with, and goes back to ignoring me.

"We're leaving soon. Rowan wanted—"

"What do you want?" she snaps at me. "I'm trying to talk to Katie about the video." Her voice lowers to a whisper, and she covers the mouthpiece of the phone. "The concept you were supposed to help me sell, but never did."

"I—"

"You better not think I still owe you a favor."

Danica sneers at me and puts the phone back to her ear, and I stand there dazed as she backs away from me. "Are you still there?" she asks Katie. "Yeah, I just—"

Her voice fades out as I watch the disaster about to happen. The clump of wet leaves clinging to the steel dock, Danica's useless fashion-forward boot about to back into them. I reach out to grab her at the same time her foot slips out from under her. She stops falling backward, backward, and I get pulled forward, forward.

"DANI!" I shriek as she yanks on my arm to save herself. And then I'm catapulting—

Off the dock—

Through the air—

Down into the pitch-black water.

Chapter 14

I NEVER KNEW that sparks could be quiet—like a silent firework that no one even knows is exploding until they gaze up at the moon and see the whole night sky consumed by burning color. A person can just be drowning in a pond, minding their own business, when the whole world catches fire.

Forests ignite. Houses burn down. One minute, you're breathing fresh air. And the next, you can't breathe at all.

Sometimes, you burn alive.

I don't know the moment I sparked, but I do know the moment I realized I couldn't breathe. And it wasn't when Danica yanked me into that pond. It wasn't when my calf got ripped open on the side of the dock. It wasn't when Mike reached down and pulled me out of the water. And it wasn't when he insisted I let him carry me on his back all the way back to the cars so I wouldn't make a bad injury worse.

I think it happened sometime during that long trek back through the woods, with my hands braced on his shoulders and his fingers curled tight beneath my thighs. I was wearing his mostly dry hoodie and a pair of extra leggings that Rowan had brought along, and all around me was his scent and his touch and his *feel*. The rough calluses on his palms. The strong muscles in his back. The lifts and dips of his stride.

I knew if I relaxed, if I lowered my chin to his shoulder and allowed my cheek to brush against his, I'd feel the scruff on his jaw. I'd feel his hair against my temple. I'd feel the soft curve of his neck.

But then he'd also be able to feel the frantic drumming of my heart. The way it pounded furiously inside my chest at the thought of that scruff, his hair, his neck, those eyes, his voice, his laugh, that smile . . .

That was the moment I stopped breathing. Something had sparked inside me, and that spark stole all of the oxygen in the world. Something about being with him today . . . about seeing his smile and hearing his laugh and feeling him carrying me through the woods . . . it did something to me. My realization happened near a tree that looked like another tree that looked like another tree—with Danica walking right beside me.

You have a crush on Miiiike, came Dee's text, and I glanced over my shoulder to see her wink at me. The whole group was walking with us, navigating the dripping forest to get to the cars before the next storm rolled in, and I hoped the flames flickering inside me weren't as obvious to everyone as they were to my very annoying, very nosy, very stubborn friend.

But she was right.

I had a crush on Mike.

I *have* a crush on Mike.

I tucked my phone into the sleeve of his hoodie and tried to remember how to breathe evenly. But all I could focus on was his hands on my legs, *his hands on my legs.*

Danica hadn't objected to him carrying me, which was surprising. And she had also apologized half a dozen times for knocking me into the water, which was even more surprising. She said it was an accident, and I believed her.

Which was why I felt like the biggest bitch on the planet for crushing on her boyfriend. While my arms and legs were wrapped around him.

He was being a gentleman. Danica was being nice. And I was being the lowest kind of low. I wasn't the kind of girl who deserved piggyback rides or apologies or favors. I was the kind of girl who developed incinerating crushes on her own cousin's boyfriend. I was the kind of girl who couldn't be just his friend. Who texted him at night. Who kept it a secret. Who ran with him through the woods when he should have been with his girlfriend.

His girlfriend. His *girlfriend.*

Danica.

My cousin.

I vowed then and there to keep my distance from Mike Madden. No more gaming. No more texting. No more late-night phone calls. No more phone calls *ever.*

"COME ON," LUKE whines over the phone four days after the pond, and I brush my teeth in front of my bathroom sink as I listen to him.

"I can't," I tell him with a mouth full of toothpaste, and he whines some more.

"Come ooon."

"I'm not playing games tonight," I argue after spitting into the sink. I feel guilty about disappointing my little brother, but he's obsessed with Deadzone Five, and I'm obsessed with avoiding Mike.

I can do it. I can get over him. I have to.

Even if it hurts more than I thought it would—more than it should. It hurts more than losing a friend, and that's exactly why I need to stay away from Deadzone. At least until this aching in my chest goes away. At least until I can sleep at night.

"And you should be in bed," I lecture my twelve-year-old brother. "It's a school night."

"I'm skipping," Luke announces, and I wipe my thumb over the pasty corners of my mouth.

"Why?"

"Because I want to."

"Why?"

"Because I hate it."

I wash my face with a cleanser wipe with one hand

while holding my phone with the other. "Is this because of that punk Grayson?"

Luke's silence is answer enough, and I sigh as I toss the wipe in the trash.

"You need to stand up for yourself, Luke."

"How? I'm the skinniest kid in my grade."

"I don't know . . . Can't you make friends with some bigger kids?"

Luke scoffs. "He's the king of the big kids. They all do what he says."

"Well . . . then can't you get Mom to talk to the principal or something?"

With a very adult sigh, my brother says, "Hailey, are you seriously that old that you don't remember what seventh grade is like? I can't just *tell my mom*."

"You also can't skip school."

"I should just drop out and be a farmer."

"A very dumb farmer," I counter, and when that isn't enough to make Luke change his mind, I say, "Look, Luke, you can't just run away from your problems. If you don't stand up for yourself, this kid's never going to stop."

"You let Danica bully you," Luke points out, and I frown as I enter my room.

"That's different."

"How?"

Well, for one, I deserve it. I developed a crush on her boyfriend, which means I deserve the very worst she can give me. And for two—"We're family," I say, and my brother scoffs.

"That's crap, and you know it."

"Yeah well . . ." With lack of a better argument, I simply order, "You're still going to school tomorrow."

"Can't you just play for a little while with me?" Luke pleads, and I stare at my computer. I can't play Deadzone with him because if Mike logs on, I know he'll play with us. Which will involve talking. Which will resurrect those damn butterflies in my stomach.

I rub the ache in my chest and say, "What about that dragon game we played before?"

"I want to play Deadzone."

"Why? I feel like being a princess tonight."

"Because I miss playing with you and Mike, but he's not on yet."

My throat dries, and I croak, "You're logged on right now?"

"Yeah."

"But Mike isn't on?"

"Not yet."

I sit down at my desk, worrying my lip. Mike texted me to ask me to play Sunday night, but I ignored him. He sent me a couple more messages as I sat at my desk frowning at my black computer screen, and then just one: Sweet dreams, Hailey.

It was the same Monday night. But last night, he didn't bother asking. I was lying in bed, wondering what he was doing, when my phone dinged. He wished me sweet dreams. Nothing else—just sweet dreams.

I didn't respond.

He's an addiction that I need to stop fueling, for my

sake and his. He told me I'm one of his best friends, and I'm trying to be a good one by not letting these feelings grow. He has a girlfriend, and even if he didn't, my feelings for him would only end in hurt feelings. For me: because I'm not Mike's type—I'm no Danica—and I'd eventually have to hear that from his own mouth. And for him: because he lost a friend he thought he could trust to not fall for him like every other girl who's ever seen him bang on the drums.

We can be friends again. Someday soon, I hope. I just have to smother these damn sparks inside of me first.

"Alright," I tell Luke as I boot up my computer. "Half an hour, but then you're going to bed and going to school tomorrow."

"Deal," Luke says before I can change my mind, and we hang up the phone to start chatting in the game. For twenty-three minutes, I almost forget about Mike—right up until his username appears on the right side of my screen.

"Luke, I've got to go."

"But Mike just signed on!"

"Sorry," I rush to say. "My stomach is hurting."

"But you promised you'd play for half an hour . . ."

"I love you," I tell him in a hurry. "We'll play again soon. Go to school tomorrow."

I sign off before he can say another word, and then I press my fingers against my stinging eyes.

I miss Mike. I miss his banter and his smile and his humor and his voice. I miss making him laugh over the phone. I miss him wishing me sweet dreams just before I fall asleep.

I crawl under my bedcovers, wondering how long it's going to take for me to stop feeling this way. If I developed this crush on him in just two and a half weeks, it should only take that long to get rid of it, right? I'm already four days in, so I should only have two weeks left. Just two weeks. That's not that long . . .

Only, Mike is leaving on tour in eleven days, and he'll be gone for six weeks. So even if it only takes me two weeks to get over him, I won't see him again for two months. And I promised myself—no more phone calls, no more private chats. So it will be at least two months until group get-togethers, two months until I can try to be Mike's friend again . . .

My phone dings with a text, and my screen lights up my dark room as I read it.

Sweet dreams, Hailey.

I close my eyes, imagining Mike thinking of me in this moment, and it reopens the hole in my chest.

Does he know I'm avoiding him? He must. Did he see my name on his screen before I logged off? If he did, I hope my brother told him I have a stomachache. I hope Mike believed him . . .

It feels like my heart is starving, and I don't know how to fix that, but it warns me that I'm wrong: two weeks isn't going to be enough.

Not enough to stop falling for Mike Madden.

Chapter 15

THREE MORE DAYS pass, and I stay away from Deadzone. I try not to miss Mike's "sweet dreams" texts when they stop coming. I do my best to ignore the hollow emptiness in my chest that makes it hard to sleep at night, to *breathe* at night. And I pretend I don't care when Dee tells me that Mike has caught the debilitating cold that Kit birthed into the world.

She says Mike is sick—well, more dramatically, she tells me he's dying. She says no one has heard from him and he's probably rotting to death on his kitchen floor. And no one else can go help him out because everyone else is still sick or recovering too. She says I should go, but I know it isn't my place. I'm only a week into Mike-addiction recovery, and I don't want to fall off the wagon now, not after how difficult these past seven days have been.

Instead, I plead with Danica.

"You should go check on Mike," I tell her one week

after the disaster at the pond, going against my better judgment to try to convince her to do what any good girlfriend would do. "The girls said he's not feeling well," I continue while she sits folded up on her bed with pink foam separators wedged between her toes. She concentrates on her glittery silver brush as it swipes over her toenail.

"He's a big boy," she counters without looking up at me.

"You're his girlfriend."

"So?"

"So, don't you even care about him?"

Danica scowls up at me. "Of course I care about him. Not that it's any of your business." She goes back to pampering her toes, snooty as ever. "I talked to him yesterday."

"And he sounded okay?"

Her pause tells me more than her mouth ever will. "He said he was fine."

"In a text?"

I sigh when she can't even deny it. "Look, Hailey, this music video is shooting in seven days. What do you want me to do, go over there and get sick?"

I just stare at her, because what can I say to that? There are so many things wrong with what she just said, I don't even know where to start.

When she notices the judgment in my expression, she makes a noise and begins blowing on her toenails. "How about this . . . How about you go over there, and you take him some tissues and some soup and whatever the hell else you think he so desperately needs, okay? Put it in a basket. Like a care basket." She gazes up at me while still blowing intermittent breaths onto her toes. "I'll give you the money. Get a can of soup, okay? Throw in some crackers. And a card. Sign it from me." She begins shaking a black bottle of top coat. "You can even sign it from both of us if you want. You don't even need to chip in. Just drop it off on his porch."

"Are you serious?"

At the disdain in my voice, Danica rolls her eyes. "Or you can ring his doorbell and hand it to him and get sick. Whatever makes you feel better, Saint Hailey."

An hour later, I'm standing on Mike's porch, on the outskirts of the city, with a woven basket hanging from my hand. Inside it: three cans of soup, one box of tissues, one bottle of nasal spray, one bottle of cold medicine, one card with Danica's name scrawled in my handwriting.

I think about leaving the basket on the porch.

I frown.

What if he's really not okay? Someone should check on him.

I lift my hand to the doorbell.

I lower it.

Am I a bad person if I make sure he's alright?

Am I a bad person if I don't?

I sigh, take a deep breath, and lift my hand again. A press of the doorbell later, my foot is tap-tap-tapping against the cement stoop as I listen to the faint sound of the bell sounding inside Mike's modest white house. I wait, and no one answers. I wait some more, and still, no one answers. I think about ringing it again, but instead, I force myself to set the basket on the porch. Maybe this is a sign. Maybe this is the universe telling me to leave.

Or maybe he really is lying facedown on his kitchen floor . . .

"Jesus," I gasp when Mike's door finally opens. My hand flies to the neck of his zipped-up hoodie on instinct, and I tug him down as I rise onto my tiptoes to press my other hand against his forehead. He's dressed in full sick gear—an oversized dark gray hoodie, long black gym shorts, and black ankle socks—and his skin sizzles against my palm. "Mike!" I scold, worry clawing at my chest.

"You probably shouldn't touch me," he warns, his voice like gravel.

He's burning up beneath my hand, but that's not the reason I pull away.

He's right. I shouldn't be touching him. I shouldn't even be here.

"I don't want you to catch what I've got," he adds as the autumn chill dries his fever from my skin. He wraps his arms around himself and shivers, the ends of his hair damp with sweat and a wad of tissues bunched in his hand.

"How high is your fever?" I worry.

"I lost my thermometer," he says through chattering teeth. His eyes are rimmed red with exhaustion, and I wonder when he last slept.

"When was the last time you took your temperature?"

"Th-Thursday?"

My brows knit at the man in front of me, then at the basket sitting on the porch beside me, then at the man in front of me again. Even sick, with days-old scruff and hair that looks like it hasn't been brushed in years, he makes that spark inside me want to flare to life, but I fight to keep it smothered in my chest.

I should leave. I should give him my basket, make him promise to take the cold medicine, and leave.

Maybe I should help him find his thermometer first, but then I should definitely leave.

I shouldn't even call to check up on him. I shouldn't even text. That's Danica's job. Not mine. I should just leave him here, freezing and sick and alone and . . .

Frowning, I rise onto my tiptoes and press my palm against Mike's forehead one last time. He doesn't object this time; he just leans into my palm and lets my skin absorb the heat he's radiating. I don't know how high his fever is, but I know it's high enough that someone should be worried about him, even if that someone is me.

"Let's go," I finally decide, pulling my hand away and nudging him back inside his door. I may still have more-than-just-friends feelings for him, but my friend feelings came first, and I'm not about to abandon him when he needs me.

"Huh?"

"Let's go," I say again, grabbing the basket from the porch. "I'm not leaving until you're better."

Chapter 16

In my twenty-three years on this Earth, my mother has never once made me soup in the microwave. It didn't matter how hungry I was or how sick I was or how much I just wanted to scarf down lunch so I could run and play outside—she has always, *always* cooked me soup in a pot.

"Anyone can throw something in the microwave," she'd lecture as she stirred homemade chicken noodle soup in the cast-iron pot that she got from her mother, who got it from her mother, who probably got it from her mother. I'd be sitting at our unfinished kitchen table, having a staring contest with the smiling ceramic pig who took up residence there and taunted me every time my nose was runny. "When you make something in a pot, you make it with love. And love is going to make you better."

In Mike's kitchen, I pour two cans of Campbell's

chicken noodle soup into a pot I found under the stove, I set the burner to medium, and I go back out to the living room to make sure he's lying down like I ordered him to.

He needs to go to bed, but I want him to eat first.

Actually, he *needs* to go to the doctor, but I lost that battle within thirty seconds of walking through the front door.

"Are you okay?" I ask, frowning at the shivering man laid out on a big plush couch against the wall. As soon as we came inside, I gave him a dose of cold medicine, I tried and failed to find his thermometer, I grabbed him a blanket, and I ordered him to lie down. Now, he's wrapped in the navy-blue fleece I found, shivering despite the sweat beaded on his forehead.

Mike tries to answer but ends up coughing instead. I frown harder, find a pillow, and tuck it under his head. Kneeling in front of him, I study the pallor of his face and the circles around his closed eyes. "When was the last time you ate?"

"Yesterday," he manages to say with his eyes still closed.

"Slept?"

"Body hurts t-too much."

A violent chill shakes him, and I gnaw on the inside of my lip. I wish he'd let me take him to a doctor, but he's right: there's probably no use. The rest of the group—with the exception of me, Dee, and Danica—went through the same symptoms, albeit less severe. This is the worst of it. He needs to sweat it out.

"This is the worst of it," I say out loud to reassure us both, and Mike nods.

I want to reach out and brush his damp hair from his forehead, or rub his arm, or . . . I don't know . . . do *something* to comfort him. But instead, I stand up, walk back to the kitchen, and stir that pot of soup. I stir it, and I stir it, and I *will* it to make him better.

Only, it doesn't make him better. Ten minutes after Mike eats the entire bowl, the entire bowl comes back up. He can't keep down cold medicine. He can't keep down juice or water or Gatorade. He shivers uncontrollably, sweats through two blankets and three sets of clothes, and refuses to let me take him to the doctor since, when I finally find his thermometer, his temperature "only" reads 102.7.

As the evening wears on and the light streaming through his windows fades, I bring him ice chips and fresh clothes, and I coax him to drink small amounts of water and chicken broth at a time. He watches hockey with his eyes closed, and I sit on the far end of the couch from him, doing my best to narrate all the small things that the sports announcer doesn't. Together, we listen to his laundry tumble in the dryer, since he was down to his last clean T-shirt and I had a feeling he might soon need another.

"Hailey," he quietly says sometime after 8 P.M., and I look over at him laid back in the reclined end of the sofa. In the dim light of a single corner lamp, he's buried under two blankets and surrounded by a fortress of throw pillows. His face is turned toward me, his cheek against the back of the couch and his brown eyes heavy with exhaustion.

"If you're going to tell me to leave again—" I start, expecting him to tell me for the hundredth time that I don't have to stay with him. But he cuts me off.

"I'm not." He pauses to let the argument seep out of me. "I'm not. I want you to stay."

"Oh," my tiny voice apologizes. "Then . . . what is it?"

Mike's weighted gaze lingers on mine, and then it shutters closed. "Nothing."

"Tell me."

Thick lashes lift to reveal those big browns again, and the air in the room thickens as the sun sinks below the windowsill. "Why'd you stop playing Deadzone?" he asks in a quiet voice. It molds a lump in my throat, and I contemplate my answer.

"Homework," I decide after a too-long pause. "I've had a lot of homework."

"Is that why you haven't responded to any of my texts?"

Unable to find my voice, I nod.

Mike studies me from two cushions away, his gaze threatening to pull the truth from where it's buried in the pit of my chest. "Do you know how I can tell you're lying?"

That lump in my throat swells and swells, and I just sit there, staring.

"Your eyes get a little wider, and your lips get a little tighter. Like you're biting the inside of your bottom lip."

My teeth immediately release the inside of my

bottom lip, and Mike eventually turns away from me. He watches the ceiling like it's going to crumble down on him. "I feel like a mess."

Thankful for the change of subject, I say, "I don't think it's time for more cold medicine."

"Cold medicine won't help," he replies with a heavy sigh, and then he turns toward me again. "Can I lie down?"

"Do you want me to move?" I ask, planting my feet on the floor as Mike begins to shift out of his blankets.

"No." He tosses a throw pillow onto my lap, repositioning on the couch until his heavy head pins it there. The protesting springs beneath the cushions drown out the sound of my heart thudding in my ears, and Mike pulls a blanket up to his neck while he continues getting comfortable. With him facing the TV, I sit there with one hand braced on the armrest and the other splayed against the back cushion beside me.

Every muscle in my body has turned to stone while my jackhammer heart threatens to crack me into pieces from within. Even my lungs have turned to granite, threatening to suffocate me while I pretend to watch TV.

"Is this okay?"

"Huh?" I squeak, and Mike turns his head on the pillow to gaze up at me, which is almost certainly how I'm going to die. Those eyes. My heart.

"Is this alright?"

"Yeah," I manage, and Mike's eyes linger on my lips before he turns back toward the TV.

I let out a deep breath slowly, *slowly.*

"Tell me your favorite pizza topping."

"What?" At the sound of my own squeaky voice, I resist the urge to slap myself. *Stop squeaking! There is no reason to squeak!*

"You don't eat meat," Mike explains. "So what do you like on your pizza?"

I still don't know what the hell to do with my right hand. Do I put it on his shoulder? His *waist*? "Um, I like black olives," I say, cupping my hand on my head like a damn idiot.

When Mike turns to question me, I pretend to be scratching my scalp. "Olives?"

"And banana peppers." Mike's brow furrows into a deep V, and I continue scratching my head until I'm pretty sure he's going to think I have lice.

"Black olives and *banana peppers*?"

With no other choice, I rest my hand on his shoulder. "It's good."

"We probably shouldn't talk about this," he says, facing the TV again.

"Why?" My hand is light as a feather.

"I'll throw up again." Mike groans, and I can't help laughing.

"You shouldn't knock it until you try it."

"Hm," he hums. "Tell me something else."

"Like what?"

"Are you a vegetarian because you don't believe in killing animals?"

I stretch the kinks out of my fingers before letting

them rest against the blanket covering his arm again. "No, I believe in the humane killing of animals. On my parents' farm, all of the animals are allowed to roam free and live long lives. I think that's okay."

"Why then?"

I can't help the quiet chuckle that shakes me, and when Mike turns to question it, I say, "Promise you won't tell Danica."

He shifts so that he's lying on his back, and his response comes quick and easy. "I promise."

With him lying this way, it's impossible to ignore the fact that *Mike Madden* has his head on my lap. I am at Mike Madden's house, on his couch, at nighttime, with his *head* on my *lap*. I pretend my heart isn't drumming louder than his professional-grade drums. It takes me a moment before I remember how to talk.

"When I was fifteen," I start, hoping I can get through this story without any more unfortunate squeaking, "my family went to Danica's house for Thanksgiving. We'd always hosted Thanksgiving dinner at my house, since my family could never afford to fly all the way down here to Virginia—" A burning blush creeps across my cheeks, and I wish I hadn't said that last part. "But that year, my uncle Rick flew us all down, and my aunt Tilly made the turkey."

Mike just watches me, no judgment in his eyes, and I breathe a little more evenly.

"Well, really, I don't even know if she made the turkey. She probably ordered it precooked or something. But anyway, her turkey was as big as a full-grown Yorkshire pi— uh . . . a really big pig. One of those huge pink ones." Mike nods his understanding, and I force myself to stop stammering. "Right. So, this turkey could've fed fifty people even after the seven of us ate our fill. It was honestly the biggest, most beautiful turkey I'd ever seen, but my mom . . . my mom had always made the turkey before, and hers had never been anything near that size, and I could see how bad she felt about it."

A frown slips onto Mike's face, and I remember the look my mom wore that day.

"I remember looking across the table, and my mom smiled at me, and all I could think was that I'd never seen her look so sad. And Danica was sitting right next to me, and she kept asking us if we'd ever seen a turkey that big, and talking about how she'd never seen a turkey even *half* that size."

I roll my eyes, remembering how oblivious she was. I even kicked her under the table at one point, but all she did was smack me and loudly order me to watch where I was putting my feet.

"And her parents weren't any better, talking about how they had to contact *special* people to get this *special* turkey, and how *special* it all was." I sigh and shake my head. "So my uncle finished carving this ridiculous turkey, and he went to put some on my plate, and I just threw my hands over my plate and said, 'Oh no, I'm a vegetarian.'"

I laugh to myself, and Mike smiles up at me.

"All of a sudden *I* was the center of attention instead of that stupid turkey, and everyone was gaping at me, and Danica got *so* mad. She kept ordering me to admit I was lying and eat the turkey, but I never did." My proud smile stretches across my face. "Because that was the day I became a vegetarian."

"You haven't eaten meat in eight years just to spite your family?"

"I guess so," I say with a chuckle, and Mike belly-laughs until he starts coughing and has to roll away from me again.

"You're amazing," he praises when he finally catches his breath, and I grin at the side of his head.

"A real rebel." One who never stayed out past curfew, didn't get a car until she was eighteen, and babysat her brother on weekends for fun.

"Tell me something else."

I ask Mike what he wants to know, and the list of things he comes up with is endless. We pass hour after hour with story after story.

He asks me why I want to be a veterinarian, and I tell him about the thirteen photos my mom keeps in a hatbox in her closet. Every year on the first day of school, she stood me on our front porch with a sign that read, "When I grow up, I want to be a . . ." And every year, that sentence was finished with "a veterinarian." The handwriting changed over time—from my mom's, to a child's sloppy lettering, to the handwriting I use today—but the dream has always been the same. I've wanted to be a veterinarian for as long as I can remember, because I wanted to care for pets that were loved instead of simply cared for. I grew up knowing not to get too attached to the chickens or pigs we owned—with the exception of Teacup, who was my birthday present for my sweet sixteenth—but it's always hurt my heart a little, knowing that they were never truly loved. So I loved our dogs and cats extra, and I've always wanted to spend my life helping people who love their animals just as much as I love mine, and to make sure that their animals stay with them as long as possible.

Mike asks me other things too—like what it was like growing up on a farm, if it's hard when the dogs get adopted from the shelter, if I plan on moving back to Indiana once I get my degree. He asks a million thoughtful questions that I answer with stories. I tell him about the sick baby goat I rescued at home and how it was the first animal I ever named. I tell him about the time I broke my arm when I cartwheeled right out of our barn's hayloft. I tell him about falling asleep to the smell of rain falling outside my window. I tell him about the poodle that got adopted from the shelter by a little boy and his family last week, and how it wouldn't stop licking the boy's face and clothes.

I tell him stories until my eyelids are drooping and my hand is heavy on his shoulder. And I notice when he begins shivering beneath my palm.

"Are you shaking again?" I ask, leaning forward to study Mike's face. In the glow of the TV, I can see the sweat glistening on his forehead.

"I'm fine," he chatters with his eyes closed.

"You're not." I glance at the clock, and my stomach plummets. "You were due for more cold medicine an hour ago." It's past eleven. Where did the time go?

"I didn't want to get up," he reasons, and I hiss when I press my palm against his face.

"You're burning up." Another big shiver rocks through him, and I push his hair away from his forehead. "Let me up."

"I'm fine."

"You're not."

"I'm comfortable."

"I'm just going to get more cold medicine," I promise, sliding out from beneath him. I curse my shitty nursing skills all the way to the kitchen, where I grab the cold medicine, a glass and bowl full of cold water, and a washcloth.

"Here," I say so that he'll sit up when I get back. Standing in front of the couch, I hand him a measuring cap full of blue medicine, and then I give him a glass of water. He drinks it down and stares up at me, waiting until I sit back down in my seat at the end of the couch.

Two seconds later, his head is in my lap again. No pillow. Just his cheek and his scruff and his breath against my jeans.

My trembling hand dips the washcloth into the bowl I set on the side table. I wring it out one-handed and gently place it against Mike's forehead. "Does that feel okay?"

His arm wraps around my legs, his fingers tucking

beneath my thigh. I couldn't wiggle out from under him now even if I tried. "Yeah."

My whole body aches from how tense my muscles are, but still, I brush that washcloth over Mike's forehead again and again, slowly and softly. I comb his damp hair away from his forehead with the fingers of one hand and follow it with the cold washcloth I hold like a lifeline in the other. "You should be in bed."

Mike's fingers slide a little further beneath my jeans, his hold on my legs growing even snugger. "I should be right here."

"Danica wouldn't like this," I blurt, because my heart is pounding and my blood is rushing and Mike's *cheek* is on my *legs*.

"Danica isn't here."

I freeze with the washcloth against his temple, and Mike turns his chin to look up at me. "It's fine." At my doubtful expression, he swears, "It's fine. Trust me . . . It's going to be fine."

I don't know if I believe him, but when he turns away from me again, I run the washcloth over his forehead. I let him hold me, and I take care of him, even though in my heart, I know none of this is fine.

Danica should be taking care of him.

She is who he should be holding.

I shouldn't have these feelings.

"I'm not her, Mike."

"I know," he says. "Trust me. I know."

Chapter 17

"I STAYED BECAUSE I had to," I tell the bobble-head zombie gnashing at me from my dashboard. "He was so sick. You should have seen him, Danica."

The bobble head nods furiously as I drive over a railroad track, its level of crazy a good match for my cousin's.

"Why didn't I call you?" My thumbs pick at my steering wheel as I try to brainstorm a good answer. "Because I didn't want you to get worried and come over and end up getting sick and having to miss the music video. I know how important it is to you."

I release the inside of my lip between my teeth, remembering what Mike said about my tell.

"Of course nothing happened. I'm your cousin, Danica. God."

The zombie judges me in silence.

"I swear! All he did was shiver and throw up all

night. I wanted to take him to the doctor's, that way I wouldn't have to hang there all night, but he wouldn't let me."

I frown in the rearview mirror when I realize I'm chewing my lip again. My dark eyebrows turn in, and my bottom lip pushes out. Unbrushed curls remind me of hours spent sleeping on Mike's couch—his head on my lap, his arms around my legs.

"I'm not lying," I say to my reflection, and then I tell the zombie, "I have nothing to feel guilty about."

He nods at me, I nod back, and I reluctantly turn left into the parking lot of the apartment I share with Danica.

I concentrate on my lip as I walk up the entryway stairs, as I turn the doorknob, as I cautiously step inside. And when Danica leaps off the couch and flies at me, I nearly throw my arms up to protect myself.

"Which color?" she asks as I flinch, thrusting a nail polish bottle in my face. "For the music video. This one, or this one?"

I stare at two identical shades of hot pink and then up into my taller cousin's dark eyes. Thrown off by her nonviolent greeting, I jam my foot far, far down into my throat. "Don't you want to know where I was?"

Danica stands with the bottles still held in the air, her eyebrow lifting into a skyward arch. "Weren't you at the dog shelter?"

"I stayed with Mike," I confess, and when her face twists with some emotion that hasn't fully formed yet, I admonish, "He was *really* sick, Dani."

I wasn't expecting this—this anger that's come over me—but it works to my advantage, because instead of breaking a nail polish bottle against the wall and stabbing my eye out with it, she lowers the bottles and asks with only a slight amount of skepticism, "Like how sick?"

"Like sweating uncontrollably and throwing up all night."

Her face wrinkles. "Ew."

"Yeah."

"How is he now?"

"Better," I answer, my hard tone softening. "His fever broke. His throat is still scratchy and he's still really weak and exhausted from being sick for so long, but he should be fine in a couple days."

Danica considers me like a viper considers a mouse, eyes attentive and muscles tight. My tiny heart races and races as I wonder if she's going to strike, or if she's going to let me live in her aquarium to play with another day.

"Well, thanks for doing that for me," she finally says, and my brain short-circuits. Did Danica seriously just *thank* me for spending the night with her boyfriend? "Did you tell him the basket was from me?" she asks.

I nod.

"Did he like it?"

I nod again, and she smiles.

"Good. Now pick a color."

I lift a random hand, point to a random bottle, and listen to Danica spend the next few minutes explaining why that color is horrible. She decides to go with the other, identical shade of pink, and I eventually escape to my room, where I plop down on the edge of my bed and stare at a pale indigo wall.

I'm Alice in Wonderland, shrinking to two inches tall as I try to solve riddles and believe impossible things.

Mike is in love with Danica, but he clings to me in his sleep.

Danica hates me, but she thanks me when I take care of her boyfriend.

I'm a good person, but my heart pounds every time I see my cousin's boyfriend. Or hear my cousin's boyfriend. Or think of my cousin's boyfriend.

I squeeze my eyes shut and inhale a deep breath, trying to clear the caterpillar's smoke from my head. I'm thinking of Red Queens and singing flowers and houses of cards—when my door flies open and the knob smashes the doorstopper right through the wall.

Danica stands there, her face a twisted mask of rage. "YOU LYING FUCKING SLUT!"

I gape at her.

"What the fuck did you do over there last night?!"

My heart hurtles over an impossible beat before careening onto its face. "What?" squeaks my dormouse voice.

"Don't sit there playing innocent, you whore! What the fuck is this?!"

She shoves her phone in my face, and I read two texts with Mike's name at the top.

I tried. It's over.

Please tell Hailey she forgot her phone.

When I stare wide-eyed up at Danica, all of her delicate features are painted a deep, furious red. "I—"

"You fucked him!"

"I didn't!" I argue. I'd stand up to defend myself, but Danica is practically on top of me.

"You are such a fucking *liar*! You've wanted him since the day you saw him! Admit it, you bitch!"

"There's nothing to admit!" I scream as I stand up, forcing Danica back. "I didn't sleep with your fucking boyfriend!"

"Then why is he breaking up with me?" she shouts back at me, her hands curling into fists at her sides. I should take them as a warning, but adrenaline is exploding through my veins.

"Maybe because you don't fucking love him? Maybe because you're a self-centered bitch who only cares about yourself!"

Danica's mouth drops open like it's about to come unhinged and swallow me whole. My body tenses in anticipation of the blow she's about to deal me, but instead of punching me, she walks over to my desk.

"Get the fuck out of my house," she orders, pushing my computer over with all of her might. It flies off the desktop and crashes onto the floor, taking my half-finished midterm exam files with it.

I stare at the computer and then at Danica, tears welling in my eyes.

"Are you fucking deaf?" she asks, grabbing a framed picture of my family from the desk and launching it at the wall behind me. The glass shatters into a million pieces behind my back. "Get the fuck out!" Danica screams, grabbing the side of my flimsy desk and flipping the entire thing over. A leg breaks off of it as it crashes onto the floor, taking my textbooks and folders with it. Papers scatter all over the hardwood, and I drop to my knees to collect them.

"You are such fucking trash," Danica snarls as she stands over me. When I reach for my biology textbook, she kicks it out of my reach. "Wait until my dad hears about what a little slut you are. Bye-bye tuition."

Tears drip onto the papers beneath my knees as I gather them with shaking hands. I don't even know why I bother—when Danica's dad stops paying for my tuition, none of it will matter.

"Say something, you bitch!" Danica screams.

"I didn't sleep with him," I swear again, my voice breaking on a sob, and Danica's laughter fills my room.

She continues calling me names and trashing my room as I grab what I can and shove it into my backpack—school supplies, some clothes from drawers that she empties onto the floor, a few personal effects that I know she'll destroy if I leave them behind. And then I grab my keys from the bed and walk toward the front door with Danica breathing down the back of my neck.

"Don't you *ever* fucking come back here," she warns as she kicks the backs of my heels. "Mike is going to realize what a worthless piece of hick shit you are, and he's going to beg for me to take him back. And you know what? I will, Hailey. Because he is *mine*, and you are *nothing*. You'll *always* be nothing."

She stops at the door, standing on the stoop as my weak legs carry me to my car. I struggle to unlock my car door with trembling fingers, my vision blurred with unshed tears.

"Bye-bye, slut!" Danica screams loud enough for the neighbors to hear when I get into my car. I spare one last glance to find her waving at me with her fingers, a venomous grin on her face. Tears stream down my cheeks as I put the car into reverse and back away from our apartment.

On the road, I think of the way her smile dimpled when we were kids. I think of how I'm going to explain to my parents that I need to move back home. I think of the waitressing job I'll have to spend the rest of my life working. I think of how tightly Mike held me last night, how he smiled at me this morning, how I'll never see him again when I'm living on a farm in Indiana. I think of all the sweet dreams I never should have had.

Another sob chokes me, and I park along the side of the road to fall completely, utterly apart.

Chapter 18

IN THE BACK of a kennel, at the back of a hallway, at the back of a shelter, I sit with my forehead on my knees and an overweight basset hound licking the sausage grease off my fingers. Somewhere under the fluorescent lighting of this hallway, I lost track of time. I'm not sure if I lost it in the first cage or the second cage or the third cage, but now here I am, at the very last cage, with nowhere else to go.

"Hailey," singsongs the shelter director, Barb, as her grass-stained Timberland boots echo down the hallway. "A strapping young man is here to see yooou."

I peek up from my knees to see her grinning from ear to ear as Mike steps into view. He looks a thousand times better than he did this morning, freshly showered and shaved in a black Dogfish Head T-shirt and well-worn jeans. Barb waggles her bushy eyebrows as she lifts the lock and lets him inside.

"What are you doing here?" I ask as she walks away, and Mike crouches down to pet the potbelly pup sniffing excitedly at his side.

"Trying to find you." He lifts his eyes from the dog to me, his expression telling me that he heard about what happened. "Danica told me she kicked you out."

"Did she tell you she trashed my room?" I ask, ignoring the way my eyes start to burn. "Or that she broke my computer? Or destroyed my desk?"

Mike sits down next to me, hesitating a moment before he wraps a comforting arm around my shoulders. The basset hound immediately lays its head and front paws on Mike's lap, its overplump tummy drooping onto the ground.

"I'm taking you home with me," Mike says, hugging me tight against his side. "I already filled out the adoption papers."

My eyes burn hotter, and a scalding tear traces a line down my cheek. "I'm driving home tomorrow."

"To Indiana?" Mike asks, shifting to look at me. I avoid his eyes. "Why?"

"I have nowhere to live, Mike."

"I just told you that you can stay with me . . ."

Another heavy tear drops onto my lap as I shake my head, because of course he doesn't get it. He doesn't know that Danica's family pays my tuition, my rent, my insurance, my gas, my *everything*. There's no point in staying here because Danica is going to make sure the money stops, and when it does, there will be nothing left but for me to go back home and pretend I never tried to drag myself out of the mud, that I never chased after my dreams.

Thirteen years of "When I grow up, I want to be a veterinarian" school photos: down the drain.

"There's no point," I tell Mike, knowing the pull Danica has over my uncle. He's a good man, but his daughter is his princess, and she's grown up knowing that. She's always had that man wrapped around her little finger, which is why she's twenty-four years old but has never once had to hold a real job.

"Why not?" Mike asks, his voice full of concern.

"Danica's not going to change her mind. It's not like I can live with you forever."

"Sure you can," Mike argues, and when I look up at him, his smile attempts to make the world right again. "We'll eat pizza, drink beer, play video games—it'll be great."

I wonder why he's being so nice to me, why he broke up with Danica, why he came here to find me, why he wants to take me home, what he'd do if I crawled onto his lap and kissed him until the sparks inside me burned the world to the ground.

He's single now. Why is he single?

"Why did you break up with Danica?" I ask with nothing left to lose, and Mike's smile flickers before it fades away.

"That's a loaded question, Hailey . . ."

I want to ask if it was because of me. The words trip over themselves on the tip of my tongue as Mike studies me and I study him. I stare up into those impossibly warm brown eyes, remembering how tightly he held my legs last night. But then I study the curve of his lips, the scruff of his jaw, the perfect way his finger-combed hair lies on his head, and I'm reminded of the girls who scream dirty promises at him from the crowd. I'm reminded of the fact that my cousin, whom he dumped, looks like she belongs on a runway in Paris. I'm reminded of my messy curls, my short stature, my thrift-shop clothes. "Tell me anyway" is all I say.

Mike holds my gaze for a moment before staring out at the chain-link wall in front of us. He takes a weighted breath before saying, "She isn't the girl for me."

"How do you know?"

"I don't love her." His eyes find mine, and I let myself get lost in them. "I'm not sure how I ever did."

"What changed?" my small voice asks.

Each question I ask feels like taking one step further out onto the plank. Eventually, I'm going to drown.

Mike continues staring down at me, his arm snug around my shoulder. His voice is low and quiet when he says, "Everything."

My heart is beating out of my chest when I break eye contact with him to stare at the frayed edges of my bootlace. My eyes travel to the hole in the knee of my jeans, the hem of my oversized sweatshirt.

I shouldn't be with him right now—because he's a rock star, because he's my cousin's ex, because there are bigger things I should be worrying about, because guys like him never want girls like me.

"She thinks I slept with you," I say, and Mike

squeezes my shoulder, reminding me that we're friends.

Good friends.

"No, she doesn't."

"She does, Mike. She said—"

"She's hurt," he interrupts. "She's angry. She wants someone to blame." I stare up at him, and he says, "She knows you better than that, Hailey. Anyone who knows you knows that you would never do that."

I'm not sure I believe him. I remember the fury in her eyes when she burst into my room like she was going to rip my heart out of my chest with nothing but fingernails and teeth.

"She knows *I* would never do that either," Mike adds when he sees the doubt on my face. "She'll cool down. You'll see. Tomorrow, all of this will blow over."

The basset hound finally manages to hop up far enough to crawl onto our laps, its heavy head a comforting weight on the tops of my thighs. I scratch it behind the ears and say, "I don't think so."

Mike scratches the dog's rump, and it kicks its leg, in heaven. "Either way, you're coming home with me tonight, Hailey. You're not sleeping in a kennel."

"Okay," I say to assuage the guilt I realize he feels. He thinks Danica kicked me out for something *he* did. He thinks I'm innocent in this.

"Danica is mad at *me*," he tries to assure me. "Not you."

I sigh.

"You're cousins. She can't stay mad forever. She'll

probably feel terrible for what she did, and she'll beg you to forgive her."

I don't tell him he's wrong, even though he is. Danica's conscience died sometime during puberty, and now she does whatever she wants without guilt or remorse. I'm sure there's already a missed voice mail from my uncle waiting on my phone. He'll ask me to call him, and I will—but Danica will have already cried to him, and my silent tears won't mean a thing.

"Okay?" Mike asks, pulling away to search my eyes. "No more talk about leaving."

I can't help the tear that spills silently down my cheek, or the one that follows it when the pad of Mike's thumb wipes the first one away. I nod in agreement, because I don't want to talk about it.

Danica isn't going to change her mind. I'll have no choice but to move back home.

Even if Mike doesn't want me to. Even if I don't want to either.

There's nothing left to talk about.

Chapter 19

It's late by the time we arrive back at Mike's house. Since I was in no emotional state to drive, he helped me into the passenger seat of his truck, and sometime during the long, silent drive, I collected the pieces of myself.

By the time my feet hit the gravel of his driveway, my last tear has long since dried against my cheek, and inside, I help myself to his linen closet. I sort through stacked sheets, blankets, and towels I washed and folded myself just this morning, and Mike ventures off to find us something to eat.

"You're not making this easy!" he shouts from the kitchen as I shake a navy bedsheet out and let it settle on the couch.

"Just find some cereal and beer," I yell back, knowing that his freezer might as well be a meat locker. When I peeked in there last night, it looked like a Tetris game of supreme pizzas and meatball Hot Pockets.

Mike pokes his head out of the kitchen, and I stop unfolding sheets.

"What?"

"Did you seriously just suggest we have cereal and beer for dinner?"

"Oh," I start, remembering that he's still recovering from his cold. "You're right. We should probably find you some soup or—"

"No," Mike says, the corners of his mouth tipping up. "I feel better. I'm starved."

"What is it then?" I ask, and he shakes his head, still smiling.

"You."

He disappears back into the kitchen, and something that feels an awful lot like fuzzy baby caterpillars rolls around in my belly as I continue making up the couch for the night. By the time Mike joins me in the living room, with two bowls of Lucky Charms and two Guinnesses, I've tucked and straightened and fluffed myself a bed that I can't wait to forget about this hellish day in.

Mike sits down next to me and hands me a bowl of cereal. "You know you're not sleeping on the couch, right?"

"Huh?" I ask through a mouthful of colorful marshmallows. I hold the bowl under my chin and try to keep milk from spilling out of my mouth.

"I'll take the couch. You can sleep in my bed."

I shake my head and swallow what I'm guessing is no fewer than twenty hearts, stars, and horseshoes. "No way. You're still recovering. I'm fine on the couch."

"Hailey," Mike says, setting his cereal on the coffee table and picking up a beer instead, "there's no way in hell I'm sleeping in that big comfortable bed while you're out here on the couch."

"It's a comfortable couch . . ."

"Which is why I'm taking it."

I furrow my brow at him, but his expression remains uncompromising—unblinking eyes over a straight-lined mouth. "It's enough that you're letting me stay here, Mike."

"No, it's not. I'm not the asshole that's going to make a lady sleep on his couch."

I snort at the idea of me being a lady. "So this is sexism," I accuse with a scowl.

"Call it what you want," Mike says, smirking as he steals a red heart from my bowl. "You're still sleeping in my bed."

I force myself to glare at him in spite of the warmth flooding my cheeks, but he continues smiling at me, and my heart skips rope behind my ribs. I ignore the double-dutch jumping and try to remain pragmatic—I want the couch, he wants the couch, but we both can't sleep on the couch. And even if we could, that would be stupid.

"Look, we're both grown adults," I say before I can overthink what I'm about to suggest next. "If you're really not going to let me sleep on the couch, we can share the bed."

"Fine," Mike immediately agrees.

"Fine," I echo while my brain screams, *OH MY*

FLIPPING GOD! Did you seriously just agree to sleep with Mike?! In his bed! Together?! Together!!! In his bed! What?! What the hell happened to staying on the wagon?!

"How are those Lucky Charms?" Mike asks, and my shell-shocked gaze drops down to my soggy oats. My mind is still screaming that I just made a huge mistake, that sleeping in his bed is only going to reignite my stupid sparks, that it's wrong, that it's going to make Danica hate me more than she already does, that she'll never know, that *I'll* know, that she's my cousin, that she never deserved him, that he's single now, that he's a rock star, that he doesn't like me as anything more than a friend, that none of this should matter, that I—

"Hailey?" Mike asks.

"Huh?" I squeak.

"What's on your mind?"

What *should* be on my mind is my education, my uncle, my tuition, my future. But the real answer is *Mike's bed*, and I am most definitely never *ever* sharing that information with him. "Your music video," I rattle, frantically changing the subject from beds to literally *anything* else. "Will you still let Danica be in it?"

"After she treated you like she did?" Mike all but growls. His fingers stop tapping against the neck of his beer, coiling tightly around it instead. "Not a chance in hell."

I take a big gulp of Guinness to calm my nerves. It doesn't go with Lucky Charms—not that any beer really could—but whatever, it's beer. "Are you nervous?"

"About Danica?"

"About the video." I crisscross my legs under me, thinking that the video seems a safe enough topic. No big bed, no angry Danica, no butterfly-winged sparks. "Have you ever made one before?"

"We made one in high school once," Mike says. "But it was just a stupid kid thing. Nothing like this."

"So? Are you nervous?"

"Nah. No one pays attention to the drummer." He takes another sip and slides forward on the overstuffed couch so that he's sitting on the edge. "All I have to do is sit in the background doing this." He holds his beer with a curled pinky as he plays the lamest air drums ever, and I chuckle.

"Just this, huh?" I set my bottle on the coffee table to mock his movements, and his mouth stretches into a big grin. "Maybe I should be a drummer," I tease. "This is easy."

"You think so?" Amusement fills his voice as I strike an invisible cymbal.

"I mean, I don't want to brag—" I let my toes drop to the floor so I can throw in some foot pedal work while I continue banging on my make-believe drum kit, "but I think I'm probably better than you."

Mike watches me act like an idiot for a while, takes one last swig of his beer, and suddenly rises to his feet. My air drumming freezes as I sit motionless on the couch staring way, way up at him. "Come on then," he says, holding a hand down for me.

"Come where?"

"My drums, Keith Moon. Let's see what you've got."

ON A STOOL in front of a massive set of polished black drums, my palms sweat around two smooth drumsticks and my feet dangle off the floor. "You're *sure* you want me to embarrass you like this?" I taunt with forced bravado, and Mike smiles wide at the challenge.

"I can't wait."

"But you'll never be able to unsee this," I bargain. "You'll spend the rest of your life like, 'Wow, what's the point? I'll never be as good of a drummer as Hailey Harper.'"

Mike laughs, his brown eyes glittering with anticipation, and I swallow hard. My grasp on the drumsticks tightens, and I wonder which drum to hit first. One of the big foot ones with The Last Ones to Know logos on them? One of the deep ones at my sides? One of the shallow drums in front of me? Dear God, there are so many drums.

I stare up at Mike, and the corner of his mouth kicks up. "Alright, Hailey Harper, how about a game of horse? All you have to do is match what I do, that way you don't embarrass me too much."

I thrust the drumsticks at him and slide off the stool like it's about to catch fire. "Let's do it," I agree, thinking, *How hard can it be to copy what he does?*

Mike smiles as he takes the drumsticks, settling on the stool like I'd settle at a desk—like it's the most natural thing in the world. The drumsticks look at home in his hands, and he looks at me with an easy smile on his face. "Are you ready?"

I nod, and Mike starts tapping one of the cymbal

things with his right hand. Just tap, tap, tap, tap, tap, tap, tap, tap . . . eight taps in an even rhythm. When he hands me the drumsticks, I lift an eyebrow at him, and he chuckles as he slides off the stool.

My grasp on the drumsticks this time isn't as white-knuckled, and I easily keep the beat Mike set: tap, tap, tap, tap, tap, tap, tap, tap.

"Nice," he praises, taking the drumsticks I hand him and sliding back onto the stool I vacate. He takes his next turn, doing the same tapping beat with his right hand, but adding in one of the big foot pedal drums. Tap/thump, tap, tap, tap, tap/thump, tap, tap, tap. He repeats this a few times, then looks up at me. "Got it?"

I nod, and he hands me the drumsticks. He lowers the stool for me before I slide back onto it, and I carefully rest my foot on one of the pedals before taking a deep breath. Mike gives me a reassuring smile, and I try to mimic what he did: tap/thump, tap, tap, tap, tap/thump, tap, tap, tap. When I do it twice without messing up, I beam up at him.

"You're a natural," he praises, and I laugh as I slide off the stool, because he is so full of crap. But my insides feel all fuzzy anyway, and my cheeks ache from smiling when he slides back onto the stool.

"I'm going to add the snare to the bass and hi-hat this time," he coaches, and I catalog these new terms in my mind, studying him carefully. "Ready?"

I nod, hoping I can get this new beat right, and

Mike plays it out for me: tap/thump, tap, tap/bang, tap, tap/thump, tap, tap/bang, tap. He plays it a few more times, giving me time to memorize it, and my fingers start itching to take the sticks from him so I can give it a try. "Got all that?"

"We'll see," I say, and he chuckles as he relinquishes the stool. I slide back onto it and chew on my lip, my confidence fading as I replay the beat in my head and doubt my coordination.

"You've got this," Mike promises, and the assuring look in his big brown eyes makes me loosen my death grip on the sticks. His hand squeezes my shoulder, and his thumb taps a beat against my skin: tap, tap, tap, tap, tap, tap, tap, tap.

"I can't concentrate with you doing that," I confess, and his thumb stops tapping, but he doesn't pull it away. It starts rubbing back and forth across my shoulder, and my thoughts turn into strings of yarn that tangle around and around and around themselves as my toes curl in my tennis shoes.

I stare up at him, and he stares down at me. No one speaks, and my heart sets its own beat: BANG BANG BANG BANG BANG BANG BANG BANG.

"You're cheating," I breathe, and Mike's mouth curves into a sly smile.

"How am I cheating?"

"If you keep that up," I warn with my heart hammering in my throat, "you're getting the H in horse."

Mike laughs and lets his hand fall away, and I struggle to breathe evenly enough to keep a steady beat on the drums. *Was he flirting with me just now? Was he only teasing? Does he know I like him?*

Oh God. *Does he know I like him?*

When my toes curl inside my shoes, the foot pedal hammer whacks the bass drum and makes me jump. "That doesn't count!" I squeal, and Mike laughs again. I poke him in the stomach with a drumstick. "That was an accident! It doesn't count."

"Fine," he agrees with a chuckle, grabbing the end of my stick so I can't poke him again. "It doesn't count." Holding the stick, he leans in closer, a playful smile on his face. "You're still going to lose."

When he lets go and crosses his arms over his chest, I turn back toward the drums and prepare to prove him wrong. My right stick taps the hi-hat, my foot pedal smacks the bass. Tap/thump, tap, tap/bang, tap, tap/thump, tap, tap/bang, tap. I continue playing, laughing when I don't make any mistakes. I grin at Mike, in awe of the fact that I'm actually drumming. Ten minutes ago, I didn't even know what a hi-hat was, and now I'm sitting here setting a beat like a legit drummer. "This is awesome," I marvel with a laugh, and Mike's smile brightens as he watches me.

"Told you you're a natural."

"Am I better than you yet?"

Mike tries to hide a smile and holds his hands out for the sticks. When I hand them over, he takes my seat and flashes me a playful smirk. "Let's see."

He starts by beating on the snare drums, and I

try to memorize the order. But then, his hands start moving too fast for me to keep track of. His sticks dance over snares and cymbals while his feet pound on the two bass drums, setting a fast, loud, impossible beat. I stand there watching, in awe of him, in wonder of how many hours and how many nights and how many years it must have taken him to get to this level. He plays this wild beat like it's easy, like it's as simple as thinking, as breathing.

Eventually, my eyes stop concentrating so hard on his hands. They move to his arms, his chest, his face. I admire the curve of his lips, the shadow of his jaw, the shade of his eyes. Those butterflies start stirring inside me again, and by the time Mike finally takes one final hard swing at his drums, I'm no different than any of the dozens of weak-kneed girls who watch him from the front row of his shows.

"Your turn," he says while I stand there breathless, and I finally come back down to Earth.

"Huh?"

He hands me the sticks and teases, "Let's see what you've got."

I sit down at the drums in a daze, and then I can't help laughing. Because yeah, freaking, right. "How about I do something better?" I ask, and Mike's eyebrow lifts in question.

"Like what?"

I spin toward him and hold the drumsticks up for him to see. Then, when I have his full attention, I start spinning them between my fingers. Five years of baton twirling has prepared me for this moment, and I twirl my freaking heart out. The sticks pick up speed, blurring as they spin between my fingers. I stand up and walk to the center of the garage studio, where I throw the sticks up, spin around while they're in the air, catch them in my fingers and immediately start spinning them again. "Got it?" I ask, echoing what Mike asked me earlier, and he laughs.

"No way. You win."

I grin and show off by tossing the sticks into the air again, planning to catch them behind my back this time, but when my phone rings in my pocket, they both clatter to the ground.

Chapter 20

IT'S DIFFICULT KEEPING up with Dee and Rowan on a regular basis, but on a three-way call after the day I've had?

Dee: "You're going to fuck his brains out tonight, right?"

Rowan: "Dee—"

Dee: "He's single!"

Rowan: "She doesn't want to be a rebound!"

Dee: "Who's a rebound? He's in love with her!"

I step outside into the freezing air, because I would rather die a slow death of frostbite or hypothermia than have Mike hear **any** of this ridiculous conversation.

"Hailey," Rowan counsels, "you know you can take turns staying with me and Dee to finish out the semester, right?"

I don't get a chance to answer before Dee scolds, "Don't tell her that! She's living with Mike now!"

"Guys—" I start, but in their bickering, they don't hear me.

"Dee, that's too fast!"

"You did it!"

"Guys—" I try again.

"That was different! I—"

"How was it different? You—"

"GUYS." Dead silence stretches on the line, and I take a deep breath. "I appreciate the offer, but I'm going home to Indiana tomorrow."

More silence.

"Guys?"

After a moment, Dee: "Why would you do something so stupid?"

And this time, Rowan doesn't rush to my defense.

"What choice do I have?" I ask as a night breeze nips at the tops of my ears. I'm standing outside Mike's front door, illuminated by his porch light and a sky of October stars. "I can't afford to stay here."

"I can probably get you a job waitressing at the restaurant where I used to work," Dee suggests. "The job sucked major ass, but—"

"And next semester?" I counter. "When Danica gets her dad to stop paying my tuition, I'll have to drop out of school. There's no way I can afford it on my own."

"But *this* semester is already covered, right?" Rowan asks, and I know she has a point. A semester at Mayfield University is more than I would have been able to hope for just a few months ago, and I know that leaving now would be a waste of all the hard work I've done over the past two months. A waste of my uncle's money. A waste of each time I bit my tongue while Danica made me earn every cent of that tuition.

But I don't want to be a burden on Rowan and Adam, or Dee and Joel, or Mike. I know they would let me stay with them for the two months left in the semester, since they're my friends, but it's because they're my friends that I don't want to let them. They didn't sign up to be donors to my charity case of a life . . . This is my problem, not theirs.

"Can't your parents help you?" Dee asks while I'm lost in thought, trying uselessly to figure another way out of leaving.

"If they could, do you think I would've spent the past two and a half months living with Danica?" I sigh and squeeze my eyes shut, already feeling the sting in my heart from saying what I need to say next. But they need to understand—they need to understand that none of this is that easy. My voice is quiet with confession when I explain, "I don't wear thrift-shop clothes because I'm eccentric . . . You two realize that, right?"

"Hailey," Rowan immediately cuts in. "First off, you're beautiful and your clothes are amazing, so shut up with that crap. And second . . ."

When she doesn't finish, I ask, "Yeah?"

"Well . . . I don't really have a second thing yet. Let me think."

The three of us stew in silence while I sit down on Mike's front porch. The cold bites through my back pockets, and in the green Ivy Tech hoodie he rescued for me the first night we met, I wrap my arms around myself.

"I'm going to research scholarships," Rowan finally decides.

"Me too," Dee agrees.

I anchor my stare on the moon, helpless as the world turns round and round and round toward tomorrow. "There's no point," I tell the two girls I've grown to consider close friends. "I've already researched them all."

"Hailey, becoming a vet is important to you . . ." Rowan starts, but I can't think of that right now. I can't because there really *is* no point. I can't because it hurts.

"I know, but—"

"I'm researching them anyway," Rowan insists, and Dee echoes the plan.

"Me too."

I want to tell them I'll miss them when I leave—I'll miss coffee with them at school, I'll miss their insane phone calls I can't keep up with, I'll miss Dee's crazy texts and Rowan's silly laugh.

"What does Mike say about you leaving?" Rowan asks, and I hold myself tighter against the cold.

"He thinks all this is going to blow over. Like Danica is going to grow a heart overnight or something."

"I still don't understand how he could spend so

many years with her and still have no idea who she is," Dee criticizes.

"She was different around him," Rowan argues.

"He knows," I say, and silence creeps into the three-way conversation. I sigh before I continue. "I think Danica was different when he fell in love with her"—the word *love* feels so gross in that sentence, but I press on anyway—"and he's just been holding out hope these past few weeks that maybe she was still that same person deep down. That maybe she'd come back to life." I know the feeling, because I've felt it myself. But Danica isn't the little girl who giggled in a chicken coop with me, and she's not whoever Mike fell in love with either.

"I think you're right," Rowan says, and the understanding in her voice makes me wonder if she knows the feeling too . . . if she knows what it's like to grieve the loss of someone who's still walking, talking, breathing. "Sometimes it's hard letting go."

"But you shouldn't hold on to a mistake just because you've spent a long time making it," Dee argues, and all three of us agree.

"I'm assuming you told Mike there's no way Danica is going to change her mind about this?" Rowan asks, and I use a frizzy brown curl to cut off the circulation of my pointer finger.

"Yeah. He offered to let me stay with him to finish the semester, but . . ."

"But what?"

"He doesn't know that it's not just the apartment

that Danica's family pays for. He doesn't know they pay for my tuition, my bills, my groceries—"

"Why don't you want him to know?" Rowan wonders, and I guess this is the part that I need to say out loud . . .

"Because it's embarrassing." Embarrassing. *Embarrassing.* I know I shouldn't feel it, but there it is. "I hate that I have to bring coffee from home. I hate that I can never buy clothes with real tags on them. Mike is this freaking rock star, and—"

"Mike doesn't care about any of that," Rowan interrupts.

"I know that, but—"

"But nothing. Do you hear me? Mike doesn't care about that stuff. Mike isn't a rock star. Mike is just *Mike.*"

As if on cue, yellow light spills onto the porch when the door creaks open. Mike pokes his head out and sees me with my arms wrapped around myself. "Hey, sorry to interrupt, but . . . it's cold. Do you want a jacket?" He holds a black canvas jacket out for me, and my heart constricts when I accept it.

"Thanks."

"I ordered pizza," Mike says. "They didn't have banana peppers, but I got you olives."

My throat is thick when I thank him again, and when he disappears back inside, I squeeze my eyes shut tight against the sting of the air.

"I still say you should screw his brains out tonight," Dee suddenly suggests, and my nose is stuffy when

I laugh. "Look," she insists, "if you really are leaving soon, I say you should go out with a *bang*."

Crickets.

"Get it? *Bang*?"

"That was so corny," Rowan scoffs, but none of us can keep from laughing. And that's why I love them—because even on my worst night, they can make me laugh. It's why I'm going to miss them, along with Mike and school and the dog shelter and everything else about this town.

Well, almost everything.

I eventually make an excuse to get off the phone, and I promise the girls I won't leave until we explore every option. I know that Rowan is going to stay up all night researching scholarships and housing solutions for me and that nothing I can possibly say will stop her from doing so. And I know that Dee's grand plan is probably to physically hold me down until she can brainwash me into marrying Mike and having a dozen of his babies, because she refuses to believe he only likes me as a friend. But I don't try to change their minds. I just let them care about me. I let them care about me because, when I inevitably have to move back to Indiana, I need to know that this mattered somehow, that all of this wasn't for nothing.

Inside the house, Mike and I sit side by side on the couch, game controllers in hand, pizza slices on paper plates beside us, beers on the table in front of us. We join a map with Kyle the PussySlayer and bomb the ever-loving hell out of him until I laugh so hard, I forget about real life. I forget about needing to leave. There is nothing but the way Mike laughs with me, the way he turns to me and smiles.

"What?" I ask sometime around 3 A.M., giggling at the expression on his face.

"I think this might just be the best night of my life."

I snort. "You've had too much to drink."

He shakes his head, that goofy smile still plastered on his face. "No, I'm serious."

"I think you mean delirious." When he just keeps grinning at me, a blush spreads across my cheeks. "You need to go to bed."

"Come with me."

That blush turns into hot, molten wildfire. "I'm not tired."

Mike sets his controller on the couch. "Come anyway."

My nose catches fire. My ears catch fire. My neck catches fire. "Why?"

"So I don't have to stay up."

"I'm pretty sure you can go to bed without me."

"Yeah," Mike says, turning a remote toward the TV and shutting it off, "but I don't want to."

Chapter 21

I'M NOT SURE what being on drugs feels like, since I've never done any, but I imagine it must feel a lot like having Mike Madden order you to go to bed with him. Reality spins, time picks up speed, and my whole body buzzes with nervous anticipation.

It's late—really late—and I'm pacing back and forth in Mike's hallway bathroom. My fuzzy blue socks eat a line into the slate-gray tile.

When I was thirteen, I kept having this recurring dream that a six-foot-tall blue mouse broke into my room to play hopscotch on my bed, and *that* made more sense than everything that's happened with Mike tonight. I pace toward the bathtub, remembering the way his thumb massaged my shoulder, the way he refused to go to bed without me. Then I pace back toward the door, remembering the way we scarfed down pizza and played war games together like twenty-year-old frat brothers. Toward the tub—how tightly he held my legs last night. Toward the door—the fact that it took him weeks to break up with Danica, even though I've been here the whole time.

His voice at the pond echoes in my mind: *You're one of my best friends now.*

I sit on the lid of the toilet and press the heels of my palms into my eyes. I'm exhausted, I'm drained, and I'm making something out of nothing. Mike rubbed my shoulder to tease me, *like friends do.* He wanted me to come to bed so we could keep talking and laughing, *like friends do.* He carried me through the woods, he picked me up from the animal shelter, he confided in me about his feelings for Danica, because those are all things that friends—really, really good friends—would do.

He'll miss me when I'm gone. But not like I'll miss him.

And anyway, even if he did like me like I like him, it's not like it would matter. He's a rock star. He's going to be ridiculously famous. He's going to have girls throwing themselves at his feet in every country in the world, starting next week when he goes on tour. Most of his life is going to be spent far away from Virginia. Far away from Indiana. Far away from me.

Maybe he was always just meant to be my one exciting story. Fifty years from now, when I'm still living on the farm my parents lived in and my grandparents lived in, when my own granddaughters have tired of a thousand boring stories about livestock and weather and crops, I'll tell them about the hot drummer I pined after during my one semester in Virginia. Maybe I'll even tell them about the night I slept in his bed. They'll probably think he's the one that got away, and maybe I'll think that too . . . but I'll smile anyway, because there are worse things than being Mike Madden's friend—I could have never even known him at all.

Ignoring the sting in my chest, I push open the bathroom door and pad down the hall to Mike's bedroom. In the dim light of a corner lamp, he's straightening the sheets of his oversized bed. His brown eyes lift to mine, dark under thick lashes in the soft lamplight. He straightens to his full six-foot-something, in a white T-shirt, red workout shorts, and black ankle socks, and it strikes me how big he is—how if he wrapped his arms around me, I could get lost in them completely.

"Which side do you want?" he asks.

"Whichever side you don't normally sleep on."

"I normally sleep in the middle." Mike drums his fingers on his leg, and I curl and uncurl my toes against the floor.

"It's your bed. You pick."

"I guess I'll take that one," he decides after a while, pointing to the side closer to the door. I nod and chew on my lip as we walk past each other at the foot of the bed. The faint scent of his cologne makes my heart ache. It smells like running through the rain, like being carried through red leaves.

Mike and I climb under his covers at the same time—me, teetering on the edge of the mattress; him, getting comfortable on his side. When his eyes find mine in that soft yellow light, I nearly roll right off the bed.

I expect him to crack a joke about how awkward this is, or ask me if I'm comfortable, or say something, *anything*, but instead, he just lies there, and so do I. In the gentle light, I let him study me, because it means I get to study him. I take in the curve of his black lashes, the golden undertones in his eyes, the strong slope of his cheek, the adorable shape of his ear. It feels forbidden, staring at him like this, being this close. But not because of Danica. It's because he's too perfect. How soft his hair looks against his navy pillow. The way it fades perfectly into the scruff on his jaw. The tempting shape of his lips.

I close my eyes and try to commit it all to memory, because I want to take this moment home with me. I want to keep it close forever.

"I missed wishing you sweet dreams," Mike says, and his quiet voice persuades my eyes to open. I find him still lying inches away, studying me with that gaze that pulls the strings inside me.

I want to ask why he stopped, but I already know the answer. It's because I stopped responding. I didn't want him to realize I had a crush on him, and I still don't. I can't spend the rest of my life wondering if that's the reason he never talks to me again once I leave this town behind.

"Me too," I say, and when my gaze twines with his, I let it. I let myself fall into those eyes, and fall, and fall, and fall.

"Sweet dreams, Hailey."

My fragile heart bangs in my chest, threatening to break with every beat. I force myself to swallow, force myself to breathe. "Sweet dreams, Mike."

When he turns off the light, I close my eyes again. And in the dark, I listen to my heart splinter beneath the weight of saying goodbye.

Chapter 22

In Mike Madden's room, in Mike Madden's bed, it's no wonder I can't sleep. Not even the light of the moon penetrates his thick blackout curtains, so there's nothing to claim my attention except the thoughts racing through my head.

Tomorrow, a call from my uncle Rick will show up on my phone. He'll recount Danica's accusations, and I'll deny them. I'll be careful not to use words like jealous, or delusional, or psychotic when describing his daughter, but I'll defend myself. I'll tell him I would never, *ever* do something like steal her boyfriend, and maybe he'll even believe me.

But it won't matter. Danica's tears have always meant more than my honesty. Like the Christmas she wouldn't let me play with her toy jeweler because she said there weren't enough rhinestones to go around.

Or the Easter I couldn't use any of the pink egg paint because she said she needed it all for herself. So I won't beg, and I won't cry, and I won't even tell my uncle about her breaking my computer, because there's no point—computers are as replaceable to him as number two pencils. Meaningless: my feelings will be meaningless. And in the end, he'll decide that if Danica doesn't want to share this town, she doesn't need to. He'll never understand how much playing with that jeweler meant to me.

The bed shifts with Mike's weight for what must be the hundredth time, carrying my thoughts to someplace closer. I don't think he's slept yet either, judging by how much he's been moving around. Lying next to him in the pitch black, I've been acutely aware of every shift, every turn, every deep breath.

"I can't sleep," his quiet voice confirms, though I'm sure it's for entirely different reasons. I can't sleep because it *hurts* to be this close to him. It's a tightness in my chest. It's a cramp in my fingers. It's the torture of being so near, but so, *so* far. It's been easier to let my mind drift to the future than to be here, now, in his bed, with him close enough to touch. I don't know if I've spent mere minutes struggling to breathe evenly next to him, or if it's been hours, but it *feels* like hours. It feels like days. Weeks.

"Why not?" I ask.

"Can't get comfortable."

I roll onto my side to face him under light blankets,

and even though I wouldn't be able to see my own hand in front of my face right now, I can sense the distance between us. "Do you want to switch sides?"

"No," Mike says, and the bed shifts again, dipping close to me. I know for certain that if I reached out even a little right now, he'd be right there. I could touch him.

"Are you sure?" I whisper, and my pillow moves. Mike's warm breath grazes my cheek when he answers me.

"Yeah." His voice is quiet, softer than the pillow we're sharing. "This feels better."

"Okay," I say, my skin thrumming with the nearness of him. It waits to be touched—for him to wrap his arm around me, or pull me close, or slide forward until his body is pressed tight against mine. But instead, he lies agonizing inches away, bringing my nerve endings to life with every single breath he takes.

If I didn't have to leave soon, maybe I *would* reach out. Maybe I'd find the shirt hanging loose over his hard stomach, and I'd fist it in my hands. Maybe I'd draw him to me and risk rejection to find his lips in the dark. Maybe in the dark, he'd kiss me back.

If I didn't have to leave.

If I didn't have to leave.

For tonight, I close my eyes, and on a shared pillow, I let my breath mingle with his, and I try to have sweet dreams.

Chapter 23

IT'S ALMOST WORSE: *not* getting the call. It means I'm constantly checking to make sure my ringer is on. It means my phone is glued to my hand. It means my nerves are on edge, my head kind of hurts, and my stomach is *very* unsure of itself.

In Mike's kitchen, I flip an omelet in a pan and turn my head to the side for a breath of non–egg scented air. This morning, I rolled silently out from beneath his covers as soon as the clock on my phone changed from 5:58 to 5:59 to 6:00, and I helped myself to a quick rinse-off in his hall shower. After brushing my teeth with a toothpaste-painted finger, I sat at his kitchen table weighing all of my options—and then I decided to cook, because cooking is easier than thinking.

Now I'm standing at his stove doing both. I know Danica is playing games, but I have no idea how long she plans on playing them. Do I go on the offensive?

Call my uncle and explain things myself? No . . . because what if Mike's right? What if I'm wrong? What if she's really *not* going to go through with her threat to ruin my life?

Yeah, right. Since when has Danica ever missed an opportunity like that? Even if I groveled at her feet right now, she'd use it as an opportunity to stomp my face into the dirt.

"Good morning," Mike says, and I look over my shoulder to see him scratching his head and yawning as he walks into the kitchen. His hair is sticking up on the side from the pillow we shared last night, and I catalog the image to take home with me: sleepy-eyed Mike Madden with bedhead and slept-in clothes. Then I turn back around before I do something stupid, like walk over to straighten his hair.

"I'm making breakfast," I announce, flipping the eggs, pushing them around in the pan—anything to keep from glancing over my shoulder again. So what if we shared the same bed? We're still just friends. He's still my cousin's ex. He's still a rock star. He's still untouchable.

I still have to move back home.

"You eat eggs?"

My breathing stalls when Mike's voice sounds from right behind me, and my whole body stiffens when his chest brushes against my back. I glance up at him over my shoulder, momentarily losing myself in those big brown eyes. While I search for my voice, he adds, "I thought vegetarians didn't eat eggs."

"Some do," I manage. "But I don't . . . These are for you."

The sleep seems to clear from Mike's eyes, the sun rising on his expression. "How'd you know I'd be up?"

"I didn't," I say, and when I reach over and pop open the microwave, he chuckles. He removes the plate stacked with two already cooked omelets, and then he grabs a fork and butter knife from a drawer and sits at the kitchen table.

"It's a good thing I'm hungry."

"They're probably terrible," I warn as I flip the third omelet in its pan. "I haven't made eggs in forever."

"I'm sure they're amazing," he says, and I glance over my shoulder to see him carving off his first bite.

"Would you tell me if they weren't?"

Mike shovels the bite into his mouth and smiles as he chews, shaking his head no. When he swallows, I ask, "Well?"

"Amazing," he repeats, and his teasing forces me to turn away to hide my smile.

I stand there wondering if he could do that for Danica—if he could find her in the middle of a storm and make her forget it was raining. And if he could, I wonder why she would ever give that up, why she wouldn't fight tooth and nail to keep him.

For a moment, I think I can almost understand why she lost her mind and broke my computer and trashed my room yesterday. But the moment passes, and I shake my head, and I remember she's a psychotic bitch.

"So," Mike says, and when he hesitates before finishing, I know what's coming next. "Have you heard from your cousin yet . . . ?"

I must have checked my phone five hundred times this morning—for a call from my uncle, for a text from Danica, for a call from the local fire department letting me know that she burned the rest of my belongings on the front lawn of our apartment. But five hundred times, there was nothing. Except one text, from Dee, asking if I got laid yet. It had a time-stamp of 7 A.M., and since I'm guessing she set her alarm solely to ask me that question, I responded by telling her to go back to bed.

Now, resting the spatula on the counter, I pat my back pockets for my phone. One, then the other. Then the right one again, the front ones, the left one, the back ones a third time. "Shit." I spin around, scanning the counters, the tables. "Do you see my phone?"

Mike stands up to help me look for it as I anxiously search the living room, the bathroom, the bedroom. When we meet in the kitchen again, both of us are empty-handed.

"Do you want me to call it?" he asks, already moving his thumbs over the screen of his phone.

I take one last look around the kitchen before nodding. "Yeah, I think my ringer is on."

A couple more seconds pass, and my ringtone begins going off somewhere in house. I head to the living room again and lose its trail while Mike heads down the hallway leading to the back of the house.

"I think it's in here," he shouts just before the linen

closet clicks open. Just a simple click, and my eyes flash wide with terror.

"WAIT!" I beg as I race for the hallway. My socks slip on the hardwood floor, but I force my useless feet to keep slipping and sliding in a desperate attempt to beat Mike to my phone. I'm a banana-peeled cartoon character, panicked as I scream, "WAIT, DON'T!"

One second, I'm careening toward the back of the open closet door. The next, that door is swinging shut and Mike is staring down at my phone. I slide to a stop two feet away from him, cursing the day I was born. I must have dropped my phone into the hamper when I threw my dirty towels in there after my shower, and now the corner of Mike's mouth is slowly tugging up, up, up while he stares down at it. When his eyes meet mine, they're full of mirth that makes me want to drop dead right where I'm standing.

"Sexy as Fuck, huh?"

Dee's name for him in my phone. God hates me. God really, really hates me.

"Dee did that!" I insist, knowing damn well that my burning cheeks aren't helping my case. My shitty excuse does nothing to erase the smug amusement from Mike's face.

"Then why are you freaking out?"

My tongue is in so many knots, I just stand there like an idiot.

"Just admit it, Hailey," Mike teases as he offers me my phone. "You think I'm hot."

It nearly drops as I tug it out of his grasp. "Whatever."

I'm walking away from him, wishing I had drowned in that stupid pond back when I had the chance, when Mike says, "What do you think is hot about me?"

"Why don't you ask Dee?" I counter, and Mike chuckles as I continue my walk of shame back to his burnt-to-a-crisp eggs. I want to hide in the pantry, or bang my face against a wall, or stick my head in the oven. Instead, I have to keep pretending that I'm not the most mortified I've ever been in my entire freaking life.

I turn off the burner to the stove and continue facing away from Mike, checking my phone while I wait for my cheeks to stop melting off. There are no missed calls or texts from my uncle, not that this day could possibly get any worse. But really, I'm just pretending to care about my phone while I relive the past sixty seconds, wishing I could have run a little faster and tackled Mike to the ground before he opened that damn closet door.

"If you tell me why you think I'm hot," he negotiates from the entryway to the kitchen, "I'll tell you why I think you're hot."

I glance over my shoulder at him before I can help it, because *did he just say I'm hot?* But Mike isn't smiling like he's joking or playing or lying. He's just leaning against the jamb—all six-foot-one, rock star hair, panty-melting eyes—waiting for me to answer him. His gaze doesn't shy from mine.

"Stop joking," I order.

"Who's joking?"

When I turn away from him again, even the tips of my ears are burning. A hot flush creeps up my neck, and I know he can see it. His footsteps move closer as I scoop his burnt omelet onto a plate, and when I turn back around, he's right there, utterly serious, waiting for me to say something.

"I have to pee," I squeak, and I thrust the plate at him.

This is my great response to Mike hitting on me. *Is he hitting on me?!* I just announced I have to pee, and now I'm rushing from the kitchen. *Oh my God, what the hell am I even doing?!*

"Your lips," Mike calls after me, and I freeze in my tracks and look over my shoulder. His eyes lock with mine, making my heart jackhammer so violently in my chest that I'm sure both of us can hear it. I hold his gaze for as long as I can—a split second—and then I turn back around to finish escaping to the bathroom.

Chapter 24

In Mike's bathroom mirror, my reflection pokes her bottom lip, wondering if Mike could have been telling the truth: if maybe he thinks I have attractive lips . . . They're not particularly pink. They're not particularly pouty. They're not particularly *anything.*

Poke. Squish. Poke. Poke.

Amber eyes stare back at me, eyebrows knitting.

I have to pee. Smooth, Hailey, *smooth.* I close my eyes and shake my head at myself. *I have to pee.* In the history of awkward girls everywhere, has there *ever* been a more pathetic response to flirting?

Was Mike flirting with me?

I remember the look on his face when I glanced over my shoulder, and I continue prodding at my bottom lip while the edge of the sink presses a line into my shins—the price of being five feet tall in a giant's home. My reflection met me only after I scaled the sink like a miniature King Kong and roosted here, where we could frown at each other in earnest.

The past two days have felt like a nightmare and a dream.

Danica kicking me out: nightmare. Mike teaching me to play the drums: dream. Waiting for a call from my uncle to ruin my whole life: nightmare. Sharing a pillow with the only man who has ever made me spark: dream. Him telling me that my lips are hot: confusing.

Confusing, confusing, *confusing.*

It's not that I've never had a guy find me attractive before. I got asked out often enough back home, and I know quite a few guys found me pretty . . . Not Danica pretty, but . . . Hailey pretty. Small-town pretty. Hand-me-down pretty.

Definitely not rock-star pretty. Not pretty enough for Mike to look at me the way he did.

But there it was: that look. It's cataloged clearly in my mind, along with the way his eyes looked in the soft light of his bedroom last night, the way his hair stood up this morning.

My teeth punish my bottom lip as I continue frowning at my wild-haired reflection. My cheeks are a little too pale. My eyes are a little too big. My eyebrows are a little too thick. All of me is a little too little.

I'm uselessly trying to tame my hair with one of Mike's combs when the doorbell rings. My hand stills as the bells echo through the house, and I hear the front door open. Then voices: Mike's and—

I round the corner to the living room and see her:

her perfect reddish-brown hair, her periwinkle cashmere sweater, the massive gift basket in her arms.

"What the hell?" Danica snarls while I stand there with a comb stuck in my hair.

"What are you doing here?" Mike asks, like it isn't the first time he's voiced the question, and Danica's eyebrows slam together as she scowls up at him.

"What is *she* doing here?"

"You kicked her out."

Danica's face whips in my direction just after I tear the comb free from my hair. "You told me you weren't sleeping with him! You fucking liar! You're such a fucking—"

"I'm not—" I start, but Mike's voice booms over mine.

"Don't you finish that goddamn sentence," he snaps, and the crazy look in Danica's eyes immediately clears. She stares up at him like a pit bull that's just realized it has a master, and Mike stares down at her like he'd like to see her put to sleep.

Danica, ever calculating, takes a moment to collect herself, and in that moment, she notices the couch. She takes in the messy sheets, the wrinkled blanket, the bed pillow on the end, and she snaps them together like puzzle pieces. The final picture tells her that I slept in the living room, that I'm not a threat, that Mike is still hers for the taking.

She makes a production of taking a calming breath and tucking her hair behind her ear. "I'm sorry." She locks eyes with me, and mine narrow. "I'm sorry,

Hailey. I just get really jealous." She laughs to herself, softly at first, and then a full-on giggle. "Look at me, I'm a mess. I just—" She bats her eyelashes up at Mike. "I've just been going crazy over the thought of losing you. I know I should have brought this sooner, but—" She lifts the gift basket as an offering. "Look, I made you a get well basket. It has your favorite soup, and your favorite cookies, and—"

"I'm not sick anymore," Mike informs her mid-sentence, and Danica frowns.

"Did Hailey give you my card with the other basket?" she asks, and Mike lifts an eyebrow.

"You mean the one that she signed your name in? I know your handwriting, Danica. You had nothing to do with that card."

"But the whole basket was my idea! I—"

"What?" Mike interrupts. "You what? You want a medal for sending someone else to the store to throw shit in a basket?"

"Why are you being so mean?" Danica pouts, and Mike sighs and rubs a line between his eyes.

"I just don't want to do this anymore." He swings his finger between himself and my cousin. "There's nothing here. I'm sorry . . . I had a crush on you when we were kids, but that's all it ever was."

Something tells me I should give them privacy, that I should back away slowly and disappear. But I'm too busy watching Danica's knuckles whiten as she strangles the handle of her care basket, and then her viper eyes are pinning me in place.

"Is this because of her?" she snarls while glaring at me.

"No."

"Bullshit," Danica spits. She glowers up at him. "Do you think I'm stupid?"

"Why are you doing this?" he asks.

"Doing what?!"

"Fighting so hard." Mike's voice is tired but steady. "There's nothing here to fight for."

"Why do you keep saying that!" she shrieks. "You're only saying that because of her!"

"This isn't about her," Mike insists.

"This is ALL about her. Tell me you don't like her!"

"Danica—"

"Tell me you don't fucking want her, Mike! I'm not blind! You think I don't see it?!"

"This is about me and you—"

"Say it!" Danica's face turns red, her voice making my ears ring. "Look me in the eye and tell me you don't have feelings for my fucking cousin!"

Mike quiets, hesitating, and then his eyes find mine across the room. Danica is staring at him, and he is staring at me, and I'm holding my breath when he says, "I'm in love with her."

Chapter 25

I'M IN LOVE with her.

Someone gasps. Me? Danica? All I can do is stand there convincing myself that I couldn't have just heard what I think I just heard. Mike is standing by the door, his hair still a mess from a night spent on my pillow, and his brown eyes make the world fall away. He says it again.

"I'm in love with her."

My lips part, and a violent scream tears through the room. My eyes dart to Danica just as she chucks her gift basket against a wall, sending soup cans rolling in every direction. She continues screaming as she balls her fists, stomps her foot, and storms out of the house.

Mike looks at me, I look at him, and I don't know what to say, so I say the only thing I can. "You should follow her."

He scratches his hand through his hair, and my

eyes beg him to go. I need a minute. I *desperately* need a minute. And when he gives it to me, closing the door behind him, I stand there trembling from my fingers to my toes.

There was no mistaking those words. He said them twice, just to make sure I understood them.

Mike is in love with me.

He's in love with me?

He's in love with me.

I sit down on the floor because my knees are too weak to hold me up, and I bury my fingers in my hair, trying to think. *When? How long? Why? How?*

Danica is going to bury me after this—absolutely *bury* me.

Mike loves me. He *loves* me.

I don't know whether to laugh or cry, so I just sit there staring at a spot on the floor. Sharing my pillow: it meant something to him. Asking me to go to bed last night: it meant something to him. A dozen "sweet dreams": they all meant something to him.

Our late-night phone calls. Our walk in the woods. The way he kept pushing his hat onto my head.

He loves me. All of it meant something, and not just to me.

When the front door opens again, Mike isn't alone. Danica walks right over to me, and from my spot on the floor, I crane my neck to stare up at her. Her makeup is smeared from tears that I'm guessing—hoping—didn't work on Mike, and when her hand drops in front of my face, I realize she's offering to help me up.

It's the scariest thing she's ever done.

"Come on," she orders when I hesitate, and I obey simply because I'm positive the alternative would involve me getting kicked in the face. I let her pull me up, and then I stand there waiting for her to push me back down.

"I'm not mad at you, Hailey," she says, and she might as well be speaking a foreign language, because none of this is making sense in my head. "I feel terrible about kicking you out."

Wait, *what?*

"I just want to go home, okay? This is all my fault."

All her fault . . . ?

Danica hasn't accepted responsibility for her actions since she was old enough to realize that her pretty smile is the equivalent of a get-out-of-jail-free card. Broken toys, bad grades, missed curfews: they've all always been someone else's fault. And it clicks for me then: what's happening. I can almost see her too-big smile hiding behind the act she's putting on, and I resist my fight-or-flight instinct. My feet stay planted in place. I'm a dormouse about to be eaten alive.

"I'm going to make this right," Danica says, and there it is: that smile.

I decide right then that I don't *want* to be eaten alive. I don't want to be fucking eaten at all.

"You're full of shit," I say, and Danica's smile vanishes. Mike is standing behind her, so he can't see the way her eyes narrow into slits.

"Hailey, I know you didn't sleep with Mike. I—"

"Oh, I know you know that," I agree. "But you're not sorry."

Danica stands there—assessing, calculating. And then she steps forward and wraps her arms around me, pulling me into a threat of a hug. Low, so that only I can hear, she whispers in my ear, "I didn't call my dad yet. But keep pissing me off, you little bitch." And then, for Mike's benefit, she says more loudly, "I mean it more than you'll ever know, okay? I want you to come home with me. We're family."

She pulls away, her pearly white smile daring me to challenge her again. One wrong word, and she'll make my nightmare a reality. She's giving me a chance to stay here, to stay in school and finish what I came here for. One chance.

"Do you need help gathering your things?" she asks, and when she starts gathering them for me, I let her.

If I leave with her now, I can finish my degree. I don't have to move back to Indiana. I don't have to leave Mike for good. I don't have to grow old on that farm.

I tell myself these things as I begin helping my soulless cousin. For the fifteen seconds it takes to finish shoving my belongings into my backpack, I avoid eye contact with the man who just told me he's in love with me. But as soon as I'm finished, my eyes find him across the room.

He's standing by the door, not bothering to hide the fact that he's watching me. "You can always stay here, you know."

"Are you ready?" Danica asks, shoving my back-pack into my arms, and when I just stand there, her tapping foot begins counting the seconds I have left until she explodes.

"Give us a minute," Mike says, and Danica dramatically wipes her finger under her eye.

"Really, Mike? *Really?*"

Mike frowns and rubs his forehead, but then he takes in the expression on my face, and something in it makes him press on. He walks past Danica and takes my hand, leading me out of the room. "Just a minute."

In the kitchen, he pulls me close enough that Danica can't hear us, and he says, "I meant what I said." His fingers stay clasped with mine, the tip of his thumb nervously circling mine as he gazes down at me. "Earlier . . . before I went outside . . . I meant it, Hailey. I need you to know that."

I want to hug him. Or kiss him. Or just cry in his arms. But instead, I simply swallow. I swallow hard, and I float on the surface of those deep brown eyes.

I believe him—however impossible it should be, I believe him when he tells me he loves me.

And I also believe Danica will never, *never* allow it to continue.

I stare up at Mike until he leans down close, eye-level with me. His voice is hushed but firm, a low whisper that sends goose bumps up my arms. "Pick up your phone tonight, Hailey. If you don't, I'm coming over."

In Danica's car, in Danica's passenger seat, I stare out the window wondering if she's going to intentionally crash the car into a tree and kill us both. She hasn't said a word, so I know something's coming. I know something's coming because I *know* Danica.

She looks over at me, and I continue staring out the window.

"When did you become the kind of girl that steals other girls' boyfriends?" she asks, shaming me.

I want to tell her that I didn't steal him—that she threw him away—but I ignore her, resting my head against the window.

"I mean, I know you don't like me, but stealing my high school sweetheart? Spending the night with him? Having him tell you he loves you right in front of me?" Danica looks back out at the road, shaking her head. "I never would have imagined you'd hurt me like that."

I know what she's doing. She's making this my fault. She wants me to accept the blame so that she can pile it on and pile it on and pile it on. And if enough is piled on top of me, I'll never be able to find my way out. She'll be the only person who can unbury me.

I swallow the "I'm sorry" creeping its way up my throat, and I concentrate on the trees blurring a path back to my prison of an apartment.

Danica glances at me again, no doubt reevaluating her strategy. "Do you believe what he said?"

One tree, two trees, three trees.

"Aw, sweetie," she says with faux concern. "You *do* believe him, don't you? You think he really loves you."

Nine trees, ten trees, eleven trees.

She sighs and pats my leg. "I should let you learn this the hard way, but I'm still your big cousin, so . . ." She glances at me, waiting for a reaction, but she doesn't get one. "Some guys just like being the hero. Mike always likes to say he fell in love with me from the moment he saw me. But do you know when that was? Third grade, when I moved to his school." She pauses her delivery for dramatic effect, and I resist the urge to look over at her. "And do you know who I was back then? I was this sad little girl who had to move away from everything she'd ever known, including her best friend."

I can't help it—my neck turns, my eyes find hers, and I get caught in her web.

"Mike likes them broken, Hailey. It makes him feel important."

My gaze slowly swings back to the window, because counting trees is easier than trying to digest anything she's saying. I don't want to believe her, and I know I shouldn't.

"You don't want to be with a guy like that, do you?"

Sixteen trees, seventeen trees, eighteen trees.

Danica faces forward again, and after a moment, she releases an exaggerated sigh and says, "Well, I guess it doesn't matter anyway."

I look at her again, alarms sounding in my head. When she turns her chin in my direction, her brows knit into a pitying expression.

"Oh, sweetie, you didn't think I was going to let you keep flirting with my boyfriend, did you?" She admonishes me with a shake of her head. "I'm doing you a favor. You realize that, right?"

"What are you saying?" I ask point-blank, tired of the charade that Danica won't stop playing. Concerned cousin. Loving girlfriend. Decent human being.

"I'm saying that if you ever see him again, call him again, even talk to him in passing again"—her mask slips away, revealing the monster underneath—"you'll be lucky if all I do is put a call in to my dad."

Chapter 26

DEE DAWSON AND Rowan Michaels are good at many things. They're good at finding replacement computers, which they claim they got for free from some guy who got it from some other guy who got it from some other guy. They're good at cleaning up trashed bedrooms and unflipping flipped-over desks. And they're good at making sure that when Mike Madden calls me when I'm in bed that night, his name shows up on my phone as "Dee-licious-andra" instead of "Sexy as Fuck Drummer."

"Hello?" I say on the fourth ring, after I stop gnawing on my thumbnail and summon the courage to hear his voice.

"Hey."

My door suddenly flies open, and when Danica points at my phone, I roll my eyes and show her the screen. Satisfied that I'm talking to her arch nemesis instead of her ex-boyfriend, she makes a face and leaves me alone.

"Hey," I reply.

"Hey."

I crack a tiny smile at the ceiling, marveling once again at how easy it is for Mike to make that happen. "How long are we going to keep saying hey?" I ask, and his reply makes my butterflies flutter.

"Until I get tired of hearing your voice."

I sigh, and I'm not sure if it's because that was such a perfect thing to say, or because of how hopeless this all is. I like Mike, he likes me, and Danica hates us both. If she knew I was talking to him right now, all hell would break loose. I'm extending a personal invitation to the very nightmare I've spent the past thirty-six hours trying to avoid.

Two years. It's going to take me at least two more *years* to finish my bachelor's degree, which doesn't even include my plans for my doctorate, and Danica plans to be here for just as long. Talking to Dee-licious-andra on the phone in hushed conversations isn't going to cut it for that long, but anything more will land me back on the farm.

Either way, I lose. Danica makes the rules, and no matter how I play the game, I lose.

"How have things been since you left?" Mike asks, and I decide to start with the good.

"Dee and Rowan helped me clean up my room."

"That's good . . . What else have you been up to?"

"Pretty much just working on all the homework that was due today so I can turn it in tomorrow."

"Danica hasn't been giving you any trouble?" Mike

asks, and I find shapes in the pattern on my ceiling. A snowman. A dog. A three-headed Hell Beast with long, sharp teeth.

"She said you only like me because I'm broken."

It feels like a confession, so I say it extra quietly. I'm acknowledging I remember what Mike said. I'm asking him to tell me if Danica is right.

"*What?*" he asks, the word a gust of disbelief. When I don't reply, he demands to know, "How are you broken?"

Instead of naming a thousand ways, I simply say, "I don't know."

"You're smart. You're in school. You're working hard for your dreams." I can hear the anger in his voice. It's like a bold underline beneath every word he says. "You're beautiful. You're funny. You're kind. You work at an animal shelter, for God's sake. Everyone loves you. How the hell are you broken?"

Beautiful. Smart. Funny. Kind. I let his words comfort me, not wanting to argue.

A sigh of frustration cuts across the line. "Look, Hailey, Danica is going to say lots of things to you because she's upset. She hasn't stopped texting me all day—"

"She's been texting you?" An unfamiliar pang of jealously flares in my chest, but Mike douses it in an instant.

"Not since an hour ago. I blocked her. But listen, just . . . don't let her ruin this, okay? You're not broken, and that's not why I said what I did. If anyone is broken, it's her, and that has nothing to do with either one of us."

I know he's right. I *know* he has to be right. "Okay."

A moment of silence passes, and I find more shapes on the ceiling. A hippopotamus. A sunflower. Half a heart.

"I want to take you out," Mike says, and my pulse quickens. "Tomorrow. Can I take you out to dinner?"

He's asking me out. On a date. A *real* date . . . Oh my God. "I have a lot of homework to catch up on," I stammer in a panic.

"What about Friday?"

"I have to work at the shelter."

"Saturday?"

"Saturday is your music video."

"Breakfast the next morning?"

My heart is hammering in my throat, pushed there by the unease thrashing in my stomach. If I say yes, I'm risking everything. And for what? Even if I ignore the fact that Mike is way out of my league, that he is my cousin's ex-boyfriend . . . he is still a freaking *rock star.* It's impossible to forget the way he looked when I first saw him: covered in sweat at the back of the stage, pounding his drums under laser-blue lights for girls who giggled his name later out on the sidewalk.

And I am Hailey Harper. Farmhand. Big sister. Yard sale frequenter. Future veterinarian, if I'm lucky. I don't belong on a stage or beside a stage or anywhere *near* a freaking stage.

I hesitate too long. Too, too long. Insecurity creeps

into Mike's voice when he says, "If you don't want to, that's fine. I just thought—"

"I want to," I rush to assure him. "I do." In my mind, I'm screaming, *You have no idea how much I want to. Sleeping in my own bed is never going to cut it again after last night!*

"But?"

I scramble for something to say. I search the shapes on my ceiling, but come up with only an overweight dolphin, a crescent moon, and a potato.

"Hailey," Mike says, "I didn't mean to throw all that at you today. It's okay if you just want to be friends. I never expected—"

"Your arms," I blurt, and absolute silence replies.

"Huh?" Mike finally says.

"When you asked me what I thought was so hot about you." I take a deep breath and close my eyes. "Your arms . . . And your eyes. And the way your left cheek dimples when you smile. And your laugh. And how good you are at the drums. And the way you carried me through the woods when I hurt my leg at the pond."

With my eyes still squeezed shut, I throw my covers off, burning up. I'm having a goddamn hot flash, I am so completely embarrassed. And when Mike doesn't respond, I lie there dying. I'm *dying.* "Are you still there?" I ask.

"Yeah," he says, his heated voice making the temperature in my room spike even higher. "But I wish I was with you instead."

I am *officially* breaking out in hives. The implication is clear in his smoldering words, and I am stripping my shirt off just to keep from self-incinerating into a pile of ash. Why is it so goddamn *hot* in here?!

"There's no way I'm leaving on tour before I see you again, Hailey," Mike promises while I practice for my audition as the Human Torch. "Come to the video shoot on Saturday, okay?"

"Okay," I agree, mostly because if I don't get off the phone soon, it's going to be a nonissue. My parents won't even need to bother cremating my remains because I'll just blow out the window where it's nice and breezy and *cold*.

When Mike chuckles, it's a miracle I manage to form a more-than-one-word reply. "What are you laughing about?"

"I can hear you blushing," he says while I'm in the midst of kicking my pants off. They're made of silk, but I swear to God, they might as well be a woolen-polyester blend right now. My legs are melting, *melting*.

"Shut up," I scold, and he laughs even harder. "I'm getting off the phone now!"

I can hear the dimpled smile in Mike's voice when he says, "Sweet dreams, Hailey."

And in spite of everything—Danica's threats, Mike's upcoming tour, my *clearly* malfunctioning thermostat—I smile too, because for the past week, I'd missed those words and the sound of that smile. I take a deep breath, I let it go, and I grin at half a heart on my ceiling. "Sweet dreams, Mike."

Chapter 27

THERE ARE GOOD days, and there are bad days. There are days when you wake up with Mike Madden on your pillow, when you realize your dreams might not be crushed after all, when you fall asleep with butterflies in your stomach. And then there are days when your professor won't accept your late homework, when you get chewed out by the shelter director for missing a shift, when you realize you forgot to log on to Deadzone to play with your little brother at the appointed time.

"I am *so* sorry," I grovel on Thursday, but Luke is unfazed by my pleading.

"That makes two," he counts. "Two times you've forgotten about me."

"I haven't forgotten about you," I assure him as I unwrap a chickenless chicken wrap in the parking lot of the Mickey D's closest to the shelter. When faced with eating in the parking lot, making my bedroom smell like French fries, or having to talk to Danica while I eat my dinner, I'll choose parking lot every time. "I've just been busy," I continue. "But I miss you." I pause with the wrap an inch from my mouth. "Like crazy."

Ever the pragmatist, Luke asks, "How do you have time to miss me if you're that busy?"

I'm chewing a mouthful of thousand-calorie goodness when I answer, "I'm going to show you how much I miss you when I squish you in front of all your friends."

He snorts. "What friends?"

"What happened to Jimmy?" I ask with more concern in my voice than I intended, and I can almost *hear* Luke's eyes roll.

"He got a girlfriend."

"So?"

"So, you know girls. No more Deadzone, no more arcade, no more fun."

I clear my throat. "Not all girls are like that."

"Sisters don't count," Luke counters, and before I can argue, he says, "Hey, did you know Mike broke up with Danica?"

I almost choke on my tomato-lettuce-mayo wrap. "What?"

"Yeah. We were playing Deadzone last night, and—"

"You were playing with Mike?"

"We play all the time. But"—I can hear the frustration in my brother's voice—"can you just listen?"

"Yeah," I say, doing my best to be patient. "What?"

"So I forget how it came up, but he told me he broke

up with Danica, and I was going to tell him he should go out with you—"

"You *didn't*," I gasp, and Luke practically growls at me.

"Let me finish."

I hold back a growl myself, and Luke waits to make sure I'm going to stop interrupting him before he continues.

"I told him I knew who he should go out with, but he told me he already likes someone else. He said she's really smart and pretty, but . . . I think you should just try to get in there anyway."

"'Get in there'?" I ask, and Luke acts like I'm an idiot.

"Yeah, like get him to like you."

I don't know whether to laugh or lecture him on the importance of minding his own business. "And why would I do that?"

"Don't you ever want to get married?" Luke asks, and this time, I *do* actually choke.

I have to set down my wrap and cough into my elbow to clear my throat, and my eyes are watering when I say, "*Married?*"

"You're twenty-three," my brother reasons, and my brow furrows at my steering wheel.

"Right. Twenty-three."

"Don't you want kids?"

"Luke!"

"I'm just saying, sis . . . I don't think you're going to find another guy as good as Mike."

My appetite disappears as I rub a spot between my eyes, use the back of my hand to wipe the mayo oil away, and take a calming breath. I'm not about to start discussing my love life with a twelve-year-old—much less one who shares my last name—so I tell him half of the truth. "I'm concentrating on school right now."

Undeterred, my brother says, "He asks about you sometimes."

"He does?" I question before I can think better of it.

"Yeah. Last night I told him about that time you tried singing to those cows to herd them. What was the name for that again?"

"Oh my God," I say. "You did not."

Luke's laughter almost makes my mortification worth it, but I'm still going to kill him. "He thought it was funny."

Kulning. It's an ancient Swedish herding call I saw on YouTube, and I sounded like an *extremely* drunk yodeler. My brother sat on the fence laughing his ass off. "And you expect him to marry me?" I groan.

"He said he thought it was cute."

At the word *cute*, I can't help smiling to myself, but I quickly school my expression back into neutral territory. "Well, I hate to break it to you, kid, but I didn't go through all this trouble just to drop out of school and start popping out babies."

"Who said you had to drop out of school just to start dating him?" Luke asks, and I realize what I've said.

It's a choice that's been nagging at the back of my

mind, one that I've been trying to ignore. And without meaning to, I already gave Luke an answer: I didn't go through all that trouble—five years of part-time community college, tons of declined financial aid and scholarship applications, nearly three months of putting up with Danica, two days of agony waiting for her to call her dad—just to throw it all away.

"Can we talk about something else?" I beg, rolling down my car window for some fresh, freezing air.

"Like what?"

"Like when you're going to get your own girlfriend," I tease to make sure Luke forgets about the current topic, and when he groans and starts trying to find his own subject change, I try to just enjoy talking to my little brother. I try not to think of Mike or impossible decisions, and I try to forget how sick to my stomach I feel. I even promise Luke I'll play Deadzone with him that night, and I do—along with Mike. The three of us play and laugh, and Luke does a not-so-subtle job of trying to convince Mike of my awesomeness. When we end the game, Mike calls me and we laugh about it, and he assures me he agrees with every single thing Luke said. My cheeks are stained red as I listen to him talk, and by the time he wishes me sweet dreams, I'm not entirely sure I'm not already living in one.

But then the call ends, and it's just me in a bed in a room in Danica's apartment. I fall asleep knowing that Mike is leaving on tour in three days, that I'll see him in two, and that it will probably be for the very last time.

Chapter 28

I'M NO STRANGER to feeling out of place. High school parties, funerals of family friends I never met, Danica's thirteenth birthday at an upscale hair and nail salon that included all of the most popular girls in her school . . . I didn't exactly feel comfortable at any of them, but never have I felt as out of place as I do walking to the pond on Saturday afternoon.

There are people *everywhere.*

I had to take a shuttle. A freaking *shuttle.* Everyone was directed to park in a massive parking lot a few miles from the location. There were signs, workers conducting traffic—I knew at the sight of bright orange cones and professionally printed GHOST VIDEO signs that I was in over my head. I parked my car in a shimmering sea of vehicles, and I tried to blend in as I followed everyone else to where the buses were picking people up.

So many people.

Pink hair, blue hair, pierced noses, mohawks, dresses, Chuck Taylors, high heels, fishnets, leather pants, tutus, leggings, belly shirts, skinny jeans, choker necklaces, tattoos. I tried not to stand out in my faded blue hoodie, five-year-old Levi's, and clearance-rack boots.

The buses eventually dropped us off at an access road on the opposite side of the pond from where our group hiked last time, and I once again had to swallow my nerves to keep my feet moving forward.

Trucks, *everywhere.* And not all small trucks, though I did think I recognized Mike's cherry-red Dodge Ram. No, *massive* trucks, fit for hauling military equipment or full-grown trees. And tractors, all kinds. They honked for people to jump away from the narrow trail to the pond as they rumbled past us, carrying all sorts of equipment that once again reminded me how *big* this video is, how *big* the band is, how *big* Mike is.

How *small* I am.

I swallowed the growing lump in my throat and continued walking, and the crowd thickened . . . and thickened . . . and thickened. I knew even before I broke through the tree line that the scene was going to be insane, judging by the way the noises grew louder . . . and louder . . . and louder. But nothing could have prepared me for what I saw when I stepped into that clearing.

Hundreds, *thousands* of people, and more still coming behind me. Most of them colorful extras for the video, but also tons of guys with headsets and black STAFF T-shirts, all buzzing around like single-minded worker bees.

I'M STANDING THERE, on the precipice of the clearing, frozen with paralyzing shock, when a hand slaps down onto my shoulder.

"How fucking sick is this!" a guy with neon-green hair and a barbell in his eyebrow cheers in my face, and I manage a mute nod that prompts him to hoot excitedly and bound away. He's like a very high Mr. Tumnus . . . I'm officially in punked-out Narnia.

I fumble my phone from my pocket before any more woodland creatures can realize I'm a human girl where human girls don't belong, and Dee's name stays on my phone as it rings and rings and rings. "Oh God," I worry out loud when I get sent to voice mail, staring around at dozens of faces I don't recognize.

"Excuse me," I blurt, catching a passing staff guy by the arm before I lose him in the chaos. He furrows his brow at me, and I rush to explain, "I'm supposed to meet with the band."

"Yeah, kid," he dismisses, already shrugging from my grasp. "You and everyone else. You'll get to meet them later."

"No," I say, uselessly trailing him as he walks away from me. "Listen, I—"

"Hailey!"

Never so happy to hear Dee's voice, I spin around

and find her in the mess of a crowd. She's not hard to spot, considering everyone else is looking at her too: at her bluish purple mini dress, her knee-high boots, her long, long legs. Long chocolate-brown curls cascade over her shoulders, and she wraps me in an excited hug. "I am so happy I won't have to kill you for not coming!"

"This is *insane*," I say, and her giddy laugh shakes us both.

"I know, right?!" She pulls away, smiling wider than I've ever seen her smile. "They told me it was going to be big, but, holy shit, just *look* at all this!"

With my trusted friend by my side, I finally take it all in, the massive scope of it all. The entire clearing has been mowed and manicured, the grass now cut to climb up only the edges of my boots instead of the legs of my jeans. Giant white generators can be heard buzzing faintly under hundreds of voices. And everywhere, breaking up the body count, is tech equipment: cranes and cherry pickers with gigantic spotlights, massive cameras attached to off-roading Segways, rolling tracks sunken into the grass. Dee starts pointing things out: Condor light, jib, Fisher dolly. I stare wide-eyed at her, and she flashes me a smile.

"What, like I can't learn a thing or two?"

The whizzing of a drone steals our attention, and my eyes follow it through the sky and into the setting sun. I squint, raise my hand to my forehead, and try to see where it went.

"Alright, listen up."

Adam Everest's voice booms from every direction, from loudspeakers hidden in the trees, and the crowd goes absolutely wild. I can hear the distinct sound of Adam trying to cover up a laugh before Dee grabs my hand and starts dragging me in the direction everyone else is rushing as they clap and cheer and scramble for a better view. "We're about to get started," Adam announces as I struggle to hold on to Dee's hand, getting swallowed alive by a mass of people much larger than me. She doesn't let me go, finagling people out of her way and then mine to keep us moving forward. "So I just want to tell you a little about the song and what we're going to be doing."

Dee suddenly stops, and when I squeeze in next to her, I see why. A rope barrier blocks us from moving forward, and beyond that is the edge of the grass. And beyond that, the pond. And beyond that, Adam standing at the edge of the steel platform with a microphone to his lips. He looks every bit the rock star in distressed black jeans and a tailored black button-down, with bracelets strung around his wrists and hair down to his shoulders, but my attention is already moving past him, to the back of the platform where Mike is sitting at his drums.

He's wearing that same Dallas Stars hoodie he wore here last time—the one that made my toes curl then, and the one that makes my toes curl now. He has a drumstick in his hand, and while Adam talks to the crowd, Mike twirls it between his fingers. A smile dances onto my face as I realize he's practicing one of the baton tricks I taught him a few nights ago.

"So that's why the song is called 'Ghost,'" Adam continues. "So the concept for this video is basically that the music is bringing you back to life. It's going to start with all of you in the forest surrounding this clearing." Adam stretches out an arm and spins all the way around. "We're going to use CGI to make you look really washed out. But as the song plays, you're going to walk from the trees, and as you get closer to this platform, where we'll be performing the song, you're going to gain color."

"The costume department has been handing out cards," Shawn announces into his own mic, stepping up beside Adam. "There are trailers back where you guys came in. They're color-coded. If you haven't already visited the trailer that matches your card, you need to do that as soon as we're done here."

"We want everyone dressed bright as fuck," Adam explains, and Shawn chuckles.

"Right. Most of you got the memo and look awesome, but if you got a card, there's a reason for it, so go to the trailers."

"No logos," Adam reminds everyone, and Shawn nods.

"No logos. If you're wearing a logo and costume missed you, go to the trailers."

Adam glances at a guy standing off to the left, who I'm guessing must be some kind of video producer.

"Are we forgetting anything?" The guy gives a thumbs-up, and Adam continues. "So we're probably going to spend a few hours doing the tree shit."

"We have to cut after every single angle," Shawn explains.

"But it's going to look sick when we're done." A few cheers fly out from the crowd, brightening Adam's electric smile. "By the time you reach the crowd that's going to form around this pond here"—Adam gestures to the water surrounding the platform—"you're going to be in full bright color, and you are going to be rocking *out*. By the time you get from there"—he points to the trees—"to here"—he points to a random girl at the edge of the water, who looks like she seriously might faint—"we want you to be out of your mind excited."

"Big smiles," Shawn illustrates. "Hands in the air, jumping up and down."

"Rocking the fuck out," Adam finishes, and when I glance back at Mike, a big contagious smile is on his face. I find myself mirroring it, my excitement for him washing over me. Even though I didn't know him when he was younger, I *know* how hard he worked for this. I can tell by the way he plays those drums, like he used to practice even in his dreams.

"Still good?" Shawn asks the producer, getting another thumbs-up.

"So when we're performing for the video," Adam says, "it's just going to be for show. You'll hear the song, through the loudspeakers, but we won't be live."

A murmur goes through the crowd, and Adam

shakes his head at Shawn. "They have so little faith." Shawn grins, and Adam looks back at the crowd. "I haven't even gotten to the best part yet."

"You should probably get to it," Shawn advises with a chuckle, and Adam smiles.

"We're going to have to get some shots of us playing, but then after that, this whole fucking clearing"—he spins around again, playing to the giant crowd surrounding him on every side—"is going to be transformed into the biggest rager you've ever fucking seen."

I flinch when excitement consumes the crowd, causing a deafening cacophony of screams and cheers. Over the roar, Shawn says, "We've got trucks coming that are going to be loaded with kegs and food and glow shit."

"And we're going to perform two songs from our next album for you guys, so you'll get to hear them before anyone else," Adam adds, and the screaming grows even more insane. I look back at Mike, my heart skipping a beat when I realize he's found me in the crowd. He smiles wide, and then, in spite of all the screaming, he starts twirling the drumstick between his fingers, showing me that he's mastered the trick I taught him.

With my cheeks blushing red, I giggle—*giggle*. And then I thank God he can't hear me.

"This guy over here is going to give you more direction as we shoot," Shawn says, pointing to the director. "So listen to what he has to say. If you haven't already signed your release form, head to that lady over there because you *need* to sign it in order to be in the video." Shawn points to a woman standing further back in the clearing, who waves. "And if you got a card from the costume crew, head back the way you came and let them fix you up."

I frown down at my boring hoodie, jeans, and boots, but Dee nudges me with her elbow and shakes her head, telling me not to worry.

"And give yourselves a big hand for coming out tonight," Adam praises, ever the energetic frontman. "You're going to be in a music video for The Last Ones to fucking Know!"

Chapter 29

MY OUTFIT IS a perfect combination of Dee and Rowan.

My zippered black ankle boots: Dee. My solid black leggings: Rowan. My I-don't-even-want-to-*know*-how-expensive leather jacket: Dee. My finger-curled hair: Rowan.

And my dress . . . my *dress*. The soft layers of tulle remind me of Rowan, but the bright, *bright* bloodred color is all Dee. And it's strange, how all of this together feels like *me*. Like a version of me I never knew existed, but which I'd like to get to know.

Standing in front of a full-length mirror in the band's personal trailer, I've never felt prettier in my entire life.

"I can't even get over how gorgeous you look," Dee praises, lifting the delicate red tulle away from my knees and watching the way it falls. Rowan brushes my bangs away from my face and smiles at me in the mirror.

"I can't believe you *made* this dress," I counter, and Dee's gaze lifts from the skirt of it, finding my reflection.

"You need to let me borrow it so I can get a grade on it for school," she says, "but after that, you can have it."

"I can?"

The question comes out as a squeak, and Dee smiles. "Of course. I made it for you."

"And you can have the shoes and leggings and jacket too," Rowan adds, and when I frown, she assures me, "Mosh Records paid for those."

"We put in a special request," Dee explains with a smirk.

"How'd you know my shoe size?"

"I checked your boots after you fell in the pond," Rowan confesses, and the girls both laugh, but I'm busy trying not to drown in emotion.

Even back then, they were planning this for me. Our scouting trip to the pond was two weeks ago, and it must have taken Dee even longer than that to make something this stunning. I can see her hard work in every stitch, every impossibly delicate layer of material. She sees my eyes welling with tears in the mirror, and she sternly shakes her head.

"Don't you dare, Hailey. If you mess up your makeup—"

Rowan laughs and fans my face with her hands. "She means you're welcome. Now calm down."

"I'm sorry—" I start, but Rowan only fans me harder.

"Don't be sorry. Just don't cry. I don't want you to mess up your makeup either. You look so pretty."

"Mike is going to die," Dee says, reminding me that I have to go back out there. I have to go back out in front of everyone—*thousands* of people, and one in particular—in a bloodred dress that's impossible not to notice.

"Are you sure he's going to like it?" I worry, and Dee raises an eyebrow at me in the mirror.

"What part of 'He is going to freaking *die*' did you not understand?"

WALKING BACK TOWARD the pond, I'm not convinced Mike is the one who's going to die. My knees are week, my heart is racing, and I'm pretty sure that Rowan's elbow linked with mine is the only thing keeping me moving.

"If this doesn't make him proclaim his undying love for you," Rowan says, "nothing will."

I reply with a nervous chuckle, because I skipped over that little part when I told the girls about Danica bursting into his house the morning after I spent the night. His words just felt too big to repeat out loud.

I'm in love with you.

And he hasn't said them since. Sometimes I wonder if he ever really said them at all, if maybe I imagined the whole thing.

As Rowan, Dee, and I walk back into the clearing, I can feel more than a few pairs of eyes on us—on Dee's mini dress and long legs, on Rowan's pretty blonde hair and blue eyes, on my bloodred dress and the black boots I'm desperately trying not to trip in.

"Oh. My. God!" A girl in a royal-blue tube top and long aquamarine skirt gapes as I walk past. "I *love* your dress!"

I smile at the expression on her face and thank her, and then, before we're too far away, I shout, "It was designed by Deandra Dawson! Look her up!"

Dee beams as she continues walking, and I do my best to do her dress justice. I swallow my nerves, I straighten my posture, and I pretend to possess her unshakable confidence as we get closer to the pond.

Closer to Mike.

He's standing with a group of fans, showing them the drumstick twirls I taught him, until one of the guys notices me over his shoulder. His eyes get wide, and when Mike follows his gaze, his do too. His drumstick slips from his fingers, dropping to the grass, and Dee and Rowan both giggle at my sides as they continue marching me to him.

He forgets all about his drumstick and meets me halfway.

"Wow," he breathes, stealing all oxygen from the air. I'm breathless at the look in his eyes, but Dee isn't impressed.

"*Wow*? Really? That's the best you can do?"

Mike glances from her to Rowan, but Rowan doesn't help him out. Instead, she grins as Dee lifts my hand into the air and twirls me around. Blushing fiercely, I spin for the man in front of me, and when Mike's eyes meet mine again, they're full of even more admiration than before.

"Try again," Dee instructs him, and he doesn't hesitate.

"You took my breath away," he says, his voice full of veneration that I don't think even Dee was expecting. I swear I hear her swoon beside me, and my cheeks are as red as my dress when she nudges me with her elbow.

"See, and you were worried he wouldn't like your dress."

There's no word to describe the color my face turns. My skin flushes itself into a brand-new shade of just-kill-me-now, and Mike's lips curve into a soft, amused smile.

"Can I take you for a walk?" he asks, and the prospect causes the butterflies in my stomach to riot.

"Don't you have to start shooting soon?"

Mike gives me an honest yes at the same time Dee and Rowan both blurt no. Then Dee gives me a gentle push forward, and before I know it, Mike's hand slides into mine.

Chapter 30

It's strange, how intimate something as simple as holding hands can be, when it's with the right person. Last summer, I held hands with Billy Lynch on the Ferris wheel at the Apple Harvest Festival. The view was beautiful: white lights strung along the streets, carnival rides flashing as they spun in the air, balloons and cotton candy swimming over the ground far, far below. And nothing. Not one butterfly, not one spark.

But here, with Mike, with nothing to see but tech equipment and unknown faces, my heart is a wild mustang that bucks in my chest. I hope my palm isn't sweating, but I really can't tell, because I'm holding on for dear life.

"What time did you get here this morning?" I ask to try to maintain the façade that I'm the kind of girl that can hold hands with a rock star. I can be cool. I can be calm. I can do words.

"Around seven this morning," Mike says, and I gape at him. Dee and Rowan told me that the video isn't scheduled to wrap until around three in the morning. That's a twenty-freaking-hour workday.

"That's insane," I say, hoping that the crew at least fed him. I should have called before I left home to find out if he wanted me to bring anything: sandwiches or coffee or a pizza or—

"Yeah, well, I mean, I didn't really *have* to be here that early," Mike says, interrupting my mental checklist. "But Shawn always has to micromanage everything, and I figured he could use the company."

It strikes me—what a *Mike* thing that is for him to say—and I realize he does this a lot: does incredibly sweet things and takes no credit for them. It makes my heart grow as I stare up at him, and when he meets my eyes, I make sure he knows, "You're a good man."

Mike chuckles and stops drumming on my hand, holding it tighter. "I'm not that good."

"Yes, you are."

He smirks and shakes his head, and when I wait for him to explain, he nods his chin toward a group of guys who are very shamelessly checking out my dress. "I'm a selfish man. I'm about to steal you from your fan club."

He tugs me toward the woods, and as I let him lead me, I spot the path we took last time.

The cabin. He's taking me to the cabin.

Last time, the entire path was lined with trees that looked like they were bleeding, they were so dressed in red leaves. Now, those leaves are withering under our feet. Each crackle weighs heavily on my nerves, reminding me that Mike is single, that he's holding my hand, that we're walking into the woods, that he told me he loved me.

None of this should be happening. He's my cousin's ex-boyfriend. He's leaving on tour. He's a freaking *rock star.* And if Danica jumped out from behind a tree right now and saw me holding his hand, she'd throw me out of our apartment, she'd get her dad to stop paying my tuition, she'd revel in the annihilation of my dreams . . . and then she'd murder me with her bare hands just for the fun of it.

Sliding my fingers from Mike's, I swoop down to pick up a vibrant red leaf, pretending that my fascination with it is the reason I pulled my hand away.

It's not that I'm afraid Danica is going to catch me here tonight—I know she won't, since Shawn told her the video was rescheduled for tomorrow—it's just that even if she doesn't catch us tonight, even if she doesn't catch us tomorrow . . . she'd catch us eventually. I'm smart enough to know that, and I care about Mike too much to pretend that I don't. I don't want to lead him on.

I twirl the dry leaf stem between my fingers, trying to ignore the loss I already feel at the absence of his touch.

"So you've been friends with Shawn a long time, huh?" I ask to change the subject, and when I look up at Mike, the expression on his face is unreadable.

He studies me for a long moment, and then he tucks his freed hand in his pocket. "Since we were kids."

"How'd you meet? I mean, I know you went to school together, but how did you end up in a band together?"

Mike holds the reaching arm of a pricker bush out of my way and answers, "He and Adam just came up to me one day at lunch in the cafeteria and were like, 'We hear you play the drums.'" He smiles warmly at the memory, continuing the story when I look up at him expectantly. "I was just sitting there drinking a chocolate milk, and they sat down in front of me and told me they were starting a band and wanted to hear me play. They rode my bus home with me after school, and I guess they liked what they heard, because we ended up spending the whole night just hanging out in my garage dreaming up this awesome band we were going to be."

I didn't know them back then, but I can see it. I bet Mike was the kind of teenager that didn't even bother brushing his hair before he went to school each morning. I can picture him with his hours-old bedhead and his fingers drumming on the side of his chocolate milk, and I can see the curiously skeptical look he'd give a lanky Shawn and Adam when they said they wanted to hear him play. It feels like a fond memory—one that makes me smile.

"It was crazy," Mike continues. "Shawn had that look in his eye even back then. Like when he talked about how we were going to make it big, I believed him.

And so did Adam. I just wanted to be a part of that ride, I guess . . . That night was the first time I ever drummed for anyone other than my mom, and here I had these two guys telling me I could be a rock star."

When Mike looks down at me, he asks, "What?"

A proud smile curves my lips, and I say, "Look at you now." A faint blush creeps under the scruff on Mike's cheeks, and I press, "Big record deal with a huge label. A massive music video with thousands of people. An international tour." I beam up at him, so proud of how far he's come. "You've gotten everything you ever wanted."

"Not everything," Mike corrects, and the serious look in his eyes feels like a challenge—Do I need to know? Do I *want* to know?

"What else is there?" I finally ask, and Mike takes his time with my question, his gaze fixed on the leaves lining our path.

"Right now?" His eyes lift back to mine, drying my throat. "Right now, I really just want to hold your hand again."

I chew on the inside of my bottom lip, weighing the consequences of what he wants against the heaviness in my heart. And then, before I can overthink it for even one more second, I stretch out my arm and wait for him to take my hand.

Chapter 31

THE WAY MIKE'S fingers lace with mine—his thumb outside of my thumb, his fingertips snug against the top of my hand—it feels like more than just holding hands, but that's what I keep telling myself: It's just holding hands, it's just holding hands.

As we walk, I ask him more about growing up with Adam and Shawn. I laugh at the way he describes a numskull teenage Joel. I get him to tell me about his mom, his dad who lives in Texas, his half sister and the turtle she had as a pet for a while. And I'm not sure why I ask all of these things, except that I don't have the willpower not to.

Mike is like a book that I can't stop reading. And even if I finished—even if I got to the very last line of the very last page—I'm pretty sure I'd want to read him over and over and over again.

We walk toward the cabin but never get there, since

we turn around when it starts getting dark. It's just a walk—a walk in the woods under a dusk-stained sky, with Mike Madden making me laugh. I'm in a pretty dress, and he's holding my hand, and nothing can go wrong—until it does.

"Oh my God," I blurt as my feet freeze on the path. My hand jerks from Mike's, and I stand there in a blind panic. "Oh my God, oh my God, oh my God."

"What?" Mike worries, looking around for a snake or a rabid raccoon or a chupacabra or something, while I just stand there paralyzed, staring wide-eyed down at my dress.

"My dress."

In the low light, Mike follows my line of vision and spots the branch with its fangs lodged in a layer of my flawless red tulle. "Don't move."

"Oh my God."

"Just stand still," Mike orders, dropping to his knees.

"Oh my God."

"It's going to be fine," he assures me. "I can get it out."

"I ruined it."

"When have I ever let you down?" Mike asks, getting to work. I brace my hands on his shoulders to keep my balance. I can't believe I snagged Dee's gorgeous, priceless, perfect dress. She didn't even get a grade on it yet, and I destroyed it.

"I fixed your hoodie, didn't I?" Mike reminds me as I stare up at the sky, praying for a miracle. "And I saved you from drowning in the pond. And I rescued you from that basset hound at the animal shelter." I tilt my chin down to give him a confused look, and he smirks up at me. "That dog was an insatiable little monster. He probably would've eaten you alive."

"Barb named him KissyPie . . ."

"Should've named him Cujo," Mike counters, and I laugh.

"My hero," I joke, and he flashes me another heart-stopping smile before returning his attention to my dress.

"So speaking of," Mike starts as he gently maneuvers the red tulle. "I was talking to Luke last night, and I was thinking . . . when we get back from tour, I'd like to play a little show at his school. Me and the guys."

"Why?" I ask in disbelief. I know he's trying to distract me from the dress, and it's working. I imagine a band as big as Mike's playing at a school as small as Luke's, and how much that would mean to my timid little brother.

"I was thinking it might help. I know he gets picked on a lot and isn't having an easy time making friends, but I bet a lot of the kids he goes to school with have heard of us. I bet they'd think it's cool that he's our friend."

Friend. Mike Madden, Sexy as Fuck rock star with thousands of people currently waiting to be in his music video, is willing to be friends with my twelve-year-old brother to help him make friends at school. When he looks up at me from where he's kneeling at my feet, all I can do is stare at him.

"What do you think?" he asks, and I tell him the truth.

"I think you're amazing."

The corners of Mike's mouth tip up, and my eyes follow them when he stands. All I can think about is how soft those lips must be, how badly I want to find out.

"I meant about the dress," he says, and when I glance down, I realize he's holding it out for me to see. He fishes his phone from his pocket and shines a light on the bloodred tulle, his fingers brushing mine as we both move the material this way and that.

There's nothing. Not one snag, not one rip, not one trace of the thorn that had promised to ruin it.

Words aren't enough when I look up at him this time. I stare up into his big brown eyes, and my gaze slides slowly back down to his lips. With my four-inch boots, they're not so far away. Mike lets my dress fall from his fingers, and—

"Mike Madden." Adam Everest's voice booms from speakers not too far away. "Mike Madden, we're going to need you to get your ass back here so we can start filming, over." A short pause. "Unless you're getting laid, over. In which case, hurry it up, over."

"I'm going to kill him," Mike decides as we both stare in the direction of Adam's voice. Mike takes in the beet-red color of my face and shakes his head. "I'm seriously going to kill him."

"After you play at my brother's school," I agree, and Mike rubs a hand down his face.

"Okay," he says with a frustrated but amused laugh. "After your brother's school. Then he's a dead man."

With a deep, heavy sigh, he takes my hand in his, and I let him hold it without argument this time. I allow myself to appreciate the way it makes my skin tingle, the way it causes my heart to pound. I commit it all to memory, since I'm not sure I'll ever feel it again.

"I bet you went to school with bedhead," I tease as we walk back to the clearing, recalling my earlier image of teenage Mike sitting in his lunchroom cafeteria.

The way his mouth twitches to hide a smile confirms it.

"I knew it," I say, and he laughs.

"I didn't really care about school. I wasn't bad at it, but I just thought it was such a waste of time. I would've rather been home gaming or drumming or skating or something."

"You skated?" I ask, and Mike grins.

"A little. I wasn't any good at it."

"But you weren't a skater?"

Drumming his fingers against the top of my hand, he says, "No. I mostly kept to myself. No one paid much attention to me until I joined the band."

I put everything I know about Mike together, and I paint a mental picture: a teenage boy sitting in classes he couldn't care less about, not interested in high school cliques but pining after the cheerleader he's had a crush on since third grade. He joins a band with the popular kids. People start to notice him . . .

"And then you ended up with the most popular girl

in school," I say out loud, and Mike stops drumming his fingers against my hand. He holds my gaze as we walk.

"We'll make sure your brother doesn't do something that dumb. No cheerleading captains for him." His hand squeezes mine, and he gives me a sexy smile that charms all my blood to my cheeks. "Only pretty baton twirlers."

BY THE TIME Mike and I break back through the trees, the entire space looks much less like chaos and much more like business. All of the extras are lining up just inside the tree line, directed by a hive of staff workers that buzz here, there, here, there. Mike leads me away from them, through the stragglers heading toward the woods.

"You!" a woman in cargo pants and a black thermal shouts at me when we're halfway to the pond, and I hold tighter on to Mike's hand, feeling like I'm breaking the rules by being with him. "I've been looking everywhere for you!"

I glance over my shoulder and then back at her, unnerved by the excitement in her smile as she bursts through my personal bubble. She grins in my face, looks me up and down, and circles behind me.

"Huh?" I manage as she completes her 360-degree inspection. That smile is even bigger when she stands in front of me again.

"The girl in the red dress. Wow, you're stunning. I

saw you walking through here earlier and—" She finally seems to notice Mike. "Wait, you're the drummer, right? Mike?"

Mike and I share a confused look.

"Oh, this is perfect," she says with a smoker's texture to her voice, clapping her hands together. "Are you a couple?" To Mike, she asks, "This girl is too pretty for just a fling in the woods, right?"

"No," I stammer, and the woman lifts a sandy-blonde eyebrow at me.

"No to the couple or no to the fling?" She dismisses her own question with a quick shake of her head. "No, look, it doesn't matter, it doesn't matter. PAUL!" She shouts over her shoulder. "PAUL, I FOUND HER!"

"I'm . . . just . . . Hailey," I stammer, at a loss for all other words. When the woman glances back at me, her smile stretches and stretches and stretches.

"Oh, no, sweetie. *You* are my girl in red." She leans down to be eye level with me, her green eyes sparking with enthusiasm. "*You* are my star."

"ALRIGHT, LISTEN UP!" Out in the clearing, Paul, the director, holds a microphone to his mouth. His voice thunders through the speakers concealed in the trees, and Dee interrupts it in my ear.

"I swear to God I had nothing to do with this."

We're standing shoulder to shoulder just inside the tree line, along with hundreds of other people. But I know that the massive camera stationed out in the clearing is pointed at me. After all, in the words of Jillian the producer, *I* am the star.

There was no convincing her that she had the wrong girl. She had her heart set on me, and when I told her I couldn't be in her video because my psychopath cousin would hate me for it, she simply held my face in her hands and told me not to let anyone dull my shine.

My *shine*? What shine?

Still, how could I argue with that?

Mike was the one who stepped in to assure me I didn't have to be in the video if I didn't want to, but everyone was looking at me, and I knew what it would mean for Dee's career for me to show off her dress, and just . . . here I am. It's an epically terrible idea, and here I am. The star.

"You really didn't put her up to it?" I accuse Dee again, even though I believe her when she insists she didn't. My teeth are chattering, and it has nothing to do with the cold.

"I promise."

"I'm going to faint," I warn through my growing nausea. The frigid autumn air feels like thick molasses hardening in my belly.

"You're not going to faint."

"I'm going to die."

Unsympathetic, Dee argues, "All you have to do is walk."

Easier said than done when my knees are shaking more than a newborn pony's.

"Danica is going to kill me when she sees me in this video."

Dee turns to me then, her flawless face illuminated by the fifty-foot-tall crane showering its white spotlight on us. "All Danica said was that you can't see Mike anymore, right?" I nod, and she says, "So tell her that your scenes were shot separately. You can even say I *made* you be in the video to show off my dress. Hopefully she'll call me to confirm." Her wicked grin reveals her violent intention, and a chill races up my spine.

"She's still going to be livid that I was in it." I can hear her now—*You took* my *idea,* my *role,* my *boyfriend.* And the thing is, she wouldn't exactly be wrong about any of it.

I'm frowning when Dee loses her devilish smile and says, "I know she has you in a tough spot, but you need to realize that a girl like Danica is always going to have something to hate you for, Hailey. She's always going to find a reason to be mad at you. I know you think you can walk on eggshells with her until you graduate, but I love you enough to tell you that you're wrong."

I want to tell Dee that she's the one who's wrong. I want to tell her that it's only two years, that I can get through two years. But then the director is finishing his speech and asking if there are any questions. And since I can't very well ask him to repeat everything he just said, I simply stand there like a deer in ten-thousand-megawatt headlights. Some staff workers get into position behind or beside cameras. A clapboard slaps shut.

And then we're walking.

Step, step, step, step. I glance down at my feet, and someone shouts, "CUT!"

"No, no, no, no, no!" Jillian complains as she marches up to me. "Who put this one here?" She shakes her head at Dee, sunglasses threatening to fly off the top of her head, and I realize she wasn't talking to me at all. Everything about Dee's stiff posture screams that she's ready to go toe to toe with the producer standing in front of her, who's preparing to get rid of her, but Jillian defuses her in an instant. "Sorry, honey, but you're way too pretty. You're taking attention away from Hailey. I need you somewhere else."

Jillian snaps her fingers, and a few staff workers rush over to show Dee where to go.

"Are you sure you don't want her to be the star?" I ask, looking over Dee's shoulder at Jillian when Dee wraps me in a hug. Jillian waves dismissively at me as she walks away, and Dee whispers in my ear.

"This is your moment, Hailey. Trust me, this is *meant* to be your moment. Show them what you're made of." She pulls away, smiles at me, and adds one more piece of *super* helpful advice. "Make my dress look good!"

She leaves me. Quite happily, she lets herself be escorted away, and then I'm just standing there *literally* shaking in my boots.

"Okay, everyone back in position!" Paul the director shouts, and everyone around me starts moving back into the trees. I follow their lead, shrinking under the spotlight. "Eyes toward the pond. Slow and steady. Backs straight. Aaand three, two—"

The clapboard slaps shut, and we start walking again. We do one take, two takes, five takes, nine takes. On the tenth take, Paul starts walking up to me, and I don't know whether to be ashamed that I let everyone down or relieved that they've finally realized I'm no star.

He's a skinny guy in skinny jeans, gray at his temples and long in his chin. "Hey, Red, listen . . . What's your name?"

Everyone is staring at me—the extras at my sides, the staff on the grass, the band out on the pond, Dee somewhere that is *extremely* not helpful to me. My voice is tiny and shy when I answer, "Hailey."

"Hailey," Paul repeats softly, smiling at me. "What's your last name, Hailey?"

"Harper."

"Hailey Harper." Still smiling, he places his hands on my shoulders. "You're my star, Hailey Harper. Jillian was a genius casting you. We love everything about you. Your dress, your hair, your walk. You've got this really sweet, really sexy vibe going, and we love it . . . but we need to work on your face."

"My face . . ."

"It's gorgeous. Your big amber eyes and your long eyelashes. I love that you went with a nude shimmer for your lips. Really, beautiful." He squeezes my shoulder. "But Hailey, you look scared to death."

An embarrassed blush stains my cheeks, and I struggle to swallow.

"Let's talk about your motivation, okay?"

"My motivation . . ."

Paul smiles and nods. "Have you ever had your heart broken?"

I think about it a moment, and then I shake my head.

Frowning, he asks, "Really? Not even once?"

"I don't think so," I say, and after a moment, a light chuckle escapes him.

"No, a pretty girl like you, I guess not. Okay, well, can you pretend? Can you think of a time you were really sad or depressed?"

An image immediately enters my mind, but it's not of the past—it's of the future. I imagine a scenario I've imagined a thousand times: having to move back to Indiana. I picture leaving school, saying goodbye to my new friends, never seeing Mike again. That last part chokes me, and I nod my head.

"Great! Okay, so tell me about it."

"Uh—" I panic, unwilling to surrender my secrets. "When my puppy died," I lie, chewing on my bottom lip.

"Perfect!" Paul says, and I've never seen someone so happy to hear about the death of a puppy. "I want you to remember how you felt when your puppy died. I want you to remember feeling like you'd never recover from that loss. And then I want you to imagine that freedom from that pain is within reach. Happiness is waiting for you on that platform over there—"

He points, and my eyes lift to see Mike standing on the platform, arms crossed over his chest, watching me. Rowan waves, and the rest of the band watch me too. But it's Mike that I focus on when the director says, "Imagine that you're walking toward that feeling. Maybe happiness is a color. Maybe it's a sound. Maybe it's your puppy. In the video, it's going to be a song. That song is going to make you love life again, Hailey. You just have to walk through the darkness to get to it.

"Okay?" he asks, and I pull my eyes from Mike to nod.

One last squeeze of my shoulder, a few last words of encouragement, and then the director takes his place behind the big rolling camera again. His fingers count three, two, one.

A clapboard slaps shut.

My eyes lock on Mike.

And I walk.

Chapter 32

It's insane, how much filming goes into a three-minute-long music video. We cut after every shot, every angle. Paul films shots of me standing in the woods, emerging from the woods, walking toward the pond. Fifty zillion takes, from at least a gajillion different cameras. Then he gets shots of me walking through the crowd that's rocking out around the pond. "Be a pebble through water," he instructs me, and I try to be a freaking pebble.

The moon gets higher and higher, and not all of the shots include me, thank God. Paul gets plenty of shots of the band playing onstage, and I enjoy just watching them as their new song pours out of the speakers hung around the clearing. Even though the prerecorded song will be in the final video, the band scraps the production team's plan and insists on playing it live for the fans, and the fans' enthusiasm is authentic. Hands in the air, wild excitement on their faces. Paul gets shots of them jumping up and down to the song, of the band playing it, and then we do it all over again for the drones that fly overhead.

The final shots are of me walking onto the dock while the band is playing, and then of me walking onto the platform after everything has been cleared off of it. It's just me walking out into the middle, and then spinning around and around with my arms spread wide and my red dress twirling out around me.

"Let it all go," Paul had instructed me. "You're in school, right? Just open up as you spin, and let your homework go, let your finals go, let your student loans go . . . Anything you can think of that's been weighing you down, just twirl around and let it all go."

With thousands of people watching me, I spin round and around and around on that dock, the night air kissing my skin as I lose myself in the feeling I've been chasing after all night. I close my eyes and turn my face to the night sky, doing as Paul directed: I let my classes go, I let my debt to my uncle go. Twirling faster, I let Danica's crushing presence go, I let her ultimatum go, and then I let her go completely. I remember Mike telling me he loves me, and this time, Danica isn't there. It's just me and him, and I feel what I should have felt when I heard him say those words. I smile at the moon, and I spin, and I spin, and I spin.

"Cut!" Paul shouts, bringing me down from starlit clouds. I slow to a stop, laughing as the world continues spinning without me. The trees blur and I struggle to find my balance, expecting Paul to bark orders for another take, but instead, he stands up from his director's chair at the end of the dock and shouts, "We got it! That's a wrap!"

He gives me a thumbs-up as thousands of people burst into cheers and applause, and I plop down on the platform, lying back while I wait for my head to stop spinning. I'm smiling at the moon when Mike's face appears in its place, and then I smile at him instead.

"You killed it," he praises, offering me his hand. I reach up to grasp it, but instead of letting him help me up, I surrender to impulse and tug him down beside me.

Mike lies on his back, his shoulder pressed against mine.

"I leave in ten hours," he says, and I reach down and link my fingers with his. I hold on, even when I know I have to let go. He was never mine to hold on to.

"I don't want to go," he confesses, and I finally look over at him. He should be happy—his band just finished shooting an epic music video, a massive party is about to start, he's going on an international tour tomorrow . . . but I find none of that in his eyes as he stares somberly over at me.

"Why?" I ask, and he holds my hand tighter.

"I haven't even gotten to take you out yet," he says, and my heart doesn't know if it wants to cartwheel or simply curl up in a ball and cry.

"Fancy restaurants are overrated."

At my failed words of comfort, the corner of Mike's mouth kicks up. "I wasn't going to take you to a fancy restaurant."

"Where were you going to take me?"

"Ice cream," he says, and at the expression on my face, his laugh lines appear.

"In October?" I ask, and when he nods, I realize I'm smiling. I can see us—side by side on a little bench outside the parlor, teeth chattering from the ice cream, Mike's arm wrapped around me to keep me warm, me laughing because of how perfect it all is.

My heart starts to ache, and Mike and I both lift our chins when footsteps begin to clatter against the steel grating.

"Sorry to interrupt," Shawn says with sincere apology in his voice. He scratches his fingers uncomfortably through his hair. "But it's time to set the equipment back up."

BACK ON DRY land, after being showered with hugs and kind words from Jillian, Paul, and the rest of the staff, I head for the long row of Porta-Pottys back up the access road. Dee, Rowan, and even Kit offered to go with me, but honestly, after being literally *surrounded* by people for the past five hours, I need some alone time.

I regret my decision almost as soon as I step back out of the Porta-Potty. The after party is in full swing—judging by the music I hear blasting back in the clearing—and waves upon waves of people are heading in that direction. I overheard Adam saying earlier that a lot more people were going to come afterward, since the band couldn't accommodate everyone who wanted to be in the music video, but I never anticipated *this* many people.

I get swallowed in the current as I make my way back toward the pond, and once I get to the clearing, I realize I have *no* idea where anyone is. I know the band must be performing out on the water, but the space around the pond is absolutely swarmed with people, and there's no way my five-foot self is going anywhere near it, not after my experience with armpit guy at the band's concert a few weeks ago. I fish my phone out of my jacket and consider calling Rowan or Dee to find out where they are, but I pocket it when I realize they're never going to hear their ringers over the blaring music consuming this entire forest.

Instead, I walk. In my red dress and my black boots, I walk through the grass and pretend I know where I'm going, which is no easy task considering that the entire space has been transformed. Fog machines that were used earlier to make the woods look eerie have been turned up to full blast, and all throughout the clearing, blue strobe lights and lasers cut through the haze. A firework explodes in the sky, and I look up to see a waterfall of white sparks fall from the moon. Cheers erupt all around me while I just stand there with my eyes pointed at the sky, mouth parted in awe.

A shiver sends goose bumps up my arms, and I lower my eyes just as a woman handing out glow necklaces passes me. The night lights up with glow sticks and glow necklaces and glow bracelets, and then the

Solo cups start multiplying, and I realize I'm nearing the kegs. And beside the kegs, food trucks advertising free pizza, free pretzels, free funnel cake. Someone carrying cotton candy walks past me, and I realize I am so, so, so incredibly lost.

I keep walking, and my eyes start playing tricks on me. I think I see Kit in the crowd, but it ends up not even being a girl—just a guy with the same incredibly smooth black hair and the same fair skin tone. And beside him, another guy with a buzzed head who *also* looks strikingly like Kit. And a few feet away, flirting with a group of girls: yet another ridiculously tall guy who looks just like Kit.

I'm walking away from the food area, rubbing my eyes and trying to convince myself I'm not losing my mind, when I hear an unfamiliar voice call my name.

"Hailey Harper," the guy repeats as he walks toward me, a warm smile on his face, "are you lost?"

He stops just in front of me, a tall twenty-something with honey-shaded eyes and dyed ombre hair—the base, the same striking cerulean color as the highlights in Kit's hair tonight.

"Do I know you?" I ask, and his smile widens.

"Sweetheart," he says, tapping his glow stick against the top of my head, "I'm your fairy godfriend."

I lift an eyebrow, and his face falls.

"Seriously? Again?" He shakes his head in disappointment and exhales a deep sigh of frustration. "What does a guy have to do to earn a reputation around here? When Kit didn't recognize me, that was one thing, but—" He pins me with furrowed brows and says, "Big gay best friend? Not ringing any bells at all?"

"Leti?" I ask, remembering stories that Rowan and Dee have shared over coffee, and his smile sparkles brighter than the flashing stage lights over at the pond.

"You *have* heard of me!" He wraps an arm around my shoulder and starts walking me to God knows where. "Those girls were going to give me a complex. Hey"—he looks down at me, and I stare up at him—"you haven't seen my boyfriend around here, have you? Kit's brother."

"Oh!" I say, relieved I'm not actually losing my mind. "Buzzed head? Lots of tattoos?"

"Mason?" Leti snorts. "No, not that one."

"Tall? Looks a little older?"

"I think you're talking about Ryan," he says with a shake of his head. "He's the oldest. I'm with her twin."

I think of the guy who was flirting with the group of girls, and I pray I'm wrong when I ask, "Muscular? Really short hair?"

"Bryce." Leti laughs, and I find myself relaxing under his arm. He feels safe in this chaos—like he's a native of this strobe-lit Narnia and can help me find my way back home.

Chin turned up in disbelief, I ask, "How many brothers does she have?"

"Too many," he says with a warm laugh as he types something on his phone. Then he slips it into his back pocket and smiles down at me again, "I'm with the one with the perfect hair and the perfect smile and the perfect shoe size and—"

"Hey!" Mr. Perfect says as he jogs toward us, and I immediately see Kit in his dark hair and his even darker eyes. He's just a little taller, with the same lean build, long lashes, and curved lips. Leti winks at me, and his boyfriend breathes a little heavy when he finally catches up.

"I've been looking everywhere for you," he says to Leti, and Leti hugs my shoulder.

"Look who I ran into."

I hold out my hand and introduce myself as Hailey, and Mr. Perfect tells me his name is Kale.

"He didn't use the fairy godfriend line on you, did he?" Kale asks. When Leti releases me to smack Kale's arm with the back of his hand, Kale laughs. "He's been planning that one all night."

"Don't listen to him," Leti orders. "Our meeting was by chance. I wasn't looking for you at all."

I look back and forth between them, but Kale just smiles at my confusion and says, "You looked amazing tonight. Kit said you were nervous, but you really couldn't tell."

"You were *gorgeous*," Leti agrees. "How do you like Dee's dress?"

"I love it," I say, lifting the part that got caught on the pricker bush earlier, still in awe that it didn't get torn. I glance toward the pond, wishing I could catch a glance of Mike through the masses of people.

"She worked really hard on it," Leti tells me. "When you were twirling out on that dock . . ." His golden eyes are full of admiration when he gives a little whistle. "Just wait until you see the video. It's gorgeous. I mean, the whole thing, really—stunning."

He pauses a moment, with Kale at his side, and then he says, "But do you know what I thought was the most beautiful thing about the whole video?"

"What?" I ask, and he grins.

"The way Mike watched you like a lovesick Romeo during every single scene."

Heat creeps into my cheeks, and Leti's smile widens just before he takes me under his arm again.

"Can I bestow some fairy godfriend advice on you?" he asks as we walk, but I'm too busy flushing red to answer him. His voice abandons its humor, full of nothing but soft sincerity when he hugs me close to his side and says, "Realize that a look like that is special. It means something."

He lets me digest that, but I already know Mike has feelings for me. I still remember the way he looked at me when he told me he was in love with me—how I could have understood his feelings by the expression in his eyes alone.

Leti pulls me from the memory when he leans down and says, "And you look at him the same way."

He winks when my eyes lock on his, and he releases me from under his arm just as we arrive near the crowd gathered around the pond.

"There's a funnel cake calling our name now, Hailey Harper," Leti says as he backs away. "But should you need us . . ."

"Did you just quote *The Labyrinth*?" Kale asks when Leti turns around, and Leti laughs as they walk into the dark.

"I have a T-shirt with that line on it."

I'M STANDING THERE alone, staring at the spot where Leti and Kale disappeared and wondering if I should have tried following them, when a hand slides onto my lower back. "Hey."

I look up into Mike's brown eyes, feeling even more lost than I did before. "How are you here?" I glance toward where Leti faded into the night, and then at the crowd jumping up and down nearby. Blue lights flash over their heads, and Adam's singing carries over the mayhem. "Aren't you guys playing right now?"

"I had a friend fill in for me," Mike says, joining his hands behind my back, until I'm just standing there in his arms, weak-kneed as I gaze up at him. "We're down to nine hours," he says, his words laced with a desperation that I feel under my own skin. "I don't want to waste them."

This is his night—his moment—and he should be onstage. But he's here, holding me in his arms, counting down each hour we have left.

My heart swells, and I don't know what to say, but Mike saves me from having to say anything at all, because he takes my hand in his and says, "Come on. I want to show you something."

Chapter 33

NINE HOURS IS probably only three at best, because this night can't last forever. Soon, the sun will rise, the magic will clear, and there will be nothing in this clearing but scraps left as a reminder—a Solo cup here, a dimmed glow stick there. But for now, there's fog under our feet, lights in the air, and Mike's hand in mine.

"What countries are you touring?" I ask as he walks me through vibrant colors and loud noises and thousands and thousands of faces.

"Canada, China, Korea, Indonesia—"

"Wow," I breathe, my voice lost under the music.

"Singapore, Malaysia, Thailand, Australia, England . . . I'm probably forgetting some."

I wonder how many thousands of miles away those countries are, and then I try not to think about it.

"Do you think you'll have Internet?" I ask, even though I know I shouldn't.

This night can't last forever.

This night can't last forever.

Mike glances down at me just as another set of fireworks explodes in the sky. White sparks rain down from black clouds, and he says, "If you think I'm not calling you every single day, Hailey, you're wrong."

He veers to the right then and leads me into the woods. We abandon electric light for moonlight, walking through bare-branched trees until the music quiets, the fog clears, and Mike releases my hand. I can still hear the band playing back in the clearing, but it feels like a world away.

"What did you want to show me?" I ask in a voice barely loud enough to hear, and Mike's answer is sure in the quiet night.

"How I feel about you."

Nervous energy thrums through me, and I sound far more composed than I feel when I ask, "And how are you going to do that?"

Mike reaches out and tucks a wild curl behind my ear, his fingers brushing a feather-light trail over sensitive skin. "Don't pull away, Hailey."

When he starts leaning in, everything in me threatens to do just what he told me not to. He's going to kiss me, and I'm so nervous, I'm panicking. He's going to kiss me. *Mike is going to kiss me!*

When he places his lips near my ear instead of doing what I thought he would, the tension in my body softens only a fraction.

"I'm more nervous than you are right now," he

whispers, and then he pulls away to search my eyes. His tentative gaze holds mine, his soft words a plea when he says, "Please don't pull away."

My heart is beating furiously against my ribs when Mike begins leaning in again, and it pounds harder and harder the closer he draws. I close my eyes on a breath, and I hold it until unbelievably soft lips brush mine. Time stops, the heat of Mike's satin mouth tests the seam of lips, and the entire world explodes around us. The fireworks have stopped, but everywhere, there are *sparks*. They consume me from the inside out—through my heart, into my fingertips—and before I know it, I'm stretching onto my tiptoes and burying my fingers in the thick of his hair.

The silence of the forest is interrupted by the low, sexy sound Mike makes when I pull against him, and I can feel the moment my sparks set him on fire. I'm melting against his hard body when his hand curls around the nape of my neck, like he couldn't bear for me to pull away right now, as if I'd even try. His tongue does this thing in my mouth that no tongue has ever done in my mouth before, and at the way I moan desperately and my knees start to quiver, his hands slide down my sides and wrap behind my thighs, lifting me into the air.

"Oh my God," I pant at the sky when the hard muscles of his stomach press firmly between my legs, and Mike drops his lips lower, making my blood rush like rapids just beneath my skin. His mouth explores the curve of my neck, and when he pulls away to gaze up at me—his face flushed, his lips kiss-swollen, and his hair a disheveled mess—the hungry look in his eyes could melt stone. Desperate for more of him, I hold his jaw in my hands and kiss him like I've never kissed anyone *ever.*

Mike's body is fire between my legs, and when I cross my ankles behind his back, squeezing him closer, I begin to tremble all around him. I'm lost in the heat of his mouth, the tension of his fingers, the strength of his arms. It feels like this moment has been building and building, and with the scruff of his jaw scraping the palms of my hands, all I want is to let go.

"Take me home," I beg, my voice rough with lust while Mike's smooth lips graze mine. He pulls away only far enough to pin me with that dilated, feverish gaze again. It's questioning, concerned, and I pin my forehead against his. Heat radiates between us—from me, from him—and I explain, "Your place. Take me to your place."

"You're sure?" he asks after a moment, and if I wasn't before, I am once he forces himself to ask those words.

Nine hours.

I answer by letting my fingers memorize the curve of his jaw, the scruff of his cheek, the soft hair on his temple. When my lips meet his, I memorize that too. I memorize the sweet way he lets me set the tone, the way his fingers tighten around my thighs with barely controlled restraint, the way he moans against my mouth when I kiss that restraint away from him.

Mike carries my trembling body halfway from the forest, never stealing his lips from mine even as branches snap under his feet, until he eventually lowers me back to Earth and takes my hand in his. The music gets louder and louder until we eventually step back into the clearing, our pace quick as we steal across the grass. Someone calls Mike's name, but he doesn't even turn his head. Instead, he leads me straight to his truck, opening the door and helping me inside. The inside light is on when he opens his driver's side door, and the flushed hue of his face sends sparks racing across my skin. His truck growls to life, and one of Mike's hands grips the steering wheel while the other slides onto my thigh.

He doesn't say a word as he drives—just keeps glancing over at me with those seductively dark eyes of his, and with every single gear change, his hand inches a little higher. It sneaks under the tulle of my dress, sliding up over butter-soft leggings, and the trembles in my body turn to desperate, needy quakes.

I squirm as his grip tightens and his palm slides slowly higher, higher. My fingers are white-knuckling the bottom hem of my leather jacket as I stare out the windshield, and my muscles ache from his teasing. I glance over at him, and he holds my gaze as his finger traces circles on the inside of my thigh, sending torturous waves of sparks to a place just a little bit higher.

"Pull over," I order once I release my lip from my teeth, already unbuckling my seat belt and turning in my seat. Mike gives me a look like he can't even comprehend what I'm saying, but I can't wait for him to understand—I'm desperate for the taste of the salt on his skin, and my lips are on his neck even before he pulls onto the shoulder.

His truck shuts off, his seat slides back, and before I can finish climbing onto his lap, he pulls me the rest of the way.

When I straddle him, he's not a rock star. He's not my cousin's ex-boyfriend. He's just *mine*. I feel it in the way he kisses me, in the way he clutches my ass and pulls me close until the heat between my legs is burning a brand against his stomach. His gluttonous hands squeeze my ass and move me against his body, just enough to torture me through my leggings, and I gasp and bite his lip between my teeth, fueled by the masculine moan that rumbles against my mouth. When I pull away, his lips follow, refusing to let me go, but I press against his shoulders until he's pinned against the seat.

I breathe heavily as I stare down at him, my small hands on his big shoulders and my knees framing his thighs. He's so beautiful in the moonlight—his dark lashes, his moist lips, and those bedroom eyes that stare up at me like I'm a goddess gracing Earth.

"You're so beautiful," he says, and I surrender to temptation, reaching out and running my fingers gently through his hair.

Mike closes his eyes, and then he captures my hand and draws my palm to his mouth. His soft kiss scorches my skin, and heat pools between my legs when he opens his eyes with the center of my palm still held against his mouth. My body trembles with need as I hover above him, and I know he can feel it.

"You deserve so much better than a truck along the side of the road," he says when he releases my hand, and I worry at the regret in his voice.

"Do you want to stop?" I ask, and he holds my gaze for just a moment before his hands slide up my thighs, grip my hips, and press me slowly, *firmly* down onto his lap. I gasp when his sex pushes against my heat, straining desperately against his jeans and my paper-thin leggings.

"No," he says, the lust in his voice soaking my panties. His hands travel beneath the tulle of my dress, feathering up my sides and making my entire body break into goose bumps. Our eyes lock when he sits up and brings his mouth within a breath of mine. "I'll give you better later."

Mike's mouth claims mine with enough heat to ignite us both, and his body awakens every one of my senses. His cock teases my sex even as his hands continue playing up my bare sides. They travel higher and higher, until he's palming the swell of my breast and sweeping his thumb across my pebbled nipple.

I gasp against his mouth, and Mike nips at my bottom lip. "You're so soft," he breathes, and when he lowers his hand and pulls away from me, my body weeps for him. "I want to see you," he says, his gaze intent even as his voice questions.

A lump forms in my throat, but I can't deny those

brown eyes that have made me melt even in my dreams. I've wondered this before—what he would look like beneath me. And now that I see it, now that I have it—I want to give him anything he wants. I want to give myself to him.

I sit a little further back, and I find the hem of my dress. With shivering hands, I start to lift it up, but Mike finishes the job, his fingers grazing the undersides of my arms as he lifts it over my head.

"Hailey," he admires, his eyes caressing my body before feasting on my breasts. I fight the urge to cover them, to hide from him, but he doesn't give me the chance. Mike takes my hands in his, places them against the sides of his neck, and shifts in his seat until I'm lying back against the steering wheel and he's taking my nipple into his mouth.

I don't recognize the sound of pleasure that bursts from my lips, or the way my fingers scratch into his hair and beg him to continue savoring me. His tongue swims across my nipple, sending waves of pleasure rippling under my skin. He sucks and pulls and pins it between his teeth while he rolls the other between smooth fingertips, and I can't help the way my hips respond to him. I grind helplessly against his cock, and it tortures us both until he's groaning against my breast and I'm moaning into the air.

"Take them off," I pant, and Mike doesn't ask for clarification before he hooks his fingers inside my leggings and helps yank them off. I take off my boots to remove the black material the rest of the way, and then

I settle on Mike's lap again, my panties damp against his jeans.

I grind against him purposefully this time, kissing him with wild lust that fogs the truck's windows, and Mike grips my ass as I do, encouraging me to ride him. I move my hips until the feel of his denim fly against my thin cotton panties steals my ability to think, until my moans are desperate cries, and Mike steals his lips from my neck to pant, "Let me inside you, baby."

Oh God. I don't know if it was the gravel in his voice or the way he called me baby, but I'm fumbling for his zipper even as he helps me out of the last article of clothing I have on. Mike shifts his jeans and boxers down in one swift movement, and then I'm hovering on my knees above the point of no return.

On impulse, I gaze down, and my eyes widen when I see the size of what was straining inside his jeans.

"Shit," he breathes as he follows my gaze, a line forming in his brow. "I don't keep any condoms in my—"

I shake my head at him, shock still washing over me. "I'm on birth control. It's just—"

I glance down again and bite my lip between my teeth, and when I lift my eyes, his expression relaxes with relief.

"Don't worry," he assures me, his fingers exploring my body with minds of their own. They pinch my nipples, and I bite down harder on my lip as my body melts for him.

I'm worried. I'm *definitely* worried. It's been too

long since I last had sex. Sex with Mike is going to hurt . . . a lot.

"Hailey," he says, and I pull my eyes from the glistening head of his enormous cock. He holds my gaze and leans forward, kissing me softly until my eyes flutter closed and his touch travels down, down, down.

Mike's tongue dances with mine, intoxicating and distracting as one of his hands grips my hip and the other slides between my legs. His fingertips find my slick, tight bud, and my knees nearly give out beneath me.

"Mike," I gasp, and he captures his name with a kiss that makes me heady. His fingers rub in slow circles, the friction melting me like an ice chip lavished by a tongue. His palm brushes my clit as he slips his hand further between my thighs, sliding a finger deep, deep into my heat.

I struggle to kiss Mike, to keep my head from falling to his shoulder, as he strokes the perfect spot inside me while massaging my clit with his thumb. He kisses at the moans coming from my parted lips, and his other hand skates up my stomach and over my breast, rolling my pebbled nipple between his fingertips. Little bolts of pleasure jolt through me from so many places at once, I don't know how he's managing it—his hand between my legs, his fingers around my nipple, his lips against my lips, his tongue between my teeth.

In ecstasy, I realize that this is what it's like—*this* is what it's like to be worshipped by a drummer.

Mike slips a second finger inside, and this time,

I can't help breaking the kiss to drop my forehead against his shoulder. I bite the slack of his T-shirt between my teeth to keep from losing control, but when he dips his head and finds the hollow of my collarbone with his satin tongue, that control threatens to slip.

I'm overwhelmed. With his fingers filling me and his tongue savoring my body, I'm consumed by electric sparks that lick me to my core. He's kindling a fire that's growing out of control, and when he carefully slides a third finger into my slick heat, pleasure-pain rockets through me.

"Fuck," I hiss as the heel of Mike's palm grinds over my burning bud, coaxing my body to melt around his fingers, to stretch to fit their width.

"Am I hurting you?" he asks, and I shake my head against his neck. My fingertips are digging into the backs of his shoulders, my body accepting him and demanding more.

"You're killing me," I plead against the sizzling column of his neck, the sound of my own voice making my nipples tighten with need.

"Come for me," Mike orders over the sounds I'm making against his skin. My sex is milking his fingers, drawing him in, begging for what's waiting in his lap.

"I need you inside me," I plead, pulling away to burn my gaze into his. I'm desperate for him, coming undone at my seams, and I can see him struggling with restraint when he forces himself to deny me.

"Come first, Hailey. It'll be easier for you."

"Please," I beg, but Mike only leans forward again,

forcing me back and taking my nipple between his lips.

"Oh my God," I groan, my heat clenching his fingers as he lavishes my breast with wet kisses and swirling licks. "Oh my God. Oh—" My breath catches in my throat and my muscles scream for release. I'm so close. I'm so fucking close.

"Now," Mike orders, and when he pins my nipple between his teeth and fills me to bursting with his fingers, I fall utterly, *completely* apart. My hips buck and I scream his name, and I'm spasming around his fingers when they suddenly leave me empty. The loss drives me mad with want, and I'm not sure if I'm going to cry or scream, when his cock presses firmly against my slick folds. I gasp as his swollen head begs entrance into my still-orgasming sex, and Mike pushes down on my hips, stretching me around his solid length.

"Hailey," he says, moaning my name like some people moan "God." But it's me who worships his mouth as his fingertips sink into the meat of my thighs, holding me in place as fireworks ignite all throughout my body. They spark in my core as I squeeze hungrily around him, milking the length of his satin cock as he begins to move inside me.

"Fuck, Hailey, you're so ready for me," Mike breathes against my kiss-bruised lips. "You feel fucking amazing. You feel perfect. Baby, open your eyes."

I struggle to open my eyelids in spite of the sensations rocking my sweat-beaded body, but when I do, I can tell my pupils are dilated and my eyes are still half-lidded. Everything is brighter, crisper, and Mike's chocolate gaze melts any parts of me that were still whole. He lifts his hands, pushing my wild hair from my eyes and holding my face gently in his palms. I know what he's going to say before he says it—I can see it in the way he looks at me, the way he touches me.

"I love you."

His eyes are locked with mine when he says it, and this time, it's just us. It's just us in the dark with him penetrating my body and my soul, and when I kiss him, he listens. He listens to everything I can't say yet.

My lips tell him that no one—*no one*—has ever made me feel the way he does. He's in my head, in my heart, and having him in my body feels like finding a puzzle piece that's been missing my entire life. He feels like a part of me, and I'm never going to come back from this. He's going to leave tomorrow, and I'm never going to recover from this moment. But tonight, I have him, and I plan on taking and giving until I can't tell where he ends and I begin.

I kiss him until Mike's hands drift from my face, caressing and teasing my oversensitive flesh until I'm stealing control. With my knees framing his thighs, I rock my body against him, loving the way that it makes his fingers flex against my ass. I tug his shirt over his head and let my lips explore his collarbone, his shoulders, the muscles of his chest. He's so big beneath me, and I want to taste every inch of him.

With every lift of my hips, my body aches for him, and with every drop back to his lap, I moan my ecstasy against his skin. The rougher I get, the more desperate Mike's hands get, until he's trying to slow my pace, trying to calm my need.

"Hailey," he warns, but I curl my tongue behind his ear and clench around his cock. I know I'm driving him crazy, and it's too much for me to resist. He wants me—I can feel it in the way he throbs inside my sex, the way he catches my lips every time they pass too close. And however wrong it is, because there are too many reasons we can't be together, I *want* him to want me. When he's on tour for the next six weeks, I want him to remember the way my tight heat pulsed around his massive cock. I want him to compare every other girl he's ever with to me, and I want him to find her lacking.

"Baby, you feel too fucking good," Mike warns again, putting pressure on my hips to try to stop me from riding him so fast. He's going to come, and I know it. And God, I *want* it. He's doing to me physically what he's done to me emotionally over the past few weeks—tugging at my strings, making me want him, and I can't deny it anymore. I *want* him to come in me. I'm hungry for the way his cock will pulse in my body, the way his eyes will look when he gives himself to me.

I pry his hands from my hips and slide them firmly up my sweat-sheened body, placing them over my breasts and squeezing my supple flesh inside his palms. Mike's eyes grow hooded as he watches me touch myself with his hands, and my heart beats out of control. He licks his lip and gives a defeated shake of his head.

"You leave me no choice."

"What do you mean?" I ask, and when I release his hands, he pinches my nipples between the tips of his thumbs and the sides of his fingers.

"I'm going to come inside you," Mike says, his eyes locked intensely with mine as he sends electric waves of heat through my taut nipples and deep into my molten core, "and then I'm going to take you home and lick your tight pussy until you melt in my mouth. And then I'm going to bury myself inside you until I have to leave tomorrow."

His unexpected words trigger every unused muscle in my body, causing me to tighten around him. Mike's cock pulses in response, and he leans in, sweeping warm kisses from my collarbone to my ear. "Say okay," he demands on a hot whisper that burns a seductive path across my skin. I never thought simple words could turn me on so much, but hearing them come from his lips, I'm catching fire on top of him.

"Okay," I breathe, gripping his shoulders as I lift myself up his thick shaft and lower myself back onto his lap.

His head buries in my shoulder and he moans, "Ride me, Hailey."

My fingers tunnel into his hair, and I grasp thick chunks of it, pushing his head back so he has no choice but to watch me. His big eyes fix on mine, his pupils swallowing the white as I lean in and capture his feverish lips with mine.

Mike moans against my mouth as I do just what he told me to—my body plays with him over and over again, taking him and letting him go, taking him and letting him go. I don't know what's come over me, but with this beautiful, talented, gorgeous rock star losing himself beneath me, I feel like a goddess, and I ride him like one.

"How do you feel so perfect," he pants against my neck as the pleasure inside me turns urgent. I feel my release building, and when Mike lifts his head to stare up at me, I capture his lips and kiss him with the fire burning inside of me.

Mike's moan rumbles against my mouth, his grip on my hips unforgiving as he pulls his mouth away and says, "Hailey."

I know he's ready to come. I know he's going to get there before me. I remember his promise.

"Come," I urge as I rock my body against his. I grasp his chin and pin my sweat-beaded forehead against his. "Mike. Come in me."

He kisses me feverishly before I can breathe another word, and between kisses, I beg him.

Please. God. *Mike*. Please.

The primal sound that he makes as he empties inside me triggers my body to explode into white-hot fire, my fingers clawing desperately into the backs of his shoulders. The heat floods out from my core and rushes into my legs, my arms, my fingers, my scalp. When I collapse against Mike, he catches me in a tight hold, gripping me as his body continues marking me as his.

His heartbeat throbs inside my heat and against my chest, and my heart swells with his arms around me. I bury my nose in the curve of his neck, breathing him in and letting him hold me. I know I have to let him go. He's a rock star. He's going on tour. His life is going to be so much *bigger* than me. And my life—my future—is dependent on me never seeing him again.

I know I have to let him go after tonight.

I just don't know how I can.

Chapter 34

I BLUSH THE entire ten-minute truck ride back to Mike's place. In the dark, with his headlights on the road, the memory of his lips sparks across my skin, and my insides pulse with the reminder of how *full* he filled me, how it felt when he moved inside me. His fingertips tattooed my body with a touch that still sears my skin.

He reaches across the center console, but instead of tracing teasing circles against my thigh like he did before I made him pull over, he simply takes my hand. He holds it tightly, and when I glance over at him, he smiles. It touches his cheeks and lights his eyes—an unguarded happiness that makes me giggle in his passenger seat. He smiles even wider, and I blush fiercely as I turn my gaze out the window.

The full moon is still high in the sky, but it's moved since we were back at the pond. The time on Mike's dash reads 4:27 A.M., which means nine hours has now become less than eight. My chest tightens, knowing that goodbye is coming, and I reach forward with my free hand to turn on the radio, hoping to drown out my thoughts.

"This next one is an oldie but a goodie," the radio DJ says. "These guys recorded a video for their upcoming single 'Ghost' over in Mayfield tonight, and I hear it was epic. Fans were invited to be a part of the shoot, but if you weren't one of the estimated two *thousand* people that were there tonight, I hear the party's still going. Check out our website for details, and in the meantime, here's one of my personal favorites. You're listening to 'Mayhem' by The Last Ones to Know, on 101 The Heat."

Mike glances over at me again as the tapping of his drumsticks sounds through his speakers, and one of the songs that his band played the first night I met him fills his truck. And it hits me with renewed force then—that he's driving me back to his place while radio stations across the country are playing his songs. That he's here holding my hand while the rest of his band celebrates the night away with over two *thousand* fans back in the woods.

I know I'm not pretty enough or special enough or just *enough* for him at all—not after seeing the crowd he drew out tonight, not after feeling how much passion, how much devotion, how much love he has to offer—but he slides his thumb across my hand reassuringly, like he's reading my thoughts and promising me I am.

When we pull into his driveway, my nerves are a wreck. I don't know how to talk to him after what we just did. Everything is different now, and I have a sinking feeling that I just messed us all up. I won't be able to laugh with him like we're just friends if we ever play Deadzone again—not with the memory of how my breasts felt beneath his tongue, how expertly that tongue flicked out to tease them.

Never in my wildest dreams did I imagine that sex with Mike would be like that—that sex in general could *ever* be like that. I can't even remember it without heat pooling in my core, without my knees squeezing together. My heart is pounding against my ribs when Mike looks over at me and says, "Don't move."

The interior light flashes on when he opens his door, and then his feet drop to his gravel driveway. He closes me inside the truck alone, and I watch as he walks in front of his still-lit headlights and circles around to open my door for me. I spin toward him to let him help me down, but Mike's hands immediately slide up my bare thighs—my leggings discarded somewhere in the backseat from when he tore them off me earlier. His rough fingers push my dress up high as he parts my thighs, stepping firmly between them.

"You don't think I've forgotten my promise, do you?"

His words replay in my head, in that same heated tone he used while he was deep inside me: *I'm going to come inside you, and then I'm going to take you home and lick your tight pussy until you melt in my mouth.*

And then I'm going to bury myself inside you until I have to leave tomorrow.

I'm biting my lip when Mike leans in and steals it from me, his tongue coaxing it from my teeth so he can pin it between his own. I moan against his mouth, and Mike reaches behind me, his big hands sliding beneath my ass and tugging me forward. I'm teetering on the edge of the seat, his body the only thing keeping me from falling onto my knees.

"I want you in my bed," his rough voice demands against my mouth, and my still-damp panties warm with renewed heat. I scratch my fingers up through the soft hair at the nape of his neck, and Mike deepens the kiss, teasing my tongue until my eyes are rolling back and it's a struggle to find my voice.

"I thought you said you want me in your bed," I manage to say, reluctantly breaking the kiss when he makes no attempt to help me from the truck. A fire is growing around us, and if we don't leave now, there will be no hope of walking away from the inferno.

"I do," he says as his fingers lift my dress over my head, exposing my body to the chilly night air. It hardens my already pert nipples and makes my flesh goose bump as Mike lies Dee's creation gently in the backseat and rakes his eyes over me. "I also want you in my truck," he says, planting a kiss beneath my ear. "And on my kitchen counter." His lips glide lower, dipping into the hollow of my collarbone until my fingertips are sinking desperately into his shoulders. "And in my shower." He leans me back until my trembling elbows are propped on the center console, and then he captures a pebbled nipple between his lips, warming it with his tongue before lavishing the other with soft, torturous kisses. My head falls back on a moan, but Mike takes his time with me, nipping and kissing until my body demands I lift my hooded eyes again to watch him. "And on my couch," he says with a smirk just before his breath skates down my body. His tongue dips into my navel, making my toes curl before he traces a trail to the hem of my panties. "And on my lawn." He kisses the moist cotton covering the apex of my thighs, and I whimper as his tongue soaks it through. He teases me through the fabric before nibbling at my clit. And then he hooks a finger inside my panties and tugs them to the side. "And my drums," he says, just before his warm tongue strokes a firm path through my heat. He circles my clit, lighting my nerves on fire, until his lips part and he sucks it gently into his mouth.

"Oh my fucking God," I gasp as Mike savors my swollen bud. He holds it between his lips and explores it with the firm tip of his tongue, making my legs shake violently as my release roars to life, building inside my core. I look down at him between my legs, and he gazes up at me with molten eyes as he devours my melting sex.

"You have no idea how long I've wanted to taste you," he says, lapping at me as he holds my gaze, and my head falls back as my knees continue to shake. My insides coil and tighten, and when Mike slides a finger into me, I nearly scream out with pleasure.

"Look at me, Hailey," he orders, and I summon the strength to lift my head as he slides another finger deep into my heat. The interior light switches off, leaving him shadowed by the hanging lamp on his garage, and the danger of this moment creeps up my spine. Even though Mike's house is set away from a back road, anyone could drive by. At any moment, headlights could appear down the road, and I'd be found reclining in the passenger seat of Mike's truck with his head buried between my thighs.

My nipples harden to twin points at the thought of it, and as Mike pleasures me with his fingers, he plants a wet kiss around my clit. "Hailey, when I kiss you—" he says, wrapping his scorching lips around my taut bundle of nerves again. The rest of me is wind-bitten and cold, which makes me focus on the fire he's burning between my legs. His lips stroke over my bud as he draws away on his kiss, only to lavish me with another, and another. "I want to know, when I kiss you, do you feel sparks?"

His fingers fuck me as he gazes up at me, baiting me with a question he already knows the answer to, but I can't form coherent words over the sounds of tortured pleasure coming from my mouth.

"Answer me, Hailey," he says, lowering his mouth to my heat again, lavishing my bud with his tongue.

Fireworks explode behind my eyes as my hips buck beneath him, and my body shatters and comes back together, only to shatter again. "Yes," I scream as my orgasm turns me inside out. Mike removes his finger to lap at me with his tongue, devouring me hungrily as I lose my damn mind. "Yes, yes, *yes*!" I scream, not caring who might be driving by to hear me. "Fuck, *Mike*!"

He lifts me up in an instant, kissing me heatedly as he carries my all-but-naked body across his driveway, up his sidewalk, and into his house. "I want your come on my cock," he growls as he lies me on his bed and crawls over me, and all I can do is kiss him as I burn alive beneath his body. He kicks his jeans and boxers off, tosses my panties across the room, and lowers himself on top of me.

"I need you," he says, and I realize he's asking for permission. His body is trembling with need for me, but he's staring down into my eyes, begging for me to welcome him into my body for the second time tonight.

"I'm yours," I answer, sliding my fingers up his neck. I hold his jaw in my hands and pull him to my mouth, kissing away the moan that rumbles from his throat as he pushes into me.

In Mike's bed, in his arms, the mood is different than it was in the truck. He moves inside me slowly, spoiling my body with kisses that make my back arch and my fingers dig into his back. He whispers that he loves me, and it takes everything in me not to say it back.

He's leaving in a few hours—I *can't* love him. I can't.

The way my heart swells as he makes love to me is a secret I keep to myself, one that exhausts me as I memorize Mike's body with my fingertips, my lips, my tongue. I lose track of time beneath him, and by the time he releases into my body, I'm not sure if we've been in his bed for two hours or two days.

When he rolls onto his side and pulls me against his chest, I snuggle in even closer. I sigh at the way he molds against me, and I fall asleep in his arms.

Chapter 35

THE FIRST TIME I slept in Mike's bed, I wanted nothing more than to reach out and touch him. I wanted to slide across his king-sized mattress, curl up next to him, and press my cheek against his chest. And when I wake up Sunday morning, after opening my eyes and remembering everything we did last night, that's exactly what I do. Since falling asleep, I've slipped out of his arms, but I slide across the bed until I'm melting against his body, relishing the way his big arms wrap tightly around me and hug me like he'll never let me go.

Mike groans contentedly and presses a kiss against the top of my head, and I can't help it—I giggle.

He loosens his hold to gaze down at me, the hint of a smile already playing on his lips. "What?" he asks, and I can't help laughing again.

"You're a dirty talker," I finally say out loud, and

the blush that stains Mike's cheeks makes my heart flip in my chest. He was a god last night—dominating even as he worshipped me on his knees. And the words that came out of his mouth, the way his voice sounded when he demanded I come on his cock—it was unexpected and so, so, *so* unbelievably freaking hot.

"Did you like it?" he asks, and my cheeks flush to match his own.

"Couldn't you tell?"

The corners of Mike's mouth tug up into an adorably sexy smile, and before I overthink it, I give in to temptation and stretch up to plant a kiss against those irresistible lips. I lower my head back to his biceps, and Mike's smile brightens as he brushes a lock of curls away from my eyes.

"I've never been like that with anyone else," he says, tucking the hair behind my ear, and I question him with my gaze. "The uh . . . dirty talk."

"You weren't like that with . . ." I trail off, and Mike shakes his head against his pillow.

"No. I never even *thought* those things with anyone else. You have no idea what you do to me, Hailey. You bring it out of me."

"Your inner caveman?" I ask with an impish smile, and Mike fists his hand in the back of my hair, applying pressure as he smirks at me. I bite my lip between my teeth, and he releases my hair to sweep his thumb across my mouth, laughing with surprise when I bite down on it.

I release his thumb to smile up at him, loving the

way his laughter touches his eyes, the way they crinkle at the corners as he gazes down at me with more love than should be possible after so short a time.

"What's on your mind right now?" I ask, and Mike lifts himself up on his elbow to let his eyes rove over my lips, my chin, my cheeks, the tiny freckle on my nose. Finally, his gaze settles on mine.

"I wish I could wake up with you tomorrow."

My throat thickens, and he kisses me softly. It's not a fiery kiss—it's a plush blanket that wraps itself around me, that warms me from the inside out. He pulls away and tames another curl that's tumbled over my forehead.

"What else?" I ask when a secret smile touches his lips.

His attention slides from my hair to my eyes, and he holds them when he says, "You're the most beautiful thing I've ever seen."

I can't stop the way the corners of my mouth turn up even as I roll my eyes. "You are such a liar."

Mike's expression sobers, his voice full of sincerity when he says, "I would never lie to you, Hailey."

I don't respond. I just stare up at him.

"Do you believe me?"

I give a small nod of my head, but it doesn't seem to ease his concern. His fingers thread into my hair, and he rubs tender circles over my temple with his thumb. "I want to give us a shot. I want this to work." He pauses like he wants me to say something, but I don't know what to say. Danica forbade it. And besides, he's leaving in a matter of hours, if not less, and I won't see him again for weeks. *Months.* We're not even together yet and he's already leaving.

"I'm going to be gone for a long time," he continues, "and you know there are fans . . . girls." I feel his fingers tense in my hair like they want to drum against my scalp. "But you only need to know one thing."

"And that is?"

"I don't want them," he promises. "I want you. I've waited for you for too long to mess this up."

"You've waited for me?" I ask, incapable of understanding. We just met. He didn't even know I existed before a few weeks ago.

"I've waited for you my whole life, Hailey," Mike says, and when a silent breath catches in my throat, he waits for me to release it. "Will you give me a shot?"

That question is so much more complicated than he knows. If Danica knew I was in his bed right now . . . if she knew all the ways he touched me last night . . .

I worry the inside of my lip, wondering how Mike and I could ever possibly work. We'd have to keep our relationship a secret from Danica, and if Lifetime movies have taught me anything, it's that secret relationships are never a good idea.

And frankly, neither are long-distance relationships. When I was eighteen, I was dating a guy named Tom, and he cheated on me after he went off to state college. Granted, I was kind of relieved, since it meant I didn't have to keep spending hours on the phone each night listening to how much he missed me, but still . . .

And Mike is going to have so much more opportunity than a frat house at state college. He's going to have girls *literally* lining up. They'll be in single-file outside of his clubs. They'll be screaming his name in the front row of his shows. They'll be standing outside of his bus, in short skirts and skimpy tops.

"What would giving us a shot entail?" I surprise myself by asking, and even though I haven't answered yet, Mike is already smiling.

"Let me date you," he says. "Don't date anyone else while I'm gone. Just me."

"You'll be on the other side of the world," I point out, and he brushes his fingers over my arm, sending goose bumps dancing over my skin.

"I could be on the other side of the universe, Hailey, and it wouldn't keep me from you."

Butterflies swarm in my stomach at the sincerity in his words, at the promise in his eyes, and in spite of my dry throat, I nod and manage a tiny "Okay."

"Okay?" he asks with hope glinting in his eyes.

This is probably the wrong decision. I'm probably going to regret it. But I started falling for Mike Madden the moment I made him laugh beside me on his tour bus, and I don't have the strength to break my own heart. Not today, not with his eyes shining with happiness, not when I'm the one who put it there.

"Okay," I say again, and Mike seals the promise with a kiss that wraps itself around my worries and makes them disappear. They'll matter tomorrow, and the next day, and the next day, but for now, this morning, there is only Mike Madden—rock star, gamer, pizza lover, drumstick twirler, beer drinker, sex god.

My boyfriend.

We'll have to say goodbye soon, but for better or worse, I know this is just the beginning.

Chapter 36

Dee: Hailey, please PLEASE FOR THE LOVE OF GOD tell us you had mind-blowing sex with Mike last night.

Rowan: And that you two weren't axed to death in the woods. . . .

Dee: Mike's truck was missing!

Rowan: Maybe the axe murderer took it.

A schoolgirl smile consumes my face as I sit alone in Mike's empty house and type back, I had mind-blowing sex with Mike last night.

Dee: OH MY GOD OH MY GOD OH MY GOD

Rowan: OMG!

Kit: Why am I in this conversation?

My face flames hot as I realize it's more than just me, Dee, and Rowan in this group text.

Unknown number: YASSSSSSSSSSS!!!!!!!

Me: Who is that?

Unknown number: HOW CAN I BE A PROPER FAIRY GODFRIEND WHEN NO ONE KNOWS WHO I AM?

Dee: Calm your tits, Leti.

Rowan: Is your car still in the parking lot back at the woods, Hailey?

Kit: Hailey, did Mike leave yet?

I finish plugging "unknown number" into my phone as Leti, and then I rub a line between my eyes and tell Rowan that yes, my car is still back at the woods, and Kit that yes, Mike just left. I know he's running late, since we dragged our goodbye out longer than we should have, but it hurt to let him go, and I could tell how much he struggled with leaving.

He gave me a key to his house before he left, insisting that he wanted me to have it just in case Danica kicked me out again. And then he told me that he'd be performing in a time zone two hours behind me tonight, and promised to call me before his show. He offered to make himself even later by taking me to pick up my car, but I insisted I could find someone else to take me, so he left me with a kiss that lingered against my lips, and I stood in his driveway watching his truck disappear down the road.

Me: Rowan, can you pick me up from Mike's place?

Rowan: Already on my way.

In Mike's shower, I let the water wash the scent of him from my skin, and my eyes begin to sting. He's going to be gone a month and a half, and my heart already aches at the thought of it. I remember how hard it was when I avoided him for the week after I realized I'd developed a crush on him, and now I have to multiply that by six.

At least we'll be able to talk on the phone . . .

I close my eyes under the water and see the way he smiled at me this morning as he lay beside me, playing with my hair. I won't *see* him again for six weeks. I won't feel his fingertips on my skin or his mouth on my lips, and after learning how good those things feel, it hurts. He's only been gone for forty minutes, and my entire body already aches from missing him.

When I answer Rowan's knock on the door, my hair is still wet and I'm wearing my borrowed leggings from last night under one of Mike's smallest T-shirts. I'm swimming in it, but it wraps itself comfortingly around me in spite of the hole in my chest and the stinging in my eyes. Rowan stands on his doorstep, taking in the sight of me before wrapping me in a tight hug.

Her eyes looked red like she'd been crying on the way here, so I hold her just as tightly. "He'll be back soon," I assure her of Adam, and she nods against my cheek.

"Mike too."

When she pulls away, she gives me a sad smile and wipes a tear from my cheek that I hadn't realized had spilled there.

"Is it always this hard?" I wonder, and she nods as she finishes drying my skin with her thumb.

"Every time."

"But you make it work?"

She nods and wipes her fingers under her own damp eyes. "It's worth it."

"How is Dee?"

Both of the girls are in the same position—left behind while Adam and Joel tour the world. Shawn is the only one who didn't have to leave someone, since Kit is part of the band.

Rowan gives another weak smile, her normally dark denim-blue eyes a shade brighter with unshed tears. "She can't really talk about it. But she'll be okay." She picks at my T-shirt, a teasing grin sneaking onto her face. "I'm pretty sure details about last night would be just the distraction she needs." I blush furiously, and Rowan laughs as she squeezes me in another hug. "I'm so happy for you."

I want to tell her that Danica is going to kill me, that dating her ex is a terrible idea, and that I'm pretty sure I've made a huge mistake. Instead, I force a smile when she pulls away, and I try to stop falling apart.

In her blue Honda Accord, she doesn't press me for details about what happened after Mike and I left the party last night. Instead, we talk about the video shoot, we talk about Dee's dress, we talk about how she met Leti and how Leti ended up dating Kit's brother. I laugh when she tells me the story of her and Adam—how she, Leti, and Adam were all in the same French class, and how everyone in the world, including Leti, had swooned over Adam Everest. But Rowan and he had history, and when they were forced to spend a weekend on tour together, they both fell and they both fell hard. Their story is one made for books, and I find myself asking how Dee got with Joel, and how Kit got with Shawn. Rowan gives me all the details over strawberry pancakes at IHOP, and when we're finally on the way to pick up my car, she turns to me and asks, "Hailey, can I be really honest with you?"

I nod, and Rowan gazes back out at the road.

"When I went on tour with the band after meeting Adam, Mike was the first one of the guys to really make me feel welcome. I was so out of my element, and I think he could tell, because he went out of his way to make sure I felt comfortable and safe." She glances over at me, and the serious look in her eyes ensures I pay close attention. "Mike is one of the nicest, most considerate, most hilarious, most selfless guys I know. He's not like other guys, Hailey. He's special."

I simply stare back at her, silently agreeing with everything she's saying.

"Anyway," she continues, looking back out at the road, "after one of the shows that weekend when I was on tour with them, he and I went to this little pizza shop and got a pizza, and we somehow ended up talking about his ex-girlfriend."

I swallow hard, and Rowan asks, "He said her parents owned a pig farm that had a strawberry patch?"

I nod, confirming that he was talking about Danica.

"We talked about her for a little bit, and I eventually asked Mike why none of the guys had girlfriends. I wanted to know why Adam didn't have one, and he told me that Adam, Shawn, and Joel didn't want one." I crack an amused smile, since they have all very clearly changed their minds, and Rowan mirrors it before she says, "But do you know what Mike said about himself?"

I wait for her answer, and she holds my gaze. "He said he hadn't found the right girl yet."

A torrent of emotions whirls in my stomach—I feel proud and incredibly lucky that he thinks I'm the right girl, but worried and pressured that I'm not.

I'm nothing special. I know he thinks I am, but I'm not.

"It's been kind of . . . *sad* isn't the word I'm looking for . . . but, I mean, Adam, Joel, and Shawn all settled down before Mike, when Mike has been the one open to finding love this whole time." Rowan looks over at me again, worrying her lip like she's trying to choose her words carefully. "I love Mike like a brother, Hailey. I want him to be happy."

I know what she's telling me. She's telling me not to break his heart. I can hear myself having this conversation with Luke's girlfriend in a few years.

"Me too," I say, and I mean it.

Mike deserves the girl he's been waiting for . . . I just don't know how I can be her, when Danica is so determined to make sure I'm not.

Chapter 37

Some days at the animal shelter make me not want to live on this planet anymore. Like days when it's time to evaluate the dogs that were rescued from a dogfighting ring a few days ago, when I have to see just how devastating human cruelty can be. Even though we're a no-kill shelter, many of the pit bulls are too aggressive to be adopted and have to be put down. And even more are simply injured beyond hope.

As part of my internship responsibilities, I help evaluate the rescues, and each time one lunges at me or goes ballistic on a plastic hand or stuffed dog, I fight back tears. I know they weren't born this way—they were *made* this way—and it's why my heart shatters every time I have to walk one of them to the back room.

I go home that night mentally, physically, and emotionally drained. I went directly to the animal shelter after Rowan drove me to my car, and it's been a terrible, long day. In the clothes I arrived at the video shoot in the night before, I sit in my apartment parking lot, wondering if I should just sleep in the backseat of my car.

I slept with Danica's ex-boyfriend last night. I had his fingers and his tongue and his sex deep inside me, and every second of it was bliss. He made me feel things that I've never felt in my life before, and that I doubt I could ever feel for any man again. And I can't help feeling like it's written all over me—like as soon as I walk inside, she'll be able to see his kisses on my neck, his fingerprints all over my skin.

I fiddle with my thumbs and fiddle with my phone, until I'm typing a text to Rowan just to keep from fiddling anymore.

Me: I'm sitting in front of my apartment.

Rowan: Any particular reason why?

Me: Scared to face the Hell Beast.

Rowan: Want to spend the night here?

I stare at the lit windows of the home I share with my cousin, knowing I can't run forever. She's in there, she's awake, and I'll have to face her sooner or later.

Me: No. But if you don't hear from me tomorrow, find out where she dumped my body.

With forced bravado, I pocket my phone and order my feet up the entry stairs. Then I wrap my hand around the knob and push it open as quietly as humanly possible. I'm hoping Danica will be in her room and that I'll be able to sneak into mine, but her dark eyes zero in on me like a heat-seeking missile that's found its target.

"Did you know Mike's band shot their video yesterday?" she accuses at me as she launches off the couch, her teeth snapping.

"Huh?"

It's all I can manage. She's invading my bubble, dressed in a tight black mini dress with her hair and makeup looking professionally done, and I know she wants to tear me to pieces. I realize she must have shown up at the clearing only to find it empty. Maybe there was a cleanup crew picking up all the trash—and Danica standing there in her dress.

I want to feel bad for her, but it's hard when she's standing in my face like a death eater about to devour me whole. With panic surging through me, I respond with the first thing that comes to mind, which is definitely *not* the detailed excuse Dee instructed me to go with. "No!"

Danica narrows her eyes. "Oh really? Then where were you last night? Did you even *come home*?"

"I was on a date." The lie comes as a surprise even to me, and Danica's eyes seethe with suspicion.

"A date with my boyfriend?" she hisses.

It takes everything in me to not shout that he's not

her fucking boyfriend, that he's *mine*, but I conquer the urge and hiss back at her. "With a guy from school. I spent the night at his place just to get away from you for a night."

Danica's face contorts into an ugly mask of disgust. "Wow, you really *are* a whore."

"Takes one to know one," I snap, and I stand there waiting for her to punch me in the mouth. Her fists are clenching at her sides, her eyes narrowed like a viper's.

"Prove it," she demands as I quiver with a mix of fear and impatience.

"Prove what?"

"Call him. Speakerphone. Fucking prove it, or get the hell out of my apartment."

I hide the panic that squeezes in my veins as I try to think of some way to get out of this. But Danica's narrowed eyes and her squared hips tell me that she's not going to buy any excuses I try on her. With my heart pounding in my chest, I pick up my phone, and I find a number.

"You vixen!" Leti answers, and I jump in to stop him from spilling last night's secrets.

"Leti, my paranoid cousin thinks I was at some video shoot with her ex-boyfriend last night." Danica's nose reddens with anger, but I press on with my veiled explanation. "Will you please tell her where I was so she'll get off my back?"

My fairy godfriend pauses for a moment that feels like an eternity, but then he effortlessly comes to my rescue. "Are you cheating on me?"

"No!" I play along. "She just thinks—"

"I take you to the fanciest restaurant in town," Leti pretend-complains. "I open your door and pull out your chair and give you a gorgeous bouquet of apricot amaryllis—" I hold my breath, wishing he would have just settled on *roses*. "I treat you like my queen, and you're fucking cheating on me?"

Danica's expression is something between suspicious and satisfied. I can tell she's enjoying the fact that she's causing problems in my fictional relationship, and I press on.

"I'm *not* seeing anyone else! That's my whole point here!" I turn away from Danica for show. "But for the record, it's not like you ever asked me to be exclusive anyway."

"Well, I'm fucking asking, Hailey. I can't stand the thought of you being with anyone else. You're special to me, girl. I want to spoil you and treat you like the princess you are to me."

I nearly laugh when I glance over my shoulder and see the jealousy that flashes across Danica's face, and I silently vow to hug the life out of Leti next time I see him.

"Are you satisfied?" I whisper-yell at my cousin, and she glares at me but lets me turn off the speakerphone and walk away. In my room, I walk to the far corner and slide down onto the floor.

"You really are my fairy godfriend."

Leti laughs. "She bought it?"

"I think she's even jealous."

He laughs harder, and I smile as I realize I can't wait to get to know him better. My circle of friends in this town keeps growing and growing, and I don't want to leave. It only cements my resolve to continue putting up with Danica, to continue trying to stay one step ahead in her game.

"I didn't even get to use my best line," he pouts.

"Use it."

"Okay, are you sure you're ready for this?"

I grin and tell him I am, and Leti clears his throat.

"Ever since I adopted that Saint Berdoodle from you at the pound, girl, I've wanted to get all up in *your* pound, kna wh'am sayin'?"

"Why are you talking like a gangster?" I ask through my laughter, and Leti snickers.

"'Cuz I've gone hard for you, girl."

We both laugh like immature ten-year-olds until another call rings on the line, and I pull the phone away from my ear to see Dee-licious-andra's name on my phone. A hot blush settles under my skin, and I press the phone back to my ear, whispering, "Hey, Leti, Mike's calling so I've got to go. Thanks for covering for me."

"Anytime, Hailey-rella."

I take a deep breath before I answer Mike's call, and then I accept it and find my voice. "Hey."

"I miss you."

Three words in his smooth baritone, and butterflies whirl in my stomach.

"You've only been gone a few hours," I point out,

wishing I had an ice pack to press against my heated cheeks.

"I know. Tomorrow is going to suck."

I close my eyes and smile, wishing I didn't have to worry about the volume of my voice as I talked to him. I wish my walls didn't have ears.

"Did you get a ride back to your car?" he asks, and I tell him Rowan drove me. I even tell him about having pancakes with her at IHOP, but I don't tell him about the serious conversation we had afterward.

I ask him how his flight was, and he tells me the band got recognized for the first time in the airport. I ask how Canada is, and he tells me about the freezing weather. I ask how preparation for the show is going, and he tells me they just finished sound check and that kids are already lining up outside.

"What about you?" he cuts in before I can ask anything else. "How was your day?"

I think back to the pit bulls I basically signed death warrants for, and my stomach sinks. "Fine," I say, knowing Mike has to go onstage soon. He doesn't have time to hear about it, and even if he did, I wouldn't want to burden him.

"Why are you lying?"

"It's a long story," I confess. "I know you don't have the time to—"

"I've always got time for you, Hailey. And if not, I'll make time. Now talk to me."

Something in his voice undoes me, and I unbottle the emotions I've been storing all day. I share it all with him—the hatred I feel for the dogfighters, the hope I have for the puppies and some of the younger dogs, the overwhelming sadness I feel for the dogs we couldn't save. I tell him about the dreams I have about the animals who never leave the shelter, and Mike listens to it all. He listens to the negative and helps me focus on the positive, asking how I'm going to rehabilitate the young dogs, and by the time I'm finished unloading the weight that's been on my shoulders since I walked into that shelter this afternoon, I actually feel . . . better. I feel like I might actually be able to sleep tonight.

"Thank you," I say as I crawl under my covers. It's nearing ten o'clock, which means it will soon be time for him to go onstage, if he's not already late. "I feel better. You can go be a rock star now."

"What if I don't want to go?" Mike asks, and I smile as I pull my covers up to my chin.

"I'm pretty sure you have to."

We both linger on the line, and I force myself to ask, "Can you do me a favor though?"

"Name it."

"Send me a picture?"

"Of what?"

"You," I answer timidly. "I don't have one."

I know I could go online. I'm sure there are plenty of pictures, videos, and interviews. Mike is famous, and I don't doubt I could find a picture of him that would make my heart melt.

But I want one for me. I want a smile from him that's *just* for me.

He agrees to send me one, and he wishes me sweet dreams. I reluctantly hang up since I know he really does have to go, and a few seconds later, a text dings on my phone.

I open the photo and smile at my screen as I stare into his warm brown eyes. He's backstage at an obviously packed show, judging from all the people I see buzzing around in the background, but his soft smile is just for me. It touches his eyes and makes my heart swell, and I hold the phone to my chest as I fall asleep that night, wishing he wasn't so far away.

Chapter 38

MIKE SENDS ME a photo every day for almost a week. We even try to video chat a couple times, but the connection is always spotty since he's constantly on the go, so eventually, we give up trying. He flew to Beijing last night, so now we're on a twelve-hour time difference. He left me a voice mail before I woke up this morning, wishing me a good day and telling me how much he missed waking up next to me. My heart ached as I listened to his voice, knowing the sun was setting where he was, even as it rose outside my window.

The memory of his fingers in my hair begins to feel like a fading dream, but I try to convince myself that his voice is enough. I miss the curve of his smile and the scent of his skin and how messy his hair looks first thing in the morning. I miss sitting next to him on his couch. I miss stealing glances across the room. I miss the warmth of his lips and the softness of his touch, and my heart aches with the loss of all these things even though I really only had them for a heartbeat in time.

Yet in spite of it all—in spite of the wound in my chest that reopens every time we hang up the phone—I feel myself falling even more for him. The distance between us gets greater and greater, but each passing day brings us closer and closer. He's the first thing I think about when I wake up in the morning, and I've never been so excited for anything as I am for the moment his name flashes onto my phone.

"LET ME USE your phone," Danica orders on Friday after my morning classes, and I glance up from my spot on the loveseat to see her motioning for me to toss my phone to her on the couch.

"Use your own phone."

"I can't," she complains as she continues holding out her hand. Her feet are propped on the coffee table, her toes spread with foam separators as her glittery silver polish dries. We've been sitting together in silence for the last half hour while she painted her nails and I worked on a mountain of homework, since I'm sick and tired of imprisoning myself in my nine-by-ten bedroom just to avoid her.

"Why not?" I ask.

"Because Mike blocked my number. Now let me use yours."

I make a face and go back to ignoring her, since

that is *so* not happening for *so* many reasons. For one, when she put in his number, he would show up as Dee-licious-andra and I'd be royally screwed. And for two, I hate her guts and there's no fucking way in hell I'm going to give her *my* phone so she can try to win back *my* boyfriend.

"Oh, come on," she argues. "You're seriously going to be like that?"

I strangle my pencil as I try to solve organic synthesis problems. I used to think that hell must be filled with chemistry textbooks and structural formulas. Now, I'm convinced it must be filled with a million Danicas painting their toes on our communal coffee table.

She sighs dramatically and lowers her hand. "I can't believe you're still mad at me."

I gape at her, and she rolls her eyes.

"It's been like two whole weeks, Hailey. What are you going to do, stay mad at me forever?"

"You called me a *whore*," I remind her. "You trashed my room. You flipped my desk. You blackmailed me. You broke my computer—"

"Do you need me to buy you a new computer?" she asks. "Is that what this is about?"

I swear I see red. My mouth is hanging open, but Danica just sits there staring at me like *I'm* the one who has problems.

"If you need me to buy you a new computer, Hailey—"

"I don't need you to buy me a new fucking computer!"

"Then what is your problem?" She sits forward and plants her feet on the floor. "You're already dating someone else, so what are you still so mad about?"

I glare daggers at the numbers in my textbook, until eventually Danica asks, "Is he hot?"

I scowl up at her, and she tries disarming me with a smile.

"Your new guy, is he hot?" When I don't answer, she pouts. "Come on, Hailey. I know you're mad that I went so crazy, but can you blame me? My boyfriend got a crush on you while he was *sleeping* with me."

It's like a slap in the face, and the worst thing is that I don't even think she meant for it to be. She was just stating a fact. An observation. A truth.

Mike was sleeping with her when he had feelings for me.

"Did you do it on purpose?" she asks, and I focus on the way her brow turns in, the unguarded way her eyes study me as she waits for my answer.

"No," I tell her honestly, not needing her to elaborate any further. I didn't make Mike fall for me on purpose—I was too busy trying to keep *myself* from falling for *him*. I never considered him developing feelings for me even within the realm of possibility. I'm still not sure why he did.

Danica nods to herself, focusing on an invisible spot on the coffee table, and then she looks up at me again, "I should hate him, right?"

I don't know what to say to that. I feel like I'm slipping over a waterfall, drowning as I fall.

Danica props her feet back up on the table and begins applying a second coat of polish. "I wish I could, but I don't. I just want him. I messed things up with him, twice, and I want another shot."

"Why?" I ask, and when she questions me with her eyes, I clarify, "Why him?"

"Because I want him more than I've ever wanted anything," she answers simply, and I give my attention back to my textbook. Or I pretend to, at least. There's a feeling of wrongness smothering me like a woolen blanket in the dead of summer, and I don't know how to kick it off.

"Can I ask you something honest?" Danica says, and I reluctantly look up at her. "What do you think made him like you?"

My throat dries, and I shake my head. "I don't know."

"Come on, you have to have some idea," Danica persists. "I'm guessing he liked the whole 'nice girl' thing, but do you also think he found you attractive?" Her gaze skips to my crazy hair for just a second before resting on my face.

"I really don't know."

My cousin sighs. "Can you come shopping with me tonight? I need to get a new number, and I want to look for an outfit that will make him remember why he fell for me in the first place." She lowers one finished foot and concentrates on the other. "I was too busy obsessing over the band's music video, and I think he felt neglected. And then you showed up with that damn care basket, and—" She dismisses the past with a wave of her hand. "I just need to make him remember why he loves me."

"I'm heading to the shelter at three," I tell her, thanking God that I keep a busy schedule.

"Then tomorrow?"

"I—"

"Look, Hailey," Danica interrupts, pausing her toenail painting to level me with her stare. "I'm going to be really honest with you, okay? We both know I only moved to this town because I wanted to get back with Mike. You know that, I know that . . . My parents probably even know that too, but they're willing to ignore it as long as I stay in school. But the thing is, if I'm not with Mike, I don't *want* to stay in school. There's no reason for me to stay in this stupid town."

She lets that sink in before she continues, and I know where she's going even before she goes there.

"And we also both know why my dad jumped at the chance to pay for you to come here too. He thinks you'll help keep me in line, be a positive influence. You're here to babysit me, Hailey, but if I'm not here, there's no reason for you to be here either."

That suffocating blanket over my face grows heavier and thicker and hotter.

"I'm not blackmailing you into helping me, Hailey. I'm just telling the truth." She swipes the tiny brush over her little toe while I tumble over Niagara, entombed in my blanket. "So will you go shopping with me tomorrow?"

"I guess I have no choice."

When Mike calls me an hour later, it's one o'clock in the morning in Beijing. I pick up the phone, still trying to recover from my talk with Danica, and I spend the first few minutes of the call barely saying a word.

"Can I ask you something?" I cut in at a random point in the conversation. I'm not even sure what he was saying, since I was too busy replaying my conversation with Danica in my head.

"What is it?"

I take a steadying breath and release my lip from between my teeth. "When you realized you had feelings for me, were you still . . . did you and Danica . . . were you two still—"

I'm stuttering over my words, trying to hold together the pieces of my own fractured heart, when Mike says, "Whoa. *Whoa.* Hailey, *no.* I would never—"

"But Danica said—"

"Said what?" Mike scoffs. "Haven't you learned you can't trust a word that comes out of her mouth?"

"She said you fell for me when you were sleeping with her," I finish, and Mike growls into the phone.

"She just won't ever fucking stop, will she?"

My end of the phone remains silent as I squeeze my lip between my fingers at the far corner of my room. I'm sitting on a bed pillow on the floor with my head against the wall and a vise around my heart.

"Hailey," Mike says, "Danica and I only slept together *one* time since she came back around. The night you waited outside my tour bus, that was the *only* time. It's part of why she's been so pissed off at me all the time, because I wouldn't do it again. It just didn't feel right. Even that night, it felt so wrong—"

"Then why did you do it?"

Mike sighs. "I didn't even feel like I was in my own body that night. I'd spent years thinking about this girl I loved, and then there she was, and she just kept throwing herself at me, and—it was fucking stupid. It was so fucking stupid. Even when I was doing it, I couldn't look at her. I had to—" Mike abruptly stops, his voice pained. "You don't want to hear this."

"I need to," I tell him, and it's the truth. Danica's words are a ghost that will haunt me if I don't pull the floating sheet away from them.

"I couldn't even look her in the eye, Hailey. I flipped her over and took her from behind, and afterward, I felt fucking sick. She fell asleep, and I just felt so *wrong*. I was so confused. When you asked about her later, I told you she'd probably be sleeping a while, but really, I just didn't want you to wake her up. I couldn't even think straight."

"Why did you date her?" I ask.

"I don't know," Mike says, and even though I'm hurting, the sadness in his voice makes me want to reach out across thousands and thousands of miles just to hold him. "Stupid reasons. I felt like I needed to see if my feelings would come back. And I felt guilty about what we'd done on the bus . . . I'm not a one-night-stand kind of guy, Hailey. I felt guilty, like I owed it to her to at least give us a chance."

I stop punishing my lip, surprised by the easy way

his words comfort me. I knew he slept with Danica that night, and while I had thought the details would hurt me, they're cool relief over my skin. And when Mike tells me he felt like he owed Danica because of the mistake he made that night—I don't know why that makes me want to hug him, but it does.

"I love you," I say, and my heart slams against my ribs. My eyes widen when I realize what I just said, and I hold my breath, curl my toes, squeeze my fingers—

"Say that again," Mike says, and the gentle need in his voice pulls the words from my mouth.

"I love you," I repeat, releasing the death grip I have on my own fingers. I uncoil them from one another and try to breathe evenly, try not to panic, try not to have a heart attack. The line is quiet for so long that my anxiety kicks back up. "Hello?"

"I want to be with you so badly right now," Mike says. "I want to kiss you and spin you around and be inside you—"

A nervous giggle bubbles out of me, and Mike growls, "*Fuck*, I want to be inside you."

Heat sparks over my skin, and I blush furiously in my dimly lit room. "I miss you," I whisper, hearing the lust in my own voice.

Mike groans. "Jesus."

Spurred on by his hungry tone, my inner vixen re-emerges, and she's wearing a bloodred dress. "Do you miss me, Mike?"

"Hailey," he warns. "I'm standing in the corner of a greenroom filled with people right now."

"Which parts do you miss the most?" I purr, and when he curses into the phone, I can't help laughing.

"You're going to find out when I come home in five weeks, baby," Mike promises, his filthy tone sparking over my flesh.

His promise keeps me awake that night as anticipation and fear prickle over my skin. I lie in the dark, thinking, *Five weeks until I can lose myself in his arms again.*

Five weeks until I could lose it all.

Chapter 39

"WHICH COLOR?" DANICA asks, holding up two dresses worth more than my left leg—one teal, one bloodred.

"The left," I say, indicating the teal one as I stand with my back against one of the marble pillars inside a high-end retail store in our town shopping center. The judgmental looks the salespeople gave me as I walked inside the store made it *very* clear that they don't believe I belong here, and they're right. One look at a price tag, and I tucked my hands inside my pockets to keep from accidentally touching anything else. With my luck, it would end up smelling like dog, and I'd have to sell my soul to Danica to buy the damaged goods.

Danica ponders my suggestion for a moment, looking at both of the dresses. "Mike has always loved me in red though . . ." She giggles and hangs the teal dress back up on the wall. "My cheerleading uniform was red, and you should've seen the way he'd watch me at football games, Hail. I think that uniform was the only reason he bothered coming."

She smiles as she continues strolling around the store, and I consider stabbing out my eardrums with a clothes hanger as I follow.

Before we got here, she told me that she plans to find a few sexy outfits for a video message she's recording for Mike in a few days, one that she believes will make him take her back. And then she's going to send it to him—to my boyfriend.

"You should try something on," she tells me as she walks around the two-story store. Soft golden light illuminates the interior, but bright stage lights are hung on the ceiling for show. This entire shop is like one big runway—one that wasn't built for the tattered tennis shoes on my feet.

"No thanks."

"Oh, come on. Shopping is no fun if we don't both try stuff on. Don't you try things on when you go shopping with your girlfriends?"

I guess maybe I would if I ever actually had the money to go shopping . . . or if I ever had close girlfriends before Rowan and Dee . . .

"You do have girlfriends, right?" Danica asks with her brow knitted.

"Of course I have girlfriends," I scoff. "I just don't really like shopping."

Danica eyes me skeptically before turning back to a rack against the wall. "We just need to find something you'd like. Liiike—oh!" she squeals, tugging a dress from the rack. "Like this! This is gorgeous. What do you think?" She holds the garment up so I can see it: a very short, very slinky pale pink dress. "Hailey, you would look *so* pretty in this."

"How much is it?" I ask on impulse, but Danica simply shakes her head.

"It doesn't matter. Do you think it's pretty?"

The truth is, I do. It's made of some soft, flowy material that I want to reach out and feel between my fingers, and the color is beautiful.

"I wouldn't look good in something like that," I answer, but Danica rolls her eyes.

"Hailey, do you like it or not?"

When I nod, she grins from diamond-pierced ear to diamond-pierced ear.

"Good. You're trying it on."

IN A FITTING room that contains a plush, embroidered, fringed freaking sitting chair and a hanging crystal chandelier, for God's sake, I set my five-dollar purse down and take a calming breath. I'd honestly rather be cleaning up dog poop than tiptoeing around this store.

I spent all yesterday evening at the dog shelter, and I worked there again this morning. With the arrival of all of the new dogs rescued from the fighting ring, the shelter is extremely overcrowded and grossly understaffed. The few volunteers who work there have been stretching themselves thin, myself included. Rehabilitating abused animals is a time-consuming process, but it's worth it to see them go home with a new family, one that will play with them and take care of them and teach them what it means to be loved.

I don't have time to be trying on dresses I can't afford, but here I am, carefully slipping one over my head. I let it slide over my skin—it's almost as soft as the dress Dee made me for the music video, but not quite—and I stare down at my socked feet before letting my eyes travel up the length of the wall mirror in front of me.

It's not anything I would have picked for myself—a cotton-candy-pink dress that's high in the front but dives low in the back. I zip up the skirt portion of it and stand there studying myself until I bend down to yank off my neon-green socks.

With my bare toes on the white marble floor, I turn this way and that. I run my hands down the skirt. I spin a little back and forth to watch it fan out around me. I smile in the mirror.

"Are you ready?" Danica calls from the dressing room across from me, and I swallow as I open the door and step out to meet her.

She takes my breath away in the bright red dress she chose, which looks like it was made just for her. It fits like a glove on top and ends at a soft hem at the middle of her thigh, and I forget all about the reason she's buying it as I open my mouth to tell her how pretty she looks.

"Oh," she interrupts, scrunching her nose at me. I close my mouth, and she steps in close enough for me to see the line between her brows when she furrows them in disapproval. "You're right. This dress doesn't look good on you at all."

I stare down at the pink dress that had made me smile at my reflection just a minute ago, and then up into Danica's dark brown eyes. "What's wrong with it?"

"Well, for one, it's supposed to end here, not here," she says, poking my thigh and then just above my knee. "I mean, I suppose you could get it hemmed, but—" She lifts her hand to her mouth to conceal a quiet chuckle. "Hailey, you've got the worst chicken legs. I figured you would have grown out of those by now."

My cheeks stain red as I stare down at my knees while Danica circles behind me.

"Even your shoulders are bony." She comes to face me again, shaking her head. "No, this dress looks terrible on you."

"Oh . . ."

"We'll find you another one," she says with a white smile before spinning around. "What do you think of mine?"

"It's really pretty," I tell her, still thinking of my chicken knees and resisting the temptation to frown down at them.

"What about the back?" Danica asks, turning away from me.

I take in her smooth, lightly tanned skin; the perfect lines of her shoulder blades; the generous slope of her curves; her long, not-bony legs. "Beautiful," I tell her, and she beams when she turns back around.

"I think Mike is really going to love this one," she says, and I force a smile to keep my face from falling. "Okay, get that hideous dress off and let's pick out something else for round two."

WE'RE ON ROUND five when Danica suggests we split up. "I'm going to check out those racks over there, but find something you like, okay? Remember, we're having fun."

Fun, I think as I walk through the store, positive that I'm being watched by security to make sure I don't steal anything. After the past four *fun* rounds of trying on dresses, I'm convinced that my knees are too bony, my legs are too stubby, my hips are too narrow, my shoulders are too pointy, my breasts are too small, my skin is too pale.

It's not like I could afford any of these dresses anyway, but they're all so pretty . . . and I guess I just wanted to look pretty *in* them.

I stop in front of a mannequin at the front of the store and chew on my lip as I admire it. She's propped up on a pedestal wearing the most gorgeous dress I've ever seen. It's sleeveless, but high-backed and long, so it would hide my bony shoulders and bony knees. The material is a soft cotton gauzelike fabric in a mist-gray color, with vibrant blue wildflowers gathered into striking bouquets throughout the pattern. The waist is cinched with a blue lace overlay, and the bottom is shaped into pretty, uneven layers lined by the same bright blue as the lace and flowers. The whole dress is stunning, and I stand there too timid to touch it.

"Oh, I *love* this," Danica says from beside me, and I snap out of whatever daydream I was in. She smiles down at me. "You should try it on."

I worry my lip as I stare back at the dress, but Danica is already snapping her fingers to get the closest saleswoman's attention. She makes them find one in my size, and then she nudges me toward the dressing rooms while she continues browsing the racks for something to try on herself.

Back in my crystal-chandeliered, fringed-chaired room, I remove my tennis shoes and socks and threadbare jeans. I tug my T-shirt over my head and unclasp my bra. I place all my secondhand clothes on the absurdly expensive-looking chair, and then I stand there staring at the beautiful dress hanging against the wall in front of me. I don't dare glance at the price tag before I remove it from its hanger and slip it over my head.

It's magic, how it molds against my curves. The V-cut top pulls my breasts up and together in a way that's sexy without being indecent, and the lace cincher hugs the curve of my waist flatteringly. The bottom drops down to just above my ankles, and I curl my bare toes against the polished floor as I stare down at it.

"Hailey, you almost ready?" Danica asks, and I hear her close and lock the door to her own dressing room.

"Yeah."

"Okay, hold on a sec."

I study myself in the mirror as I wait, wondering if

Mike would think this dress is as pretty as I do. Would he think I'm pretty wearing it?

I consider looking at the price tag, but instead, I simply smile at myself in the mirror. Maybe I should snap a picture with my phone. Maybe I should send it to him.

"Alright, you ready?" Danica calls, and we both step out of our dressing rooms at the exact same time—wearing the exact same dress.

I freeze when she emerges in my soft gray fabric and bright blue wildflowers—her skin a shade tanner, her legs a lot longer, and her long copper hair cascading softly over her shoulders while mine curls wildly around my face. The bottom hem hits her shins at a much more flattering spot, and I notice all these details as she steps forward with a smile on her face.

"What do you think?" she asks, and honestly, I think I want to cry.

Danica turns us both toward the gold-rimmed mirror at the end of the hallway, and I see just how ridiculous I look standing next to her. She looks like a runway model born for this catwalk of a store, and I look like a beggar child who snuck in to try on her clothes.

"I think you found the perfect dress," she praises as she watches herself walk toward the mirror and away from it again. She beams as she closes the distance between us, her lips turning up and her eyes sparking prettily. "Mike is going to die when he sees me in this."

She bends down to hug me tightly before disappearing back inside her fitting room, and behind my own closed door, I try not to tear the dress as I rush to pull it over my head.

I know Mike will think it's beautiful, but pretty dresses like this weren't made for girls like me.

They were made for girls like Danica.

Chapter 40

"SHE'S NOT THRIVING. She's losing weight," my boss says two days after my hellish shopping trip with Danica. I hook my fingers into the chain-link cage as I frown at the mutt balled up in the corner. She looks like a golden Chow mix, but her ice-blue eyes make me think part Border collie or Siberian husky.

"Was she one of the bait dogs from the fighting ring?" I ask, and Barb nods solemnly. Along with the pit bulls we seized a week and a half ago, we rescued a few bait animals—animals that would have been used to help train the pits to fight and kill. The rabbits and kittens went to other facilities, but the puppies and our golden Chow mix stayed here.

"When she got here, her snout was duct-taped shut, but they didn't break her teeth or anything, so she can eat . . . She just won't."

"Who's been her primary caretaker?" I ask, since all

of the volunteers were assigned their own group of new arrivals. The plan was for the dogs to bond with one new person before we started switching things around to get them properly socialized.

"Gabe," Barb answers. "He has to carry the poor baby outside just to get her to use the bathroom. Otherwise, she just pees on herself. She's too scared to leave her cage."

"How old is she?" I wonder through the emotion in my throat, and Barb shakes her head.

"Two, maybe three. She's a little old for a bait dog. We thought maybe she was stolen from someone, but she's not chipped, and no one has reported a dog like this missing." Barb sighs heavily over the sound of other dogs barking throughout the shelter. Their noise echoes off the walls, terrifying our poor golden. "My guess is she was a stray they picked up and decided to use."

I crouch down as I stare into the cage, wishing the dog would stop tucking her head under her body. If she doesn't adjust, she's never going to get adopted. "Can't anyone foster her?" I ask, even though I already know the answer.

"Beth tried," Barb says. "But she has other dogs, so it wasn't working. Goldie here wasn't aggressive or anything—she was just terrified. She ended up urinating and defecating in the house just like she does in her cage. Beth and her husband tried kennel training her, but then she wouldn't come out of the kennel. It was just too much."

I nod in understanding. Beth is almost as tiny as I am, and I can't imagine her trying to pick up a urine-soaked golden Chow and carrying her outside for every single bathroom trip.

"How is she on walks?" I ask softly, still holding out hope that the golden will at least glance in my direction.

"She just balls up until Gabe brings her back inside," Barb says. "He's doing his best with her . . . but we don't call you the dog whisperer for nothing, Hailey."

I glance up at Barb from where I'm still crouched in front of the cage, and she gives me a weak smile.

"What do you want me to do?" I ask.

"I don't know. But I know you'll figure it out."

THAT NIGHT, AFTER ordering the meatiest, greasiest, grossest thing on McDonald's menu, I sleep in a cage. With a McDouble unwrapped and resting on my lap, I sit at the opposite corner of the cage from the golden Chow, and I try coaxing her out of her shell.

I had tried offering her a piece of warm burger, but she only shivered in fear. Then I tried simply sitting next to her, but when I realized she wasn't going to stop shaking, I moved to the opposite corner.

I talk to her about how much I miss my boyfriend. I tell her about his tour, about the pictures he's sent me from Canada and China and Korea, about the food he's eaten in those places and how I really hope I get to try kimchi someday. The burger grows cold as I tell her how pretty she is, as I make up fictional stories about the life she's going to live once she gets adopted (beloved dog of a movie star, furbaby of a billionaire, spoiled pet of a sausage heiress), as I tell her about all the animals I miss back on my parents' farm. We chat about Teacup the pig and Harley the horse and Moose the bull, and eventually, I give the dog a name: Phoenix, since I pray she rises from the ashes.

I don't normally give the dogs names, since I'm always afraid of getting too attached, but Phoenix deserves a name, and a strong one. She eventually untucks her head from her body, watching me with her chin on her front paws as I talk. And when I run out of things to say, I offer her more burger, and I sing. She doesn't come to me, but her tail wags ever so slightly, so I lower the burger and continue singing. And when I run out of songs, I hum songs I make up myself.

I'm sleeping when I feel something wet on my hand, and my eyelids sneak open to see Phoenix sniffing at me. Her cold nose pokes at my knuckles, and I stay still as a statue as she inspects me. I don't even know what time it is, but the sharp ache in my back tells me that I've spent more than a couple hours sitting on the concrete floor.

I ignore the pain in my spine as I continue watching Phoenix check me out. She sniffs the burger but ignores it, smelling my shirt, my pants, my hand again. She nuzzles her nose under my palm, and I hold my breath. She nuzzles her nose under further, and I gently move my fingers against her fur.

Phoenix lets out a sharp cry at the movement, and I jerk my hand away, fearing I hurt her still-patchy snout, which just a week and a half ago had still been wrapped in duct tape. But as soon as I pull away, she pushes against me again, crying even louder when I try to yank my hand away again. Eventually, I realize she's crying because she's scared, because she wants me to protect her, and I pull her big body into my lap as she yelps and whimpers and cries.

"It's okay," I croon, trying to soothe her. "It's okay, pretty girl. I've got you. I've got you. Good girl. You're such a good girl."

I hold her as she trembles in my arms and tries to push herself even further into the circle of my body, and I don't know when I start crying, but at the back of that kennel, I cry along with her. My tears drip onto her golden fur as she leans on me for support, as she gives me her trust, and I try to show her a lifetime's worth of love in the way I squeeze her against me, the way I pet my hands over her precious face.

I hold her for hours like that, letting her lick my face and my arms and my hands as I pet her. I continue talking to her—about the meaning of her name, about the importance of eating, about the fact that I'm a vegetarian. She eventually falls asleep in my arms, and I don't leave until the following morning, when Barb arrives back at the shelter and orders me to go home. She smiles in spite of the sternness in her voice, thanking me for staying overnight but insisting I can't live there, and I cry on my drive home about the panicked look in Phoenix's eyes when I left her at the shelter.

For the next few days, I spend absolutely all of my free time there. If I'm not at school, sleeping, or taking care of necessary things like homework or personal hygiene, I'm working with Phoenix. On the third day, I get her to let me walk her the whole way outside, and it's such a huge step, I call Mike to celebrate as soon as I get the chance.

"This is Mike," his voice mail says. "Leave a message."

"Hey," I start, shouldering my phone as I rush onto campus to try to make my first class on time. I'm speed-walking down a sidewalk with a messenger bag slipping from my shoulder and a rock wiggling around inside my shoe. "I know you're probably onstage right now, but I just wanted to tell you I finally got that dog I told you about to go outside today. All on her own!" I smile and try to shrug the messenger bag back up onto my shoulder. "She still won't let anyone else touch her, but . . . I'm just really excited, and I wanted to tell you."

My smile starts to slip when nothing but silence replies, and I realize how badly I wish I could tell him my news in person, or at least have him on the other line of the phone. It's been so hard matching up our schedules this past week, and even though Mike has sent me flowers—which I was *extremely* lucky he sent to my work instead of the apartment I share with Danica—they only made me miss him more.

"Alright, well . . . I hope you're having a good show. I miss you. Maybe we'll get to talk later . . ."

I hang up the phone and concentrate on walking. To dull the ache of missing him, I focus on the things that I still have: school, work, Phoenix. But the more I focus on these things, the more distant Mike seems to get.

I don't have a boyfriend who is thousands of miles away . . .

What I have are dying flowers, a voice mail I know by heart, and boyfriend who's never here.

Chapter 41

ON FRIDAY AFTERNOON, Rowan and Dee kidnap me for ice cream and a funny movie, and I realize how much I needed it. My entire waking life has been spent either rehabilitating Phoenix or missing Mike—missing him during meals, during showers, during the quiet time before sleep. He calls me every day on the phone, or at least leaves me a voice mail or two, but it never feels like enough. It feels like eating gluten-free bread or sugar-free doughnuts. It's just not the same, and it's not what I really want.

On Friday night, he asks me out on a date, and a smile sneaks onto my face as I lie in my bed with my phone to my ear. "How are you going to take me on a date when you're a million miles away?"

"Ninety-seven hundred," Mike corrects, and I chuckle.

"You're keeping track?"

"Sometimes," he admits, and I can hear the bashful smile in his voice. "It's not that far. The moon is over two hundred thousand miles away, and man managed to travel that distance. You're only a flight away. You're practically down the street."

"Then I wish you'd come visit me," I say, unable to stop myself but hating the sadness that creeps into Mike's reply.

"Me too. I've never felt this way on a tour before."

"What way?"

"So . . ." He searches for the word. "Homesick. So *homesick*. I've missed my house before. My bed, my TV . . . But those things don't even matter anymore. I just want to hold you."

I know what he means, which is why there's nothing I can say. Talking about missing him isn't going to change the fact that I'm not going to see him anytime soon.

"Only thirty more days," he says, and I close my eyes. "So will you please go on this date with me tomorrow?"

"Where are we going?" I play along.

"My house. Normally, I'd pick you up in my big red truck . . ." His voice lowers, sending heat prickling across my skin. "You remember my red truck, don't you?"

I blush fiercely at the memory of all the things we did inside it—on the side of the road, and then in his driveway with the door hanging open—and Mike chuckles.

"You play dirty," I say, and his tone smolders.

"If I remember, Hailey, that's just how you like it."

Oh God. I groan and climb out from under my covers to open a window, letting the late October chill extinguish the fire blazing beneath my cheeks while Mike's sexy, confident laugh sounds against my ear.

"This is no way to ask a girl out on a first date," I scold so he'll stop trying to kill me with his deliberately sexy voice, and Mike laughs a little harder before he stops teasing.

"Okay. So my place, seven o'clock. Does that work?"

"What do you have planned?" I ask as I slip back under my covers, excitement thrumming through my veins.

"A surprise" is all he'll tell me, and for the first time in two weeks, I fall asleep looking forward to tomorrow.

Don't forget your key. Text me before you go inside.

Mike's text is the first thing I read in the morning, and it reminds me that today is our first date. I smile in the mirror as I brush my teeth, because even if he won't be there for it, he's taking me on a date, and the knowledge that Mike—Mike!—is taking me on a real date fills me with all sorts of giddy, girly freaking excitement. I tell Phoenix all about him that day, about his smile and his laugh and how skilled he was at teaching me to play the drums. And I leave the shelter early enough to shower and put on some non-dog-scented clothes, even though Mike won't be there to smell me.

At seven o'clock on the dot, I text him to tell him I'm in his driveway, and a second later, a video chat request appears on my phone. My eyes flash wide, since Mike hasn't had reception strong enough for a video chat since he left. It's been two entire weeks since I've seen him, and nervous butterflies swarm in my stomach.

The video chat rings three times before I muster the courage to answer it, and my heart slams against my ribs when I finally accept his call.

Mike's face instantly appears on my phone, and I don't know if I want to laugh or cry. The warmth that rushes through me when I see him makes it undeniable: I love him. I love him so much it hurts.

"Hey," he says, a sexy smile on his face, and a nervous, giddy, happy one sneaks onto my lips to smile back at him.

"I thought you weren't going to have good reception for a few more tour stops?" I ask, and he smiles wider when he hears my voice.

"I wasn't. I tracked down a special SIM card."

"Do you have tonight off?" I ask, and Mike shakes his head. He looks like he's in a hotel room, and I wonder what Indonesian city he's in, or if I could even pronounce it.

"No, just a few hours," he says. "But we don't have any flights or press this morning, so I'm all yours until sound check."

"Shouldn't you be out exploring the city? Seeing the sights?" I ask, feeling guilty for keeping him.

"No. I should be taking my girl on our first date."

He smirks at the blush that hides the faint freckles on my nose, and my cheeks stain even redder at the sexy way his mouth quirks up.

"I've missed making you blush," he says in that irresistible tone of his, laughing when I turn the phone away so he can't see me fan my cheeks.

When I finally turn the phone back around, the happy look in his deep brown eyes is enough to melt my heart. "Okay," he says, "pretend I'm opening your door for you, because I'm a gentleman like that."

I chuckle as I climb out of my car, and when I get to his front door, I use the key he gave me. Inside, he instructs me to go into the kitchen, and I immediately spot the massive bouquet of oversized sunflowers sitting in a pretty crystal vase on the counter.

"These are for you," he says, as if he's handing them to me, and my smile is unguarded as I let the sweetness of his gesture make me fall even more in love with him.

"How'd you get these?" I wonder as I brush my fingers over their summery yellow petals, and Mike tells me about a florist he found three towns over.

"They delivered them to Rowan," he explains, "and she brought them to the house for me since Adam and Shawn left my spare key at their place."

"I bet Adam and Joel hate you right now," I say with a laugh, knowing Mike is putting them to shame. They've done sweet things for Rowan and Dee—

flowers, chocolate, postcards—but nothing like planning a romantic date from ten thousand miles away.

Mike grins. "I'm sleeping with one eye open, trust me."

When a knock sounds against the front door, I startle and stare wide-eyed at the back of it.

"Dinner," Mike explains. "I hope you're hungry."

I open the door to find a teenage delivery boy standing there with a pizza in his hands. He hands me the warm box, tells me the tip is already covered when I frantically search for money in my pockets, and wishes me a good date.

In Mike's living room, I set the pizza on the coffee table and open the box, lifting an eyebrow when I see the toppings. "Half pepperoni?" I ask, wondering if he forgot I'm a vegetarian. The other half is my absolute favorite though—banana peppers and black olives.

Mike turns his phone so I can see the pizza on the bed beside him—half pepperoni, half banana peppers and black olives, just like mine. "I'm not too stoked about these banana peppers, myself," he complains, and I laugh.

"Why didn't you just get me banana peppers and olives, and you pepperoni?"

"Because this is date," he insists. "And since this is a date, we're sharing."

I fight back the happy tears threatening to spring to my eyes, grabbing a paper plate and napkins from the kitchen while Mike tells me how he had to special-order the banana peppers and have them shipped to the hotel so he could have them as a topping. It makes me realize he's been planning this for a while, and once again, I feel weightless as I fall.

We talk and tell stories about our days as we eat our pizza, and I laugh at the face Mike makes when he tries a piece from my half. After two slices, I'm full, and he tells me to check the back porch. In front of his patio door, I find a box filled with souvenirs from all the places Mike has been—Canada, China, Korea, Indonesia. There is even some Indonesian candy called Berri Bonz, and Mike tells me he's held off on trying it since he wanted us to try it together.

We both pucker up at the sourness of the candy, and I laugh hard when Mike's eyes start to water. Eventually, our eyes stop welling from the sourness, and start welling from how hard we're laughing. He teaches me a game called *semut, orang, gajah*, which is basically the Indonesian version of rock, paper, scissors, and I almost forget that he's not with me—that he's still on the other side of the world.

The hours pass quickly—too quickly—because before I know it, it's eleven o'clock my time and someone is knocking on Mike's hotel door. He sighs heavily and stares at me through the phone. "They're saying it's time for sound check."

"That's a shame," I joke to keep myself from begging him not to go. I can tell Mike is struggling enough without me adding to it. "I'm pretty sure you were going to get lucky."

He gives me a half smile, and I return it. "Really? On our very first date?"

"It was a damn good date," I tell him, and his smile stretches just a little wider.

"You really liked it?"

"I loved it," I assure him, taking a deep breath to soothe my stinging eyes. "Thank you."

"I'll take you on even better ones when I get home."

"I believe you."

Mike's voice softens when he says, "I love you, Hailey."

"I love you too," I tell him, my heart already twisting from the goodbye I know is coming.

"Sweet dreams, baby."

"Have a good day."

THAT NIGHT, I don't have it in me to leave Mike's house. In his room, I help myself to one of his giant T-shirts, and I crawl under his covers. His pillow still smells like him, and I smile against the soft cotton when I realize he ate banana peppered pizza and sour candy for breakfast, since our date started at six o'clock in the morning for him.

His hair was damp, his face was clean-shaven, and he was wearing a T-shirt and jeans, which means he'd woken up ridiculously early just to shower and get ready for our date. He ordered me flowers and candy and made me feel like I was traveling the world with him, and I don't know how I got so lucky to deserve a man so thoughtful, but I never want to let him go.

Not even if Danica is determined to win him back.

Not even if he has girls pining after him in every country of the world.

I want to keep him.

But with Danica's threats hanging over my head and two years of school left before I graduate, before I can get a decent job and apply for an assistantship to cover my doctorate, I'm just not sure how I can. In twenty-nine days, Mike will want to take me on real dates, and it will be impossible to keep him a secret.

Chapter 42

"You never came home last night," Danica accuses with a devilish smirk when I finally return home to our apartment Sunday evening. After leaving Mike's place this morning, I spent the afternoon trying—and failing—to get Phoenix to let anyone else pet her, and my brain is so fried, I can't even think of anything to say.

"I, uh—"

"Have you slept with him?" she asks, and my face goes slack with panic.

Danica laughs and sets down her textbook, and while I should be relieved she's actually studying for once in her life, I'm too busy trying to decide if I should run back out the front door before she can catch and gut me like a pig.

"Oh, come on, Hailey, don't hold out on me," she pouts. "My sex life is dead until Mike comes home.

I'm trying to be good and not cheat on him, but I need details."

She's clearly not referring to Mike, so I search my brain . . .

"You mean Leti," I guess, and Danica raises a perfectly shaped eyebrow.

"Is there someone else?" At the panic that flashes across my face again, she sits forward on the couch. "Oh my God, two?!"

"No, no," I stutter. "I just, I didn't think you remembered him."

"Hailey Harper!" Danica scolds. "Stop lying. You're terrible at lying."

I make sure my lip is relaxed and freed from my teeth when I say, "I swear, just Leti."

Danica narrows her eyes at me, but then her mouth curves into a satisfied smile. "Okay, so what did you two lovebirds do last night?"

"Just hung out . . . ate pizza . . ."

Her face falls. "*Pizza?* Seriously?"

I think of the half of a pepperoni pizza I had to throw out this morning, since Mike had eaten his half in Indonesia, and I give her a genuine smile. "It was fun."

"Did you at least have some *real* fun afterward?" she asks, and when I don't answer her, she says, "You *have* slept with him, right?"

Again, I stand there with my tongue tied.

"Oh my God! Hailey, you're not a virgin, are you?"

My face is bright red when I throw up my hands.

"No! God, no." I drag my fingers through my hair as I go to the kitchen for a glass of water, and Danica trails gleefully behind me.

"You had me worried there for a second." She hops up on the counter, perching her toes on the edge. "So when was it? Where was it? Who was he?"

"Who was what?" I ask after gulping down some much-needed water.

"Your first. You've never told me."

"Oh." I drink more water to stall, wondering when Danica and I suddenly became best friends. Eventually, my glass turns up empty. "Um . . ."

Danica grins as she waits.

"A guy named Will. Senior year. Barn."

"Barn sex," she chides with a friendly laugh. "How romantic."

I smile and let her teasing relax me. "You?"

Her smile softens, her brown eyes warming with memory. "Junior year. Prom. Mike."

My heart skips a painful beat, and I choke out, "Mike?"

"Don't sound so surprised," Danica says with another laugh. "Mike and I started dating when we were fifteen, Hailey. Who else would it have been? We were both virgins. We gave our virginities to each other.

"It was pretty romantic, actually," she continues while I just stand there frozen in hell. "He got us a hotel room, and I think he was even more nervous than I was. His hands shook as he struggled with the ties of my dress." She smiles with her cheek resting on her knees. "It was so adorable."

"I've never had anyone make love to me the way he made love to me," Danica says, and the acid in my stomach crawls to the back of my throat. I should have known Mike was her first, but I . . . just didn't think about it. I still don't want to think about it. I desperately need to get out of this kitchen, or I'm going to be sick on her silver toes.

"I just didn't expect him to be so *big*—" she continues, and I thank God when my phone rings in my pocket.

"Hello?" I answer, walking away from Danica before she can notice the pallor that's spread across my face. I listen to Luke tell me about some new achievement he got in Deadzone Five, and I reel from the realization that Danica was Mike's first, and she was his.

Even though I wasn't in love with Will, I'll never forget the way the barn smelled of freshly cut hay that night, how nervous he looked as he tore open the condom, the quiet way he told me that he thought I was the most beautiful girl in school.

Just like Mike will never forget how beautiful Danica looked in that hotel room, how he struggled with the ties of her dress, how it felt to be inside her—and he loved her, so the memory will mean so much more to him. Fifty years from now, he'll still carry it with him.

They were each other's first loves, first times, first heartbreaks. And I can't help feeling like an intruder as I fall asleep that night, imagining the way he loved her.

"Did you know Mike and Danica lost their virginities to each other?" I ask Rowan and Dee on Wednesday afternoon at the campus coffee shop. I've spent the past three days trying not to think about it . . . and then I've thought about it, and thought about it, and thought about it.

"Ew," Dee says, her face scrunched with disgust. She sets her coffee down and pushes it all the way to the other side of the table.

"How do you know?" Rowan asks, and when I don't answer, Dee looks back and forth between us before pinning her eyes on me.

"Did Danica tell you that?"

I worry my lip, and Dee growls.

"Hailey, what did I tell you about listening to her? That girl is poison. *Poison.* If you start buying into her lies—"

"She wasn't lying though," I interrupt in defense of my cousin, and the corners of Dee's mouth turn down. Eventually, Rowan shakes her head.

"It doesn't matter if she was lying or telling the truth, Hailey. You know she's just telling you this stuff to get under your skin."

I stare down at my coffee thermos, because I'm not so sure. She was gossiping with me like we had never stopped being friends, like we were just two roommates talking about boys. I remember her easy laugh and her bright eyes, and I grip the thermos until the heat bites into my palms. "He'll never forget her," I say, and when I look up at Rowan, her blue-jean eyes are filled with sympathy.

"Of course he won't. She was his first love."

"Do you know what I remember about my first time?" Dee cuts in, finally pulling her coffee mug back to her side of the table. "I remember he lasted about two seconds, and it was horrible." She grabs a sugar packet from a container at the center of the table and begins shaking it violently. "It was like he didn't realize that *water* is required to go down a waterslide. The fucker just dove right in. I know your first time is supposed to hurt, but I swear to God, I had first-degree vagina burn."

Rowan chokes on her coffee as she laughs, trying not to spit it out, and I can't help cracking a smile.

Dee empties the sugar into her coffee and stirs it with a tiny straw. "Everyone's first time is horrible. I mean, Ro's was apparently pretty nice, aside from the whole being impaled on Adam's Viking-sized cock thing."

Rowan laughs harder and smacks Dee's arm, and my smile widens as I watch them together.

"I bet Mike only lasted two pumps," Dee continues. "Three, tops. Guys never set any endurance records their first times. I bet Danica even bitched him out about it afterward, because you *know* how she is."

I smile until it becomes too difficult to keep it on my face. "You don't think I'm a bad person for coming between them?" I ask, and Dee's perfect eyebrows slam together.

"Come here," she says, curling her finger to motion for me to lean across the table.

"Why?" I ask as I start leaning in. *Do I have something on my face?*

"Because clearly you need some sense slapped into you."

Rowan grabs Dee's arm out of the air, and I jump wide-eyed back into my chair.

"Hailey," Rowan says, releasing Dee's arm when I'm out of slapping range. "This is exactly what we've been trying to warn you about. Danica is going to do whatever she can to come between you and Mike. He didn't break up with her because of you—he broke up with her because she's horrible. She treated him like garbage. I mean, come on. Even if he wasn't with you, would you really want him with *her*?"

I'm shaking my head before I even realize it. "No."

"Right. Because you love him." Rowan smiles. "You want him to be happy."

I nod, and she reaches across the table to squeeze my hand.

"*You* make him happy. He loves you. It doesn't matter who his first was, because she's not his *only*. You could be his last, and the last is the one that counts."

"Damn, Ro," Dee says, relaxing in her chair. "That was beautiful."

Rowan smiles at me and lets go of my hand. "Do you feel better, Hailey?"

I nod, even though I'm not so sure. Because even

though everything they said makes sense, my heart still stings like it didn't hear a word.

"Hey," I eventually say to change the subject, since I know my feelings are something I'll have to wrestle with on my own. "Would either of you be interested in adopting a dog?"

Rowan and Dee remain silent for a while, until they eventually allow me to shift the conversation. They both tell me what I already guessed—that their apartment building doesn't allow pets—and I frown as two more doors close for Phoenix. They insist they'll ask around though, and I thank them as I think of my sweet golden Chow, who still won't walk beside anyone but me.

She's the only creature I tell all my secrets to—the only one who knows how much I'm struggling.

I miss Mike with every beat of my heart, every breath that fills my lungs. While he's living his dream, I'm drowning trying to reach mine. And I don't know how I can ever get it unless I'm willing to give him up.

Rowan is right. Mike deserves to be happy. But how can I make him happy when my own happiness is so out of reach?

Chapter 43

FOUR WEEKS.

It's been four weeks since I last saw him.

In Phoenix's cage, I tap my finger against a calculator, crunching numbers. I've tried to work this out a thousand different ways—a way I could give up my uncle's financial support and still finish getting my degree. I've accounted for theoretical jobs and maybe-possible scholarships. I've calculated living expenses and textbook expenses and miscellaneous expenses. I've added the numbers with my car and car insurance, without my car and car insurance, with Internet, without Internet, and it all comes out the same.

Not possible. Without sizable savings, which would take me years of living at home to accrue, it's just not possible.

"Hailey," Barb says, lifting the lock on the cage and coming in to sit next to me. Phoenix immediately skitters to the other corner of the cage, curling into her usual ball, and Barb frowns. "I need to talk to you."

"Okay?" I ask, setting my calculator down and staring up into the solemn face of my supervisor.

"We're transferring some of the dogs to another shelter this evening. We're over capacity, so they've agreed to take them in." She hesitates, and my heart constricts as I realize what she's about to say. "We're going to send Phoenix to them. They're a smaller shelter, so—"

"No," I say, already shaking my head in denial.

The corners of Barb's mouth sink down even further. "She's not adjusting, Hailey. I know you've gotten her to eat, but she's not putting on weight like she should. And she still won't let anyone else touch her. She's been here for almost a month—"

"I'll work with her more," I promise, but Barb simply shakes her head, pity filling her moss-green eyes.

"How? You're here every single day, Hailey. You do your homework in her cage. I know you want to help her, but this isn't healthy . . . I'm doing this as much for you as I am for her."

Tears fill my eyes as I stare across the cage at Phoenix, her glacial blues peeking out from under her paw as she watches us. I've tried everything I can for her. Even Rowan has come to the shelter, and we've tried to take her on walks together, but Phoenix hasn't opened up to anyone but me. I know that moving her to another shelter won't help—she'll close back down, she'll stop eating again, she'll stay curled in a ball until they realize she's never going to get better.

"I'm taking her home with me," I decide, and Barb pats my arm.

"Hailey—"

"I'm taking her home, Barb. You're not sending her away."

"You can't save them all, honey," Barb says, giving my arm a motherly squeeze. "I love you for trying. You know we adore you here. But you can't get too attached to the dogs, or we won't be able to keep you on staff."

"Then fire me," I say, already packing up my things. Barb could drop me from my internship for this, but I'm hoping—praying—she won't. "I love you too, but"—I point at the damaged dog still cowering in the corner—"I'm taking that dog home with me, and nothing you say is going to convince me to leave her."

IN MY CAR, I gaze out the windshield with my hands on the steering wheel and Phoenix sitting timidly in my passenger seat. I stare over at her, and she stares back at me. "Well, shit."

I walked her out of that shelter with no plan and no place to take her, and now we're just sitting in the parking lot, stuck. I know I can't take her back to my apartment, because I already discussed fostering Phoenix with Danica a couple weeks ago, and she reminded me that our lease strictly states no pets. I could always take her there anyway and keep her there low-key until

I figure out something else to do with her, but I know that would end in disaster; even though Danica has been less horrible than usual lately, I don't doubt she'd open the front door to let Phoenix "run away" if Phoenix dared touched one of her precious shoes or five-hundred-dollar purses.

"Shit," I repeat as I stare over at the dog I've grown to care for over these past few weeks. I've watched the fur grow through the injured parts of her snout. I've watched her eyes clear as she learned to trust. I've watched her tail wag excitedly when I praised her for finally being brave enough to go to the bathroom outside.

She chased a ball yesterday—really actually chased it across the shelter yard—and I can't let her go back to being a dog who's too scared to run or play or live.

She crawls across the console to sit on my lap, and I rest my forehead against the soft fur of her shoulder. "Why couldn't you let anyone else pet you?" I groan, and her tail slaps back and forth across my gearshift.

With a sigh, I lift my head, and she starts covering my face with sloppy dog licks until I nudge her back to her side of my car. "Where am I going to take you?"

She barks, and I take a deep breath before turning my key in the ignition. I pull out of the shelter parking lot, and I take her to the only place I can.

"BETTER TO ASK for forgiveness than permission," I convince myself as I walk Phoenix through Mike's front door. I called him but got his voice mail, and then I decided it's probably better to just *not* ask if he's okay with me keeping Phoenix at his place. I have no other options, and it's only temporary until I can find her somewhere else to live. He's my boyfriend, and he once told me I could live with him, so . . . that includes my dog too . . . right?

"You better be good," I warn Phoenix as she begins sniffing every surface of Mike's home—his couch, his coffee table, an old pair of tennis shoes he left by the front door. I half expected her to curl into a ball in some random corner, but instead, she tentatively explores the place, and when she realizes no one else is here, she starts wagging her tail and trots from room to room.

I sit on the couch watching her, wondering how in the hell this is going to work. This is just one more ticking time bomb I have no escape plan for. I'm winging life by the seat of my pants, and eventually, I know everything is going to blow up in my face.

For now, I try to ignore my growing anxiety, and I watch Phoenix chase shadows around Mike's living room, sniffing every nook and every corner.

When he calls me, I answer on the second ring. "Hey."

"Hey," he says, and my heart does that thing it always does lately when I hear his voice—it aches, like it's not sure if it wants to open up or shut down. "Sorry I missed your call. I was lugging my stuff up the stairs to my new hotel room. The elevator in this place is scary as shit."

"What floor are you on?"

"Six," he says, and I relax with a laugh.

"You carried your suitcase up six flights of stairs?"

"So did Shawn and Kit. Adam and Joel were the only ones dumb enough to ride that rickety elevator."

"I bet they're happy they did," I tease, but Mike just laughs.

"I doubt it. They're still stuck in there."

"They're *stuck*?" I gasp.

"The hotel has mechanics coming to get them out. The manager keeps trying to convince them it's good luck to get stuck in that elevator."

Through my laughter, I ask, "Shouldn't you be keeping them company?"

"I was going to, but they yelled at everyone to shut up so they could get some sleep in there." He yawns into the phone, and even though it's only two o'clock in the afternoon where I am, I yawn tiredly after him. "We flew all night. Everyone's exhausted."

"Do you have off tomorrow?" I ask.

"I wish. We have a show tomorrow night and press the following morning, but we have the rest of the night off after that. Then we fly to Australia, and the schedule is going to get really crazy."

"You should go see the city while you can," I say as Phoenix sniffs at my knee. I rummage a chew toy out of the purse I dumped on Mike's coffee table, and I toss it across the room for her.

"I miss you," Mike replies, and I know what he's really saying: that he'd spend his entire work-free evening talking on the phone to me if I let him.

"Go try the food so I know what to add to my food list," I say, and he chuckles. In every city, Mike has told me what local foods he thinks I'd like, and we've kept a running bucket list of foods I need to try. "What country are you even in now?"

"Malaysia. Which is only ninety-five hundred miles from you."

"Getting closer," I say as I pull my knees up to my chest in my corner of Mike's oversized couch. There are less than two and a half weeks until he comes home, but I still have no idea what I'm going to do when he gets here.

He still doesn't know about Danica's ultimatum. He has no idea that she gave me an impossible decision to make: Mike or school. Mike or my career. Mike or my future.

When he left, I had asked him not to send flowers to my apartment or anything. *If Danica calls you*, I'd told him, *don't mention me, okay? I don't want to rub our new relationship in her face. She needs time.*

It wasn't a total lie, but really, *I'm* the one who needs time. I need two more years of it, until I no longer have to depend on Danica's family to get me through school.

"I can't wait to take you out," Mike says, and a heaviness settles over me. I know he's not going to be okay with never being able to pick me up from my apartment. I know he's not going to be okay with never being able to be seen with me in public. I know he's not going to be okay with being my secret, and I know he deserves better than what I can give him. He deserves a beautiful, smart, wonderful girl who doesn't have to choose between him and everything else she's ever wanted.

"Did Danica send you her video yet?" I find myself asking, and I listen to Mike settling into his new room as he answers me.

"Yeah. A few days ago. Why?"

My brows knit, and I pick at a tiny hole in the knee of my jeans. "You didn't mention it."

"Oh, sorry," Mike says. "I didn't know you wanted me to."

I had told Mike about the video, and that Danica changed her number. But I couldn't give him her new number to block, since then she'd know I was still talking to him.

"What did you think of her gray and blue dress?" I ask, remembering the mist-colored dress I had tried on in the fancy fitting room, and how gorgeous the blue wildflowers printed on the fabric had been. I had felt beautiful in that dress until I walked out to see Danica wearing the same one.

"I didn't watch the video," he says. "I just deleted the message and blocked her new number."

"Oh."

"Did you really think I'd bother watching it?"

"Aren't you at least curious about what she has to say?"

There's a long moment of silence, and then Mike asks, "Do you know how many times I've thought about Danica since leaving?" I brace myself for the answer, and he says, "None. Not one. Do you know how many times I've thought about you?"

I barely have time to wonder before he answers, "I think about you all the time, Hailey. Do you know what I do before bed each night? I pull up this picture I took of you the morning I left. You were sleeping, and I know that makes me a creep, but I don't care. You were so damn beautiful, I just wanted to stare at you forever. So I took a picture, and every night, I look at it to remind myself that you're what I'm coming home to. That I'll get to see you like that again because I'm the luckiest fucking guy alive to have you at home waiting for me."

I'm speechless when he emphasizes, "I don't think about Danica, Hailey. I never think about her. She doesn't even cross my mind. If I'm thinking about a girl, it's you, because you're the only girl for me."

I'm silent for a long time while I try to calm my cartwheeling heart. And when I speak, I take the easy way out and crack a joke. "You took a picture of me sleeping?" I say with mock offense.

Mike chuckles. "You were covered up by the sheet, I promise."

"Creep."

"Worth it."

I smile at the way my heart flutters, and Phoenix jumps up on the couch beside me as I listen to what sounds like Mike fluffing a pillow on his end of the line. "Are you allergic to dogs?" I ask as I debate making Phoenix jump down. She lays her front paws on my lap, and I scratch her behind her ear.

"Why?" Mike asks.

"Just wondering . . ."

"That's pretty random."

"I like random."

"Hailey, if I was allergic to dogs, I don't think I could date you."

I bark out a laugh, knowing damn well I smell like dog ninety percent of the time, and Mike snickers against my ear. "You're such a jerk!"

"You set 'em up, I knock 'em down."

I'm still laughing when he says, "I love you, Hailey."

"I love you too," I say with a pink-tinted smile on my cheeks.

"Sixteen days."

"Sixteen days," I agree, petting a dog that shouldn't be here and carrying a decision I can't make

Sixteen days until I have no choice.

Chapter 44

I THOUGHT IT was lonely inside Phoenix's cage at the back of the shelter . . . but in Mike's house, with his big couch and his big bed and all of his very-Mike things, it's so much lonelier. He's everywhere—in his soft bedsheets, in his oversized TV, in the Teenage Mutant Ninja Turtle figurine he has sitting on his mantel (Michelangelo, of course). He's everywhere except really here.

I spend most of my time at his place, since I still haven't found anyone else to take Phoenix in (and if I'm being honest with myself, I haven't looked very hard), and every minute I spend in his house, with him on the other side of the world, makes the hole in my heart grow and grow and grow. After he leaves Malaysia, his schedule gets as hectic as he warned me it would. The texts become fewer and the calls grow further apart.

It's a mid-November Saturday, less than a week

before Thanksgiving, when my brother says, "I miss Mike."

It's been over two days since I last spoke to him myself. We've tried, of course—with him calling me, or me calling him—but after forty-eight hours of phone tag, I'm beginning to feel less like I'm missing him and more like I'm mourning him. For the past five weeks, I've felt like the calls and the texts weren't enough—like I needed more, always *more*—but now that I'm not getting them, they feel like everything. Which leaves me with nothing.

"I finally find some time to play Deadzone with you," I admonish Luke as I sit on Mike's couch with a game controller in my hands, "and all you're going to do is complain about missing Mike?"

"You suck tonight," Luke counters, and as if on cue, my player gets shot in the head for the umpteenth time.

"Sorry," I sigh, knowing he's right. I'm distracted.

Mike will be home in eight days, and even though I miss him more than I've ever missed anything in my life—even though all I want in this world is to hug him and kiss him and feel his arms around me—it feels like too soon. I still haven't figured out a way to continue dating him without having school pulled out from under me, and the thought of losing either one of those things has kept me up at night. It's given me nightmares I can't remember when I wake up near tears in the morning. But I can feel it—the stress that roots in my muscles and sits there like a toxin as I sleep.

"Do you miss him too?" Luke asks, and I know he's

still sneakily trying to push me into the relationship he has no idea I'm already in.

"Yes," I admit.

"Because you have a crush on him?"

"Because he doesn't talk as much when we play Deadzone," I quip, my player re-spawning as Luke laughs.

"Do you think he has groupies?" my little brother asks, and my throat dries.

"Yeah."

"Even in Asia and Australia?"

"Everywhere," I say, unable to deny how big the band is getting. Their new record label is promoting the hell out of them—I've heard them on the radio, I've overheard classmates talking about them at school, I've seen ads with the guys' faces on them posted in the campus coffee shop. Rowan has even complained about all of the people coming out of the woodwork, trying to be her friends simply because she's Adam Everest's girlfriend.

"That's so cool," Luke says as he dominates the game. He's racked up so many headshots, Mike would be proud. "I should get him to teach me to play the drums."

I smile sadly, remembering what a good teacher Mike was when he taught me in his garage. "Why, you want to be a rock star?"

"Hell yeah," Luke says as Phoenix makes herself comfortable on my bare toes. She's been doing really well since I brought her to Mike's house, eating plenty and making herself at home. She hasn't chewed or peed on any of his things—thank God—but I still have no idea what I'm going to do with her when he comes home next Sunday. "Who wouldn't want to have girls begging to be with them?"

"I thought you didn't like girls?" I ask, and my brother's tone makes it clear he thinks I'm an idiot.

"I'm *twelve*," he informs me with his signature preteen snark. "Someday I'll be Mike's age, and then all I'll want is to get laid."

I don't know which is worse—imagining my brother as a typical twenty-five-year-old male, or imagining my boyfriend as a typical twenty-five-year-old male. I make a face.

"I don't think Mike's like that . . ."

"Well, he should be," Luke argues, oblivious to the way he's making the stress under my skin thicken. "What's the point of being a rock star if you're not going to act like one?"

"I thought you wanted him to date me?"

"Would you?" Luke asks as we meet up in the map and begin scouting an enemy base. "If he asked you, would you go out with him?"

"He's Danica's ex . . ." I say, wishing I had never brought this up.

Luke sighs. "Yeah, I guess you're right."

"I am?"

"I *do* know the difference between right and wrong, Hailey," Luke complains. "I know that would be a messed-up thing to do."

My heart plummets to the floor, and my character dies five more stupid deaths before Luke and I finally call it quits. His words play over and over again in my head, and I have a sinking feeling he's right. About everything.

Mike should be enjoying his new fame, not spending all of his free time calling a hand-me-down farm girl back home, one who can't even afford pretty dresses or new boots. He could date singers or supermodels or actresses. He could date singers *and* supermodels *and* actresses.

And as for Danica . . . I *know* that me being with Mike is messed up. From the moment I saw him the night we waited outside his tour bus, I told myself to stay out of it. Out of her business. Away from her boyfriend. I know I'm the worst kind of person for letting myself fall for him, when he wasn't mine to fall for.

He was *hers*. He was my cousin's boyfriend.

And over the past five weeks, she's made it perfectly clear: she wants him back.

"DO YOU THINK she's prettier than me?" Danica asks the following afternoon while I try to help her study for a history exam she has coming up. It's necessary I keep up appearances at our apartment, but for the past hour, I've been the only person looking at her textbook since she's been too busy looking at her phone.

"Who?" I ask without glancing up, and Danica thrusts her screen in my face.

"Her."

My eyes refocus to see a picture of Mike, his hair a little longer than the last time I saw him in person. He's continued sending me a picture a day, but it's always a little shocking to see how much he's changing on tour—how his hair is getting messier and his face is becoming more chiseled. He has his arm around a pretty Asian girl with long black hair and rose-pink lips, and she's kissing his cheek as he smiles.

"Who is that?" I ask, my brows furrowed at Danica's screen.

"Some girl following Mike around the world," she says. "She's posted tons of pictures. Do you think she's pretty?"

"She's following him around the world?" I ask, bitterness stirring in the pit of my stomach as I notice how tightly she's pressed up against my boyfriend. Her lips are on his cheek, his hand is on her bare shoulder, and I'm sitting countless time zones away.

"Hailey," Danica snaps. "God, can you answer me? Do you think she's prettier than me or not?"

I stare up at my cousin, at the look of impatient concern on her face, and try to rein in my emotions. "I don't know. No?"

Danica huffs and pulls her phone away. "These girls are way too pretty," she complains, showing me another picture. This time Mike has his big arms stretched way out, and there are like *five* girls squeezed up close to him. They're all absolutely gorgeous, and if Danica told me they were all her best friends from high school cheer camp, I would believe her, if not for the look of supreme annoyance on her face.

She swipes to the right, and there's another girl with Mike, and another.

I feel like I'm swallowing rocks as I sit there trying not to let my emotions play out on my face. Sharp stones sink down my throat and sit heavy on my heart.

Danica sighs heavily as she pulls her phone back in front of her to continue swiping through pictures, and I gnaw on the inside of my lip as I turn my attention back to her textbook.

I knew there would be girls at the band's shows, but it was this abstract thing I could force myself not to think about. I didn't picture their perfect hair, or their perfect lips, or their perfect curves. Now I can see their faces—their ridiculously gorgeous faces—and my stomach roils in protest.

"I wonder if he's slept with any of them," Danica says, and the nerves in my lip scream in pain when I clamp down on them.

Danica places her phone facedown on the table and turns a thoughtful gaze on me. I forget about her exam as I stare back at her, wondering what she's thinking.

"He's getting really famous," she says. "There are going to be more girls and more girls, and they're only going to get prettier and prettier."

Those rocks sitting on my heart grow heavier, until they're stabbing me with every heartbeat.

"He's not ready to settle down yet," Danica says. "I know he thinks he is, but he isn't."

All I can do is sit there hoping my face betrays none of what I'm feeling.

"That's why he left me," she explains. "He was telling the truth when he said it wasn't about you. It was about *him*. He doesn't know what he really wants yet."

"What does he really want?" I ask as my mess of a heart struggles to keep itself whole.

"To be a rock star." Danica taps her fingernail on her phone case, and then she shakes her head. "If you want to date a rock star, you have to be okay with it."

"Okay with what?"

"The girls," she says. "I mean, obviously I wouldn't have been okay with *you*, because you're my cousin, but, like, the girls on tour. He can have other girls, as long as I'm the one he comes home to."

"You mean you'd let him sleep with other people?" I ask, disgust warring with the disbelief on my face.

"I love him," Danica snaps, the look in her eyes leaving no room for argument. "So yes, Hailey, I would. Being with Mike isn't like being with other guys. He's a rock star."

"You think he'd do that?" I ask in a voice that continues getting smaller and smaller.

Danica nods. "I think he just wants someone to tell him it's okay. And I'm going to do that for him. If I don't, we'll never last—even if he resists years of temptation, he'll always think about all those beautiful women he passed up, and he'll end up resenting me for holding him back."

I feel like I'm suffocating as I sit there listening to her.

"That girl with the long black hair?" she says. "The one kissing his cheek? He wants her, Hailey. There's *no way* he doesn't want her. I mean, did you see her? She's hot as hell. And if he wants to know what it's like to be inside her, who am I to deny him?"

"I think Mike just wants to find the right woman," I say, trying to reassure myself.

Danica shakes her head. "He's a twenty-five-year-old man, Hailey. With gorgeous women begging to do *anything* he wants them to. He could have his dick sucked every second he's not performing, by any girl he wants. He's not used to that, but eventually, he will be. And he's going to fuck them one way or another. The only question is if he's going to feel guilty about it afterward. If I love him through it and encourage him to experience those women and all the perks of being a rock star, he'll love me for it, and he'll be with me in the end."

Acid pools at the back of my throat, and I try to keep from losing my lunch.

"Not everyone can handle being with a rock star," Danica says. "But I can. Because I love him *that* much, Hailey."

I stare down at Danica's textbook, imagining him with that girl . . . I imagine him turning into her kiss, capturing her mouth, lying her down on a hotel bed in some distant country thousands of miles away.

I tell myself Mike would never do that. I tell myself Mike would never *want* that.

I know him better than Danica does . . . She's wrong.

She's *wrong*.

I tell myself that over and over and over again.

Chapter 45

Hey, baby. Sorry I missed your call. We were at sound check. The venue here is massive. I think Shawn said it holds like thirteen thousand people, and we're almost completely sold out. If you're not already in bed when you get this, call me back. I miss you.

Hey, Mike. It's Hailey. I was in the shower when you called. You're seriously going to be playing for thirteen thousand people? That's so insane . . . I'm going to try calling you again in the morning, but if I don't get ahold of you, take a picture for me, okay? I miss you too.

I was an idiot and forgot to turn my ringer back on after sound check. [sigh] I guess you're already in bed. [pause] Seven days, Hailey. Have sweet dreams.

Hey, Mike. It isss . . . 9 A.M. here. I guess you're already onstage. I wish I could be there. I bet you're killing it. Call me before you go to bed, if you get a chance.

Hailey, where are you? I feel like I'm going through withdrawal . . . We just finished up the gig. I'm in a cab heading to the hotel. The guys are making fun of me for missing you so much . . . Call me back.

Hey. Sorry, I was in class when you called. I have like fifteen minutes until my next one, so if you get this, call me. If you're already sleeping . . . I love you. Have sweet dreams, Mike.

I am so fucking sorry, baby. My phone went dead and I forgot my charger at the fucking hotel. [frustrated sigh] I miss you so fucking much. How long are classes? Like an hour and a half? [long pause] I'm just going to wait up, okay? Call me when you get out.

As I WALK out of Campbell Hall, I listen to one ring, two rings, three rings, four rings—

"Hey," Mike rushes to say on the other end of the line, urgency pushing through the grogginess in his voice.

"Did you fall asleep?" I ask, tucking a pencil behind my ear as I walk to the commuter parking lot.

"Yeah. Shit. What time is it?"

"Five A.M. your time. Do you want to go back to sleep?"

"No, no." Mike yawns, and I hear the rustling of covers. "I'm awake."

Guilt gnaws at me, knowing what a huge show he just played, and I say, "You should get some sleep—"

"Don't you miss me?"

The truth is, the sound of his voice makes me feel empty, like my heart is missing from my chest and I don't know where to find it.

"You know I miss you," I say, even though the words don't feel like enough. I miss my parents and my brother and my potbelly pig, Teacup, but the thought of them doesn't make me want to sleep in a dark room all day.

"Then talk to me."

"I wish you were here."

"Me too," Mike says, the sadness in his voice matching my own.

"Five days," I remind him, because in this moment, I need it to be only five days. I don't care about Danica's ultimatum or the fact that Phoenix is still living in his house—I just want to hug him, feel him, kiss him, hold him.

"Ten." A deep sigh pushes through the phone. "We added two more European tour stops on the way home. Shawn thought it would be a good idea, but I really didn't want to, Hailey. I just want to come home to you . . . But it's only five extra days . . ."

"Ten days?" I ask to make sure I heard him right, and Mike growls at the hopelessness in my voice.

"I should've told him no."

"No, no, it's a good idea." I force the words of assurance from my mouth, even as my chest grows yet more hollow. "I mean, they're on the way, right? Might as well."

Mike exhales another frustrated sigh. "I hate being so far away from you."

"How many miles?" I ask to try to cheer him up.

"Too fucking many."

I open my car door and sit inside, my eyes focused on my steering wheel, while my mind is somewhere else. "How often do you have to do this?"

"Tour?" he asks.

"Yeah."

"Usually a couple months out of the year."

"Every year?"

I watch students walk past my car, one after another, while I wait for Mike's answer. Eventually, he says, "You can come along. Next time, come with me."

"I have school," I say, hating the way the hopefulness in his voice disappears.

"Oh, right."

Someone honks their horn behind me, and I glance in my rearview mirror. With an irritated growl, I say, "I've got to go. Some asshole is honking for me to give them my parking spot."

"Tell them to fuck off," Mike says, and I throw my hand up between my seats.

"Fuck off!"

Another long honk, another angry growl. "I've got to be at the shelter in twenty minutes anyway. I should go."

"Forget the shelter," Mike says, but the fight is gone from his voice.

"I'll call you in the morning," I promise. "You don't have a show tonight, right?"

"No, just some appearance at a record store or something."

"Okay, I'll set my alarm and call you around eight, okay?"

"Okay," he relents.

"Try to get some sleep. And make sure you have your ringer on."

"I love you, Hailey."

"And remember to send me a picture."

"I love you, Hailey."

"And hug a koala for me sometime before you come home."

Mike chuckles. "I love you, Hailey."

"I love you too," I say, a soft smile touching my lips even as I flip off the still-honking asshole behind me.

"Ten days," he says, and my smile slips away.

"Ten days," I say, putting my car in reverse.

Chapter 46

ON MIKE'S TEAR-STAINED pillow, sleep doesn't come easy. After we got off the phone, I worked a two-hour shift at the animal shelter, had a quiet dinner with Phoenix, and crawled into his bed, where I finally let go of the emotion I'd been holding in. It's not an ugly cry, full of convulsions and sobbing—it's a hopeless cry, one where hot tears escape the corners of my eyes to slide over my cheeks and onto a cold pillowcase. I fall asleep and wake up over and over again, until I'm not sure if I'm in a dream or in reality, and both feel like a nightmare.

Mike gave me five extra days—days I didn't want—to figure out how to fix things, how to keep him *and* school. But the problem is, there is no way to fix this, and there never was. I want to choose happiness, but happiness is two pieces of my heart that are pulling in different directions.

When the sun forms a dim outline around Mike's blackout curtains, I finally give up on sleep and make a pot of coffee. I take Phoenix out to let her use the bathroom before opening my laptop on Mike's kitchen table. And then, coffee forgotten on his counter, I look up Mike Madden.

I find all the pictures Danica showed me—and more, and more, and more. Not just pictures of him with girls, but pictures of him with guys, other bands, famous people I recognize. There are pictures of Adam, Shawn, Joel, and Kit too . . . performance pictures and promotional pictures and pictures with fans. The sheer volume is overwhelming—because there is my boyfriend, smiling in hundreds, *thousands* of pictures.

I sit there for so long that my laptop idles and my screen goes black, and then I see my reflection: wild hair, big eyes, an unguarded frown on my face.

I swipe my fingers across the touchpad to get it to go away, and then I look Mike up on YouTube. The most recent video is from a few days ago, and I click it.

"Are you excited?" a female voice with an Australian accent asks a bunch of girls standing outside of an enormous city building. The sky is bright blue, and all of the girls are gorgeous. Different shades of sunshine-yellow hair, white smiles, pretty makeup.

"I'm freaking out!" a girl with rose highlights says with a laugh.

"What about you, Amy? Are you excited?"

"I'm dying," Amy says, pulling the camera in close. "*Dying.*"

"Who are you excited to see?"

"All of them," she says with a devastatingly beautiful smile.

"Pick one. Say you get to go home with one. Who do you pick?"

Another girl's hand shoots up into the air. "Adam! I call Adam!"

"You can't call Adam," the camera girl scolds. "Adam is mine."

"Bitch, I will cut you," the Adam fan says, and the girls all laugh.

"Shawn or Mike," Amy finally decides, and my stomach drops to my feet. "Probably Mike."

"Why Mike?"

"Uh, have you seen him?" Amy asks, and the camera girl giggles.

"You think he's hotter than Adam?"

"*Way* hotter than Adam," she says, taunting Adam Fan, who launches onto her back. They're all joking around when one of the other girls suddenly gasps.

"Oh my God. Is that them?"

The camera swings wildly around, and a chorus of screams erupts from a long line of people as Adam, Joel, Kit, Shawn, and Mike walk down the line, talking to people as they do.

Camera Girl spins the camera around so we can see her wide blue eyes. "Oh my God, oh my God, oh my God!"

"Hey," Adam says when he gets to the girls, and Adam Fan suddenly becomes absolutely speechless.

"We're making a YouTube video," Camera Girl announces, and the corner of Adam's mouth tips up as he looks into the camera.

"Oh yeah?" He reaches out and takes the phone from her, turning it around to capture her blushing cheeks. "Have you gotten this huge line of people?" he asks, and Camera Girl nods as Adam backs up further to capture the true scope of the line, which stretches as far as I can see and then wraps behind the building. "How's everyone doing tonight!" Adam yells, and the line cheers wildly. "Are you excited for the show?"

More screams, and then Adam winks into the camera before turning it on Shawn.

"What about you? You excited?"

Shawn pushes the camera away so we can see more than just his green eyeball, and Adam laughs as he turns the camera on Kit. "Excited?"

"This show is going to be sick," Kit says as she ties back her long black hair, and Joel slides in front of her.

"Joel, you excited?" Adam asks, and Joel smiles brightly into the camera.

"I'm hungry."

Adam's braceleted hand reaches out to push Joel out of the way, and then the camera lands on Mike, who's busy checking his phone. "Mike, how much do you love Australia?"

"Huh?" Mike says, lifting his eyes and pocketing his phone.

"Australia. Thoughts?"

"The toilets don't actually flush counter-clockwise, so I'm pretty bummed."

Adam is laughing when he turns the phone around again. "There you have it, folks. Pretty bummed."

"They have good steak though!" Mike amends as the band goes inside and Adam stays outside interviewing people in line about toilets. Eventually, he mumbles, "Whose phone is this?" and the video cuts to black before Camera Girl's face reappears on my laptop screen.

"Adam Everest just touched my phone," she squeals, panning to the shell-shocked faces of her friends. "He hugged you!" she tells Adam Fan, whose face is burning bright red.

"I can't believe he hugged me."

"You're never showering again, are you?"

Adam Fan shakes her head furiously, and Amy laughs.

"I still say Mike is the hottest."

The girl beside her nods. "And he smelled *so* good."

"He did smell pretty amazing," Camera Girl agrees. She spins the camera around to tell viewers, "Guys, I know you can't smell this video. But trust us on this. Mike Madden smells fucking amazing." She closes her eyes and sighs. "I can't believe we just met The Last Ones to Know."

"And they were all *really* awesome," Amy says, and the rest of the girls agree.

They talk about the band some more before the doors open and the video ends, but all I can think about is Mike on his phone. I know he was looking to see if I texted or called him—I know it in my bones—but he should have been enjoying the sight of all his fans. He shouldn't have been oblivious to the girls swooning over him. He should have been *there*, instead of a million miles away.

I'm letting him waste his days in hotel rooms and his nights on the phone, but for what? When he comes home, I won't be able to give him the relationship he wants. He won't be able to pick me up for dates, or kiss me on my porch, or even sit at the same table with me in restaurants—because Danica will always be watching. I know Mike wants to find "the one," and maybe he will—maybe she'll have blonde hair, maybe she'll have an accent. But she won't be me, because I'm his ex-girlfriend's cousin. I can't give him what he deserves, and I never should have pretended I could.

When I summon the strength to call Mike at eight o'clock (morning for me, night for him), the aching in my heart has grown sharp, like the tip of a blade that's slowly plunging deeper. I listen to his phone ring once, twice, three times, four times—

"This is Mike. Leave a message."

"Hey, Mike," I say, my voice cracking with emotion. There are ten days left before he comes home, but that's ten days too many. I've already wasted enough of his time, and the longer I pretend that things could ever work between us, the harder it's going to be to accept that they never, ever could. "It's Hailey . . . Listen, I—"

Another call interrupts my voice mail, and I answer Mike on the other line.

"Hey," he says. "Sorry, it's loud as hell in here."

"Where are you?" I ask, because I'm weak and I need to hear his voice.

"Some record store party in London. The place is called, uh—"

As Mike tries to remember the name, someone starts talking to him. A few someones, if the multiple female voices are anything to go off of. I hear laughing.

"Sorry about that," Mike says. "No one seems to know where the hell we are."

"You should go," I say, nearly choking on the words.

"Huh?"

"You shouldn't call me anymore," I say with tears streaming down my cheeks.

"Hailey?"

"Go have fun, Mike. Be a rock star. Be happy."

"Baby, what the hell are you talking about?" I hold in a sob, and Mike says, "Hailey, you're scaring the shit out of me. What's going on?"

"This just isn't working," I say with my whole heart shattering into pieces. I think of Danica's ultimatum, the dreams I had before I moved here, the dreams Mike has had since Adam and Shawn approached him in a middle school cafeteria. I think of the faces of dozens of girls on the Internet. I think of Danica and how pretty she looked in that wildflower dress. I think of my brother back home and the way the words *messed up* sounded in his voice. I think of my mom's hatbox and the thirteen first-day-of-school photos inside it. I think of my broken desk and my broken computer, and Danica's soup cans rolling across Mike's hardwood floor. I think of him staring at his phone in front of a long line of people, and me holding mine to my ear as someone honked at me to leave my parking spot. "You deserve to be happy," I manage through the emotion clouding my eyes. "I just want you to be happy."

"I *am* happy," Mike argues. "You make me happy."

I shake my head against the tears burning lines down my face. I should have done this before he left. I shouldn't have hung out with him on his bus. I shouldn't have played Deadzone with him late at night. I shouldn't have stayed with him when he was sick. I shouldn't have let him kiss me in the woods.

I never should have fallen in love with him at all.

He's been waiting for the girl he'll spend the rest of his life with, and now it's time for me to let him find her.

"I'm so sorry," I say, and I hang up the phone.

Chapter 47

I THOUGHT I'D fallen apart when Danica trashed my room and I believed my time in this town was up, but nothing—nothing—compares to the way I fall apart when I hang up on Mike. Phoenix whimpers at my feet as I cry into my arms, my entire body racking with sobs that have been piling inside of me for weeks.

Rowan was right when she said the last love is the one that counts. But I was never meant to be Mike's last. Someday, he'll be married to a beautiful wife, and she won't have the entire world standing between her and loving him. She won't have vindictive cousins or ultimatums, and she'll be able to give him the life he's always dreamt of. They'll have beautiful kids and a beautiful house and a beautiful life—but I won't be her. He'll barely remember me, even though I will never, ever forget him.

There weren't sparks before Mike, and there

won't be sparks after Mike—because I carved my heart out of my chest the day I fell in love with him, and now it's walking outside of my body, thousands of miles away.

I have no heart left to give.

Instead, I have a gaping hole, and that emptiness inside me makes me cry until my head is throbbing and my eyes are swollen. And through it all, my phone rings and rings and rings. Within fifteen minutes, I have twenty missed calls from Mike, nine missed calls from Rowan, twelve missed calls from Dee, six from Kit. When Shawn starts calling me too, I finally pull myself together enough to answer the phone.

"Hailey, what the hell is going on?" he asks. "Mike just left for the airport."

"The airport?" I ask, alarm overwhelming the rawness in my voice.

"Yeah. Look, I'm sorry, I don't know what's going on with you two, but . . . Fuck, Hailey, I'm really sorry, but we have a huge show in Dublin tomorrow. We fly out in the morning. He has to be here. You need to call him. Can you please call him?"

"Okay," I agree, absorbing Shawn's panic.

"Thanks," he says, but I'm already hanging up the phone.

Mike answers even before the first ring stops sounding. "I'm coming home."

"Mike, don't." My voice breaks with the fresh tears filling my eyes. It was hard enough doing this once, it's going to kill me to do it twice.

"I'm already in a cab, Hailey. I don't even have my suitcase. I have my wallet and my passport and you're not talking me out of this, because I'm not fucking losing you."

A sob steals the breath from my lungs, and Mike says, "Why are you doing this, baby? Just talk to me."

"I can't," I cry, pulling my knees to my chest in the corner of his kitchen. Phoenix licks at my tears, but I hunch my shoulders and turn away from her.

There are a million reasons why Mike is better off without me, but I can't tell him the one reason, the *one* single reason, why I would be better off without him. I can't tell him that Danica made me pick between him and school, because then he'll know I'm just as bad as her. She made me choose between money and love, and it should have been an easy decision, but it wasn't.

"Yes, you can," Mike assures me. "You can tell me anything, Hailey. I love you . . ." There's a pause, and then he says, "Baby . . . did you cheat on me?"

"No!" I say as I wipe my fingers over my eyes. "Mike, *no*, I would never do that."

"Is this because we added extra tour dates?"

"No," I assure him through a runny nose and scratchy throat.

"Then what?"

"I'm not worth this," I say through a new wave of tears. "You should've tried that Indonesian candy with the guys. You should've seen how those girls looked at you last week."

"What girls?"

"The ones outside your Perth show, at the front of the line. They posted a video on YouTube and—"

"Baby, you can't look at the stuff on the Internet. It'll drive you crazy."

I squeeze my eyes shut, trying to escape the pages of images I looked at this morning. The girls in Australia, the girls in Malaysia and China and Korea, the girls in the U.S.—years and years of girls. Girls taller than me and curvier than me and, just . . . *more* than me. Smoother hair and prettier clothes and a million other reasons why Mike should be with them instead of me.

"Do you think I don't worry every day that you're going to meet someone while I'm gone?" Mike asks, shocking me into opening my tear-filled eyes. "We live in a college town, Hailey. You go to school every day with frat guys and future CEOs. I'm terrified you're going to meet someone better than me, smarter than me—"

I want to tell him that there's no one better than him, no one smarter than him.

"I've never taken a college class in my life," he says. "The only thing I know how to do is play the drums."

"I don't want a CEO," my small, broken voice assures him.

"Then tell me what you want, baby."

My heart aches as I think, *I want to hold his hand in public. I want to kiss him under the glow of my porch light. I want to cheer for him at his shows. I want to love him without repercussion. I want to be with him without Danica's shadow hanging over me. I want to be enough for this beautiful man I don't deserve.*

"You," I tell him, and Mike sighs.

"Even if I'm a drummer? Even if I have to tour?"

"Yes," I answer without needing to think about it, because drumming isn't just a job to Mike. It's who he is. He's the drummer of The Last Ones to Know, and I would never want him to be anyone different.

Mike lets out a breath of relief, but it does nothing to soften the guilt hardening in the pit of my stomach. Yes, I want him. But wanting him doesn't change the fact that I can't have him, not if Danica gets her way. And Danica *always* gets her way.

"I know it's hard waiting," he says, "but I told you even before I left, Hailey—I don't want anyone else. I only want you. I'm thankful every day that I fell for the wrong girl, because it led me to the right one. It was always meant to be you."

I shiver with the absence of his arms around me, and he says, "I know you don't believe me when I tell you how special you are, but remember, all it took was a red dress for over two thousand people to not be able to take their eyes off of you."

"That's only because I was the star," I say, remembering the way I spun around and around on the steel platform for Mike's music video.

"You were the star for a reason, Hailey," he says. "You're a light in the dark. And the only person who can't see that is you."

Mike's phone beeps, and he curses. "Shit. My phone is going dead."

I close my eyes, and more tears squeeze through my lashes.

"Hailey . . . I'll talk to you soon, okay?"

"Okay."

"Can you wait for me?"

My lips part, but the call drops before they can form an answer. One dead battery, and he's gone—thousands of miles away again—and all I can do is try to breathe in spite of the overwhelming hopelessness digging its claws into my chest.

I DON'T CHANGE out of my pajamas after getting off the phone with Mike. I don't shower. I don't go to my classes. If it wasn't for Phoenix, I wouldn't even get out of Mike's bed.

I text Rowan and Dee to tell them I'm okay and that I need to spend the day alone, and since they have no idea I'm camping out at Mike's house with my vagabond dog, they have no choice but to honor my wishes.

Thanksgiving is tomorrow, when I'll have to put on a brave face and spend time with family, but for today, I'm off the map, and time passes slowly. I spend countless hours watching daytime TV and old cartoons from Mike's bed, and he does call just like he promised he would, but for only two short minutes. Just long enough to ask me how I'm feeling, listen to the lie I tell him, and then have to run again.

I'm curled up under his heavy comforter when the sun sets, its yellow halo around his curtains fading to dark blue, to gray, to black. With Phoenix sleeping in her usual spot out on the living room couch, I'm alone in the dark. I close my red-rimmed eyes against his pillow, wondering how I got here.

When I moved to Mayfield, the plan was simple: do my best to get along with Danica, excel in all of my classes, try to make sure she didn't party her education away, make something of myself. A boyfriend was never part of the picture—much less my cousin's rock star ex, who I have fallen madly, irreversibly, desperately, soul-crushingly in love with.

I've never been this girl—one to cry herself to sleep in the same pajamas she wore to bed last night. But here I am, completely raw. My eyelids have been rubbed sore from all the crying I've done today, so I can't even touch them when more tears begin to spill onto Mike's pillow.

I wanted sparks, and I got them, in the form of a man who kindled an inferno inside of me. If I let it burn, it will destroy everything. But if I put it out . . .

I'll miss his warmth. I'll miss his heat. I'll miss the way he consumed me, the way he made me burn.

I can't give him up, but I can't keep him, and in ten days, I won't have a choice.

Under Mike's covers, I think about playing princesses with Danica when we were little girls—how we dressed up in tiaras, wore sparkly dresses, and planned to marry our one true loves . . .

They were always princes—they were *always* princes.

But what happens when they're not princes? What if they're a rock star—just *one* rock star—and we both want him for ourselves?

Chapter 48

It's late when the bed stirs, and my mind is fuzzy from sleep when comforting arms wrap around me—big, strong arms that snake around my waist and pull me close.

"Mike?" I rasp as he nuzzles his nose into the crook of my shoulder, his stubble abrading my skin. I'm sure I must be dreaming . . . but I can feel him—his rough jeans against my bare legs, his hard chest molding against my back. I can smell him too—a familiar scent that makes my heart slam against my ribs as I turn in his arms. In the soft glow of a nightlight I brought from home, I find his warm brown eyes, and my breath catches in my lungs.

Mike smiles and tucks a long curl behind my ear.

"How are you here?" I whisper, a flood of emotion washing away my voice as my eyes begin to water.

"I told you I was coming home, didn't I?"

At the warmth in his eyes and the soft curve of his smile, a sob escapes me, and Mike pulls me tighter against his chest. I grip the back of his T-shirt, terrified he's going to disappear. "I told you not to," I cry, holding him tight enough that I can feel his heart pounding against my cheek.

"Nothing you could have said would have kept me from you," he promises, his chest rumbling against my ear, and quiet sobs escape me as I tremble in his arms. My body still aches from the crying I've done all day, and now a new wave of emotion racks me from the inside out.

Mike rubs my back. He kisses my hair. He hushes me as he picks up all of my broken pieces and tries to put them back together. It's like he took my heart with him when he left, and now he's put it back in my chest. In his arms, it can finally beat again.

It took him all day to fly here—I know, because I've spent countless hours these past few weeks looking up flights to wherever in the world he was, and I've daydreamed about being able to afford visiting him. Twenty hours to South Korea. Twenty-seven hours to Indonesia. Twenty-four hours to Australia.

Ten hours from London, not counting the time it must have taken him to purchase tickets, get through security, wait for his flight, drive home.

"How'd you know I was here?" I ask with my ear still pressed against his heartbeat.

"I didn't," he admits, trailing his fingers over my back. "I came home to change clothes, and then I was going to throw little rocks against your window or climb your lattice or something romantic."

I smile against his shirt. "My room is on the ground floor."

"Then I'm glad I found you in my bed," Mike says, combing his fingers gently through my hair.

"What about your tour?" I ask as I let his closeness make the past five and a half weeks disappear. In this moment, nothing else matters—only that he's here. That he's holding me. That I can touch him. That I can feel him.

"I have to fly back in a few hours."

I pull away far enough to look up at him, and he gazes down at me like he would have flown around the world a thousand times just to hold me like this. "You flew all day just to spend a few hours with me?"

Mike brushes another stray curl away from my face, his fingers threading into the hair behind my ear. "I would have flown all day just to spend a few *minutes* with you, Hailey."

He brushes his thumb over my cheek, like he's memorizing the softness of my skin, and his eyes scan my lips, my nose, my forehead, my chin—as though he's checking to make sure I'm exactly as he remembers.

I don't wait for him to finish searching my face before I kiss him. I shift on his mattress and touch my lips to his, and Mike's fingers in my hair immediately pull me closer. My lips part, and my body melts against him as he unleashes five weeks' worth of wanting into one slow, consuming, bone-melting kiss.

We should be talking. I should be making the most of the short time he has here. But instead, his leg is wedging between my thighs and I'm tugging him with me as I roll onto my back. I kiss him desperately, not letting either of us up for air, and the unguarded moan that escapes his mouth as I scratch my fingers over his scalp makes my whole body tremble with need. My hips lift to tempt him, and Mike's hand slides down to catch the underside of my knee, hiking it up so that my leg is wrapped behind his back. He grips my ass, tugging me against the erection I've created, and I moan against his mouth as my core turns to molten lava. His lips drop to my neck, and he lavishes the column of my throat with satin kisses that threaten to make me erupt. All I want is for my clothes to disappear, for my skin to blaze against the heat of his body.

Mike's hand is greedy against my silk shorts, kneading my ass as he makes my panties wet for him. I'm falling apart, and all he's done is touch me over my clothes.

"Mike," I beg, and he doesn't hesitate to give me what I want. His fingers slide up to hook in the waistbands of my shorts and panties, and he tugs them off in one easy movement. His finger slides down through my slick heat, and his mouth claims the gasp that bursts from my lips.

"Is this what you need, baby?" Mike asks as he traces circles around my tight bundle of nerves. It feels like every one of my cells is reaching out to him, begging for his attention, begging to be touched. "Tell me,

Hailey," he gently demands. "I flew across an ocean to take care of you, but you need to tell me what you need."

"Yes," I groan, my fingers sinking into the firm muscles of his back. My entire body feels wound too tight, and with every circle Mike draws around my pulsing bud, I wind tighter and tighter and tighter.

"Say it," he whispers in my ear, and my toes curl beneath his sheets.

"I need you. I need you to touch me."

Mike gently pinches me between his wet fingertips, stroking me delicately with every slick pinch. My knees begin to quake, and he settles beside me, using his heavy jean-clad leg to pin my right knee to the bed, leaving me open and exposed. "What else?" he says, his warm breath fanning over my ear as he touches and strokes and teases, readying me for him.

"I need you inside me," I whimper as he drives my body to the edge. I'm teetering on a cliff, clinging to him even as I beg him to push me off it.

Mike presses soft, warm kisses below my ear as he continues priming me, and I can't help the sounds I make for him. Desperate moans, tiny whimpers, sharp gasps of pleasure. His tongue traces down to the hollow of my collarbone, and my eyes roll back in my head, my muscles aching with tension.

"Not yet," he says when I'm close to coming. He pulls away and shifts between my legs, raking both hands up my body to strip me of my oversized shirt. He tosses it onto the floor, and then he sits back, letting his hungry eyes rove over my flushed face, my pert breasts, my smooth stomach, my bare sex. When his eyes find mine again, they are full of heat that makes me want to cover my breasts—or play with them.

"You are so fucking sexy," he says, his fingertips drawing feather-light patterns over the tops of my thighs.

Encouraged by his words, I slide my hands to my breasts, and I fondle them with him watching. I glance at the bulge straining in his jeans, and I bite my lip between my teeth as I pinch my nipples between my fingers, teasing him.

Mike's voice is rough with lust when he says, "I planned to kiss every single inch of your body when I came home from touring. But I don't think we have time." He leans down and kisses my fingertips, coaxing them away from my breasts. "So I think I'll have to settle for everything from here"—he wraps his soft lips around my nipple, lavishing me with his tongue—"and here"—he slowly drags wet kisses to my other breast, drawing it into his scorching mouth. "To here," he finishes, meeting my sex with his fingers and applying electric tension. Every nerve in my body sizzles to life as I thread my fingers into his hair, encouraging his mouth to continue exploring my body.

Mike carries through with his promise, spoiling every inch of me from my breasts to the junction of my thighs. He watches me watch him as he strokes his tongue over my sex, nibbling and kissing and suckling until I'm nothing but a whimpering mess of need on his bed. When I think I can take no more, he pulls away from me to kick off his jeans and boxers, and I force myself to be coherent enough to watch as he pulls off his T-shirt.

My eyes feast on his chiseled biceps, his sculpted shoulders, his hard chest, his flat stomach, and then he's settling over me and I can feel him between my legs. He kisses me feverishly while his swollen head presses against my sex, and when I'm moaning against his mouth and arcing against him, he finally begins pushing inside me.

It isn't like last time—he didn't enter me with his fingers first, so there's nothing to prepare me. The only help he offers now is the way he kisses me—ravenously, without giving me time to think. He devours me with his lips and with his hands, and it all helps distract me from the way my body stretches around him as he pushes his sex inside of me.

"Oh my God," Mike groans, struggling to keep his composure as he enters me, and I wrap my legs behind him, slowly pulling him the rest of the way inside my body.

When he's sunken fully inside me, I pulse around him, and his cock throbs in answer. Mike rests his forehead against mine, his eyes closed, and I plant soft kisses against his closed lips. When he opens his eyes, there is so much love in them, I almost start crying again.

"You undo me, Hailey," he says, and a tear slips out of the corner of my eye.

"I love you," I tell him, and he wipes my tear away, smiling. It's the first time I've told him in person, and the words feel healing—freeing.

"I love you too," he says, kissing me as he begins moving inside me again. His kiss isn't fire or torture or teasing—it's love. I feel it in my chest, in the way my heart beats against his while he makes me remember how perfectly we fit together.

It's like he was made for me. *Just* for me.

Mike makes love to me until I shatter around him, and then he releases inside me and tells me over and over again how much he loves me, how much he missed me, how much he needs me. I say it all back, and I mean every word.

I love him. I missed him. I *need* him.

It's still dark outside when he tugs me against his chest and wraps his arms around me. I smile contentedly as I play the little spoon to his big spoon, and eventually, my eyelids grow heavy.

"Get some sleep," Mike orders when my body jerks to fight off sleep for the fifth or sixth time.

"I don't want to," I argue, my groggy voice betraying me.

Mike hugs me tighter, his breathing steady against my back. "I'll be here when you wake up."

"But you're leaving soon. I don't want to waste the time we have."

"This isn't wasting it," he says, linking his fingers with mine and hugging our arms tight against my body.

"We should talk," I counter, feeling a peacefulness I shouldn't. Danica's threat is still looming over us. But right now, it feels so far away.

"What do you want to talk about?" Mike rubs his thumb over my hand, since his hands can never be still, and I smile against our pillow.

"I don't know . . ."

"Good talk, baby. Now get some sleep."

I chuckle and try to think. "Uh, how was your flight?"

"Long."

"Was it worth it?" I ask, and within seconds, I get my answer in the form of a growing erection that Mike presses against my ass.

"I suggest you talk about something else unless you seriously don't want to get any sleep."

I let out a soft chuckle and nibble my bottom lip, tempted. "Sorry."

Mike's hand lifts to my mouth, and even though he's behind me and can't see me, he frees my lip from my teeth. "Liar."

I laugh, and he snuggles me closer. The hard length pressing against my body is starting to direct my thoughts to a very dirty place, so I force myself to change the subject. "Where was your favorite place on tour?"

"Probably the market in Seoul," Mike answers after thinking about it for a while. "The food was amazing and the vendors were really friendly. It was kind of like Chinatown in New York, but so much better."

I have no basis for comparison, since I've never been to Chinatown . . . or New York . . . "That sounds really cool."

Mike rubs his thumb over my hand again. "Bali was really beautiful though. We made a stop at this one beach . . . It was a private little cove surrounded by massive rocks covered in the greenest plants you've ever seen. The sand was like powder, it was so soft. And the water was as warm as bathwater."

"It sounds gorgeous," I say, wishing I could have seen it with him.

"I'll take you there someday," Mike promises with his chin resting on my shoulder. "There are tons of resorts all over the island. Even those kinds with the little wooden huts that sit out on the water. We can spend our honeymoon in one of them."

Mike stiffens at the same time I do—right when he says the word *honeymoon*. We're quiet for a while, and his thumb starts drumming against my hand.

"Are you planning on proposing to me?" I tease, butterflies soaring wildly inside my stomach.

"Maybe in Australia . . ." Mike answers. "In the Capella Sunflower Fields in Queensland."

"Did you go there?" I ask, and all of Mike's fingers begin twitching, drumming against the top of my hand. He shakes his head.

I swallow, realizing what he's not telling me. He didn't go there—he looked it up.

"Would I get to hug a koala afterward?" I ask to lighten the conversation, and he shakes his head again.

"Nope. We'd hug one before."

"Why before?"

"It'd guarantee a yes," he says, and my whole body relaxes with a laugh.

"You think I'm that easy?"

"Okay," Mike dramatically relents. "Two koalas."

I laugh again and elbow him playfully, and he sighs contentedly as he pulls me tighter against his body. Every inch of me is squeezed against every inch of him, and I close my eyes and smile against the pillow.

"I'd buy you a house with a white picket fence," Mike says, and my smile widens.

"What would the house look like?"

"Pretty. Lots of trees and flowers. Window boxes on every single window. A big deck for me to grill out back. A place for you to grow banana peppers in the yard. Like . . . seven bedrooms."

"Why so many bedrooms?"

"For the six kids we're going to have."

I bark out a laugh. "No way."

"Five," he amends.

"Two."

"Four."

"Two."

"Ten," he argues, and I laugh hard. He presses a kiss against my neck before nuzzling his chin back in the crook of my shoulder. "Two," he agrees softly, and I smile in spite of the butterflies wreaking havoc inside my stomach.

"I hope they have your smile," he says, and I close

my eyes and picture it—a little boy and a little girl, both with my smile but Mike's big brown eyes.

My heart aches as I realize how much I want that. I want the white picket fence. I want Mike grilling out back. I want an obscene amount of bedrooms, and I want one of them to be ours. I want to lie with him like this at night—every night. I don't want to let this go.

I *can't* let this go.

I turn in his arms, and with our cheeks pressed against the same pillow, I allow acceptance to wash over me: I *can't* let this go. Even if I lost him, even if I made the biggest mistake of my life and gave him up, I would fight to get him back. I would *fight* for him. Even if it meant giving up school for a while, I would never stop fighting to keep him.

Because he doesn't want a rock star mansion and fancy cars. He wants a pretty house with a banana pepper garden and kids with my smile. He wants *me*. Wild hair and tattered hoodies and all.

"I love you," I say, and Mike reads my expression. He doesn't know I just made the biggest decision of my life, but I hope he can see it in my eyes—that I choose him, that I will *always* choose him.

"I love you too," he says, and when he kisses me, there is love, and there are sparks, and there is the promise of a future that I will no longer allow *anyone* to threaten.

Mike Madden is mine, and I'm keeping him.

Chapter 49

WHEN I WAKE a couple hours later, at two in the morning, I'm alone, and I panic. In Mike's T-shirt and a pair of underwear, I throw off the covers and rush from his room, thinking he already left. It's still pitch-black outside, but I missed him. He let me sleep, and now it's going to be nine more days before I see him again. A lifetime.

"No," I say, fighting off tears. I flick on lights as I search the house, but I can't even find Phoenix. She's not on the couch. She's not in the kitchen.

"Mike?" I ask as I investigate room after room. "Phoenix? Come here, girl!"

Silence answers me, and I stand in his living room with my hands on my head, wondering if I've finally cracked and lost my damn mind. There's no sign of Mike—except the T-shirt I'm wearing. I lift it to my nose to see if it smells like him, and I'm still standing there sniffing it when the front door opens.

Mike walks in, wearing a fresh shirt and holding a dog leash in his hand, and the loose fabric drops from my hands.

"Good morning," he says with a bright smile, letting Phoenix off her leash and walking over to wrap me in his arms and give me a kiss on the head. Phoenix stands by our side, wagging her tail excitedly.

In shock, I search Mike's eyes. I forgot to tell him about Phoenix living here last night, and now he's . . . walking her? She's letting him walk her? She let him touch her?

"We met when I came in last night," Mike explains, dropping down to scratch Phoenix behind her ears. She eats it up, pushing the top of her head against his chest. "I think she likes me."

I watch them together—Mike petting her head, Phoenix licking his face, him coaxing her onto her back, her letting him scratch her tummy.

My hand flies to my mouth, and when Mike looks up at me, tears are welling in my eyes. "Baby," he says, quickly rising to his feet. "What's wrong?"

"She's letting you touch her," I say, watching as Phoenix nuzzles Mike's leg for more attention.

Mike's brow furrows before he gazes down at her—at the golden Chow who weeks ago was balled up in a cage, drenched in her own urine. "Wait, is this the dog? The one you rescued from the dogfighting ring?"

I nod as scorching tears drip over my cheeks, and

Mike glances at Phoenix again before tugging me into his arms. "Why are you crying, Hailey?"

"I don't know," I sob, wishing I could stop. "I'm happy."

Mike chuckles and rubs my back. "Are you sure?"

"Yes," I sniffle, pulling myself together. I step back and hold my hand out for Phoenix, patting her nose when she pushes it into my palm. "You're not upset she's here?"

Mike sits on the floor, and Phoenix immediately squeezes her big body onto his lap. He smiles as he pets her, and her tail swings wildly over his leg. "No, I owe her one for keeping you company while I've been away. Did you adopt her?"

I frown, not knowing how to answer that question. "They were going to send her away, but I couldn't let that happen, so . . ." I take a heavy breath. "I don't have anyone to keep her."

"I'll keep her," he volunteers without hesitation, petting her as he gazes up at me.

"Mike . . ."

I stop myself, unsure of how to finish that sentence. Before last night, I would have talked him out of it. I would have felt guilty that he offered to help, and I would have rejected the favor . . . But I really *don't* have anyone else to keep her, and she's *on his lap*. The dog who wouldn't let anyone else touch her is sitting on his lap, wagging her tail excitedly. I don't know if it's because she got used to his scent by living in his house before he came home, or if it's just because Mike is impossible not to like, but she's clearly as in love with him as I am, and who am I to take that away from her?

"Are you sure?" I ask, giving Mike one last out, and he glances at Phoenix only to get a surprise lick to his nose.

His answer comes in the form of a deep, happy laugh, and I fall even more in love with him. "Yeah," he says as he wipes Chow slobber off his face. "We'll share her, okay?"

"So we have a dog?" I ask, and I don't know why that question stokes the butterflies inside of me, but their silken wings tickle the inside of my stomach.

"We have a dog," Mike confirms, tugging me down next to him.

MIKE AND I pack as many laughs, smiles, and kisses as we can into the forty-five minutes we have before he has to leave. I lament that he has to spend Thanksgiving so far from home, but he assures me that waking up with me in his arms this morning more than made up for it. I make him promise to try to track down some turkey lunch meat in Dublin so that he and the guys can at least have turkey sandwiches, and we make plans for me to try his mom's green bean casserole next Thanksgiving.

He gives me a nice kiss before he gets in his truck to leave, and then he gets back out of it to pin me against the door and kiss me breathless. I'm a boneless mess when he finally drives down the dark road, through the trees that separate his house from the city. I watch him disappear, touching my fingers to my lips and closing my eyes, smiling in the dark.

Just a few hours ago, nine days seemed insurmountable, and I didn't feel like I could get through them. Now, I can actually breathe when I think about them. Nine days—it's not that long. Mike knows I'm waiting for him, and now *I* know I'm waiting for him too. I'm not waiting to give him up—I'm waiting to launch myself into his arms and pay him back for how flustered he made me against the side of his truck.

In his living room, I sit on his overstuffed couch with my legs pulled under me, and I bite my thumbnail between my teeth. With my decision made, there's just one big detail to take care of.

Danica.

I'm supposed to meet her at our place in a few hours so we can carpool to her parents' house for Thanksgiving dinner. It was her idea, not mine, and I frown as I think about how nice she's been recently. It started with her taking me on that shopping trip, and then it became me helping her with her homework; her excitedly asking me about my smoke-and-mirrors boyfriend; us watching TV together on the same couch. When we've talked about boys, I've pretended that her Mike wasn't my Mike, and I've ignored the guilt that knocked against my stomach with every little lie I've had to tell.

I haven't worried about Mike wanting her back, since he's made it very clear that will *never* happen—

with me or without me—but that hasn't stopped Danica from trying. She's changed her phone number at least three times since he keeps blocking her, and she has all sorts of grand plans for when he comes home from his tour. I've listened helplessly as she's shared them with me—how she plans to bake him his favorite cookies; how she's going to give him a scrapbook of pictures of them in high school; how she plans to be in the front row of his next show at Mayhem, wearing the lowest cut top I've ever seen in my life.

In a way, I feel sorry for her. She lost the best man she ever could have had, and even though she already regrets it, one day she is going to regret it to her core. I don't think she truly loves Mike—not like I love him—but one day she is going to realize that *he* loved *her*, and she's going to know that it's her fault she lost him.

He'll be with me. Maybe we'll even have our white picket fence by then. And even though I feel bad for the heartache and regret she'll feel about that, I'm not willing to sacrifice him for her. If he wasn't with me, he *still* wouldn't be with her. She lost him twice, and that's not my fault. She doesn't deserve him—she *never* deserved him. And even though I'm not sure I deserve him either, because he's a fairy tale prince in a rock star's body, I'm keeping him.

I tell myself that over and over again as I drive to my apartment in the same clothes I wore to Mike's house two days ago. Danica will think I spent both nights at Leti's, and I'll let her think that until after Thanksgiving dinner. I don't know how she's going to react when I tell her that I'm in love with Mike and that we're in a serious relationship, but I know I don't want to find out until after we no longer have to be in a closed space together. She deserves a nice, drama-free holiday with our families as much as I do, so I'll tell her after we get home. And I'll pack up my things beforehand, just in case she decides to go crazy again. If I have to live at Mike's, I know he'll be okay with it. And if I have to drop out of school for a while, I know *I'll* be okay with it. I can find a job around here until I find some way to re-enroll—because there *has* to be a way for me to do it on my own. I have to believe that, and I have to believe I'll find it. Eventually.

Positive thoughts: I'm confident, I'm powerful, I'm strong . . . I'm also fifteen minutes late since my feet aren't as brave as the rest of me.

"I was just about to call you," Danica says when I finally gather the courage to step inside our apartment. She smiles, and I force a smile back.

"Sorry," I say as I head toward my room. "I just need to change real quick, and then I'm ready to go."

"Busy night?" she teases as she follows me, and I swallow my nerves.

"Yeah, sorry. I overslept."

Danica plops down on my bed as I pull clothes from my dresser, and when she makes no attempt to give me any privacy, I take them to the bathroom in the hall.

"Were you at Leti's?" she asks through the door, and my throat thickens as I slip a fresh top over my head.

I glance in the mirror and release my lip from my teeth. "Yeah."

"When am I going to get to meet him?"

I hop into a clean skirt and force a brush through my hair. "Uh, soon."

"You should go on a double date with Mike and me when he gets home," she says, and I hesitate with my hand on the knob. God, how can I face her? Mike is on my skin. He's in my body. I should have showered before I left his place, but I didn't want to. I didn't want to erase the memory of his touch so soon.

I take a deep breath, forcing another smile as I finally open the door. "Ready to go."

Danica grins and follows me to her car. I try to turn on the radio, but she stops me. "Let's talk," she says, pushing my hand away from the dash. "I haven't seen you in a while."

"What do you want to talk about?" I ask, glancing into her mascara-framed eyes.

"I want to talk about Leti some more," she says, the corners of her mouth turned up.

"Oh . . . what about him?"

"You've been spending a lot of time at his place," Danica notes, and I straighten my skirt.

"Yeah."

"It's like you're practically living there."

"I guess . . ."

"Seems like things are really serious between you two."

"Yeah . . ."

"Are you in love with him?"

I swallow the lump in my throat. "Uh, I . . . um . . ."

Danica pats my knee. "Oh, sweetie. It's okay. Of course you are." I search her expression, and she gives me a sad smile. "You two have been inseparable lately."

My toes curl painfully in my special-occasion flats, matching how uncomfortable I am.

"But listen," Danica says, pulling her phone from her cup holder. I wish she would watch the road, but instead, she fiddles with the device in her hand. "I need to show you something, okay?"

I wait, and she eventually hands me the phone. And when I look at it, my eyes flash wide.

"Do you know who that is?" she asks as I stare at a picture of Leti kissing Kale on the mouth, and I nervously shake my head. "That's your boyfriend's profile picture."

"Oh."

"It was easy to look him up," she says. "Leti isn't exactly a popular name. Did you know he's gay?"

My eyes are saucers when I stare over at her.

"You didn't know your boyfriend was gay?" Danica asks, and I shake my head.

"See, that's interesting," she says with a smile.

"Interesting?" I croak.

"Why wouldn't Kit tell you that your boyfriend is actually dating her brother? That's who's in the picture—Kale Larson. Why wouldn't your BFFs Dee or Rowan tell you?"

"Kit's brother?" I ask, trying to gauge how much Danica knows, and she bursts out laughing. She throws her head back, her laughter filling the car as it picks up speed.

"Hailey, you're so fucking dumb. You can't lie to me. Did you really think I didn't know?"

Her laugh is like ice shooting through my veins, and I realize she's playing with me.

"What do you want?" I ask, and my cousin smiles at me—a glass smile that threatens to shatter and slice me to pieces.

"I want to know where you've been."

She's holding all the cards, and I can't tell if she's bluffing. I search for a tell, a crack in her serpentine smile . . . "You know where I've been," I venture, and Danica's penny-brown eyes shine.

"Hm," she hums. "Do I?"

I say nothing, refusing to be a pawn on her board.

"I think you've been at my boyfriend's house," she finally accuses, and I stare out my passenger-side window, knowing the game is finally over. This isn't a conversation I wanted to have before Thanksgiving dinner—much less in a moving vehicle that Danica could drive off a bridge on a whim—but I've never been in control of this game. Danica has always been in the driver's seat, and I resign myself to watching the trees we leave behind.

"Aren't you going to say something?" she asks, but I continue resting my forehead against the glass, ignoring her. "Typical Hailey. Clam up like a coward the minute shit gets real." I don't take her bait, and she snaps, "Fucking say something, you stupid bitch!"

"*My* boyfriend's house," I correct her. I lift my head and level her with my stare, and Danica's face reddens as she glares at me. I don't back down, and she eventually looks back out at the road, her jaw ticking furiously.

"You think you're pretty fucking special, don't you?" she snarls as I look back out the window. "Congratulations, you got to be the pathetic side bitch waiting at home for a rock star who's fucking everything with legs thousands of miles away."

Her words don't bother me. Maybe a couple days ago they would have, but now, they roll off me. Mike's touch is still on my skin, like a coating that makes me unbreakable.

"You're such an idiot, Hailey. We're on a family share phone plan, for God's sake. I have the password. I know you never stopped talking to him." Her voice is pouty and mocking when she says, "Poor little Hailey. Sitting by the phone."

She laughs loudly, and I sit quietly, wondering how slowly a car would need to be driving in order for a person to jump out of it safely.

"I even know he came home last night." I glance at her, and she grins wickedly. "He's famous, Hailey. Word spreads fast. But I decided not to break up your little party. Do you know why?"

Silence answers her, but she presses on.

"Because it doesn't matter. None of this matters. What, do you think you're going to grow old with him? Let me guess: white picket fence, golden retriever, two-point-five kids?" She snickers, and steel shutters close over my expression.

"I'm not playing this game anymore, Danica."

"Oh, this isn't a game, Hailey. This is war."

"You've lost."

"Have you forgotten who pays your bills?"

My heart drops, because a small part of me—a very small, very naïve part—had hoped that when I told her about Mike after Thanksgiving dinner, she'd try to understand. She'd be hurt, but maybe the time we'd spent together recently would matter to her. Maybe she'd care about how I felt and what I had to say. Maybe she wouldn't try to ruin me.

Instead, she's known about us this whole time. She's been planning this the *whole* time. And now, her gloves are off.

"What are your parents going to think when they hear you've decided to throw away your education for a boy you barely know?" Danica asks, and I imagine the disappointment on their faces. "What about your brother? What kind of example are you setting?

"I'll make sure my dad never offers to pay for him to go to school, either," Danica threatens. "No use throwing away money on the same redneck family twice."

My blood boils, but I bite my tongue. If I respond to her now, there is going to be more than a war in this car—there is going to be a bloodbath. Literally—because there is a psychopath behind the wheel, and I don't doubt that she'd kill us both just to spite me.

"Is Mike really worth losing everything for?" she asks, and the answer is yes. Yes, he's worth it.

Of course I want my brother to go to school, but maybe education in this country will be different in six years. Maybe he'll have more financial aid options. Maybe my parents will win the lottery. There are lots of maybes, and right now I need to worry about myself. For once, I need to put myself first. I can't go back to being the girl who wears pajamas for three days straight, skips her classes, and cries herself to sleep at night. My heart isn't whole without Mike, and I'm not breaking myself into pieces again.

I don't tell Danica any of that, though. Instead, I stare out that passenger side window.

"What's he going to think of you when he realizes you're nothing but a gold digger, Hailey?" Danica presses. "Because that's the plan, right? Live with him, let him pay all the bills. Maybe he'll even pay for you to go to school."

I would *never* let him do that. Never.

"You have nothing to offer him," Danica says. "Nothing, Hailey. You're not even pretty. It's actually kind of embarrassing. It's why I didn't want you at my thirteenth birthday party, you know. My friends all made fun of you that night after you fell asleep in your ratty little sleeping bag, and I convinced them you were adopted so they wouldn't think we were related."

I think back to that night, and I remember my tattered purple sleeping bag. I remember the girl I was, with her rebellious curls and her gentle heart. I remember sleeping alone in a corner while the other girls stayed up gossiping, because even back then, I knew I wasn't one of them. And I want to go back in time, hug that little girl, and tell her to stop caring so much. I want to tell her that in ten years, she'll meet the love of her life, and he'll think she's prettier than all of those girls combined.

And I tell myself that now. I hide the smile that grazes my lips as I remember the way Mike kissed me against his truck this morning. Nothing Danica can say can take that from me—can take *him* from me—so I stare out the window, thinking of him, as she spends the next half hour trying, and failing, to tear me apart.

When we pull into her parents' driveway, I immediately try to open my door, but Danica hits the child locks. "Look, Hailey . . ." She sighs dramatically. "I'm willing to give you one more chance. I know you didn't have any friends as a teenager, so maybe this is your rebellious phase or something, I don't know. But if you call Mike and break things off, if you tell him he belongs with me and not you, I won't tell my dad about any of this."

I just stare at her, and she smiles.

"I'm even going to be nice and give you time to think about it." She unlocks the doors and gives me one last smile before stepping out. "You have until the end of dinner."

Chapter 50

IF MY FAMILY's farmhouse in Indiana is a Best Western, Danica's family's house is a Ritz-Carlton. Light brick with white shutters and tall, white columns. A circular driveway made of smooth, white stone. More points on the multi-tiered roof than I care to count. A large balcony off to the side, and a two-story arch framing the entry. Perfectly trimmed hedges, and an oversized autumn wreath hanging on the red front door.

I climb the stairs behind Danica, but before either of us can reach the top, my little brother bursts from the house. "HAILEY!" he shouts, practically running Danica over as he bounds down the porch stairs. His lanky arms wrap tightly around me, and I squeeze him back with all my might. He's grown since I've been gone—by summer, I bet we'll stand eye to eye.

"Did you miss me?" I ask, trying to recover from the hellish ride here, and Luke makes a noise before hastily letting me go.

"No."

I smile at him, and he cracks a smile back. "Liar."

Luke gives up the fight and hugs me again, and I hold him tight until he's ready to let me go. He glances over his shoulder to see that Danica has gone inside. "Mom made me wear khakis," he complains with his thick brows knitted and his chunky glasses slipping down his nose. I use my pointer finger to push them back up, and the disdain remains on his face.

"If I have to wear a skirt," I say of the purple knee-length skirt I'm sporting, "you have to wear khakis."

"Do you think Aunt Tilly has ever worn jeans?" he asks, stoking another smile out of me. She married my uncle Rick before we were born, but she didn't grow up on a farm like he or my mom or dad did. She and my uncle met in college, while my mom and dad met when they were kids—in the town they grew up in, that their parents grew up in, that I grew up in.

"I don't know. You should ask her."

Luke snorts. "You should see the size of the turkey she's cooking."

I sigh as we climb the stairs. "How's Mom?"

"You know," Luke says, and he doesn't need to say more. The turkey my family always cooked for Thanksgiving dinner was just enough to feed our extended family of seven, while the turkey my aunt Tilly cooks is enough to feed an entire town. As soon as we enter the house, I can tell how my mom's day is going by the defeated look on her face.

"You look beautiful," I tell her as she squeezes me

close. My mom stands only a half inch taller than me, with hair just a little straighter and eyes just a little lighter. She's wearing a floral lavender dress she bought for a friend's wedding three years ago, and I pull away to admire it. "Is this new?"

My mom smiles like she knows what I'm doing, and then she pulls me back in for another hug and kiss on the cheek, enveloping me in the familiar rose-scented perfume that she only breaks out for special occasions. It reminds me of a lifetime of Easters, birthdays, and Christmases all at once. "How was the drive here?"

I groan, still feeling battered by the hour I had to spend listening to Danica trash literally every aspect of my life. My body, my clothes, my dreams. She even tried to make me feel bad about volunteering extra time at the shelter. How dare I spend my free time "playing with dogs" while her dad is working hard to pay all of my bills.

Nevermind the fact that he pays all of her bills too, while she spends her time skipping classes, talking on the phone, and wasting his money on purses and shoes. It took everything in me to not tell her so, but Mike is coming home in nine days, and I'd like to still be alive when he gets here.

"You need something to eat," my mom decides, hooking her arm around my waist and leading me through the high-ceilinged foyer. The sound of her short black heels echoes off the walls, and in the kitchen, I make a beeline to where my dad is sitting.

He pats my arm as I lean down to hug him from

behind, the scent of cherry chewing tobacco in his front shirt pocket reminding me of home. "Tell me something good," he says, a little tradition between him and me, and I struggle for a moment to think of something.

I'm dating a rock star, Dad. Every father's dream, I know. I'm dropping out of college for him. I'll probably have to move in with him and wait tables for a few years. He wants to knock me up with ten of his babies.

I clear my throat, and my dad glances at me over his shoulder.

"Uh," I stammer as I stand back up, "you know that dog I told you about?"

My dad looks around the kitchen for it as I hug my aunt Tilly and then my uncle Rick. "Hailey Marie, if you expect us to take home another dog—"

"I found her a home!" I interrupt, and my mother lets out an audible sigh of relief.

A chuckle escapes me, because they know me too well. If Mike hadn't come home last night and offered to keep Phoenix, I would have brought her along today and begged my parents to take her home with them. I wasn't sure she'd ever adjust to life on the farm, since she shuts down around other animals, but I was hoping maybe the dog whisperer gene runs strong in my family, and my brother could coax her out of her shell.

Luckily, Mike came to my rescue, a white knight on a white plane.

"Thank the Lord," my dad says, melting back into

his high-backed chair. He looks so strange wearing khaki pants and a button-down shirt that's buttoned the whole way up, but it's a concession he makes for my mother, and it's one of the reasons I love him so much.

My uncle Rick chuckles beside Danica at the end of the breakfast bar, looking much more comfortable than my father in his own dress pants and fitted blue button-down shirt. Even in his own home, he looks ready for business, tall and confident with not an ash-brown hair on his head out of place. He smiles at me at my dad's reaction, and I smile back.

Danica glares at me, and my smile disappears.

"Hailey, your mom tells us you volunteer?" my Aunt Tilly asks as she begins carrying dishes to the dinner table in the other room. My mom assists her, and I jump in to help.

"Yeah," I answer, trying to ignore the daggers that Danica is glaring into the back of my head while I carry two bowls in my hands and another on my arm. When I turn around to retrieve another dish, she's picking a marshmallow off the sweet potato casserole, helping herself instead of anyone else. "Ten hours a week count toward my internship, but I help out as much as I can," I say.

"That's so sweet of you," my aunt Tilly replies with a genuine smile on her face as she passes me on her way back to the formal dining room. Her dark hair is pulled back into a low bun with stray bits of hair escaping, and she's in a skirt-and-blouse combo that probably came from a store like the one Danica took me to—one with crystal chandeliers and fringed stools in the fitting rooms. But her voice is kind, and her words are heartfelt. Even though she's always been a somewhat flighty woman, I've liked her. When Danica and I played princesses when we were kids, Aunt Tilly always made sure we looked and felt like *real*, true princesses. When we played tea party, she let us use actual china teacups.

As we set the table, Aunt Tilly asks me all of the usual questions about working at the shelter—what I do, if I like it, if it's hard saying goodbye to the animals when they find their forever homes. I tell her all about it, with everyone else jumping into the conversation where they can, and when we finally sit down to dinner, my aunt turns her questions to Danica. "Have you ever thought about volunteering?"

"At the shelter?" Danica asks with an indignant eyebrow raised.

"Hailey," her dad says, holding out a serving of turkey for me. Years of explaining that I'm a vegetarian has taught me not to bother bringing up that I'm a vegetarian, so I hold my plate out to accept it.

"Thank you," I say, and he moves on to my brother as Aunt Tilly answers Danica's question.

"Yeah. It sounds nice. You could go with Hailey."

"I'm too busy studying," Danica says from the seat across from me. "I think I'm going to make dean's list this semester."

It's a flat-out lie. I've seen the grades on her exams, and frankly, I'll be surprised if she doesn't fail out of half her courses just from skipping class so often. But my aunt Tilly doesn't know that, and when her face lights up, Danica smiles at her. "Really?" my aunt asks, and Danica nods happily.

"I think so. I've been working really hard."

She doesn't even flinch when she says it. No lip biting. No eye twitch. A chill trickles down my spine, and Danica's white smile turns on me.

"Hailey's been a really positive influence. She's helped me study for a lot of my tests."

I'm paralyzed by that smile. She might as well have grown fangs.

My mom gives me a proud pat on the back, and the laugh lines in Danica's cheeks deepen when my mother's touch startles me.

"That's wonderful," my aunt Tilly praises, beaming at us both in turn. "Hailey, will you make dean's list too?"

"Of course she will," Danica answers for me. "Hailey is super smart. She barely needs to study to ace all of her exams. Her chemistry teacher even asked if she'd want to be a tutor next semester."

My food sits untouched on my plate as I stare at Danica, wondering what she's up to. I told her that bit of information a few weeks ago, but she acted like she didn't even hear me. Why is she complimenting me? Why is she being nice?

"Wow," her dad admires. "You must have really impressed him."

"Yeah . . ." I tell Danica's suspicious smile.

"Are you going to take him up on the offer?"

My eyes swing to my uncle, and I start stammering. "Oh, uh . . . I don't know . . . I mean, it's a volunteer position, so . . ."

"It would probably look good on your résumé," my dad says, and I turn my eyes to his end of the table. He chews a bite of turkey, waiting for me to say something.

"Yeah."

"Have you started thinking about where you want to do your senior internship yet?" my uncle asks, and my head swings back and forth as I stutter more answers to his and my dad's questions.

"What about a specialty?" my aunt Tilly asks. "Have you thought about that yet? Like livestock, marine animals, birds . . ."

"Small animals," my mom offers from beside me. "Isn't that what you were thinking, Hailey?"

I nod, and Danica's voice is pure sunshine when she says, "Hailey's wanted to be a small animal vet since she saved that little kitten at Patoka Lake."

Everyone at the table chuckles as they remember. I'd found the tiny kitten in some tall grass, and I spent hours searching for its mom before I finally brought it back to our tent with dirt and tears smeared on my face. It wouldn't stop crying, and I thought for sure it was dying without its mommy. My parents assured me it would be okay, but before I handed it over to the nice people at the nearest animal shelter, my six-year-old self demanded to talk to the veterinarian on staff, who assured me that the kitten was in good health and would be adopted in no time at all.

"Little Oliver Twist," my mom recalls with a laugh, remembering the name I gave it, and Aunt Tilly smiles at me.

"You were always such a sweet little girl, Hailey." She squeezes Danica's shoulder. "You both were."

"Hailey's going to make a great veterinarian," Danica praises. "It's what she was born to do."

Everyone agrees, and guilt creeps into the pit of my stomach. They're all so proud of me, of the things I've done and the things they believe I'll do. And I'm going to let them down, every single one of them.

I frown at the turkey on my plate, and when I lift my eyes, I realize Danica hasn't touched her food either. She's just smiling at me. Smiling brightly, happily, triumphantly—and it dawns on me, what she's doing.

She's trying to make me remember how much being a vet means to me, how proud everyone is. She thinks it will make me forget how much I love Mike . . .

She has no idea how determined I am to have both. My dreams are nothing without the warm way he smiled at me in his living room this morning, the scorching way he kissed me against his truck.

"I've been seeing someone," I announce, watching Danica's eyes flash with warning.

"Hailey—"

"Really?" my mom practically gasps. "Who?"

All eyes are on me—my mom's, my dad's, my

brother's, my uncle's and aunt's. And Danica's, burning a hole through me.

I look at my mom and my dad, hoping they can see how much this man they've never met means to me. "I'm in love with him."

"Who is it?" my mom asks again, and this time, I look at my aunt and my uncle before my eyes settle on my seething cousin.

"Hailey." She hangs my name like a threat in the air, and I push past it.

"His name is Mike," I say. "He's Danica's ex-boyfriend."

"WHAT?" my brother shouts, pieces of chewed dinner roll flying out of his mouth. He latches on to my shoulders, his eyes huge behind chunky black glasses. "MIKE?! ARE YOU SERIOUS?!"

I turn away from him as my aunt Tilly asks, "Mike the drummer?" She looks at Danica, who clenches her fists on the table. "Mike from high school?"

"Hailey stole him from me," Danica accuses, and my mom's worried eyes find me while my brother's grin threatens to stretch right off his face. His hands are flattened on the table, and I swear to God he's bouncing in his seat.

My aunt Tilly, still with her face pulled at Danica, says, "You broke that poor boy's heart . . ."

"You stole her boyfriend?" my mom asks with measurable horror.

I shake my head in spite of the guilt I still feel over what happened. I know Mike says he would have broken up with Danica with or without me, but that doesn't change the fact that he fell in love with me while he was with her.

"They were broken up," I tell my mom, and myself.

Danica overhears me and presses her hands against the table, leaning forward to better scream in my face. "You made him fall in love with you!"

My brother squeals giddily, and my uncle groans and rubs a line between his eyes. "Is this why you wanted to go to Mayfield?" he asks Danica, and her face transforms into a mask of vulnerability.

"I love him, Daddy!"

My uncle rubs his eyes, and Danica points a finger at me.

"She slept with him behind my back!"

With my face blushing beet-red, I say, "Never while you were together . . ."

My dad's cheeks flush to match mine, and my brother throws his head back and laughs hysterically.

"Dad," Danica pleads, "I don't want her living with me. I can't see them together." Tears flood her eyes, and I can't tell if they're real or forced, but her father's face softens, and I know what's coming.

This is the moment. This is the moment when he tells me he won't support me any longer, and that I'll have to move back home with my parents. I won't, of course—I'll move in with Mike. But school will have to wait, and so will the dream I've had since Oliver Twist.

"Hailey," he says, his deep voice drying my throat, "isn't there some kind of . . . girl code or something, about dating a family member's boyfriend?"

Unable to deny it, I nod my head. "Yes." I look at Danica, at the angry tears in her eyes, and I say what I've been wanting to say since the moment I realized I'd fallen for her boyfriend. "I'm sorry. I never meant to fall in love with him."

My dad nods and smacks his hand against the table. "Well, there you have it," he says, a simple man with a simple solution. I almost hate saying what I need to say next.

"I'm not going to stop seeing him though . . ." I look from my dad's disappointed expression to my uncle's. "I'm sorry about the way things happened—I never meant to fall for Dani's ex—but I'm not giving him up. I tried, and it felt like I'd ripped my heart out of my chest." My eyes swing to my mom, to the sympathetic look she's giving me. "He's the sweetest, kindest, most amazing man I've ever met. He loves me more than anyone could ever deserve, and I want to spend the rest of my life with him."

It's a big thing to say. And I realize that as I'm saying it. And every word of it is true.

"I want her gone," Danica cries while her mom rubs her back. "I just want her out of my life. I want her gone so I can move on."

My uncle sighs heavily as he stares at what's left of the turkey at the center of the table. He stares, and he stares. "We'll talk about it after dinner," he decides.

"What's there to talk about?" Danica shrieks, and my uncle's voice hardens.

"Danica, we'll discuss it after dinner."

"There's nothing to discuss! She's horrible, Daddy! She ruined my life!"

My uncle Rick groans and sets his fork back on his plate for the second time. "That boy called you a thousand times after you broke up. You haven't mentioned him for years. Why would you want him back now?"

I hold my tongue, but my brother doesn't.

"He got a big recording contract with the biggest label there is," he volunteers with his mouth full of stuffing. It might as well be popcorn, with the way he's shoving it into his mouth and watching the show. "He's famous now."

My uncle and aunt frown at Danica, and she completely falls apart. "That has nothing to do with it," she sobs, but her parents continue studying her.

I hate that I can't tell if her tears are genuine or not. I don't know whether to feel sorry or angry. I wish I could fix her—this broken thing that she grew into.

"Hailey," my uncle finally says, and I tear my eyes from Danica, holding a deep breath in preparation for what's coming. "You're going to need to move out."

"I understand," I say, avoiding the looks my parents are giving me. I can't bear to see the disappointment on their faces. I hope one day they'll understand. They loved the farm, and they never left it. I love Mike, and I'll never leave him.

Their happiness is a place, but mine is a drummer with warmth in his eyes and sparks in his smile.

"I'll make some calls," my uncle adds, "and see if I can get you into the dorms."

My heart hurtles over a beat as I stare at him, wondering if I really heard what I think I just heard, and Danica's anger slices across the table.

"What? No! Dad! She doesn't deserve it!"

"I'm sorry you're upset, honey," my uncle Rick says, and Danica's hands start shaking. "But you two are adults, and you'll have to work it out. I'm not going to pull anyone out of school over some boy."

"You're just going to keep paying for her to finish? After what she did to me?" Danica yells, and the unmoved look on my uncle Rick's face confirms it. I don't know what to think, or what to feel, so I sit there with my heart pounding violently against my ribs.

"I HATE YOU!" Danica screams at me, pushing her chair back viciously as she rises to her feet. "I FUCKING HATE YOU!"

"Danica," her mom pleads, but Danica storms from the room. She leaves us sitting there in awkward silence, with everyone looking from me to my uncle and back again.

He sighs, and then he picks up his fork for the third time and holds it as he contemplates his food. His eyes drift to my plate, and he calmly says, "Eat your turkey, Hailey."

I pick up my fork. And for the first time in eight years, I eat my turkey.

Chapter 51

DURING ONE FAMILY dinner when I was a teenager, two of our horses broke out of their stables to get their freak on literally *right* outside of our dining room window, and that family dinner was *still* not as awkward as this one. The conversation turns to weather, business, school—all sorts of normal, safe things . . . while my mentally unstable cousin sits upstairs in her room probably planning how she's going to disfigure and dismember me without getting caught.

I hand-wash the china after dinner, and my brother dries the dishes, mostly, I suspect, so that I don't get butcher-knifed in the back while I'm standing at the sink. He asks me if Mike and I will get married, and he points out that if we do, Mike will be his big brother. I tell him not to get his hopes up since I'm pretty sure Danica is upstairs taking out a hit on me as we speak.

I wash dishes until there's nothing left to wash. And then I wipe down the counters. And then I sweep the floors. And then . . . I hide like a coward in the powder room. Sitting on the closed toilet, I pull my phone out and text Rowan and Dee and tell them what happened.

Dee: OH MY GOD HELL YES

Rowan: YAY!!!!

Me: I feel sick.

Dee: What's the evil bitch doing now?

Me: Probably plotting my death. I need to get out of here. Any chance you guys are close to Downingtown?

Dee: No. We're up near Fairview.

Rowan: Hold on, I'm texting Leti and Kale. I think they're at Kale and Kit's parents' place.

I chew on my thumbnail and tap my foot against the stone floor for just a few seconds before another text comes through.

Leti: We're on our way. What's the address?

I'm about to type the address when a knock sounds against the door, and I clutch my phone to my chest.

"Hailey?" my mom asks, and I stop white-knuckling the device in my hands. "Are you okay?"

"Yeah."

"Are you sure? You've been in there a while . . ."

"Be right out."

"Okay . . ."

Her footsteps fade away, and I send the address to Leti as quickly as I can. When he tells me he'll be here in about twenty minutes, I decide that's twenty minutes too long.

After cautiously peeking into the sitting room and finding it Danica-free, I step in and announce that I'm leaving.

"What? Why?" my mom asks, but she's frowning like she already knows.

My aunt Tilly frowns the same way. "But you just got here . . ."

"I'm not feeling well," I tell them honestly, and my pragmatist father chimes in from where he's sunken into a recliner.

"Didn't Danica drive you?"

"A friend is picking me up," I tell him. "He'll be here in a few minutes. He's already on his way."

Everyone frowns at me in silence—especially my brokenhearted little brother who I know isn't ready to say goodbye to me just yet—and my uncle stands up and motions for me to follow. "Let's talk a minute before you go."

My feet are heavy as I obediently follow him back to the kitchen, and he serves us both slices of pumpkin pie that sit untouched on a pair of porcelain plates.

"So," he says, his eyes so like my mother's. Sometimes, when I take notice of his fitted shirt and his pressed pants and his shiny shoes, it's hard to imagine that he grew up on hand-me-downs and yard sales, just like my mother and just like me. All three of us were raised on the same plot of land, but I have a difficult time picturing him in a T-shirt with dirt under his fingernails.

He considers me for a moment, and then he goes to the fridge for a can of whipped cream. "I remember when you and Dani were little girls," he says with his head in the fridge. "You both wanted to grow up and marry that mermaid's boyfriend . . . the Disney one."

"Eric," I offer, and my uncle stands up from behind the fridge door.

"That's the one," he says, spraying dollops of cream on both our pumpkin pie slices. "One time, you two argued over him so bad that Dani started crying, and you hugged her and told her that you'd marry Simba instead."

He smiles warmly at the memory, and I struggle in the wake of the emotions stirring inside me. Part of me misses being that close with Danica—misses the innocence of arguing over Disney princes—but was it always that way? Was I always so willing to give up my happily-ever-after for her?

I'm expecting my uncle to lecture me about fighting over a boy, to tell me how trivial it all is and how someday it won't matter. But instead, he holds my gaze and says, "You've always been like a daughter to me, Hailey. I know we don't see each other much anymore, but your happiness is very important to me and Tilly."

A lump forms in my throat, and I couldn't speak if I wanted to.

"I know that you and Danica have grown apart, but that doesn't make you any less a part of our family. I see a lot of myself in you."

"You do?" I ask in a quiet voice, and he stares down at our pie, finally realizing that we don't have forks to eat with. He busies himself with getting them, but once again, neither of us moves to eat.

"The farm was always your mother's dream, not mine," he finally says. "She loved it. She loved rising with the sun. She loved helping with the livestock. She even loved driving the tractor into town and flipping off everyone who beeped at her along the way."

"She still does that," I say with a chuckle, and my uncle laughs.

"I didn't mind all of it," he tells me after a while. "But I didn't love it like your mom did. She and your dad loved that town, but I loved the idea of finding new towns, bigger towns. My heart was never on that farm, and correct me if I'm wrong, but I don't think yours is either."

I shake my head, and he nods his understanding.

"It was really hard for me when I went to college.

My parents didn't understand why I'd bother, and even though I had a scholarship, I couldn't afford new clothes or anything like that. I used to eat canned vegetables in between classes because that was all I could afford to bring for lunch."

I imagine a lanky kid, taller than my brother but with the same big eyes, trying to navigate a college campus with no clue what he was doing. I imagine him trying to thrive in a world he'd never been a part of, and I feel like we'd be friends.

"It was a long time ago, but sometimes it feels like just yesterday," my uncle continues, and he takes a deep breath. "Your mom told me that you know about me bailing out the farm, and I'm sure you've wondered why I didn't give your parents the deed."

I don't argue, and he nods in silent reply.

"It's because it's my childhood home too, Hailey. I love your father like my own brother, but he's terrible with finances and always has been. He's a farmer, not a businessman, and it's important to me that the farm stays in our family, so I'm making sure it does."

I take a moment to consider all he's telling me, and then I assure him, "I understand."

"Do you?"

I nod, and he sighs in tired relief.

"I wanted to offer to pay for you to go to school a long time ago, but it wasn't really my place. A man wants to be able to provide for his own family, but . . ." He stops himself and taps his fingers against the counter. "I'm rambling. Look, the point is that you don't need to worry about me suddenly deciding to stop paying your tuition. And don't tell me you weren't worried, because I could see that you were."

I frown, and my uncle frowns back.

"I can't say that I approve of you dating my daughter's ex-boyfriend, but . . ." He becomes conscious of his volume, lowering his voice. "I always liked him, and I can tell you really care about him."

I nod, and my uncle nods too.

"You're going to have to move out of the apartment you have with Danica. I doubt she'll stick around there long anyway, now that Mike is out of the picture. But I don't want you living with him—you need to focus on school, and I want you keeping your grades up."

When I say nothing, he notices.

"Was that your plan?"

"It was a temporary plan," I stammer, and my uncle considers me.

"Temporary is fine. Next semester, you'll be in the dorms. Agreed?"

"Agreed," I say, closing the distance between us and hugging him so he can't see the relieved tears springing to my eyes.

My uncle's shirt is crisp against my cheek as he pats my back. "I'm proud of you, Hailey. You're going to accomplish great things."

"Thank you," I tell him, hoping he knows I'm thanking him for more than the compliment. I'm thanking him for being the first in our family to brave a new life, for being the first to go to college, for paving the way for me. I'm thanking him for loving me, for caring about me, for not forgetting about his family or his roots. I realize why he sees himself in me, because I can now see a bit of myself in him—I can see myself in twenty years, still caring deeply about the farm and the family that shaped me into who I am.

"You're welcome," he says, hugging me until I let him go.

IN THE SITTING room, I hug my mom, and she assures me that she's going to find a way to fly me home for Christmas. I hug my dad, and he assures me that he won't make Teacup into bacon even if she eats his very last shoe. I hug my uncle, and he assures me that he'll get me into the dorms next semester. I hug my aunt, and she assures me that she'll talk to Danica.

I hug my little brother, and he insists he's coming along.

Luke begs and whines and negotiates with my parents, while I stare at the stairwell waiting for Danica to fly down it on her broomstick. I haven't seen or heard from her since she told me she hated me at dinner, but seeing as how I'm still breathing, I know this isn't over.

Desperate to leave while my lungs are still working, I tell my parents I'll drive Luke the hour and a half back to my uncle's house before it's time for them to fly home on Saturday, and they finally agree to let him leave with me. He bounds up the stairs to the guest room to grab some clothes, and I stand by the front door, chewing on my lip and tapping my fingers against my leg and curling my toes in my tennis shoes.

There's no way it can be this easy. Danica would sooner burn this whole house down than let me leave it unscathed. It's not in her to lose. She doesn't know how.

When I hear footsteps thundering down the upstairs hallway, my whole body tenses, but then Luke appears at the top of the stairs and jogs down them, flinging open the door to freedom. He steps onto the front porch, and I follow. The door closes behind me, and we take the stairs quickly. Leti isn't here yet, but we don't stop walking.

"Where are we going?" my brother asks, but I really have no idea. Away from here. Away from the front door.

"That way," I say, pointing down the street. I pull out my phone and text Leti to meet us at the end of Danica's road, and I'm sliding the phone back into my pants pocket when it finally happens—

"Leaving without saying goodbye?"

Danica's voice cuts through me, and I turn around to see her walking down the sidewalk to where my brother and I have frozen in our tracks. My fight-or-flight kicks in, demanding that I flee, that I run as fast as I can. But Luke is standing beside me, and I've run for long enough.

"Goodbye," I say, and Danica gives me an icy smile. It's chilling, how cold she looks as she steps in front of me. The pretense isn't there anymore—the façade is gone, and so are her thousand pretty masks. There is no compassion or vulnerability or kindness in her eyes—only cold hatred, and I realize that even if I *did* run right now, she'd chase me down. This ends here, on a quiet sidewalk in front of her neighbor's house.

"No hug?" she taunts in a sap-sweet voice, and I sicken of her games.

"What do you want?"

"What, I can't want a hug from my cousin?"

Years on a farm have taught me never to turn my back on a dangerous animal, but in this moment, it's all I can do. I turn away from her, and I tug Luke with me. "Let's go."

"I'm going to make your life a living hell, you know," Danica promises, but I keep walking.

"You've already tried."

"I haven't even started," she threatens as she stalks my every step, refusing to let me escape from her.

I glance at Luke, at the impressionable look he's giving me, and I stop in my tracks. I'm running. I'm *literally* speed-walking down the sidewalk instead of teaching my little brother to stand up for himself. His school is full of Danicas, full of Graysons, and Luke needs to learn not to run.

I steel myself, and I turn around. "Okay, Danica, enlighten me. What are you going to do? Cry to your daddy some more?"

Her eyes flash with anger, but I know this battle has just begun.

"You think you're something special, don't you?" she snarls, and my response comes quick.

"No, I think I'm average. But *Mike* thinks I'm special, and that's all that matters to me."

Danica's laugh is a humorless white cloud of air between us, her expression glacial as she says, "Do you think of me when you're being his little slut?"

"I don't think of you at all," I lie.

"Not even when he fucks you?" Danica asks, not caring at all that there is a twelve-year-old standing beside us. I don't answer, and she smiles. "I guess you must be used to it, getting all of my old trash. My toys, my dresses, and now my boyfriend. You can have him, Hailey. He'll never make love to you in a way that he hasn't made love to me first."

"At least he can look me in the face while he's doing it," I snap, remembering what Mike told me about having to do her from behind the one time they did it on the tour bus.

Danica's whole face burns red as she hisses, "What did you just say?"

Her fists clench at her sides, and I know it's time to get the hell out of here. I grab Luke by his elbow and spin us around, and Danica's breath is hot on my neck when she screams in my ear, "What the fuck did you just say to me, you bitch!"

When I turn back around, she's right in my face. "Say what you want, Danica! Say it so I can fucking leave! You want to tell me how poor I am? How ugly I am? Do it, because once I leave here, this is done."

"You think you're just going to live happily ever after?" she sneers. "Hailey, I'm going to make your life on campus so miserable, you're never going to finish school."

"How?" I ask just to get it over with. "What, are you going to sleep with my professors and get them to give me bad grades?"

"I have friends," she threatens with a smile.

"So, what? You're going to start rumors about me? About how I'm a whore? How I have STDs? What, Danica? Tell me."

Her jaw ticks as I guess her evil plan, and I roll my eyes.

"I used to go to high school smelling like manure with holes in my clothes. My snow boots freshman year were tennis shoes with bread bags tied over them. If you think I give even the tiniest shit what a bunch of frat boys and sorority girls think of me, you're wrong."

"Oh, you poor thing," Danica mocks with an exaggerated pout. It twists into a smile, and she taunts, "What did Mike think of my dress, Hailey? The one with the blue flowers you loved so much."

My blood boils under my skin, but I force a smile back. "That stupid video you sent him? He didn't even watch it. And even if he had, I'm sure he wouldn't have liked it as much as the red dress I wore when I starred in the band's music video."

White rage flares across Danica's face, and she hisses, "You're lying."

"I'm a terrible liar," I remind her, echoing something she's told me a thousand times. "Look at my face. Does it look like I'm lying?"

One minute, she's studying me—my eyes, my mouth, my serious expression. The next, blood is exploding against my teeth, the force of her fist knocking me backward. I fall from the unexpected blow, and my brother drops to his knees to help me. My rattled brain is still trying to register what just happened, when he starts to rise to his feet, anger rolling off him.

I latch on to Luke's elbow to keep him from getting involved, and when I'm confident he's not going to throw everything my dad ever taught him about not hitting girls out the window, I force my legs to lift me back to my feet.

Adrenaline is pulsing through me so rapidly, my whole body is shaking. I'm so angry, I want to cry. I want to scream so loud it hurts, and then I want to fall apart on the sidewalk. Instead, I meet Danica's furious glare, and I make sure she hears me. "You're the ugly stepsister, Danica. You try so hard to be the princess, but you're hideous inside. Your daddy is the only man who's ever going to love you."

Angry tears glisten in her eyes as she clenches her fists at her sides. I wait for her to punch me again, but when it doesn't happen, I wipe my sleeve against my bloody lip and turn away from her. "She's not worth it," I tell Luke when he holds his aggressive stance, and he eventually lets me pull him away.

I hope the blood in my mouth is enough. I pray my swollen lip was what she needed. If she needed to knock me down, fine, she knocked me down—

"This isn't over," she calls after me as I walk away,

and I close my eyes, knowing that words will never be enough to stop her from wreaking havoc on my life. It will never matter to her how many times she knocks me down, because I will *always* get back up.

When I turn around and walk back to her, her eyes have dried, and her face is vicious. The little girl I knew in Indiana is gone, possessed by a coldhearted bitch who's spent the past few months manipulating me like a puppet.

"You have something you want to say to me?" she barks, and I look her straight in the eye.

"Yeah," I say, channeling years of lifting hay bales and mucking stalls and wrangling horses. I spit a mouthful of blood on the sidewalk, and I fist my hand like my daddy taught me. "You punch like a little bitch."

When I pull back my fist, I pull it back far. And when I punch Danica in her startled face, I punch her as hard as I can.

Chapter 52

IF MY LIFE was a fairy tale, I suppose I would have knocked Danica out on that Thanksgiving afternoon four months ago. She would have fallen on her ass, the hit would have been clean, and I would have stood over her victorious, noting a look of surrender in her eyes.

Instead, there was blood *everywhere.*

Danica's nose crunched against my fist, and the scene that followed was like something straight out of a horror movie.

"Oh my God!" I gasped as I dropped to my knees beside her on the sidewalk. She was bawling her eyes out, holding her nose as blood streamed over her fingers. "I'm so sorry!"

"I think you broke her nose," my shocked brother said as Danica cried hysterically, and my hands shook as I panicked, not knowing how to help her.

"Get Mom and Dad!"

My brother ran back to the house, and I stripped off my favorite hoodie—the Ivy Tech one that Mike rescued for me the first night we met—and used it to try to stop the bleeding. I pushed her hair back from her face, I rubbed her back, I told her over and over again how sorry I was and how it was going to be okay.

WE HAVEN'T TALKED in the months that have passed since that day. Danica dropped out of school even before the semester ended, and I heard she's dating a doctor now—the one who fixed her broken nose. My mom told me he's a few years older than her, with a big house and a fancy Porsche, and I guess he was enough to make her forget about rock stars, because Mike hasn't heard from her either.

I'm watching him beat the drums now, a slow, easy rhythm as the guys do a lazy afternoon sound check. Mayhem is empty save for the band, a few staff members, and me, Rowan, and Dee, but outside, a line is already stretched around the building. It's The Last Ones to Know's first big show since their music video for "Ghost" released and the single went platinum, and tonight, one of the few bands bigger than they are is opening for them as part of the celebration, so the show sold out within minutes.

While I spent the night in Mike's arms, fans slept on the concrete sidewalk outside this building waiting to see him play, and a chill dances up my spine as I watch him. He yawns and plays the drums with one hand, and I smile, remembering that I didn't exactly let him get much sleep when I came over last night.

I'm living in the dorms now, just like my uncle promised, but I still spend most of my time at Mike's place with him and Phoenix. We make the nights count, and during the days—when I'm not volunteering at the shelter, volunteering at the college learning center, or frantically scribbling down notes in class—I'm usually hanging out with my new roommate, Macy, who is super nice, if not a little awkward. She's the total opposite of Danica—quiet and reserved but a great study partner—and I'm extremely thankful I was roomed with someone who complements me so well. Rowan and Dee freaked out when they discovered she's my roommate, since she was apparently Dee's roommate freshman year, and I couldn't help laughing at the thought of poor Macy trying to hold her own with Deandra Dawson. We had even more in common than I thought, and when I found out that she had even met Mike before, she told me how lucky I was to have such a nice boyfriend, and I couldn't help agreeing.

After walking over and wrapping my arms around my very nice, very tired boyfriend's neck, I press my chest against his back and tease in his ear, "Tired? Do you need me to take over?"

Mike chuckles before spinning around and catching me by the waist. He tugs me into his lap and spins us back around, slipping his drumsticks into my hands. "Yeah, considering it's your fault I can hardly keep my eyes open."

I barely have time to think of a witty reply before Dee and Rowan start cheering from where they're sitting at the other side of the club, at the bar. Rowan has a mountain of homework spread on the bartop, and Dee is helping herself to a shot of something she probably shouldn't be drinking considering it's only two in the afternoon, but she texted me this morning to let me know that the red dress she made me for the music video is going to be the star feature in her school's fashion show in New York, so the girl has a damn good reason to celebrate.

"Woo!" Rowan shouts, lifting her hands in the air. "Go Hailey!"

"Let's see what you've got!" Dee encourages, toasting me with the shot glass in her hand.

I cast a nervous glance at Mike, but his smile is electric. "Don't hold back now, Animal."

My next glance is at Kit, and she smiles at me. "Pick a song."

"Uh . . ." Over the past few months, Mike has given me a few drumming lessons, and I try to think of an easy one. "How about 'Rooftops'?" I ask, thinking of the slow song Shawn wrote for Kit. It's ridiculously complicated on the guitars, but easy on the drums, so Mike has used it as a good practice song, and Kit's face lights up when I request it.

She smiles at Shawn at the other side of the stage, and he smiles back before nodding at me.

"Are you ready?" Adam shouts at Rowan and Dee, and Rowan finally puts her pencil down, spinning around to give her boyfriend and his band her full attention. Dee screams her enthusiasm, and Joel laughs as he adjusts his guitar strap on his neck. Adam smiles over his shoulder at me, his gray-green eyes up for anything. "Ready when you are, Hailey."

I swallow hard, and Mike's pep talk comes in the form of a shoulder rub that helps calm my nerves. I take a deep breath, he drops his hands, and I play the drums with The Last Ones to Know. Kit plays rhythm guitar, Joel plays bass, Shawn plays lead guitar, and Adam steps up to the mic to start singing one of the band's most haunting, beautiful songs.

I slip the sticks into Mike's hands for the more complicated parts of the song, and even when my beat is slightly off during the easier parts, the band pretends not to notice. Mike's chest against my back, his lap beneath my legs—it makes me feel like I can do this, like I can do anything, and when I finish, Rowan and Dee give me a standing ovation.

"WE LOVE YOU, HAILEY!" they shout in unison, and I laugh as Dee puts her fingers in her mouth, her loud whistle filling the whole room.

Mike hugs me tight and plants a kiss against my cheek, and the smile that splits my face makes me think of how far we've come since I first watched him play in this exact spot six months ago.

For Christmas, he surprised me with plane tickets home to Indiana, and it was the best Christmas I've ever had. We flew out the day before Luke's school went on winter break—along with Rowan, Dee, and the rest of Mike's band—and they played a killer show in Luke's junior high gym that the kids are still talking about. The day after the show, I brought them all home and introduced them to Teacup, who promptly tried to devour Dee's sparkly purple pumps.

The band flew home a couple days later, but Mike stayed with me over the holiday. He played gin rummy with my dad, braided pie crust with my mom, and built a snowman with Luke. We opened presents together Christmas morning, and that night, Mike and I sat up in the hayloft together, cocooned inside a mountain of blankets, watching the sun set over the snowy fields.

"I can't believe you bought Luke a drum kit," I said for the hundredth time, and Mike hugged me tighter. I was sitting between his legs with my head resting against his chest, admiring the orange ribbons weaving patterns above the snow.

"The kid wants to be a drummer," Mike stated proudly, and I smiled out the open hatch.

"He wants to be like you," I corrected while he played with the tips of my fingers beneath the heavy flannel blankets.

"What's wrong with that?"

"Well, for one," I said as he flirted with the butterflies in my stomach, "you're annoyingly handsome."

Mike's chest shook against my back as he laughed. "Is that right?"

"Yes. And you're maddeningly talented."

"Oh no."

"And irritatingly romantic. I mean, really, Mike.

Making me watch the sunset in your arms? You're the worst."

He laughed and nuzzled his chin into the crook of my shoulder. "Can you ever forgive me?"

"I'm not sure I can," I teased, and Mike's fingers slipped under the hem of my shirt, caressing my stomach as they snuck higher.

"Are you sure?"

I turned my head into him just as his fingers found the delicate lace cups of my bra, and when he captured my mouth with his, I forgot what I needed to forgive him for. He made love to me under those blankets, up in that hayloft, and it was so much different than when I'd lost my virginity in that same barn. It was beautiful and romantic and full of fireworks, and when I fell asleep in his arms that night, I was sure that there was nowhere I'd rather be than on that farm, in that hayloft, with the man who was showing me one day at a time that happily-ever-afters really do exist, even for hand-me-down farm girls like me.

We flew home after the holiday, and Mike took me to meet his mom. My stomach was in knots for nothing, because she immediately gave me a bone-crushing hug and told me how much she already adored me. She had Mike's warm brown eyes, and I took to her instantly, knowing she had raised the man I wanted to spend the rest of my life with. She told me all sorts of stories about Mike as a kid, and the more his cheeks flushed as she told them, the more I fell in love with him, which I couldn't have imagined was even possible. His mom made me promise to come back to try her secret fudge cookie recipe soon—with or without her son—and I promised I'd return the very next weekend, and I did.

I'm still sitting on Mike's lap at his drums, with Dee and Rowan clapping wildly at the bar, when a voice across the room loudly asks, "What are we cheering for?"

A guy probably only a few years older than me grins widely as he strolls confidently toward the stage, and his presence alone tells me that he must be the lead singer of the opening band tonight: the infamous Van Erickson of Cutting the Line. He has jet-black hair, dyed a sparkling silver at the tips, and the cocky smile on his face screams "rock star."

"Hey!" Adam shouts back, launching off the stage to pin Van in a hug. Shawn climbs down a little more sensibly, followed by Joel and Kit—and Mike, who wraps his hands around my waist to help lower me to the floor

Van's bandmates and a pretty pair of girls enter behind him, and after everyone is finished getting reacquainted, Mike introduces me. "This is my girlfriend, Hailey."

"Oh," Van says smoothly, the corner of his mouth lifting into a smirk, "the girl in the red dress needs no introduction. We've seen the video. We're all big fans."

My cheeks burn as red as my dress in the music video was, and Mike's arm grows snugger around my shoulder. Van shoots a smile at him and reaches out to shake my hand.

"I'm Van."

"Nice to meet you," I say, and when I shake Van's hand, he chuckles.

"No wet willies—I like her already!"

Kit snorts and punches him in the arm, and Van laughs as everyone starts gravitating toward the bar.

"Mike's waited a long time for you, Hailey," Van says in parting as he leads the way, and Mike smiles down at me as we fall behind.

"Can I show you something?" he asks in a hushed voice, and when I nod, he steals me away.

OUTSIDE, IN THE March chill, I sit on the metal railing lining the steps leading down from Mayhem's side door, and Mike's hands wrap around the metal beside my thighs. He frames me with his strong arms, sculpted from beating the drums since he was old enough to hold a pair of drumsticks.

"What did you want to show me?" I ask, and a bashful smile plays around his perfect lips.

"How I feel about you?"

My cheeks dimple when I remember him using that line just before our first kiss, and I crawl my fingers up his shoulders as he steps in closer.

"And how are you going to do that?"

When Mike starts leaning in, my heart pounds in my chest just like it always does when I know he's going to kiss me. I close my eyes, breathless, but then his cheek brushes against mine.

"Don't pull away," his sultry voice whispers in my ear as the wind blows my wild curls from my face, and when his lips graze mine, I don't. I melt against him as he takes his time, and I feel the sparks ignite all around us. They fire against my lips and inside my chest and up and down my skin—until I'm molten lava, his for the shaping.

Van's words echo in my mind: *Mike's waited a long time for you, Hailey.*

But as the sparks consume me—as they consume us both—I think of the happily-ever-after I've dreamt of since I was old enough to dream, and I realize I've waited for him too.

I waited for my prince, I found him on a stage, and I'm going to hold on tight to him until the very, very end.

Epilogue

Mike

FANS SLEPT OUTSIDE Mayhem last night. While I slept in my warm bed with my girl in my arms, dozens of kids lined up and slept outside on the sidewalk to guarantee a prime spot in the pit. The guys and I watched from backstage as the doors opened and they rushed in, a stampede of fans racing for the metal railing. Within minutes, Mayhem was packed from the stage to the bar, and even though we've played sold-out shows before, this one felt different.

They'd slept outside. In March. I still can't get over it.

The first time the guys and I played Mayhem seven years ago, we were just a desperate garage band trying to make a name for ourselves. The owner couldn't decide if he wanted this place to be a nightclub or a concert venue, so he built a stage, installed a bunch of high-tech lighting, made room for a DJ booth, and called it both. Mayhem: the name of a place that has no idea what it's supposed to be, and the club we've called home since we moved here right after high school graduation.

None of us ever considered settling for a nine-to-five. We never even thought about it. We just grabbed hold of this dream with both hands, and we formed a silent pact to follow it wherever it led us.

Since then, it's led us around the country. It's led us around the whole world. And now it's led us back here, to the same familiar stage, under the same blue and purple lights. They flash around me as I pound the drums for the wild beast in the pit. There are so many faces in the crowd tonight, I can't even make them out. I play my heart out for the animal: the thrashing creature down below that grows restless with every hit song we play, every famous chorus we hit.

Famous—our songs are *famous*. The kids sing every word by heart. I set the beat to the rhythm of their feet as they jump up and down, a sea of bodies rocking out to songs we wrote—the songs that Adam and Shawn and Joel and Kit and *I* wrote. Some of these songs were written while we were all still in high school, back when none of us could have imagined playing for a crowd this big or fans this loyal.

They slept on the sidewalk. *They slept on the freaking sidewalk.*

Cutting the Line opened for us tonight, and Cutting the Line opens for no one. But Van Erickson stood at the front of that stage introducing us each by name: Adam Everest. Shawn Scarlett. Joel Gibbon. Kit Larson. Mike Madden.

Walking across the polished black floor to my drums tonight felt different than it had for the sold-out shows in China and Australia and England. It felt . . . it felt like *we'd made it.* It felt like *I'd* made it. And as my muscles burn and my sticks bang furiously against the drums stacked in front of me, I realize that feeling has as much to do with the girl waiting offstage for me as it does with the hundreds of fans screaming our names from the pit.

Hailey Harper: I never even saw her coming. I was so sure I'd never end up with one of the girls waiting for me outside our tour bus, but there she was, waiting alongside my high school girlfriend on the night that changed my life.

I was an idiot for hooking up with Danica that night, and I was an even bigger idiot for taking so long to realize we weren't worth a second shot. But the mind has a funny way of playing tricks on you—like when you go to a theme park as a kid and you think it's the greatest place in the entire world, but then you go back as an adult and you realize the rides are shit and the food is toxic.

I started falling for Hailey that night—the first night we met—but I didn't realize it until weeks later. I should have spent those weeks wanting to rekindle my relationship with Danica, but all I wanted to do was talk on the phone to her cousin, play video games with her cousin, hang out with her cousin. I convinced myself that Hailey was just a really cool girl and that we were just meant to be really good friends, but I couldn't get her out of my head. I'd lie in bed at night wishing I was with her, or that I could at least hear her voice, and the day we scouted the pond for the music video, everything finally clicked.

I knew even before we got to the clearing. The whole walk through the woods, I couldn't stop stealing glances at her, and I felt like such an asshole. It's not like she was *trying* to get my attention—she was wearing a baggy hoodie, loose jeans, and old boots—so why the hell couldn't I stop looking at her? My hand twitched to free itself from Danica's and latch on to Hailey's, and the more Danica talked, the more frustrated I got. She complained the whole hike to the clearing, and then she wouldn't shut up about being the star of our video, and the whole time, Kit just kept giving me looks like, *I told you so.*

She and the entire band had been on my case for weeks, and I should have listened, but when I saw Danica outside of the bus that chilly night back in September, it all came rushing back. All of it. The pain, the doubt, and even a shadow of the feelings I'd had for her in high school, the crush I'd had on her since third grade. She was the prettiest girl in our school, and she's still beautiful—but not like Hailey. She doesn't have Hailey's sexy curls or Hailey's kind heart or Hailey's contagious spark, and when I walked into the woods with Hailey that day at the pond, I knew I was in trouble.

We'd stopped at a fallen tree, just before it started to rain, and as she sat on top of it . . . God, I wanted to kiss her. I should have felt terrible about it, but I couldn't. I couldn't even think—not of Danica, not of anything.

All I could do was stare at Hailey's lips and wonder how soft they'd feel against mine.

Thank God it started pouring rain, or I probably would have fucked everything up. Hailey made me laugh my ass off as she screamed about manatees and koalas and God knows what else as we raced to the cabin, and as I sat on those dusty wooden floors with her, watching the world fall apart outside, I realized I was the happiest I'd been in a long, long time.

So I stuck my hat on her head. That was my genius move. I stuck my hat on her head, walked her back to the clearing, and made a silent promise to figure out my feelings. I was pretty sure it was time to call it quits with Danica, but then Hailey fell in the pond, and then she stopped responding to my calls and texts, and then I got sick, and . . . honestly, it's a miracle we ever figured things out.

"This next song is called 'Ghost,'" Adam shouts from the front of the stage, and when the crowd goes wild, he chuckles. "Sounds like you've heard of it?"

"I think most of them were in it," Shawn quips into his backup mic, and Adam grins at him and then the rest of us before turning back around.

"Scream if you were in it."

A smile stretches across my face as Mayhem fills with the rafter-shaking roar of our fans, and I glance at Hailey to find her eyes wide with surprise and her lips parted in awe. As if she can feel me watching, she meets my gaze, and my smile widens as I twirl a drumstick between my fingers—showing off a little even as I try to assure her that, in spite of all the fans and fame and noise, I'm still the same guy who squeezed into her pink bunny pajama shirt last night just to see her laugh.

I know sometimes this "rock star" thing is a lot for her to process—sometimes it's a lot for *me* to process—but beneath these blinding lights, I'm still me. I'm still me, and I'm still hers, and nothing is ever going to change that.

"Now sing it with me if you know the words," Adam instructs the crowd, and I take my cue, setting a rhythm on the drums as I remember the night we shot this music video.

I knew I was going to kiss Hailey that night. I'd broken up with Danica, and I was supposed to leave on tour the next morning, but there was no way I was stepping foot on that plane until I'd kissed Hailey at least once. It was all I could think about as I watched her shoot scenes in that sexy red dress. I just wanted to steal her away, take her face in my hands, and see if I could make her feel the sparks she said she'd never felt before.

I had no idea I'd never felt them either, but as her fingers scraped over my scalp and her body moved against mine as I kissed her in the woods—as she kissed me back—I felt like I was on fire, and I was sure my heart was going to explode in my chest. My heart, my body, my mind: they were all consumed by her, and now, when I glance at her standing offstage, smiling at me like only she can, I feel the same way.

The girl is fireworks. She doesn't even have to be doing anything special. She can just be sitting on my couch in a pair of cat pajama pants and one of my Guinness T-shirts, playing Deadzone with a pizza slice balanced on one leg and Phoenix's front paws resting on the other, and all I want to do is drop to one knee in front of her and ask her to spend the rest of my life with me.

I might have already asked if I didn't know that Adam is planning on proposing to Rowan in Paris in a few months. We have a show set up, we're bringing the girls with us, and he already bought the ring months ago. I don't want to steal his thunder, but as soon as he pops the question, I'm not waiting. I'm not planning the rest of my life based on anyone else except me and Hailey—we've done enough of that already.

Back in December, when I asked Hailey if she planned on spending Christmas with Danica's family, she finally told me everything she'd been keeping from me while I was on tour. She told me about Danica's ultimatum and how much she struggled with the decision, and she confessed it like she thought it would make me love her less, when really, it would have made me love her more, if loving her more was possible. I couldn't believe that she had been faced with that choice—her lifelong dream or me—and she had chosen *me*. And when she told me about Danica punching her in the mouth, I was ready to lose my shit—right up until Hailey smiled wide and told me she punched Danica back, and that she broke her damn nose.

My girl. Badass street fighter. She never stops surprising me.

It's one of the reasons why my grandmother's wedding ring is currently burning a hole in the glove compartment of my truck. I asked my mom for it a few days after she met Hailey for the first time, and her eyes filled with happy tears as she removed it from her antique wooden jewelry box and slipped it into the palm of my hand. When I was in high school, I thought I'd someday give that ring to Danica, but it never felt like the right time, and I doubted my mom would give it to me anyway, considering how passionately she hated my girlfriend. Now, every day that I don't put that ring on Hailey's finger feels like an eternity too long.

I try to concentrate on my drums, but I can't. I try to concentrate on the crowd, but I can't. I try to feel the heat of the lights pouring down over my shoulders, but I can't. All I can feel is the way my heart is knocking against my ribs at the thought of that ring and what Hailey might say when I give it to her.

I glance over at her again—standing with Rowan and Dee in the shadows of backstage—and she gives me a little wave. She's wearing tennis shoes, tight jeans, a The Last Ones to Know T-shirt, and an oversized hoodie tied around her waist—and she's the most beautiful sight I've ever seen. She claps her hands in encouragement, and I have no idea how I'm going to wait five more months to put a ring on her left hand. But then she smiles—brighter than any star I've ever seen—and I *know*: I can't. There's only one thing that would make this night more perfect, and I can't wait even one more day to do it.

"I WANT TO set them off tonight," I tell Shawn after our encore, and his green eyes widen.

"Tonight?"

I nod, and Shawn glances at Adam, Joel, and Kit, who meet us backstage at the opposite side from the girls.

"You want to set them off right now?"

"Tonight?" Joel interrupts, his eyes even wider than Shawn's. "Now?"

I look at Adam and ask, "Is that okay?"

The corners of my childhood friend's mouth pull way up, and he claps me on the back before yanking me into a hug. "You've waited long enough, man. Tonight's all yours."

I hug him back, and when Shawn yanks on my shoulder, I hug him too. I hug Joel, and I hug Kit, and when I finally meet Hailey at the other side of the stage, I take her hand in mine. "Come on, I want to show you something."

IN MY TRUCK, my fingers race as quickly as my thoughts. I know Hailey picked me over school, but is she sure she wants me for the rest of her life? Does she want to grow old with me like I want to grow old with her? Does she picture the same picket fence, the same porch swing, the same orange sunflowers growing outside our bedroom window and the same banana pepper garden planted out back? My fingertips drum a mile a minute against my leg, and when Hailey looks over at me, she says, "You seem nervous."

"How?"

She reaches over and clasps her fingers with mine, and I try to stop fidgeting. "Just leftover excitement," I lie. "Tonight's show was awesome, wasn't it?"

Hailey's eyes light up with her smile. God, she's beautiful. "I never thought being in the pit could be so much fun," she says, and I squeeze her hand, remembering what a blast we'd had watching Cutting the Line.

Before the show, Adam had asked what she thought of us when she first watched us perform at Mayhem back in September, and Hailey groaned as she recalled "Armpit Guy" and the terrible time she'd had with Danica. I decided she needed a better memory, and I convinced two kids right up front to let me and Hailey take their spots in exchange for backstage passes. I helped them crawl over the railing, and then I lifted Hailey up and set her down in the pit, front and center. I hopped in after her and stood at her back, my arms protecting her on both sides, and when Cutting the Line came out, the crowd went absolutely insane. I've always been more of a balcony guy than a pit guy, but as my body got pinned against Hailey's backside, I decided this was one show I was definitely going to enjoy.

We jumped up and down together, screaming lyrics

Hailey learned on the spot, and the harder she laughed, the harder I laughed with her. By the time it was my turn to take the stage, I was so full of happy energy, I felt like I could float right up to my drums.

"That was definitely the most fun I've ever had at a show," I tell her, and Hailey smirks.

"You just liked that you got to dry-hump me for an hour."

I can't help chuckling as I hold on to her hand. "It was my favorite part."

She blushes in spite of her teasing, and I brush my thumb over her hand as I stare back out at the road.

"Where are we going?" she asks, and my thumb gets restless again, threatening to start drumming against her knuckles.

"Wait and see."

FIFTEEN MINUTES LATER, we pull down the access road leading to the pond, and I help Hailey out of my truck before sticking my head back inside the passenger door to reach inside my glove compartment. "I think I've got a flashlight in here," I tell her, and I rummage around before closing the glove compartment and joining her outside. I hold the flashlight with one hand and sneak the other into my pocket.

As we walk, I tell her, "I came up here after I got back from touring to make sure they cleaned up, and I found a generator they left up here."

Hailey looks up at me, and I slip my hand from

my pocket to wrap my arm around her. "They just forgot it?"

"Seems like it."

"Did you tell them?"

"Yeah, but they never came back to get it."

We reach the clearing, and I tell her to wait for me as I walk inside the tree line to where I know the generator is hidden behind some branches. I flip a switch, and the whole forest flickers to life.

Hailey's mouth is hanging open when I emerge from the woods, and I smile as she admires the million white Christmas lights I've hung in the surrounding trees. It's been my day project—when I haven't been writing music or practicing with the guys, I've been buying out Home Depot's holiday lighting section and becoming an expert light hanger.

"Wow," Hailey breathes, and I take her hand in mine as we stare around the clearing.

"Do you like it?" I ask. I had planned for far more lights than this—by the time I brought her out here this summer, I wanted this place to look like it was filled with millions of tiny fireflies. But so far, I've only managed to hang lights in the trees immediately surrounding the clearing.

"It's beautiful," Hailey admires, and the tightness in my chest relaxes. "Did you do this?" she asks, and I start walking her toward the pond.

"Yeah."

"Why?"

"Because I knew you'd like it."

I steal a kiss as we continue walking, and each step we take toward the steel platform in the middle of the meadow makes my heart pound harder, and harder, and harder.

The fireworks start going off just as our feet hit the dock, and I don't know how Shawn timed it so perfectly. They explode in the sky north of the clearing: whites and blues, purples and greens, reds and oranges, and Hailey is so awe-struck that she doesn't even notice when I slip my hand from hers. She walks all the way to the end, staring up at the spark-filled sky.

Hailey

ONE AFTER ANOTHER, fireworks light the night sky. A boom, a rain shower of colored light, and then the sound of sparks trickling down from the full moon. Vibrant purples and greens and blues and reds. It's stunning, and when I turn around to find Mike, the sight of him down on one knee takes what's left of my breath away.

He stares up at me with those beautiful brown eyes, a sparkling diamond ring held between his fingertips.

"Hailey," he says as tears spring to my eyes and the last of the fireworks rain down behind me. My heart is pounding wildly, and my knees begin to tremble. "I feel like I've been waiting for you my whole life, and now that I've found you, I never want to spend a day without you. I want to go to bed with you at night. I want to wake up with you in the morning. I want to wrap you in my arms every time I find myself smiling for no reason." Happy tears spill over my lashes, and Mike smiles warmly up at me. "I want to give you a lifetime of laughter and love. I want to give you sparks and my last name and a house we can grow old in." I beg my knees to continue holding me up, to support me long enough to hear every perfect word coming from Mike's perfect mouth, and I watch as he takes a small, nervous breath. "Hailey Harper, will you marry me?"

"Yes," I say without hesitating, and Mike's whole face lights up with joy I feel in my own heart.

"Yes?" he asks, his voice a mix of awe and disbelief.

"Yes," I repeat, memorizing the way he looks in this moment. In fifty years, when he and I are old and gray with children and grandchildren and great-grandchildren, I want to remember every detail. I want to remember the way the moonlight is hitting his hair, the way the winter chill is staining his cheeks, the way his fingers are trembling as he holds out his ring—*my* ring. And I want to remember the way my heart is hammering excitedly against the walls of my chest—because no Prince Charming, no fairy tale knight, could ever beat the sight of Mike Madden down on one knee.

With my body quivering just as much as his, I drop to my knees and wrap him tightly in my arms. This is the biggest decision of my life—and it is also, by far, the easiest. "Yes, I'll marry you."

I kiss Mike with tears trickling down my cheeks,

and when I pull away, his eyes are shining too. He slips the ring onto my finger, sneaking kisses as I admire it.

"Do you like it?" he asks, and I nod, at a complete loss for words. The ring is beautiful, a sparkling round diamond cradled inside an ornate, vintage setting. The off-silver band is petite on my finger, and the diamond shimmers like a reflection of the full moon I loved so much as a little girl, the same one hanging above us now.

"It was my grandmother's," Mike says, and I lift my gaze to his heart-melting smile. "But I think it was always meant for you."

With the ring on my finger, I take his face in my hands. My fingertips slide into his hair, and he pulls me closer as I kiss him. I kiss him under the night sky, with our entire lives ahead of us, and later, as we lie on the dock staring up at the stars, Mike plays with my left hand.

"When Adam started dating Rowan a year and a half ago," he says, "I was a little jealous."

I glance over at him, watching him stare up at the sky.

"Not because I wanted her." He looks over at me and smiles reassuringly. "She's like my kid sister. But just because I wanted what he had with her, you know?"

I wait for him to continue, and he stares back up at the glinting stars.

"And when Joel got with Dee, I wanted what he had. And when Shawn got with Kit, I wanted what he had. But you know what I've realized?"

I continue staring at him, and he turns his head to meet my eyes.

"I don't want what they have."

"What do you want?" I ask, and the corners of Mike's mouth tip up softly as he twirls the ring on my finger. He shifts onto his side, propping himself on his elbow and lifting my hand to his mouth.

"I want you," he says, pressing a kiss against my finger, just above my engagement ring. "I would've waited my whole life for you, Hailey. It's always been you."

He brushes the hair away from my face, and I stare up into his breathtaking eyes, thinking of the war I fought to win him. I would've fought it a thousand times over for the way he's looking at me now, for the way his ring feels on my finger.

"I love you," I tell him, and he gives me that smile I've fallen so completely, hopelessly in love with.

"Enough to spend your whole life with me?" he asks, and I lace my fingers with his, making a silent promise to never, ever let him go.

"Enough to spend eternity with you."

I close my eyes when he kisses me—and everywhere, there are sparks.

Acknowledgments

FOR THE LOVE of my life and the real man Mike Madden was named after: my pizza-loving, beer-drinking, video game–playing husband, Mike Shaw. Thank you for working long days and then coming home and letting me throw a baby into your arms so I could write this book. I will forever appreciate all of the sacrifices you've made and support you've given me as I wrote this entire series. Thank you for a life full of love, laughter, and sparks.

For my mom, Claudia, who grew up wearing bread bags as snow boots and always made sure that her children had better. Thank you for making sure that I always had all the options in the world. And thank you for supporting me in all of them. You gave me the courage to follow my dreams, and you instilled in me the confidence to achieve them.

For my critique partners, Kim Mong and Rocky

Allinger, who I am lucky enough to call my best friends. Thank you for forever being my biggest supporters and fangirls. Your encouragement is what keeps me going during the times in my writing process when I want to print out my manuscript just to set it on fire. I'd be a hot mess without you.

For Marla Wilson, whose excitement for my books makes me hurry to write them. Thank you for "getting" Hailey, for your encouraging feedback, and for believing in this story.

For my editor, Nicole Fischer, who always supports my grand visions and graciously allows me to go 34,000 words over word count. Thank you for standing by every single book in this series and helping me make sure they were the very best they could be.

For my agent, Stacey Donaghy, who loved "Teddy Bear" Mike Madden from the beginning. Thank you for being my friend and advocate. None of this would have been possible without you.

A special thanks to DJay Brawner, filmmaker to the stars and my music video consultant. Thank you for being so kind, humble, and incredibly informative. You gave me the knowledge and confidence to make the band's music video truly epic. I'm so grateful that you emailed me back, and I feel very honored to have had you as a consultant on this book.

Thank you to the entire team at HarperCollins, who have been extremely flexible and supportive throughout this entire series. You took this big dream I had, and you brought it to life in extraordinary fashion.

And finally, thank you to my amazing readers, who waited so patiently for Mike and Hailey's story. There really are no words for how much your support has meant to me throughout this entire series, over the course of the past two years. Your encouragement and loyalty has been unwavering, and I am so beyond thankful to have every single one of you as a reader.

Tons of love, especially, to all of the rock stars in my Facebook group, Jamie's Rock Stars. Interacting with you is truly one of my favorite parts of this job. I write each book with you in mind, and I adore you for being a part of this journey with me.

And to my Roadies, who helped me put this story out into the world with a bang: Ashley Amsbaugh, Gina Behrends, Jodi Belshaw, Krista Davis, Erin Duffy, Felicia Eddy, Valerie Fink, Melisa Gette, Sarah Green, Kathy Lemke, Erica Limon, Casey Knittig, Denisha McPherson, Denise Prause, Nicole Reiss, Lauren Resch, Anne-Marie Simard, Hope Smith, Gabby Sotelo, Ashley Speakman, Summer Webb, and Mary Beth Witkop. Thank you for being so hardcore. You girls are amazing.

For every reader who loved Adam, Joel, Shawn, and Mike. For every reader who loved Rowan, Dee, Kit, and Hailey. For every reader who loved Leti and Kale. For every reader who loved Ryan, Mason, and Bryce. For every reader who loved Van . . .

Thank you. Thank you from the bottom of my rock star–loving heart.

And finally, thank you to my amazing readers who waited so patiently for Mike and Hailey's story. There really are no words for how much your support has meant to me throughout this entire series over the course of the past two years. Your encouragement and loyalty has been unwavering, and I am so beyond thankful to have every single one of you as a reader.

Tons of love, especially, to all of the rock stars in my Facebook group, Jamie's Rock Stars. Interacting with you is truly one of my favorite parts of this job. I write each book with you in mind, and I adore you for being a part of this journey with me.

And to my Roadies, who helped me put this story out into the world with a bang: Ashley Arshaugh, Gina Behrends, Jodi Belshaw, Kalista Davis, Erin Duffy, Felicia Eddy, Valerie Fink, Mellie Getty, Sarah Green, Kathy Lemke, Erica Linton, Casey Kittig, Dena McPherson, Denise Prause, Nicole Ross, Lauren Reedy, Anne-Marie Simard, Hope Smith, Gaobe Sotelo, Ashley Speakman, Summer Webb, and Mary Beth Witkop. Thank you for being so hardcore. You girls are amazing.

For every reader who loved Adam, Joel, Shawn, and Mike. For every reader who loved Rowan, Dee, Kit, and Hailey. For every reader who loved Peter and Kale. For every reader who loved Ryan, Mason, and Bryce. For every reader who loved Van.

Thank you. Thank you from the bottom of my rock-star-loving heart.

About the Author

A resident of South Central Pennsylvania, **JAMIE SHAW**'s two biggest dreams in life were to be a published author and to be a mom. Now, she's living both of those dreams and loving every minute of it. When she's not spending time with her husband and their young son, she's writing novels with relatable heroines and swoon-worthy leading men. With her M.S. in Professional Writing and a passion for all things romance, her goal is always to make readers laugh, cry, squirm, curse, and swoon their pants off, all within the span of a single, unforgettable story. She *loves* interacting with her readers, and she always aims to add new names to their book boyfriend lists.

http://authorjamieshaw.com/
https://www.facebook.com/groups/jamiesrockstars/
https://www.facebook.com/jamieshawauthor/
https://twitter.com/authorjamieshaw/

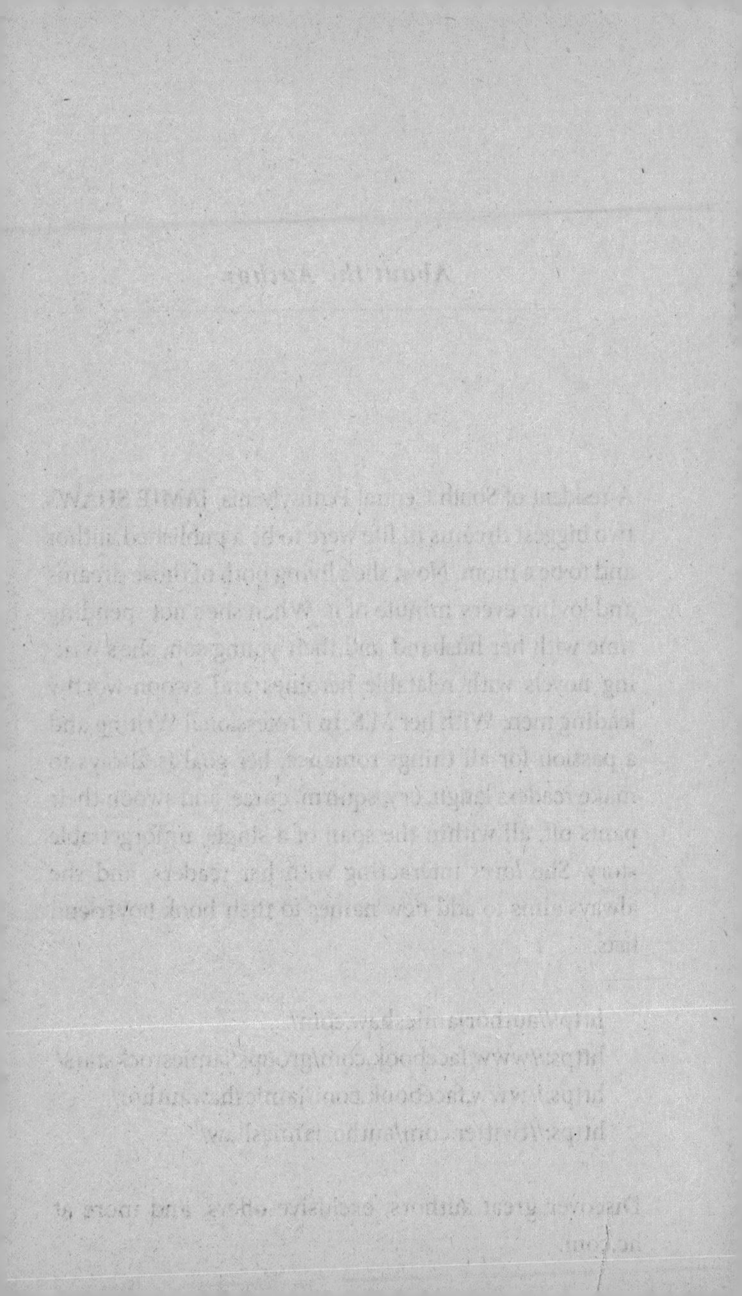

About the Author

A resident of South Central Kentucky, JAMIE SHAW's two biggest dreams in life were to be a published author and to be a mom. Now she's living both of those dreams and loving every minute of it. When she's not spending time with her husband and their young son, she's writing novels with adorable heroines and swoon-worthy leading men. With her M.A. in Professional Writing and a passion for all things romance, her goal is always to make readers laugh, [illegible] and [illegible] their [illegible] off, all within the span of a single, unforgettable story. She loves interacting with her readers and she always aims to add new names to their book boyfriend lists.

http://authorjamieshaw.com/
https://www.facebook.com/groups/jamiesrockstars/
https://www.facebook.com/jamieshawauthor
https://twitter.com/authorjamieshaw